An Albert Payson Terhune Reader

The stories and illustrations in this book were taken from (mostly) pulp magazines of the 1910s and 1920s, and are considered in the public domain. Anyone with reason to believe otherwise is asked to contact the publisher. Original publication information is included in the Appendix.

Profound appreciation is expressed to Kathryn D. George for proofreading, and for numerous helpful suggestions for this book.

The editing, arrangement and presentation, new coloring of covers, comments in the Appendix and any other new material in this book is Copyright © 2015 by Rodney Schroeter. All rights reserved. Except for brief passages for critical articles or reviews, no portion of this book may be reproduced in any form or by any mechanical, electronic or other means, now known or hereafter invented, including photocopying, 4-dimensional AI matrices, xerography and recording, or in any information retrieval system without the express written permission of the publisher. Faithfully memorizing the text of this book, in whole or in part, is heartily encouraged, in preparation for the day when books are outlawed.

The stories in this collection are works of fiction. All names, characters, places and scenes described herein are the results of the author's imagination and genius. Any resemblance to actual persons, living or dead, is purely coincidental.

These stories were published at a time when political correctness had not yet caused serious cultural and moral corruption. Certain ideas, terms and social conventions found herein are no longer considered acceptable (some for rational reasons, others not). A secure, rational reader (the kind of reader for whom this book was lovingly compiled) will understand that, and not give the matter further thought.

An Albert Payson Terhune Reader
ISBN: 978-0-9967194-0-7

Book compilation and design by Rodney Schroeter.

The Silver Creek Press
PO Box 334
Random Lake WI 53075-0334

rschroeter@silentreels.com

An Albert Payson Terhune Reader

With the original illustrations from the source publications

Compiled by Rodney Schroeter

Silver Creek Press

2015

The Coney Island Riddle

Chapter I.
An Odd Quest.

"SIT still! Don't speak! Look straight in front of you."

Now, I defy any man on earth to hear a low-voiced command like that without starting.

I started. In fact, I jumped.

But the voice broke sharply upon my involuntary motion.

"Sit down!" it repeated, a ring of anger in the low-pitched tone.

Instinctively I obeyed, but it was not in mortal nature to obey the order to "look straight in front," when the voice came just behind me.

I turned.

I was sitting on a bench by the Battery Park sea wall. My day's work—my week's work—was over. It was Saturday afternoon. I was a stranger in New York.

I had been in the city only a week, and I had spent that week in hard work. Now that the half holiday had come, I did not quite know how to spend it.

I had left the office at one o'clock, eaten a dairy lunch, and then had strolled aimlessly southward down Broadway.

The day was broiling hot. The streets were almost burning to the feet. The high, cañonlike walls of the skyscrapers reflected back the heat waves. Not a breath of air was stirring.

The street was packed with hurrying men. I alone, it seemed to me, had nowhere to go. The patch of green at Broadway's end had caught my eye. I had strolled into Battery Park, and had sat there watching the blue waters.

All New York and its myriad places for summer outings—places of which I had dreamed a thousand times in my "small-town" home—lay around me. Yet I sat there, homesick, puzzled, undecided where to go for a holiday.

Just then I had heard the voice.

I stared about, in growing bewilderment. On near-by benches lounged an immigrant or two and a few loafers. But surely none of these had addressed me.

Directly behind me stood a little portable tool house of green matchboard. The sort that the park workmen shift from place to place, according to their needs.

If the voice came from mortal lips—which I was beginning, rather creepily, to doubt—its owner must be in that tool house.

I got to my feet, meaning to go around to the door on the opposite side or else to shove back the green-shuttered window nearest me. But the voice halted me in my tracks.

"Sit down!" it commanded again. "Sit down, and look straight in front of you!"

I hesitated. It was not wholly pleasant to be ordered about like a trick dog by some one I could not see. As I stood, irresolute, the voice continued in a different key:

"If you don't obey the rest of Mr. Barham's orders any better than this, you may as well go back to Vermont. There's no future for you with Barham & Cuyp. I give you that as a free tip, Mr. Arthur Dallam."

I sat down again with some haste. Not so much through any conscious impulse of obedience as through sheer amazement.

For, not only had the voice addressed me by my own name, but it had even spoken of the law firm where for a week I had been a clerk; it had referred also to my eccentric employer himself.

This was beyond all possible understanding. I knew not a soul in New York except my landlady and the one or two office acquaintances I had made. Yet—

"That's better!" approved the voice. "Now, listen to me. And, when you answer, speak low and without moving your lips."

"Who are you?" I muttered, controlling with difficulty my face and tone. "What do you want? How do you know my name and the name of the firm where—"

"Where you are a clerk, and where you hope for a chance at the next vacancy for head clerk?" finished the voice. "It is my business to know things. It's Mr. Barham's business to know things. And he knows them. That's why he's one of the foremost lawyers in America to-day, as well as the most eccentric. If he were less eccentric I shouldn't be talking to you now."

"I suppose you think you know what you're talking about," I made answer, "but it's Greek to me. If it's a joke please—"

"I don't make jokes. You came to Mr. Barham a week ago. You came well recommended. You had just been admitted to the bar. You wanted a chance in Barham's office. He gave it to you and promised you quick promotion if you made good."

"Yes, yes! But—"

"Barham is eccentric. But there is a point—and a keen one—to most of his eccentricities. He likes you. He likes your work. But he wants to test you to make certain you are the right sort of man for him. He has a way of testing employees."

Now, this was true. And I knew it. It was common talk among lawyers. Barham had many uses for his clerks and juniors. And he proved such men's ability by odd methods that often seemed to outsiders absurd, but which, none the less, managed to show the mettle that was in an employee. There were dozens of quaint anecdotes afloat concerning these tests.

"So I'm to join the seemingly silly mystery of it all. What am I to do?"

"Unless you can manage to show more self-control than you did when I first spoke to you," was the answer, "I'm afraid there is no use in your trying to do anything. You'd only fail. And Mr. Barham has no use for failures."

I heeded the rebuke less than I should otherwise have done, because I was racking my brains to identify the voice. I knew now it must belong to one of my fellow workers at the Barham & Cuyp office. But I had known them all too short a time to fix the identity.

"I will do my best," I said, a little sulkily, for I am not fond of mysteries.

"Good," approved the voice. "Now, listen carefully: You will sit where you are for two minutes longer, looking out to sea, and not once turning around. Then you will get up. Under your bench you will find a satchel. I slipped it under there just after you had sat down. You will take it—without opening it—to Coney Island. There, at precisely nine o'clock to-night, you will give it to a man who will be waiting for it on the Concourse, just about one hundred yards beyond the spot where the Concourse merges into Surf Avenue.

"This man," continued the voice, "will be on the seaward side. He will be dressed in gray, and will have a short red beard. You cannot mistake him if you keep your eyes open. He will wear a white golf cap. Go up to him and say 'Barham.' If he answers 'Cuyp,' hand him the bag quietly and walk away. If he does not give the right answer, explain that you mistook him for a Mr. Barham; and keep on looking for the right man. Now, is that clear?"

"I am to go to a point on the Concourse—whatever that may be—on the seaward side, about a hundred yards beyond a street called Surf Avenue. I am to be there at nine o'clock to-night, and to look out for a red-bearded man in gray clothes and a white golf cap. I am to say 'Barham' to him. If he answers 'Cuyp,' I am to hand him the bag. Well? What, then?"

"That is all."

"All?"

I am afraid my tone showed my disappointment. I had counted on some test of wit, nerve, or resource. And lo! I was being dispatched on mere messenger-boy work!

All this silly mystery and secrecy about the carrying of a satchel to Coney Island.

My unseen interlocutor seemed to read my chagrin.

"I am sorry," sneered the voice, "that Mr. Barham did not choose to select you to rescue some fair damsel from a dragon or to blow up the Sub-treasury or to kidnap the Statue of Liberty, instead of giving you such a humble task; but I have found that he knows his business. If he has set you this task it is because, for some reason, the task is worth accomplishing. When you've worked for him as long as I have, you will begin to realize that he has brains. Almost as many as you, Mr. Dallam. Shall I go back and say you refuse?"

"No," I said curtly; "I will do it."

On second thought, I saw the wisdom of his reproof. Who was I that I should question the plans of a genius like Barham? If he chose to regard this messenger-boy work as a "test," I ought to be grateful that so simple a task had been assigned me.

"Very good," commended the voice. "Remember every detail. Guard that bag as if it held the crown jewels of England instead of waste paper and leaden weights. And speak to no one about your mission. Good-by."

It was hard, unbelievably hard, for me to refrain from turning and going around to the door of the tool house for just a glance at the man. But curiosity had to give place to ambition. And I was ambitious to succeed. I meant to carry out every simple detail of the foolish test.

So I sat there, staring out over the sparkling bay. The day was hot, as I have said. Men sitting near me were nodding, or else sound asleep. I wondered—

Had I, too, dozed and dreamed this fantastic, improbable thing? Half convinced that I had, I got to my feet. I was almost ashamed to look under the bench for the bag the dream voice had spoken of.

Yet I did look. And there it was! A battered, yellow-brown leather "half-size" suit case. The sort people sometimes take to the beach to hold their bathing suits, brushes, and towels.

I stooped and picked it up. It was heavy. Then I looked about for a Coney Island boat.

My test had begun.

Chapter II.
To An Unknown Land.

I had never been to Coney Island. So the wonder resort was completely unknown territory to me.

I knew no more where Surf Avenue or the Concourse might be than the whereabouts of some public square in Tibet.

I had a dim idea that one could reach Coney Island probably in an hour or so. It was not yet two o'clock. I was not due at the trysting place until nine. Yet I resolved to put in the extra hours in seeing the Coney sights.

I boarded the boat with a throng of people. They were of all sorts and conditions—from the tired, fat, shirt-waisted mother, with three noisy children, a picnic basket, and two sand pails, to the overdressed office boy and his perfectly attired best girl.

"Candy butchers" dived through the jolly crowd, peddling indigestibles to eat and drink. A trio of dark-faced musicians whanged popular airs out of tired-sounding string instruments.

Everybody was talking loudly, as a rule. Everybody seemed to wear a broad grin.

A frail-looking camp stool collapsed under a fat man's weight, and the laugh that rose could be heard as far as the half-mile-distant shore.

Another man's straw hat was whisked from his head and overboard by a vagrant whiff of sea wind; and the victim served as target for a second laugh.

By some miracle I had secured a camp chair, during the wild scramble for those rare commodities. I also secured a place by the rail, fairly well forward, where the sea wind slapped my hot face and a girl's hat feather gouged at my eyes.

I fell to watching the panorama of land and water as we sped southward, and the traffic that strewed the bay's broad, blue breast. The bag was tucked safely between my feet, one heel jammed tight on each side of it.

I felt a trifle downcast. In this throng of pleasure seekers I seemed strangely alone. Everybody else appeared to be with a sweetheart or a friend, or was part of some jocose group. I was alone; and one can be as much alone in a crowd as on a desert island.

A tow-headed young man, with a flaring yellow-and-red tie, a checked suit, and vivid yellow shoes, was crossing the deck in front of me, trying to worm his way through the press toward the rail. A very fat man—the same whose chair had smashed—happened to turn suddenly, as the other passed. The two came into violent contact. The young fellow lost his balance under the shock, and would have sprawled headlong had I not caught him.

"Thanks, bo!" he remarked, nodding at me as he readjusted his hat, and then glaring murderously at the fat man. "That human roundhouse sure gave me a jar."

"Are you hurt?" I asked.

"Not much, I guess," he returned, rubbing one shoulder. "My paint's a bit scratched, but my cylinders seem to be all right."

Instead of continuing his journey across the deck, he calmly picked up a camp stool, from which another man had momentarily risen to greet a friend, whisked it over beside my own stool, and sat down beside me.

"Alone?" he asked.

"Yes," I said.

"Same here," he vouchsafed. "Traveling to Coney all alone is 'bout as merry as watching other folks get Christmas presents."

"Why did you come, then?" I asked.

"Me? Oh, I was pretty sure to scrape up an acquaintance with some one on the boat; I gen'r'lly do. I ain't particular who I travel with."

The compliment was dubious, but I overlooked it. He continued:

"So when I saw you sitting here like a man at a funeral I thought to myself: 'Old Gloomy Gus needs cheering up.' And as I'm one of our best little cheerers, I fluttered across. Ain't butting in, am I?"

"No," I laughed.

There was something engaging about the chap, and his odd form of speech was new to my rural-bred ears.

"Some folks," resumed my new acquaintance. "Some folks say it's dangerous to get into talk with strangers. Maybe it is, at that. I lost a watch that way once. But I don't feel scared about talking with you."

"Thank you," I laughed.

"You see," he continued, "I'm not wearing a watch to-day. By the way, my name's Shayne. Bat Shayne. What's yours?"

"Arthur Dallam," I told him.

"H'm!" he commented. "While you was picking out a book name, why didn't you call yourself Montmorency Cholmondeley, or something else with class to it? But a man's got a right to any monaker he chooses, I s'pose. Going for a swim?"

"I don't know. Perhaps. Why?"

"I thought maybe you had bathing togs in that bag. Looks like it."

"No."

"No? Well, it's none of my business, as you was about to repartee, but why else should a man lug a valise to Coney? I'd as soon think of wearing yellow shoes to a wedding. What's the use of cluttering up your hands with a satchel? If ever you need both hands, it's at Coney."

"What for?"

"To hang on with. That bag'll get in about seven hundred people's way before you've walked a block, and by the time you've taken it along the line for the chutes and the scenic and the gorge, and the rocky road and Pike's Peak, and a few other hang-on-for-your-life stunts, it'll be more in your way than a reformer at a prize fight. Always carry it when you go to Coney?"

"I've never been to Coney Island before," I confessed.

He turned square about and stared at me, wide-eyed.

"Well, I'll be eternally and teetotally frazzled!" he gasped, at last. "You ain't stringing me?"

"No, I'm—"

"What branch of the Tall Timbers did you let loose of, when you fell into little old New York?" he asked. "Never been to Coney? Say, bo! I'm a bird at picking winners. And this time I've picked the star of the whole bunch. Gee, but I'm glad I tied up to you, brother. It'll be more fun than a dogfight in school to do Coney with a greenhorn. We'll see the el'phant and we'll hear the owl. Those eyes of yours will tumble sideways out of your face at the things you'll see. How are you fixed?"

"Fixed?"

"Yes. Got a kickful of iron men, or only working the pike end of it?"

"Once more, please," I begged him, "and this time say it in English."

"I asked you," he explained, with the bored patience of one teaching a stupid child, "if you're flush or broke. If you're going to hand it out in bunches or going to squeeze Lincoln's face off every time you spend a cent."

"Oh, I see. I've got about twelve dollars with me, and—"

"For twelve bucks, a man that knows the ropes can buy all Coney and have it shipped to his home address. I'm kind of glad I met you, son. There's the Promised

Land!" he broke off, pointing.

In the interest of our talk I had forgotten to watch the shore. Now I saw we had swung around a long finger of sand spit and were approaching a line of gaudy and garishly shaped buildings that rose out of a stretch of yellow sand and split the blue sky line in a marvel of fantastic silhouettes.

And, out to greet us, came a veritable rush of sounds—bands and orchestrions in fifty keys and a hundred tunes; the noise of many voices, the shouts of bathers, the cries of venders and barkers.

The City of Pleasure glowed white and rainbow-hued in the torrid sunlight. A rush of sea air and a line of snowy surf flashed against it. To my unaccustomed senses there was a thrill, a sparkle, an indefinable atmosphere of mirth that swirled around and over and through the whole place.

The stir of it all infected the passengers on the boat, whose earlier gayety had begun to die down. There was a rush for the gangway.

I stood up. Some one, passing, brushed my camp stool aside, and it fell with a clatter. Instinctively I turned to look at it. As I did so, the people surged eagerly forward, for the boat was warping in to the long pier.

The jostle almost swept me off my feet. I was carried on with it for several yards before I could brace myself to make headway against that laughing, pushing, roughly happy crowd.

Then, as a sudden idea flashed across my brain, I plunged through the mass with the speed and brute force of a football player, scattering indignant people to left and right, my elbow driving fiercely into one man's ribs, my raised forearm thrusting another fellow aside, my mad haste barely allowing me to escape collision with women and babies.

For it had dawned upon me that the bag—the bag on whose safe-keeping my hopes of advancement all hung—had been at my feet when I was shoved backward, and that now it was either being trodden under foot or had been stolen by some unscrupulous passenger.

I regained the spot, as well as I could figure, where I had been sitting.

No trace of the bag.

As well look for a needle in the traditional haystack as for a mere half-length suit case in that whirlpool of humanity.

It was lost! And through my own heedlessness. Was there ever such luck?

Chapter III.
Lost And Found.

Through the fast-emptying boat I ran like a madman, upsetting chairs, running against people, deaf to protests and growls; searching everywhere for that wretched bag.

I peered in corners and under benches. I glared suspiciously at every one who carried a parcel of any sort. I asked questions; then hurried on without waiting for a reply.

The bag was nowhere to be found!

I cursed my lot. I, who had scoffed at the simplicity of Mr. Barham's test, now saw my own folly in a pitiless light.

I had longed for a chance to make good. And now—

I found myself on the pier, still rushing back and forth aimlessly, like a lost dog, looking at every one and seeking a glimpse of the thief.

I ran into one man blindly. He caught my arm and shook me. I turned on him, eager for a chance to vent my rage and self-contempt on somebody. But, as I turned, I recognized him.

It was Bat Shayne, whose existence I had wholly forgotten in the excitement of the past few minutes. He still held my arm, and grinned quizzically into my scared face.

"What's your hurry?" he drawled. "This ain't the way to get the fun out of old Coney. If you run around much longer in circles you're liable to catch up with yourself."

"Let me go!" I panted, pulling free. "I'm looking for—"

"For this, by any chance?" he asked, holding up my bag.

With a groan of utter relief, I snatched it from him and clutched it as though it were a life preserver.

"It's real cute of you to thank me so polite," he observed. "Bless you for them kind words."

"Excuse me!" I said, in tardy remorse. "I do thank you. More than I can say. How did you ever find it?"

"You'd left the bag laying there. I picked it up for you. I tried to give it to you. But the only times I could get sight of you you were running around bowling over everything that wasn't stationary. I couldn't catch up with you. So I came down here and waited till—"

"What a wall-eyed fool I am!" I laughed.

"And then some," he amended. "I'd hate to see you in a real scrape. You'd be like old Al Fitzpatrick, who fell into the horse trough and yelled out: 'I'm all right. I can swim. But save the women and children!' Say, bo, that bag must be pretty valuable, from the way you hug it. Full of diamonds or just stuffed with measly little piker government bonds?"

"Neither," I answered. "It holds nothing more important than my chance of promotion."

"If that's a riddle—" he began doubtfully.

"It is," I answered, "but I don't know the answer."

"We're wasting time," said Bat, evidently giving up any effort to solve my puzzling speech. "Here we are. There is Coney. Let's get together. How about a swim before we take in the sights?"

"The bag," I protested.

"You'd look fine giving it a surf bath," he returned. "But they knew you was coming. So they built a place where you can check it."

"I don't like to let the bag out of my hands," I demurred.

"Why, folks check tons of joolry at those bathing joints; and wads of bills that a goat couldn't carry on his back. It's as safe as a jail. Say, bo, where are you taking the silly bag, anyhow? Or did you just bring it along for company?"

"I am taking it to a man I am to meet here at nine o'clock," I answered guardedly.

"And you're taking a running start by bringing it here at four? Gee, what a stunt to make a man do on his afternoon off!"

"I am not made to do it," I contradicted. "I do it of my own accord."

"Your own accord?" he echoed. "You lug that heavy thing around all day when you don't have to? Why, man, it's as foolish as coaxing a mosquito into your room!"

"Come on!" I said, half ashamed. "I'll check the bag, anyway, while we have our swim."

We left the pier, and found ourselves, in a few minutes, on the busiest, oddest, noisiest street I had ever seen. Broadway was a suburban lane by contrast.

People in gay attire thronged and pushed. Barkers and hucksters shouted. The smell of frankfurters, fresh popcorn, and other eatables was heavy on the sultry air.

"Hot-dog" venders cried their wares. At open booths men pulled red and white and green candy by machinery. Souvenir shops, stores of every garish sort; merry-go-rounds and other places of amusement lined the sidewalks. Down the center paraded wagons with the signs of "attractions" painted on them. Everywhere was the blare of music.

"What street is this?" I asked Shayne.

"Surf Avenue," he told me.

"Anywhere near the Concourse?"

"Nope. That's way up east, toward Brighton. Why?"

"I just wanted to know," I evaded, making mental note of the direction, against the time I should deliver the bag there to the messenger.

"See that big, bare, charred place up there? To the right and eastward? That was Dreamland. That's all there is left of it. Gee, but that sure was some fire! At night, too. Made all the sky look like a pink veil thrown into a pail of ink. I could see it from New York. I feel kind of sad when I think of that dandy white tower all gone to blazes. I pulled wires for three years to get a season pass to Dreamland. At last I got it. Next day the whole thing burned down."

We had reached the bathing pavilion. There I checked the bag, together with my watch and money, putting the two last-named articles in a big manila envelope and writing my name across the back.

I received in exchange a numbered metal tag on a thick rubber band. I followed Bat Shayne's example of putting this band around my neck, feeling just a little like a licensed dog as I did so.

It was my first swim in surf; and it was so gloriously exhilarating that I stayed in the water for a full hour. To an inlander like myself there was an unspeakable charm about the stinging slap of the breakers and the swirl of foam and green water.

At last, dragged almost bodily from the sport by Shayne, who was blue-lipped and chattering, I ran up the gangway with him toward the rows of dressing rooms.

"Get a good rubdown," Bat exhorted me, as we hurried along; "then climb inside your clothes as quick as you can. After that, we'll get warmed up by swatting the hammer game a while. Its a big mallet, and you hit a cushion with it; and if you hit hard enough the bell rings. I've seen strong men who couldn't make that bell ring and I've seen cripples that could. It's all a trick, a knack. Throw all the strength and weight and force into the last six inches of the stroke. I studied that out for myself."

In ten minutes I was dressed, and standing by Bat's side at the "Valuables" window. I turned in my numbered tag, and in return got the envelope containing my watch and money. Then the attendant went to a set of larger compartments, and returned with a satchel which he shoved across the counter toward me.

It was a half-length suit case. But, at first glance, I saw it was not mine. It was newer, and of a different shade of brown.

I pushed it back.

"You've got the wrong bag," said I.

"Only bag in that compartment," he replied; "and that's the number your check calls for."

"It's not mine!" I insisted angrily.

"It's the one your check calls for," repeated the man, with some impatience. "Take it and step aside. You're blocking the line."

"I tell you," I cried, "it's not mine."

"What's up?" queried Bat. "Are you in the allooring rôle of trouble hunter again?"

"There's been a mistake!" I declared, sick at heart. "This man has given me the wrong satchel. I—"

"That's what t'other fellow said," put in a boy who was lounging near by, waiting for some slow-dressing companion who had not yet appeared.

"What's that?" I demanded, whirling about to him.

"A guy in a gray suit, white golf cap, and red whiskers came here after his swim," said the boy. "That was maybe five minutes ago. The man at the window shoved him a bag. The red-whiskered chap said 'twasn't his. The window man said it was, and wouldn't hear 'no' to it. At last the feller with the whiskers takes the bag and says 'It isn't mine, but it cannot be worth any less, for mine's got nothing but an old extra bathing suit in it. So I'll take this, since you won't give me my own.' And off he goes."

"I s'pose the attendant got the two bags in the wrong pigeonholes," suggested Bat. "They look alike, and any one—"

"You say," I broke in, turning to the boy, as a memory flashed across me, "you say he had a red beard, a white golf cap, and a gray suit?"

"Yes. He—"

I waited for no more, but bolted wildly from the pavilion, leaving the other bag behind me.

Apparently the very man to whom I was to deliver the original bag at nine that night had accidentally come into possession of it. And I meant to scour Coney Island until I should find him.

I had been intrusted to hand him the bag at the Concourse and Surf Avenue at nine that night. And I intended to do it, even if I had first to take it away from him. I knew he would probably remain in Coney Island until then, as he was to meet me at nine. And I intended to carry out this latest item of the involved affair.

Call me a fool if you will; but all my temper and determination were up. And I was not going to confess myself beaten without a fight.

Chapter IV.
Still In Quest Of Trouble.

"What's the mad rush this time?" queried Bat Shayne, as he caught up with me. "The bag again?"

"Yes. I must find it."

"Looks more to me like you must lose it. Losing that bag is getting to be a habit with you."

"I must find it," I repeated. "It means everything to me. I must find it and give it, at nine to-night, to a man who—to the man who has it now."

"You talk like a man in a cave!" he snorted. "Are you dippy, or only just sunstruck? A man's got it, and you've got to find him and give it to him? Ain't you afraid of meeting yourself on such a fool errand?"

Briefly, as I hastened along, scanning every face, I told Bat Shayne the whole story. From time to time, as I talked, he looked sideways at me, as though seeking some hidden joke.

But my manner must have convinced him, for as I finished he said:

"You're up against it, son. As far as I can see, the test ends here and now. You were told to give the bag to that man at nine o'clock. It isn't six yet, and he's got it already. What more is there to do?"

"To fulfill the test," I answered doggedly.

"But—"

"I'm going to find that man and get the bag from him. I'm convinced he doesn't know it's the same one he was to receive from me at Surf Avenue and the Concourse. Otherwise he would not have demurred when the attendant at the baths forced the bag on him. In any case, my test required me to give him the bag at a certain place, at a certain hour. I mean to do it."

"Take it from him and hold it till nine p. m. and then hand it back? It don't make a terrible lot of sense. But I get your idea; and I kind of like you for it. There's a few better things than sense, in this old world. And one of 'em is grit. I'm going to help you, if you'll let me."

"Thanks, old man!" said I, in real gratitude.

"Two heads are better than one," he went on, "especially when one is a trouble hunter's head. Maybe the two of us can run across him somewhere. It's a hundred-in-one shot, but we'll try it. I know Coney pretty well. Alone, you'll get lost and tangled up in no time."

"But," I demurred, "you came down here for a good time. It isn't fair to spoil your outing by making you—"

"Spoil my outing?" he echoed. "Why, bo, you'll be giving me the outing of my life. I can stroll down the Coney line any old time. But it isn't every day I can be runner-up in a trouble hunt. Even if we don't find the measly bag, we'll have the fun of looking for it and for the gent with the crimson alfalfas and the white lid. And if we do find him—Gee, it'll be more fun than a catfight in jail to watch you try to separate the guy from his satchel. Oh, cut out the cold, cold fear of spoiling little Reginald's day. You're handing me the time of my life. Now, we've pretty well glanced over Surf Avenue. S'pose we take a turn at the Bowery and then drop into the parks. He'll be in some of those places most likely."

There is no need to go into wearisome detail as to the events of the next few hours. To me, they are a sickening, confused memory. We scoured Coney Island's tumultuous streets, its restaurants, its parks. Everywhere we stared until our eyes burned for a man with red beard, white cap, and gray suit. Thousands of gray suits we saw, a few red-bearded men, and two men with white golf caps. But never the right combination at the same time.

Day had turned into night—the noisy, blaring, glaring, garish Saturday night of the vast summer resort. The streets and parks were packed. Fast movement became impossible. As the crowd thickened I realized more and more the rank hopelessness of my search. Yet, ever, my stubborn determination made me press on, regardless of throbbing head, aching feet, and tired body.

I had been so ambitious to do well at the Barham & Cuyp office. My chance had come. There might never be another. And I was not going to give up, so long as one spark of life or hope remained. Meantime, my watch's hands crept relentlessly on toward the hour of nine—the hour which would mark the death knell of my high hopes.

We strayed into a big amusement park, which, in view of what befell us there, I will not name. It was our third visit to the place in three hours. The park was crowded and unspeakably bright and gay. A hundred amusement enterprises were in full blast.

The chutes sent boatfuls of squealing people whizzing down the long incline and splashing into the miniature lake. The scenic railway's roar was mingled with the cries and delighted yelps of passengers as each steep dip sent the car plunging downward.

An open-air animal show was drawing a crowd. A miniature railway with a baby engine bore groups of children through mysterious tunnels on a narrow-gauge track.

The Old Mill boats were massed at one end of a tiny artificial stream. People would board the boats and be pushed off into the darkness; into a succession of "wonder scenes" and dense gloom.

This amusement device somehow appealed to me rather than some of the more spectacular sports. In spite of my haste and worry, I hated to glance a second time at the boats and at the little knot of waiting people.

At the moment there chanced to be very few persons patronizing the mill boats. A lion in the animal show near by had taken into its head to give an exhibition of roaring. And the hideous sound had drawn most of the "floating" crowd to the spot, leaving adjacent sports ill-attended.

I glanced carelessly at the mill. Then, with a cry, I ran headlong toward its inclosure, followed by the puzzled, vainly questioning Bat.

For, stepping toward the foremost boat, I caught a glimpse of a gray-suited man, wearing a white golf cap. A slight motion of his head showed me his profile. He had a pointed beard, vividly red, and in his hand he carried—*a half-length suit case!*

I wasted no time explaining or inspecting. I was almost afraid the fellow might vanish into thin air. Past the entrance to the mill I dashed, leaving the pursuing Bat to pay for both of us.

Fast as I ran, I never once took my eyes from the object of my search. I saw him step lazily into the first of the waiting flat-bottomed barges. He was its only passenger. As he got aboard I noted a second man—taller, heavier, clad in blue serge—hurry forward and grab at the bag carrier's shoulder.

The grasp fell short, and the other did not even see that some one had tried to stop him. He went straight on, into the boat, and seated himself in the center thwarts.

The man in blue serge stepped into the boat in pursuit. The red-bearded man glanced up, took one look at his pursuer, then, without a word, ducked nimbly under the blue-serge arm and at one bound was out of the boat, leaving the bag behind him on the seat.

The man in blue stooped to snatch up the bag before chasing his escaping victim. At this moment, I, having reached the boat, bounded aboard and grabbed the bag.

The impetus of my jump almost upset the man in blue. It also jarred the boat loose from the attendant's boat hook.

Freed, the light barge plunged into the tunnel, borne on the strong current. The attendant on the bank, with a yell, jabbed for it with his boat hook, and missed it.

Into the underground darkness we swirled, the strange man and I grappling together furiously for the bag.

Chapter V.
Fight In The Dark.

It was an odd situation, had either of us had time to consider it. But neither of us had. Here were we, two men who, until a minute earlier, had never seen each other, fighting desperately in the utter blackness of a handmade underworld, for possession of a bag whose contents I thought neither of us knew.

The Old Mill boats are broad, flat, and almost shapeless. They are built to glide along a rapid stream that is almost no wider than themselves, through a succession of twists and mazes, until at last they come out at their starting point.

A fleet of these boats are launched in succession. No pilot or attendant is aboard them, as there is ordinarily no danger of hitch or of upset, and as the current carries them safe to their destination.

The banks of the tunnel are interspersed, here and there, in the darkness, by electric-light grottoes wherein weird or pretty figures are displayed. Fairy-book scenes or little flower gardens are shown.

In the blackness we fought silently, the big man and I. He was taller and his weight was greater. But I was younger and had won something of a local repute as a college athlete. Moreover, my sudden onslaught had taken him by surprise. So the fight was not as one-sided as it might seem.

I had leaped aboard and had seized the bag. The jar of my feet landing in the bottom of the boat had not only wrenched the barge away from the detaining clutch of the boat hook; but had thrown the blue-serge man off his balance. Nevertheless, even as he fell, he kept his hold on the bag. And I had much ado to keep from losing my own grip on it.

He regained his feet, and sought to tear the suit case away from me. I hung on like grim death, and strove in turn to wrench it away from him.

The boat swayed and pitched dangerously under our stamping feet and swaying bodies. To keep one's equilibrium in such circumstances was difficult indeed. Back and forth we reeled, tugging, twisting, striking. I have seldom imagined a less scientific, more awkwardly haphazard combat.

After my hours of despair, worry, and vain search I would no sooner have relinquished my hold on that miraculously discovered suit case than I would have relinquished the privilege of breathing. My opponent seemed equally determined, and he fought like a wild cat, speaking no word, wasting no time in argument or threat. We were simply like two primitive men battling murderously in the bowels of the earth.

It never once occurred to me in the excitement of the moment to question or try to explain the scene I had witnessed between my foe and the man with the red beard.

I did not even wonder who this big newcomer might be or his possible reason for seizing the bag, nor why, at sight of him, the other man had fled like a scared rabbit.

All that concerned me just then was to get back that bag and to be, with it, at the trysting place by nine o'clock.

After hours of despair, the possibility that I might yet succeed in the test, and win promotion, put new life in me. Here was a chance to atone in full for my earlier carelessness and ill luck. It was my last chance, too, and I meant it should carry me to victory.

To and fro we staggered, clawing at the bag's slippery sides, smashing wildly with doubled fists, in the darkness, at each other's bodies.

A twist of the tunnel brought us momentarily into a dazzling brightness. We were passing a grotto with spangled sea nymphs posing on mica rocks, under a bunch of arc lights. We became, thus, for an instant, visible to one another. I could see the red, tense face of my adversary, and I struck fiercely at it.

A lurch of the boat as we entered a new area of gloom sent my fist blow whizzing past his broad shoulder. The motion enabled him to wrench the bag from my free hand. He whirled the suit case behind him with one hand, while with the other he rained blows at me as I sprang forward.

I threw my arm about him in a high football tackle, his fist grazing my cheek stingingly as I grappled with him. My onrush threw him again off his balance. He threw back one foot against the stern of the boat to brace himself. The bit of carved wood, against which his heel struck, snapped under the shock.

Backward we reeled, close gripped in each other's arms. The boat slipped forward, and together my foe and I tumbled into the abyss of racing water behind the stern.

We were overboard, and again in pitch blackness.

Chapter VI.
Into Nothingness!

Into the swirling water we fell with a mighty splash.

After the heat of the tunnel and of our fight, the water seemed icy cold. It made me gasp and strangle, this sudden, involuntary bath.

But it did not make me loose my grip, nor did my enemy loose his. Dimly I realized that he was grasping me with but one arm. So I knew instinctively that he was still hanging onto the bag with the other.

Into the water, I say, we fell. Entangled in each other's furious embrace as we were, we could not swim a stroke. This, I felt, must mean swift drowning. But I was too full of the rage of battle to heed this. Drowning or no, I would not cease my quest of the bag.

Then—ridiculous anticlimax—it dawned on me that we would not drown at all; for we were rolling about in the water less than two feet deep!

The current was strong, and dashed over us. But the artificial stream was just deep enough to float the flat boats.

My foe realized this, I think, almost as quickly as did I. For he scrambled to his feet and, bag in hand, sought to dash down the shallow channel to the far-off entrance.

But before he had taken two strides I was upon him. And again we fought, this time in a slippery wooden river bed with the water churning about our ankles.

With my left hand, I caught the biceps of his free arm. Then, with my right I struck, using my full force and sending my shoulder after the blow.

My fist caught him somewhere on the lower jaw, dazing him. He reeled backward, dropping the bag.

On the instant I was upon my knees amid the swish and rush of water groping for it. My hand came into accidental contact with the wet leather handle.

I gripped it, got to my feet, and, at a step, had gained the narrow bank that lay between the water and the tunnel wall. The bag was once more mine, though water-soaked and battered.

Before I could decide on my next move, my foe had recovered his half-dazed senses. By the faint glow from a distant grotto he located me, and flung himself upon me.

I struck at him with the heavy bag; but he ran inside the blow, and gained a hold on my throat and shoulder.

My feet went from under me on the slippery bank, and together we crashed backward with terrific force against the solid wall of the tunnel, just as once more I whirled the bag aloft and struck.

To my amazement, the wall gave way, as my shoulder banged backward against it. The bag, this time, had caught my adversary squarely on the top of the head and brought him to his knees like a stunned bull.

But I had no time to do more than vaguely note this, for, the tunnel wall collapsing behind me, my own impetus hurled me, satchel and all, through the aperture and out into—what?

A section of the wall had broken down, with a rending, crackling sound, precipitating me through the hole. I felt myself falling—about three feet. Then I landed with a soft bump in a heap of sand.

I picked myself up, grasping the bag, and stared dazedly about me. Above, the moon was shining. This, and the Island's distant street lights, showed me I was in a sandy, vacant lot—a sort of back yard of the park.

In front of me stretched away a low, snakelike building of some sort, with boarded sides. A newly made gap in these boards showed me where I had fallen through.

Then I understood. The snakelike, twisting structure was the exterior of the Old Mill tunnel. I had hit against the inner side and the thin boards had given way.

I was dripping wet from head to foot. I glanced at my watch. It was still going. Four minutes before nine.

I heard a sound from within the tunnel. Then I saw the man in blue serge trying to force his greater bulk through the narrow opening my body had made.

I waited no longer.

I turned and fled; climbed a fence, found myself in an alleyway, and thence dashed out into Surf Avenue. I still had two minutes' time in which to keep my tryst. And I meant to keep it.

Toward the Concourse I dashed, running madly down the center of the street, dodging vehicles, scattering the people afoot.

Chapter VII.
At The Meeting Place.

There are many wondrous and fantastic sights at Coney Island; yet I doubt if any of the local spectacles were queerer or more outlandish than was I as I raced eastward along the middle of Surf Avenue that night.

I was hatless, of course. My clothes were streaming wet. My crimson tie had "run," and was sending a ruddy rivulet down the front of my white negligee shirt. My collar lay limp as a handkerchief. My shapeless boots "squnched" at every step.

Tight to my breast I hugged the soaked, dilapidated, little suit case, clasping it as a half back might hold the ball when bucking the opposing line.

People stopped to stare after me. Autoists honked an angry warning. Women laughed or screamed. Boys threw things at me. As I sped on, I heard one man drawl:

"He's advertising some show—the 'Big Flood,' or something like that."

Up Surf Avenue I tore, shoving, dodging, ducking, ever hastening at top speed. After an eternity—that probably occupied little over a minute—I found myself within a step or two of the meeting place.

I dropped into a walk, and glanced at my watch. It still lacked thirty seconds of nine o'clock.

I was on time. I had fulfilled the test. It was no affair of mine that the other man was not likely to keep the tryst.

No, I had not the faintest, remotest idea that my man would appear.

Nor did I care in the very least whether he put in an appearance or not. My orders had been to be at that very spot with the bag at nine o'clock. I was there. It was nine o'clock.

I resolved to wait fifteen minutes or so, then go to the nearest telephone and call up the Oriental Hotel, where I remembered Mr. Barham was spending the summer. I would notify him that I had carried out his commands, that his messenger had not appeared, and ask what he wished done with the bag.

I was not a little proud of my exploit and grateful at the luck that had backed it. I had, twice that day, wholly and apparently hopelessly, lost the treasured bag. Twice by sheer good fortune I had found it again.

A third time I had fought for its possession as for my very life. And, through a combination of luck and pluck, I had won out at last. I recalled that the Voice had told me Mr. Barham had no use for a failure. Well, whether through good fortune or merit, I at least had not failed. I—

My somewhat vainglorious reverie was suddenly broken short. Directly in front of me, and hurrying in my direction, I saw the man with the red beard and the white golf cap.

Nor was he late to the appointment. For it was barely on the stroke of nine. He came along, scanning the crowd, to right and left, somewhat furtively, it seemed to me. I stepped up to him.

"Barham?" I remarked carelessly, repeating the arranged password as though I were merely inquiring if that were his name.

The man's small, shifty eyes took in my whole appearance at one glance, his gaze resting long and wonderingly upon the wet, discolored bag. Then he answered, giving the correct countersign:

"Cuyp!"

As he spoke, he reached out his hand for the satchel. I surrendered it to him, heartily thankful to get the miserable, tricky, elusive thing out of my possession.

But I could not forbear saying:

"Since you had this so long, I wonder you didn't keep it."

His bright little eyes widened in genuine surprise.

"Was this the bag I was lugging about?" he exclaimed. "I had the tip to meet you here at nine. There was a lot of time to kill, so I 'did' the Island. I had the bathing suit and a pal's in a bag. And the bathhouse people shifted the bag on me. So I hung onto this on the chance there might be a reward offered. There was no good place to open it. So—"

"Then why did you drop it and run," I queried, "when that big fellow—"

I got no further. The red-bearded man's eyes dilated in sudden fright. He was not looking at me, but over my shoulder at some one.

In another second he had thrust back the heavy satchel into my hands, had wheeled, and was running away with the speed of a scared rabbit.

Before I could speak or move, two men had seized my shoulder from behind, while a third snatched the bag from me. Two more men sped past me after the flying, white-capped runner.

Wondering if this were some new development of the test, I wriggled about to face my assailants. The first of them that my eye fell upon was the man who had just seized the bag. He was my old enemy, the blue-serge giant. Now, he looked well-nigh as disreputable as did I.

He was hatless, and his blue suit hung limp and dripping about him. At sight of the fellow, my former rage stirred within me. I tried to step toward him.

Then, for the first time, I noted that the two men who held me were uniformed policemen. Over their shoulders peered the scared face of Bat Shayne.

"Dallam!" called Shayne before any of the rest of us could speak, "where does Barham live? Quick? D'ye know his phone number?"

"He's at the Oriental, down near here somewhere," I answered.

Scarce waiting to hear my reply, Bat sped away.

"Come along, young feller!" ordered one of the policemen. "Cap'n wants to see you. Sure this is the man, Flagg?"

The blue-serge-suited man nodded, adding:

"Didn't we see him slip the bag to Phony Jack just now? And look at his wet clothes. He's the one; I'll swear to him."

"If this is a joke—" I began, dazed.

"If it is," retorted Flagg, "then State's prison is a side-splitter. Come along with him, boys. There's a crowd collecting."

I saw it was no use asking questions just then, and it would have been doubly idiotic to resist. Moreover, I was utterly bewildered. It was my first experience with the police, and I had heard that in such cases it was best to go quietly.

So, through the gaping, questioning crowd, I suffered myself to be hustled, and on down to the police station. There, at a desk, an officer took my pedigree, and, without having time to ask anything, I was hustled into a back room. There the two policemen, with Flagg and a burly, purple-faced police captain, gathered about a table on which the wet satchel had been laid.

Flagg stepped forward, and with a bunch of skeleton keys proceeded to test the bag's lock.

"Leave that alone!" I cried, finding my voice. "It belongs to my employer. I—"

"Shut up!" growled Flagg.

The captain echoed the order, adding perfunctorily the old formula:

"Anything you say'll be used against you at your trial."

"My trial!" I yelled. "My trial for what?"

"I've got the right key at last," broke in Flagg, who had been fumbling over the bag. "Found it inside of ten seconds. One long ward and two short ones. I'm an artist at this game. You or Duke would have had to go through the whole bunch."

He clicked the key in the lock as he spoke, and threw back the top of the suit case. I made an involuntary movement of protest. But, even before the nearest patrolman could lay a restraining hand on my arm, I had stopped from pure amazement, and stood glaring, dumfounded.

For as the dingy leathern lid was raised, disclosing the contents of the bag, a gleam of soft, yellow radiance seemed to flood the smoky room.

There, tumbled loosely in the cavernous interior of the bag, was a heap of golden substance that gave back the electric light from a hundred rounded angles.

Gold cups, gold trays, gold plates, gold table utensils lay there, jumbled in careless profusion.

And this was the treasure I had been carrying about carelessly—losing, finding, fighting for, giving away in response to a silly password!

Before I could speak, the door of the room opened again, and two men came in. One was Bat Shayne. The second was my employer, Mr. Barham.

I turned on the latter in hot indignation.

"I fulfilled the test, sir!" said I, "but another time it might be well to give me an inkling of what I'm carrying. Gold plate is a trifle precious to risk in the hands of an untried clerk. Have I made good, or haven't I?"

Barham looked at me keenly. Then he replied: "Yes; you've made good. Your friend here told me the story as we came along. Did you really think I would set any employee such an idiotic test?"

"But—" I began.

"Let me explain," he intervened.

And he did explain. So did the captain; so did Flagg, the plain-clothes detective. In fact, everybody seemed to be explaining all at once to everybody else. From the babel I gleaned the following odd facts:

A few nights earlier, Mr. Barham's house in New York had been robbed. A clerk, discharged from the office the day of my arrival, was one of the gang. The burglars had been scared away before they could do more than loot the dining-room buffet of its gold plate.

They had taken this to be melted, but Barham had set the police upon their track so quickly that none of the local men who make a business of melting down stolen gold and silver dared touch the job. The discharged clerk and his two accomplices next tried to smuggle the treasure across to New Jersey or to Long Island, but the identity of all three was suspected.

And, as ferries, tunnels, stations, and bridges were watched, none of them dared leave town with the plunder. The clerk had gone that Saturday noon to the Battery to catch a Coney Island boat, thinking to smuggle himself, unnoticed, on board with the holiday crowd and to get the loot to Greenpoint, Long Island, where one of the gang already awaited him. But, nearing the dock, he had seen a plain-clothes man watching the boat. Finding himself blocked, the thief had not known what next to do.

In his quandary he had espied me sitting on a park bench. He had seen me arrive at the office the day of his discharge, and knew who I was. Seeing in my inexperience and ambition a chance of getting the gold plate safe to his confederate in Greenpoint, he had slipped into the tool house behind my bench, and had proposed to me the "test."

As soon as he had seen me depart with the bag, he had gone to a telephone and called up his accomplice in Greenpoint—the red-bearded man in the golf cap—and had bidden him to go to Coney Island and meet me according to the instructions I had received. The red-bearded man was to take the bag from me and carry it to a "fence" in Greenpoint, who would see to the "melting down."

Ten minutes after my boat sailed for Coney Island, the ex-clerk had been arrested. Under pressure he had confessed.

Flagg, who knew the red-bearded crook by sight, had been hurried to Coney Island to catch him. Like myself, he had scoured the resorts for the fellow, and had at last come upon him at the entrance to the Old Mill. Taking me for an accomplice of the thief, Flagg had summoned police aid, when I had escaped from him, and had given chase.

Bat, following close on my heels, had caught enough of the idea, from what Flagg said to the policemen during the pursuit, to realize how I had been duped. So he had posted off to Mr. Barham with the whole story.

Yes, I had been a fool, Mr. Barham said so himself. But he also said I had been a plucky, resourceful fool.

And—I got my promotion. Yes, I got it as the result of a test set me by a thief. As Bat Shayne wisely remarked afterward:

"A man who had any sense would have bungled the whole thing, and the bag would have been lost for keeps. If I had my life cards to play over again, I'd play 'em with my eyes shut. There's always something nice hangin' around loose for folks who are long on honesty and short on wits."

But I forgive Bat. He's a fine fellow at heart.

The Blizzard Juggler

"OF course," conceded Pierce, "it is an experiment."

"An experiment?" echoed Mallock. "About as much of an experiment as if an avalanche fell on me!"

"Then you're not going to try?"

Mallock replied:

"Of course I'm going to try! Providence doesn't give a bulldog jaw like mine to the sort of fellow who will sit calmly down and let an avalanche bury him. No! I'm going to try to fight my way upward through it. And if I get to the top I'll sell it as real estate. But," he added bitterly, "I'd be a born fool if I didn't realize I haven't one chance in ten thousand."

"If you go into the battle with that spirit," observed Pierce, "you're beaten before you start."

"I am? Well, before I'm through, the world at large will know there has been a battle. Now help me lock up the store. We'll both be the better for a good night's sleep. In the morning we will renew the discussion."

But Joe Mallock did not begin his much needed sleep as quickly as he might have done. Instead, when his assistant had gone, he placed paper, pen, and ink on the oilcloth-covered counter, drew a lamp nearer and began his daily letter to The Girl. These letters were usually of no interest save to their recipient. But on this night he had much to say.

I can't leave town Sunday, for I am going to be busy day and night from to-morrow on. Let me tell you in just a few words what has happened:

You know how hard I've been trying, for over a year, to make Mr. Cauldwell take me in as partner? I've explained that I am doing the *real* work of the store; that it is *my* plans and ideas which have nearly doubled his business; that I've refused three good offers out of loyalty to his interests. Well, I spoke to him about it again to-day, just as he was starting for New York on his semiyearly "buying trip." What do you suppose he said? He grunted and answered me:

"Young man, there may be sense in what you say. Or there may not. I'll make a deal with you. My profits on this store average $120.00 a week. You claim that, as partner, you could double those profits. I'll give you a chance. I'm going to be gone two weeks. Show me $480.00 net profits when I get back and I'll take you in as equal partner. Fail to do it and you must pledge yourself to stay on here as manager at $28.00 a week for three years longer, with no further talk of partnership. Is it a bargain?"

It took my breath away. Then I saw the trap. In early January our business nearly always falls off. It never yet has risen at that time. It's the slack season between the Christmas trade and the Easter. Mr. Cauldwell's profits drop to $90.00 or

$80.00 a week. There is no earthly chance of bringing them up to $120.00, to say nothing of doubling that. He knows it.

Yet, if by a miracle I *could* do it, I know Mr. Cauldwell will keep his word and make me a partner. If I *can't* he'll expect me to keep mine. That's the sort of man he is. You'll think me crazy, I suppose, but I've accepted the challenge. Pray for a miracle!

P. S.—Mr. Reuff, our real competitor here in Smithville, is already beginning to lay himself out to catch the extra custom, as he always does whenever Mr. Cauldwell goes away. Delightful prospect! To-morrow morning my campaign begins.

Mallock was up and busy in the bitter gray January dawn. Before Pierce and the other clerks appeared, he had set out a new and attractive window display; and, after careful figuring, had arranged a series of alluring, stenciled price-lists across the top of the street-sign, where their big lettering could not help but catch the gaze of passersby.

Then defiantly he glared across the street at the store of Reuff & Co. He knew his own windows and prices were far more tempting than Reuff's. And as the tide of early morning shopping set his way, he began to take heart.

But an hour later, Pierce drew him to the door and pointed across the street. There, over the top of Reuff's sign, hung a glaring array of prices, similar to Mallock's, but with a uniform ten per cent reduction.

"The first gun in the fight," observed Joe calmly.

"In the massacre, I'm afraid," answered Pierce. "See, the wind is already setting the other way. Our store's emptying and Reuff's is filling."

"Copy out a duplicate list of prices!" commanded Mallock

"To equal his? We *can't!* He's down to cost already."

"Do as I say. This is my *fight*. If I cost Mr. Cauldwell anything by my reductions, I'll pay him out of my own savings. And, while you're about it, slice off five per cent from the prices."

Never had there been such a shopping day at Smithville. People told each other of the rival stores' reductions and every one turned out to profit by the slaughter of rates. At noon, Reuff made another five per cent cut; and a little later Mallock followed it with a similar one.

At closing time, Reuff's ponderous figure rolled into the Cauldwell store. Mallock met him at the entrance.

"Well, Mr. Reuff," he said pleasantly, "what can we do for you this evening? I suppose you've come to buy something that can't be bought across the street. Very wise. Many people do that. Our assortment is—"

"Say, you young idiot!" puffed Reuff, "what d'ye mean by cutting rates like this? You'll have your boss bankrupt."

"That's our affair," answered Mallock.

"You've lost money to-day," grumbled Reuff. "So have I. This sort of thing will clean out both our stocks and leave us broke. What do you say to starting fresh to-morrow with the old prices? No use cutting each other's throats. We'll take down those cost-signs and go on as before. Is it a bargain?"

"Y-e-s-s!" reluctantly agreed Mallock, trying to hide his joy at the let-up. "I suppose so."

When Reuff had gone, he sat down and scribbled an order to a New York wholesale house for a replenishment of the stock that the day's "sacrifice sales" had depleted.

"How do we stand?" asked Pierce.

"Biggest day's business since December 24th," replied Mallock, "and not one penny of profit," he added grimly.

Next morning both rivals had removed the alluring prices from above their signs. Mallock was glad of the breathing-spell, and set about concocting new ideas for trade.

"What's up?" queried Pierce at eleven o'clock. "This is the slackest day we've ever had."

"Everybody bought yesterday."

"And everybody's buying to-day," retorted Pierce. "But they're buying at Reuff's. I'm going to drop over there for a look."

Five minutes later he came back.

"What do you suppose the old fox has done?" he asked Mallock. "Made a general mark-down on all sorts of goods. It's advertised on a big placard *inside* the door where we can't see it from here. Prices higher than yesterday, but low enough to cause a stampede from here."

"I might have known that a kid like myself had no chance at cunning against a veteran like Reuff!" growled Mallock. "I'll win out yet, though! He's taken a trick. The next is mine."

But the next trick was *not* Mallock's. Nor the next. Nor the next. When it came to sheer craftiness, he was as a child in the hands of the older, wiser man. At last he saw this himself.

"I've played the fool!" he confessed to Pierce, at the end of the first week. "If I'd gone ahead, doing the best I could, without thinking anything about Reuff or his store, I could have kept up a tolerable average of profits. But I lost sight of the real issue and tried to fight Reuff on his own ground. Here's the result."

He held up a slip of paper—the store's weekly "statement." Pierce glanced at it; then whistled long and low.

"Net profits $38.75!" he exclaimed. "The lowest in ten years. Old Cauldwell will foam at the mouth! I'm afraid this is good-by to your chance of that partnership. For the next three years it'll be $28.00 a week for you, instead of $120.00. Quite a tidy bit of difference!"

" You old Job's comforter!" cried Mallock. "There's a week yet. And—"

An envelope was handed to him. He tore it open, disclosing a bill of lading.

"Good!" said he. "We're pretty low in stock. I sent for full replenishing a week ago. The things ought to have been here yesterday. If—Hello! Our wholesalers must have gone insane. What do they mean by saying here, 'The unusual size of your esteemed order caused a delay of'—I ordered the usual—good Heavens!" he broke off. *"Look* at that bill of lading!"

Pierce glanced at it over Mallock's shoulder.

"Three car-loads!" he gasped. "Three *car-loads*. What on earth—why, that's enough provisions and staples to supply this whole county. Their shipping-clerk ought to be fired for such a blunder!"

Mallock did not hear. He had reached the telephone-booth at a bound and called up the New York wholesalers by long distance. In ten minutes he came out of the booth.

"Well?" asked Pierce.

"Well!" rejoined Mallock. "It's *their* mistake, all right. They got our orders mixed with one from a big Chicago supply warehouse. The Chicago things are coming— in three jammed car-loads—into the Smithville freight-yards at this very moment, I suppose. And *our* dinky little order is rattling west to Chicago. The wholesalers say they will rectify the blunder. But—"

"But what? You lose nothing by it."

"You don't understand. Our stock is practically exhausted. Already we are out of a lot of things. And people are going to Reuff's for them. Before our new supplies can get here by freight we'll be cleaned out as dry as a whistle. And Reuff will get every dollar's worth of trade. That'll mean—"

"Why not take some goods from those three car-loads? They're consigned to us."

"Because if we break into a consignment, we'll have to take it *all*. That's the rule, and you know it as well as I do. Mr. Cauldwell would be tickled to death, wouldn't he, if I did a thing like that and saddled him with four times as many goods as he had storage for? It'd be worse than going short. No, I'll have to take my medicine."

"The poor partnership!" sighed Pierce. "It—"

"Hang the partnership!" broke in Mallock. "I'm past thinking of that! It's gone for good and I won't whine over getting the worst of a bargain. It's Mr. Cauldwell's interest I'm thinking of now! This will not only mean a big cash loss to him, but a lot of the temporary trade that goes to Reuff's will stay there. Oh, I'm in a sweet mess! Here I try to prove myself worthy to be a partner in this concern, and in one short week I threaten to wreck my employer. I don't know what's come over me!"

"It's *luck!*" pronounced the other. "Luck runs in streaks, good and bad. And when a mere boy like yourself says: 'I'll take Fortune by the throat!' then old Dame Fortune is apt to be the one who does the throttling. But maybe Reuff is short of stock, too. He may—"

"Not he. At the station yesterday he said he expected a half car-load of staples in by to-morrow. He never lets himself get caught in a corner. It's *I* that am stuck."

"To make things pleasanter," said Pierce, "it's beginning to snow. That'll mean light trade all day and *no* trade for the evening. Maybe we can skimp along on the stock we've got, after all."

"Another bit of Job's comforting!" assented Mallock. "See, Reuff's store is running up a snow sign: *'Rubbers and umbrellas. Special sale to-day.'*"

"Why don't you run up one, too? Take advantage of the bad weather and—"

"And advertise things we haven't got? There are just the three umbrellas and four pairs of rubbers in the store. And one of those umbrellas was left here by mistake to-day. I'm the original Mr. Uppagainstit."

"How about your bulldog jaw now?"

"It's just looking for a new enemy to grip! I'm not down and out yet."

"From where I sit, you're a fine imitation of it," consoled Pierce.

"Look at that snow! It's just like a baby blizzard."

The "Baby Blizzard" proved a thriving infant. By noon it had waxed to "man's size." By dusk, the streets lay deserted, and choked with six-foot drifts. A sixty-mile-an-hour gale howled through the empty thoroughfares, shaking trees and houses and whirling before it a flying mountain of snow. Not since 1888 had such a storm swept Smithville.

By six o'clock the telephone and telegraph wires were down. By seven all railroad traffic ceased. The last link with the outer world snapped. Smithville and its outlying villages were as utterly isolated as if they had been built around the north pole.

Late the following day, when the storm momentarily slackened, folk crept out of their homes and beat a cautious way through the snow-drifts to the nearest food dispensaries. It had been a mild winter thus far and many people were still wearing "fall weight" clothing. This defect they hastened to repair.

Before night every particle of food and clothing of the scanty stock that had still remained in Cauldwell's store was gone. People leaving the gutted emporium surged across to Reuff's. The snow was still falling. Scared citizens, fearing starvation, clamored to buy any sort of food at any cost.

"If our consignment had come in on time," grumbled Pierce next morning, "we could have done a land office business. Reuff is selling everything at double prices and clearing up a pile. The old scoundrel is wringing his hands because his new shipment was held up by the blizzard, and hasn't—Hold on! Where are you going? You'll freeze to death, chasing out into that storm without hat or coat. Where are you off to?"

"To take old Mrs. Fortune by the throat again," roared Mallock, over his shoulder. "To set the bulldog jaw into another grip!"

He was struggling with the snow-jammed back door of the store as he spoke.

"I don't understand," muttered Pierce.

"You don't, eh? I'm going to the freight yards and order that three-car consignment sent here in a rush. Railroad connection won't reestablish for another four days or more. And I'll sell those car-loads at a profit that'll mean future customers to the store as well as the partnership to me. The miracle has *happened!*"

He was out and away in a swirl of white, powdery snow.

"Good old Mallock!" said Pierce to himself. "Fate's fighting for him at last. He could make a fortune by selling those provisions at famine rates. But the big hearted idiot will charge his hungry, shivering customers just the regular prices. Or, maybe, less. I know him!"

The front door blew open a little later and Reuff's huge figure in its bearskin overcoat lurched in.

"Where's Mallock?" he demanded.

"Out," was Pierce's curt reply.

"I got to see him in a rush," went on Reuff eagerly. "Where's he gone?"

"Just across to the freight yards," said Pierce airily. "You see, the blizzard's caused a bit of a rush on our goods. And as we're beginning to get low, he's stepped over to order one of our three car-loads of stuff sent around. We've plenty to last out. How about *you?*"

Under the folds of the big fur coat Reuff wiggled uncomfortably. But, for once, his need was too great for evasion.

"I want to make a deal with him for some of those goods," he mumbled, as if the words hurt him. "I'm sold out. There's no use lying when everybody knows it. I'm sold out and my next consignment is snowed under somewhere between here and New York. I heard yesterday about that blunder of the wholesale house and how Mallock's stuck with three car-loads of stuff. I thought, maybe, I'd help him out by taking half of it off his hands, as a neighborly good turn and—"

"And not lose all your customers to him?" finished Pierce. "Real kind of you, but just a wee bit too late."

"You don't understand," declared Reuff. "I—"

"No? Perhaps not. But Mallock does. Here he is! Joe, Mr. Reuff is over here to pay a neighborly call and help you out by buying half your three car-loads of—"

"I'll pay you market rates for half of 'em," interposed Reuff, facing Mallock excitedly. "And—and I'll pay you ten per cent over that if you'll let me have *all* of 'em."

"Good idea!" approved Mallock. "You'll pay market rates to keep your store open while Smithville's snowbound. And you'll pay ten per cent more if you can corner the provision market, so that we'll be put temporarily out of business and you can charge your starving customers double or treble rates? Fine idea!"

"You—you insult me!" blustered Reuff.

"No, I don't," rapped Mallock. "I don't think a man who will charge needy people double rates during a blizzard, as you've been doing, can be insulted. You want those three car-loads that are consigned to us. Is that right?"

"Yes," returned Reuff sullenly.

"Suppose they don't happen to contain the quality of goods you ordered?"

"I don't care. At a time like this, a man can't pick and choose the kind of food and clothes he sells. I offer you a ten per cent advance—"

"And I refuse it. Good day."

"Hold on!" implored Reuff. "Don't get hasty! I'll make it fifteen per cent—"

"You can't have it."

"What then? Make me an offer."

"I make no offer. I don't want to sell. If you buy, you do so on your own insistence. *But*—if you *do* want to buy, the contents of those three cars are yours for—"

"For what? Make a price, man! Quick! There's no time to lose. How much?"

"For just the face value of their bill of lading. Not one cent more."

"Mallock!" yelled Pierce, "you're plumb crazy! He—"

"Shut up, Pierce!" squealed Reuff, jumping up and down in glee. "You're witness to what he said! I get the whole three car-loads at reg-lar price. No advance. No—"

"At cash terms," interrupted Mallock. "Here is the bill of lading. You can see the price named."

Reuff glanced at the sum total at the bottom, grunted and replied:

"About average prices, I should think. Maybe a trifle more. But that's all right. Cash, you say? Here's my check. Let Pierce take it over to the bank and get the money, if you're afraid it ain't good. I'll wait here. When he comes back you'll give me a bill of sale, and—"

"Mallock," exclaimed Pierce, holding the check doubtfully, "you're doing a criminally foolish thing! You're giving this man a corner on all the local provisions. It'll be an awful knock to Cauldwell's future trade. He—"

"I'm boss here, Pierce," said Mallock quietly. "Go and get that money."

Muttering and scowling, Pierce obeyed. When he came back, Reuff had made out a bill of sale and was reading it to Mallock.

"'*Contents of the aforesaid three cars,*'" he finished as Pierce came in, "'*as named in accompanying bill of lading.*' No use in my inventorying them now. The total's what you want. That all right?"

"Yes," returned Mallock. "I'll sign it as soon as I count the money. By the way," pausing, pen in hand, "will you sell the things to your customers at regular market rates?"

"Think I'm a dummy?" snorted Reuff. "Not me! I'll clear three hundred per cent off'n this deal. If folks want food, let 'em pay for it. That's what I say."

Mallock sighed, affixed his signature to the bill and tossed the papers across the counter to Reuff. The latter gathered them up. At the door he turned.

"Young feller," he chuckled, "you may be a good wood sawyer, but you're the punkest business man I *ever* met. You had a chance to make a fortune off 'n them car-loads by selling at famine rates, or even by selling 'em to *me*. I'd have paid double their value sooner'n not get 'em. As it is—"

"As it is," said Mallock cheerily, "you've paid just what the wholesalers charged *us*. So we've given you your money's worth, and there can be no kick on either side. That's *my* way of doing business. Good day."

"Mallock!" cried Pierce, as the door closed behind Reuff. "You've thrown away the chance of your life! Thrown it away with both hands!"

"How so? The sales we'll make during the next week will bring up our average, and more than give me the $480.00 extra I needed to become a partner. Mr. Cauldwell never breaks his word. The partnership's mine!"

"But the store stays shut till our next batch of stuff comes from the wholesalers! You can't sell what you haven't, got, And Reuff—"

"Not necessarily. At the freight yards I found half a car-load of provisions, clothes, etc., that Mr. Cauldwell had evidently ordered shipped here when he got to New York. It's new stuff and he didn't mean it to be used yet. He probably found he could save cash by buying in some one's entire stock. But it will serve to keep this store going till the railroads are open again. It came in on the last train before the blizzard. That's why I didn't know it was there till I went over to the station just now.

"I've ordered it carted up in a rush. It ought to be here in half an hour or less. And as we're the only concern in town with staples for sale, I figure out that our profits will not only give me the amount I need for the partnership, but leave a good margin besides. To sell half a car-load, in four days—even at market rates— with no competition—"

"No *competition?*" mocked Pierce, "only three car-loads of it! Reuff has six times the stock we have. The trade has set his way for two days, and—"

"It will set *our* way in less than an hour. Reuff's is closed and will stay closed till—"

"Closed? With three car-loads of—"

"Of 'patent paints,' 'white lead,' 'mixing oils,' 'fixatifs,' 'driers,' 'French putty,' and 'imported camel's hair paint-brushes'! All those things are good in their way, but there won't be much feverish trade in them, during a famine week."

"What on earth are you talking about? The three car-loads—"

"Consists of painters' supplies, ordered from Chicago. If Reuff hadn't been in so much of a hurry to rob us, he would, perhaps, have read the invoice instead of only the total. But he knew the sort of goods our wholesalers ship us, as a rule, and when he heard these things were consigned to a Chicago *'supply* house,' he naturally thought it referred to *provision* supplies. The total was about the same, luckily, as it would have been for the same amount of food, etc. He knows better by this time, if he's read the inventory or gone to the freight yards. I found it out, the first crate I examined. Then I looked over the bill-a-lading items for the first time, and—

"You know the rest."

"I—I see! I—"

"So will Reuff. If he cares to sell white lead and paint-brushes at treble rates to hungry people, he may make a handsome profit. If he doesn't the consignees in Chicago will, of course, take the stuff off his hands at regular rates. So he'll lose nothing—except a week's trade. You heard me warn him the stuff might not be what he wanted. And you heard me refuse to sell it at an advance. He can't complain. If he does, we'll be too busy to listen. For here comes the first van-load of provisions. And about fifty people are following it to this store. They're bringing my partnership! They and the rest of Smithville."

"Say!" gasped Pierce, gaining his breath again, "I've heard that honesty is the best policy. But you're the first man I ever heard of who could make it pay *dividends!* Here's to the firm of Cauldwell and Mallock, Blizzard Jugglers!"

"Come in, Mr. Reuff," invited Mallock, as his speechless, purple rival stamped into the store, "anything we can sell you? We strive to please."

The Justice of the Sands

BLAKE, kicking a double tattoo against the ribs of his mule, breasted the last of a series of ridges which gave that particular sweep of the Syrian Desert the look of a huge ploughed field.

Behind the rider, and indeed in every direction, stretched away the miles of red-yellow sand, now smoothed into flat plains, now humped into ridges and dunes. For the desert is as full of inequalities as is any other region. And more so, since the sand shifts before gale and simoon into as many and as weird formations as drift snow.

Blake's mule, head hung and ears aflop from crass fatigue, toiled dolefully up the ridge, dislodging tiny avalanches of sand at every plunging step of the heavy going. Blake himself was in little better case than his mount. His canteen was empty; his eyes were blurred and stinging from glare and from flying sand-particles; his throat was throbbing with thirst; the sun hammered mercilessly through his pith helmet and pugaree. Also he was frightened—terribly frightened. For nearly a month he had been in sick fear.

Squinting, he could see at the ridge's crest a stark figure against the blue-and-copper of the sky. The figure, as the mule plunged stumblingly toward the summit, gradually took to itself such hazy details as a dirty white robe, a torn red burnouse, a *kafieh* head-dress wherein tarnished tinsel was twined, a thin brown face that peeped from under the *kafieh*-folds, a long flintlock whose butt snuggled into the bearer's arm socket while its egregious length of muzzle found rest on the sand.

Toward this moveless Arab, Blake had been shaping his course for two hours, indeed, ever since he had caught an uncertain glimpse of him through the pulsing heat-waves along the eastern skyline. And now when the figure was a bare hundred and fifty yards distant, the rider lifted his right hand high above his head, palm forward, in the universal peace-sign.

Scarce waiting to see the salute returned, Blake twisted nervously in the saddle and scanned the yellow-red miles behind him. Yes, the Spot was still there. And somewhat nearer, it seemed, than when last he had looked—the black spot that had at first differed from the heat-spots which swam and danced before Blake's tired eyes only by the fact that it kept in its approximate place along the sand and did not pirouette in air at every move of the inflamed eyelids.

Early that morning—his third morning out from Damascus—Blake had first seen the Spot. And, though it was then tiny and amorphous, he had felt instinctively what it was—had felt and had trembled and gone ill with terror.

He had known it was no wandering camel or beast of prey. How he had known it, Blake could not have told you. Perhaps by the mystic sixth sense of the fugitive, to whom all men are pursuers.

Yet he had known. And every toiling, tediously hurrying hour since then had deepened his conviction. The Spot was moving, as he himself moved; in the same direction, and, it appeared, faster. It was even beginning to take form.

Blake turned his gaze again toward the near-by summit. And there, instead of one figure, stood a half score, all in robes of white or yellow or gray and with burnouses whose red folds displayed varying degrees of uncleanliness.

"Good!" muttered Blake, addressing his worn-out mule—a habit three days of desert solitude had taught him. "That means their camp is near. Probably in the hollow beyond the crest. The first one was a sentry—just as I hoped he might be. He signaled the others to come up."

He slid awkwardly from his mule, his cramped legs well nigh buckling under him, and lurched forward on foot for the few yards of deep going that separated him from the stolidly waiting Bedouins.

"*Salaam Aleikum!*" he croaked, his voice coming gratingly from dry throat and drier lips. "To your tribe, peace and the countenance of Allah the Compassionate!"

He spoke in halting Arabic, barbarous of accent and further impeded by the drouth that gripped his throat. Yet his words were evidently intelligible to the men to whom he spoke. For their looks of studied uninterest changed ever so little. And from several of them came in irregular chorus the conventional greeting:

"*Naharak-saïd.*"

"My day is happy for beholding you," panted Blake. "I come to you as a guest, throwing myself upon the eternal Guest Law of the Desert. Do you receive me, oh brothers of eagles?"

A dozen arms were raised in the peace-sign. In an instant the group had broken up its stiff formation, and its members were crowding about the guest. One of them led the mule forward. A second and third made as though to kiss Blake's sun-blistered hands. Forming an escort of honor about the stranger, they led him over the rise and down the farther slope.

In the Desert, both policemen and restaurants are less than infrequent. To atone for this dual deficiency, the Arab tribes—as far back as the days of Genesis—framed the solemn Guest Law, the law whereby every wanderer who claims the right must be succored and protected by whatsoever tribe whose camp he may chance upon. It is a law unbroken and unbreakable. To it, Blake had just appealed; nor appealed in vain.

Down the slope his hosts escorted him to where a village camp of black goat-hair tents nestled under the lee of the dune, the summer camp of some tribal "family," detached for the time from the main body of its people.

There were perhaps twenty-five tents in all—low, black, long—in the camp's single "street." A knot of veiled, blue-robed women and staring, half-nude children clustered at the street's end to see the newcomer arrive. Several men came forward from tent-doors to swell the welcoming party of escorts.

In front of the largest tent a spear, driven into the earth, denoted the residence of the Sheik. Toward this tent Blake's new hosts led him. Within, cross-legged, upon a red morocco camel saddle, sat a tall, slender man, aquiline of nose, lofty of cheekbone, delicately high-bred of face and expression. He rose gracefully as Blake drew near, and came halfway to the entrance to meet him.

Blake, summoning to his memory certain scraps of Bedouin etiquette that he had chanced to pick up during an earlier two-year sojourn in Alexandria, halted in the doorway long enough to kick off his dusty low shoes. Then, touching his breast and forehead with the fingers of his right hand, he advanced toward the Sheik.

The latter, meeting him halfway, stooped in proud humility to kiss the guest's hand. Blake had sense enough to remember the next move—which was to withdraw his hand from the impending caress and raise it to his own lips.

The conventional phrases of Oriental welcome being spoken and replied to, the Sheik and Blake seated themselves on a gaudy carpet, spread upon the bare ground of the tent. A few of the chief men of the tribe followed their example. The rest loitered inquisitively outside.

The Sheik clapped his hands. Almost on the moment, the curtain separating the main room of his tent from the "kitchen end" was pulled aside and two veiled women came in. One bore on a tray a tin pot of coffee, surrounded by handleless cups; the other a huge platter containing a stew of goat flesh and lentils and flanked by loaves of hot, unleavened bread and little dishes of curds and of strained honey.

Then, fingers serving the double rôle of knife and of fork, the feast began.

The meal over, Blake lay stretched on the carpet strip, sucking at a bubble pipe. The coolness and half darkness of the tent, the full meal he had eaten, his unwonted feeling of safety after peril—all made him wax expansively talkative.

"My host," he said, "how shall I call your name when memory brings with it gratitude?"

"I am Yusef, Sheik of El-Maghrib," was the reply, the host forbearing to commit

the gross breach of etiquette of inquiring a guest's name.

But Blake made up for any such reticence. Lazily sprawling there, drawing in great mouthfuls of cool smoke, the terror that had so long gripped him banished, he began his Odyssey.

"I am an American, oh Sheik Yusef," he said, in his vilely ill-accented, hesitating Arabic. "My name is Blake. Oswald Blake."

"May peace rest upon your house," courteously interposed the Sheik.

"I speak your language," went on Blake, inclining his head in recognition of the Bedouin's courtesy, "because for two years, as a young man, I was bookkeeper in the Messagerie bank at Iskendería. Later, I returned to my own land, where I found high service with another banker. Of late, enemies sought my ruin. They would have cast me into prison. I fled. Whither should I go but to the East that I loved? So hither I came. To Damasch-us-shem. But an emissary of mine enemies tracked me. I had word of his coming and I fled into the desert. Three days have I wandered, knowing that soon or late I should meet some tribe of El-Badawi, who would grant me the guest right and guard me from my pursuers."

"By the Guest Law you are inviolate, *howaji,*" returned the Sheik, "and your foes become forthwith the foes of El-Maghrib."

"It is as I hoped," said Blake, "and from my heart I thank you. My mule fell, in a sand hole, a day's journey to westward, and my canteen spilled. If I had not met your men to-day I should have been jackal-meat by the morrow. Under this sun, thirst is torture."

"My tent and all I have is yours," formally replied the Sheik; yet Blake half-fancied there was more courtesy than cordiality in Yusef's tone.

A Bedouin halted at the tent door and called out something. The words were spoken too rapidly for Blake to catch their import. But Sheik Yusef straightened himself to a sitting posture and waited expectant. Uneasily, dreading he scarce knew what, Blake raised himself on one elbow and blinked out at the blinding glare of the afternoon sun.

Another moment and the square of merciless light was blocked. Several Bedouins stood there. Among them and a little to the front was a man whose aspect would better have accorded with a New Hampshire hill-farm than with the Syrian Desert.

Long he was, rather than tall, leathery and seamed of visage, large of hands, enormous of feet. His costume was of shiny black "diagonal." On his grizzled head, thrust well back, was a dusty black derby. The heat that had so nearly killed Blake seemed to have made far less impression on this creature of bone and gristle. The saddled Syrian pony that cropped sparse desert-grass in the open space just behind him seemed far more exhausted and heat-stricken than did he. Blake eyed the stranger with grinning bravado—even as, at a great distance, on the desert, he had viewed him with panic fear.

Sheik Yusef rose, as before, and came forward to greet this newest guest. But the stranger paid no heed to the action. His keen little eyes had fallen on Blake. One stride of his long legs brought him towering above the half-recumbent figure of his fellow-American.

"Oswald J. Blake," he said, his nasal voice hoarse with much dust, "you're my pris'ner. Here's the warrant; and here's the extradition papers, all properly viséd by the authorities in Damascus. Get up and come along."

Blake's grinning face had gone a bit white. But now he laughed in derision that was not wholly feigned, as he answered, without stirring:

"My friend, this is not the Detective Bureau at New York Police Headquarters. This is the Syrian Desert. I am a guest in a Bedouin camp."

"I don't care a hoot where you are," snapped the New Englander. "I was sent after you and I've got you. Come along."

"Thanks," said Blake lazily. "But I'm fairly comfortable where I am."

The detective thrust one hand into his hip pocket. At the gesture Blake turned swiftly to the Sheik, who, with his tribesmen, stood looking on in dumb wonder.

"Sheik Yusef!" he exclaimed. "This is the pursuer of whom I spoke. He would drag me to prison. Help me."

The Sheik spoke a brief word of command. The lank New Englander, half-turning to learn the cause of an ensuing movement on the part of the men around him, found himself gazing alternately into the black mouths of five flintlock guns. His hand left his hip pocket and both arms went straight upward over his head with a promptitude that was all but galvanic.

Blake leaned back again with a blissful smile.

"Belden, my friend," he chuckled, "you're in the wrong pew. I told you this wasn't Police Headquarters. Better clear out. It'll be healthier for you."

The New Englander scowled around the circle. He glowered at the leveled guns. Then his angry little eyes sought out Sheik Yusef.

"I take it," he snarled, addressing the Sheik, "that you're the chief of this outfit. Well, sir, let me tell you, I'm Ezra T. Belden—formerly of Plymouth, N. H., at present attached to the Central Office Detective Bureau in New York. I've got a warrant here for this man's arrest on a charge of embezzling $275,000 from the Aaron Burr Savings Bank of New York City, where he was cashier. And here's his extradition papers, signed at Damascus by your own government. Look 'em over, if you like. I've tracked this crook halfway across the world. And now is the time I take him back with me. So just ask these fellow coons of yours to put down their artillery, will you?"

Belden's harangue, voiced in flawless provincial New Hampshire English, was as the notes of a horse-fiddle to the ears of Sheik Yusef and his tribesfolk. The Sheik turned to Blake:

"What does your enemy say?" he queried politely.

"He says," answered Blake, "that he stamps upon the Guest Law and that he terms all Badawi as brethren to swine."

A growl ran through the knot of listeners. The Sheik's high-bred face went livid under its brown tan. Darting a glance at the gun-bearers, he opened his mouth as though to give an order. But Belden interposed.

"I don't know what this man's been telling you, chief," he said, "but I'll lay dollars to doughnuts it's a lie. Say!" —lifting his voice, "is there anybody here who can talk a few words of English? If there is, I'll make it worth his while to act as interpreter. Savvy Inglese? Hey? Anybody?"

The Sheik hesitated. Guessing at the sense of Belden's appeal, or perhaps belatedly doubting the entire accuracy of Blake's translation, he called loudly:

"Ohe, Halil! Halil-ibn-Nassar!"

From the rear of the little crowd that fringed the tent door, a man elbowed his way forward.

"Halil," commanded the Sheik, "ask this *feringhee* if indeed he likened the men of El-Maghrib to unclean swine?"

In limping English Halil repeated the query.

"No!" snorted Belden. "I don't know who Maghrib is or whether he's a swine or not. Quit your silly questions and do some interpreting for me. It's five dollars—six *mejidie*, you understand?—in your pocket, if you do some good, quick translating. You know enough English to do it?"

"Yes, *howaji*," answered Halil. "For five years I was donkeyman at El-Caire, to the Inglese—while I worked to pay off the debt of my father and to release him from the Khedivial prison. Five years of slavery—I, a son of the Desert!"

"Never mind your family history. Tell the chief there that I'm a detective—a police official—come to take this man away. Tell him my papers are in good order, signed by the authorities at the *serail* in Damascus. Say he'll get into a peck of trouble with the Turkish Government if he blocks me. And tell him for the land's sake to make those fellers stop p'inting their gaspipe guns at me."

Halil translated, more than once interrupted by a protest or wrathful correction from Blake. The Sheik, civilly motioning Blake to be silent, made reply:

"Sheik Yusef of El-Maghrib bids me to say," translated Halil, "that this man is his guest. And by Guest Law of Desert he cannot give him up to Law. Likewise that in the desert and in the camp of El-Maghrib, he and not the Turks is the government. He refuse."

"If he means he's the local Justice of the Peace," persisted Belden, "I'm willing to show him my papers. He can countersign 'em if he likes. About every other official in Syria has done it. At a *mejidie* per sign. They look like an autograph album. I—"

The Sheik asked a question. Blake sprang up to interpose; but before he could prevent its transmission, Halil had repeated it to Belden.

"Sheik Yusef says what has this man done? What is his sin?"

"Done?" returned Belden. "Oh, nothing much. Just stole a trifle over $275,000 from a bank in New York. That's all. By my reckoning, $275,000 comes to something like 350,000 silver *mejidie* in your money."

Halil's jaw dropped. Unsteadily he eyed Belden, searching to know if this were some sample of Occidental humor. But the detective was very evidently in earnest. And Halil—shamefacedly, as one who tells what cannot be believed—translated to the Sheik.

"Maschallah!" gasped Sheik Yusef, to an undercurrent of exclamations from the throng outside the doorway.

Everyone looked at Blake, then at Belden. The former suddenly felt the stirrings of that ebullient vanity which ever dogs the true criminal.

"It is true, oh Sheik Yusef," he corroborated. "It is quite true as to the sum. But not that I am a thief. I was treated unjustly. My rightful wage was withheld. They gave me a beggarly pittance instead of the salary I merited. For years I endured it—the slavery, the poverty, the hopelessness of it all. Then I—"

"Three hundred and fifty thousand *mejidie!*" bleated the Sheik.

"Then I rebelled," proclaimed Blake, working himself up to a fine glow of indignation. "The directors were rich. I was poor. They loafed. I slaved. Yet they laughed when I asked for rightful reward!"

"Three hundred and—"

"So when the chance came, I took what would make me and would not break them," went on Blake. "A sum that will repay my years of ill-recompensed labor and give me the rest of my days in plenty. By sharing the deficit among themselves, the directors can make it up without pinching their pockets. To them it is a trifle. To me it was *life!*"

He was on his feet now, carried away by his own oratory—the more so since the former looks of cold civility toward himself in the faces of the Sheik and the tribesmen were now replaced by something akin to awe.

Of the financial details he had been expounding, they understood little and cared somewhat less. One glaring, tremendous fact, though, was in the minds of all: This barbarian, who spoke their tongue so ill, had somewhere, somehow, managed to steal a fortune—a fortune compared to which their own petty lootings of caravans and of rival tribes were as the merest nothings. Wherefore, to the arch-robber those outlawed minor robbers of the desert did due mental reverence.

Their utmost net gains, from the rather more than neighborly interest they were wont to take in other tribes' cattle and in the goods of ill-guarded caravans, must needs mount up for years before reaching so fabulous a sum as three hundred and fifty thousand *mejidie.*

As the cross-roads grocer might eye John D. Rockefeller, as some French village mayor might have eyed Napoleon, so did these children of the sun lavish mute tribute upon the genius of their guest.

Ezra T. Belden observed the changed demeanor of the tribefolk toward his intended captive and, by handing six silver *mejidie* in advance to Halil, induced the latter to recover sufficiently from his trance of veneration to put into English the gist of Blake's boastful speech.

"Tell 'em," exhorted Belden, when he had heard, "tell 'em this man didn't just rob a board of fat directors. Tell 'em he robbed a lot of poor folks—depositors that a ten-dollar bill looks mighty big to. Tell 'em the news of Blake's get-away with the $275,000 brought a run on the bank and pretty near ruined hundreds of people. Tell 'em all that; an' see then if they'll keep on gawpin' at him like he was Teddy Roosevelt and Caruso rolled into one."

Halil made shift to translate to the Sheik so much of the New Englander's exhortation as he himself could understand. The reply had no visible effect on the Bedouins. The sufferings of the robbed were no novelty to them.

Bound though they were by immemorable law to feed and protect any stranger who might come to their camp, they were never in the least dilatory in relieving of his goods any promising looking traveler whom they might chance to meet abroad in the desert. To his bedraggled, impoverished appearance, no doubt, had Blake owed his escape from attack, that day, long ere he could have reached the borders of the camp.

To the Arab mind, the outward and visible sign of a foreigner's wealth is the size of his caravan or equipment. Blake and Belden, having none, had passed for folk too poor to be worth robbing, at the risk of later government interference.

Blake laughed in the detective's face, a hearty, wholesouled laugh.

"My sleuth friend," he scoffed, "you've done a neat bit of work tracking me across Europe and across the desert. I'll grant you that. But, now you've done it, you'd better start back while the going's good. I'm among friends here. And I'm going to stay among 'em—a year, if it's necessary—till I can see a good chance to square myself at home, or to slip over to some non-extradition port. These Bedouins aren't going to give me up. It's against their laws, for one thing. And, for another, you've just made me a hero in their eyes. They're in the same general line of business themselves. There's hardly one of these tribes that isn't outlawed by the Turkish government. That's why I struck out for the desert."

Belden made another appeal, through the interpreter.

"Tell 'em," he ordered, "that unless they give me my prisoner, I'll have a regiment of Syrian cavalry out here after 'em in two shakes. And Uncle Sam'll send a warship to Beirut, into the bargain."

"I will translate if you wish, *howaji*," responded Halil. "But to what good? By law we must protect him while he is our guest. The Syrian cavalry we have all times eluded with ease—when we have not ambushed it. And your Uncle Samuel—on whom be peace!—is far away—whoever he may be. And his ships cannot sail the sands."

"Tell 'em, that as sure as my name is Belden, I'm going to get this man. I get what I go for. I'll get him if I have to track him clear through to Persia. They'll save time by giving him up."

Laboriously, Halil sought to convey the message to Sheik Yusef. The detective listened closely, trying to catch its sense. At one point he broke out crossly:

"*Persia*, I said. Not Bersia."

"No use!" scoffed Blake. "The Arabs have no letter 'P' in their alphabet; and they couldn't pronounce it if they had. With them, the 'P' is always 'B.' Don't let it rile you."

The detective's translated threat aroused scant interest in anyone. The Sheik indeed did not seem to hear it. Athwart his smile of reverential admiration had shot a glint of cunning. He addressed Blake, smoothly.

"Assuredly, oh *effendi,*" quoth he, "to bear away so vast a treasure as three hundred and fifty thousand *mejidie* were a task worthy a *djinnee.* And to bear it across seas to our land were still greater labor. But perchance you buried it before you left your country."

"Buried it!" sneered Blake. "For any cheap detective to dig up? Not I. I brought it along."

The vanity that made him boast made him also deaf to the possible import of a sibilant gasp that met his statement. Taking the sound for one of admiring wonder, he bragged on:

"Buried it? I'm no fool. I didn't bury it and I didn't bank it. I did the only sane thing. I brought it with me. A thousand or so in my pockets for expenses. The rest is *here!*"

He accompanied the last word with a gesture that indicated his own anatomy from shoulder to waistline. The Arabs looked puzzled. The Sheik stared at the somewhat bulky upper body of the American, then ventured:

"It is a jest, perhaps? The thinnest of mankind could not carry so much as five thousand silver *mejidie*—to say naught of 350,000—in money belts around his body, without becoming as round as a war-drum. And you are not overfat. My guest is pleased to be merry."

Blake unfastened the breast of his waistcoat and shirt, briefly revealing, beneath, a swathing of waterproof silk. Then, reclosing the front of his shirt, he answered:

"The money is not in silver, but in much handier form. You know nothing of our currency, here, so I can't well explain. The cash is in compact, portable shape. In gold certificates and—"

"Gold!" cried the Sheik. "It grows plainer. Gold leaf and gold dust and perhaps in your native gold coins. I begin to understand. Yet—little as I know of gold's weight, I can scarce see how so huge a sum can be pressed in so small a compass."

"I can't explain," said Blake, shirking the tedious explanation of the paper money theory and the national credit system, to a semi-savage. "You would not get my meaning. But the cash is there. Girt around my body and protected by the silk."

"Son," drawled Belden, "if, as I gather from your antics, you're showing these coons where your loot is cached, you're a bigger fool than I took you for."

"Thanks for your loving care of my interests," retorted Blake. "But I know the East. While I am these peoples' guest, I could strew their camp six inches deep in diamonds; and not a man or woman or child would lay a finger on one of them. Moreover, the whole tribe would fight to the death to protect me and my treasure.

That's their law. A fool law, but a convenient one—for me. A law that's never been broken."

"I don't know the desert laws," grunted Belden. "But I know just a little about human nature. And if a crowd of men were looking at me the way these poor benighted heathens are looking at you this minute, I'd grab my watch and wallet with both hands and holler for a cop."

For an hour or more, Belden continued, through Halil, to exhort the Sheik to give up Blake. Courteously, yet firmly, the Sheik refused. He grew taciturn at last; and, from fatigue, Belden desisted.

Night drew on. The herders began to troop back to camp, driving before them from the bleak "pasture hills" a line of black goats, broad-tailed sheep, lean kine, donkeys and camel-calves. Camp fires twinkled through the dusk. The evening meal was served, the Sheik insisting on regarding Belden as his guest on equal terms with Blake.

Soon after supper came the "night-cap" cups of coffee—black, bitter, full of grounds. Then the camp quieted. Belden lay awake for a time, just within the door of the Sheik's tent,—where he, like Blake, was lodged,—listening to the snores of the Arabs, the sniffing of pariah dogs that prowled from tent to tent, the howls of wolves and the yappings of jackals amid the far-off sand-hills. At last, the detective could no longer fight off sleep, although some occult instinct seemed to bid him to do so. And he slept like a dead man.

The hot beating of the sun in his face roused Belden. Blinking painfully, he sat up and stared stupidly about him. He was wont to wake quickly and easily, with all his faculties alive. But now for a full half-minute he sat, gripping his aching head, before his brain was clear and the events of the preceding day stood out in their proper order. Then once more he glanced about him.

He distinctly recalled going to sleep inside the doorway of the Sheik's tent. Yet now he lay on the unsheltered sand, the sun broiling him mercilessly; not a tent was in sight.

His eyes swept the surrounding valley and dunes in vain, for glimpse of human figure or of last night's camp. So far as he could see, he sat alone, in the center of illimitable leagues of red-yellow sand. No camp, no Bedouins, no animals, no vestige of yesterday's scenes.

At last his perplexed eyes fell and were caught by something stretched close at his side—the body of a man: Oswald Blake.

Blake lay on his face, just as, by the dying firelight, Belden had seen him settle himself for sleep the night before. Yes, and there, three feet farther on, were the fire's charred remains.

"Blake!" growled Belden, his throat dry as a kiln. "Blake! Are you dead, man? Wake up!"

He shook the inert figure. Blake groaned heavily. A second, harder shake, and the sleeper opened bloodshot eyes and looked dully upward. At sight of Belden he started up and half-drew a revolver from his coat. And then, as though paralyzed, he sat rigid, gazing open-mouthed about him.

"The camp!" he sputtered. "The *camp?*"

Belden was studying his surroundings.

"That hole is where the spear stood," he mumbled. "And there's the stake-holes of the chief's tent. There's the picket line where the hosses was tied. There's,"— craning his neck and rising and walking to a bend in the dune, "there's Blake's mule and my pony still tethered where they were last night. Same place. But no camp."

He returned to the still bemused Blake.

"Look here!" said the detective. "I've got the hang of this, I think. You're sure about that Guest Law? You're dead certain the Bedouins are obliged to protect a man as long as he's a guest in their camp?"

"Of course," muttered Blake. "But—what's happened? Where—"

"*This* has happened, son," announced Belden. "They couldn't touch you or the

dough while you were in their camp. They couldn't drive you out of their camp or rob you in it. So they hit on the simple trick of taking the camp off you and lugging it away somewhere. You ain't in their camp now, nor liable to be again. But that's not saying you ain't liable to meet up with your yesterday's hosts plenty soon."

"What!"

"Our critters are still tied over there. The chief stuck to the law, you see. Wouldn't touch you or yours—or me or mine—while we were in his camp. Get a move on! Something seems to tell me we'll stay healthier if we cut loose in the direction of Damascus without wasting any too much time. Lord, but I've got a thirst that some fellers would give fifty dollars for! And I know why I've got it. It's the coffee. They hocussed it. Hasheesh, or something. It tasted rank. But it kept us asleep. Look!"

He pointed excitedly, as at something behind Blake. The latter slowly turned to see what had so startled his usually steel-nerved pursuer. As Blake turned, Belden deftly pinioned his arms behind him and, with a motion born of long practice, relieved him of his revolver.

Before Blake's dazed senses fairly grasped the situation, there was a harsh click and something cold closed around his right wrist. He looked down, to find his right hand manacled to Belden's left. The thief's overwrought nerves collapsed. He began to cry; weakly, gaspingly. Terror was once more at his throat.

"Mr. Blake," said the detective, "you're my pris'ner. Come."

Dizzily, stumblingly, Blake allowed himself to be led to where the mule and the pony were tied. On the pony's back were a small pigskin of water and a large parcel of food.

"I thought they'd come handy on the return trip," explained Belden, as he gave Blake a swig of the lukewarm water and helped him onto the mule's saddle. "That's why I brought along such a lot. I couldn't be sure just how soon I'd overhaul you."

Glancing at a pocket compass, Belden set the two animals in motion. The detective's lean face was tense. Keenly, he surveyed every quarter of the horizon.

"We'll give 'em a run for it, anyhow," he said, half under his breath, as he belabored the lazy mule once more. "I started out to bring you back, Mr. Blake, and I'm going to. If those coons butt in, anywhere along the route, they'll find my middle name's Trouble."

Blake, who had drunk two cups of "night-cap" coffee to Belden's one, still rode as in a nightmare. Slowly, very slowly, the drug mists were clearing from his brain. But even now he only subconsciously realized his shift of condition. Sleepily, he clung to his saddle pommel. Headache and nausea were his only clear perceptions. And far behind these, the Fear that made him sob convulsively now and then.

For an hour the captor and captive rode on, almost in silence. Then, as they mounted a ridge that stood above a mass of small surrounding hillocks, Belden's pony lifted its head and whinnied. From a dozen directions the whinny was answered.

In front, behind, on every side, were Arabs—perhaps two score in all. Slipping from sand cuts and from behind hillocks, they seemed to have risen out of the ground. They hemmed in the two Americans in a huge irregular ring. Some were mounted. Some were afoot. Sheik Yusef, on a rawboned stallion, was a little in advance of the rest. They made no move to attack, but remained moveless, alert, guns in hand.

Ezra Belden dragged Blake from his mule and himself slipped to the ground beside him; the mule and the pony affording a partial barrier for them. Belden's automatic pistol was in his hand. Tucking it under his arm, he drew forth Blake's revolver.

"Here's where we make our stand," he said very quietly. "We're two Americans. For the moment, we'll just forget one of us is a cur who robbed widows and orphans; and we'll remember only that we've got to show a passel of heathens how white men can fight for each other."

"They'll—they'll kill us if you fire on them," babbled Blake, his nerve gone. "Put up your pistol and surrender. They won't harm us, then. Sheik Yusef's my friend, my host. He—"

"They won't kill us if they can help it," drawled Belden. "They aren't too ignorant to know that a foreign power would raise hob if two of its citizens were slaughtered in cold blood. And even Arabs aren't looking for unnecessary trouble. But they want that money you were fool enough to blab about. And they mean to have it."

"Oh, I'll give it to them!" wailed Blake. "I'll—"

"But *I* won't," snapped Belden. "I won't give 'em a nickel of it. I promised to bring you back, and the money with you. And I've got a way of keeping my promises. Look out! They're moving in on us. Here, take your gun back. Can you use it with your left hand? I haven't time to dig out my keys and unfetter you. Aim low, and don't waste shots."

Thrusting the captured weapon into Blake's trembling hand, Belden leveled the automatic across the pony's saddle and took careful aim at Sheik Yusef's chest.

"Don't shoot, I tell you!" howled the frantic Blake. "They'll butcher us like cattle if you kill one of them. I know what Bedouins are. Our only chance is to surrender. Don't—"

Belden pulled the trigger. But the jerk from Blake's writhing body destroyed his aim. The bullet whined high. The New Englander turned on his prisoner with a snarl.

"Stand still, you coward! Don't wiggle around like that!" he cried. "I'll—"

He got no further. Blake's uplifted pistol butt descended full on his head. The stiff derby partly broke the frenzied blow and in turn was hopelessly broken. But the blow, deflected as it was, served to double Belden's legs beneath him and to send him on hands and knees, senseless, at Blake's feet.

Dropping his revolver, Blake raised his unfettered hand in the peace-sign. And the Arabs closed in.

There was no violence. There was need for none. Blake, chattering in fear, the drug and wrenched nerves combining to make a pitiable weakling of him, alternately flattered and entreated them in his worst Arabic. The Bedouins paid no heed. Pausing only to note in mild surprise the odd steel contrivance that linked the screeching captive to the unconscious Belden, they went swiftly to work.

In little more than a second, Blake's garments above the waist were stripped from him. The tight-folded silk bandage was laid bare. With eager hands Sheik Yusef tore asunder the silk and ripped it from the thief's cringing body. Then from the eagerly crowding circle of Arabs went up a yell of utter dismay.

"What found we?" (Halil, the interpreter, told the story long afterward to a crony in El-Kanah tribe). "What found we? Laugh! Laugh till you burst! The tale of treasure was a *feringhee* lie. Within the silk was no hoard of gold. Not a silver *mejidie*. Not a copper *metallik*. Naught save row upon row of crackling or greasy sheets of paper,—some yellow, some green,—whereon were pictures and numbers and letters in an unknown tongue.

"Sewn to the silk's innermost side were these oblongs of paper. More than a hundred of them. Perhaps more than two hundred. We had no heart to count them. Nor was there cause to count. For of what value is colored paper? Perchance they were amulets sacred to the *feringhee* gods. I know not. To *us* they were of no use.

"In his first rage, Sheik Yusef was for slaying the liar and his comrade too. But the long and lean man who lay in a faint had spoken of some alliance with the *serail* at Damasch-us-shem. And the Sheik had no wish to be harried needlessly by the Basha's cavalry, during the grazing season. So, at the last, we rode away and left them."

Away rode the cursing Bedouins, while Blake clutched lovingly at the strip of waterproof silk, which Yusef had hurled back at him. The big-denomination bills sewed to the inner surface were intact. Not one of them was so much as torn.

Then, craft coming to the aid of greed, the fugitive glanced at the inert figure shackled to him, and stooped quickly to pick up one of the fallen pistols. But before he could touch the weapon, a lean, sinewy hand snatched it away.

Belden, who for the past minute or more had been unobtrusively in full possession of his recovered senses, scrambled in leisurely fashion to his feet, the pistol in his free hand.

"And now, son," he drawled, settling the wrecked derby far back on his head, "if it's quite the same to you, we'll be starting on again for Damascus. I guess the road's clear the rest of the way."

The Shrimp

THE Shrimp upset the boat. It was by far the most natural—in fact, the only possible—climax when, sailing before a half-gale, he had "come about" with a single twist of the tiller and a simultaneous yank of the sheet. The flattened sail stood athwart the wind. There could be but one result.

The good little fourteen-foot cat-boat, unused to such vile treatment, had resented it by throwing herself down flat on the lake's face, like an angry child, and, in the same gesture, tossing the Shrimp's hundred-and-ten-pound weight and five feet, three inches, of stature lightly out into the water.

The Shrimp came up a full ten feet from the capsized cat-boat. And the Shrimp could not swim.

To his credit, he did not thrash about and at once absorb more water than the first involuntary gasp had introduced into his system. Instead, he flopped awkwardly over on his back and with absurd yet creditably slow gestures began to move his hands and feet. He had read somewhere that this was the correct thing to do.

As a matter of fact, the Shrimp was in no grave peril. The boat had overturned a bare fifty yards from shore. Yet the woman on the rocks, at sight of the mishap, had cried out involuntarily in fear; and had sprung to her feet, urged by the world-old, hereditary instinct to face peril standing.

The man who lounged beside her rose more slowly, with the lithe laziness of perfect strength, towering a head and neck above her, though she was tall.

"Oh Lord!" he groaned in mock despair. "He's at it again. We ought to tether him. Don't worry, Hera. I'll fish him out."

As he spoke he was moving to the rocks' edge. And at the last word he dived, not so much as waiting to kick off his moccasins. His head, its tumbled yellow hair abnormally sleek and glistening, came to the surface, a second later. With long, unhurried strokes, swimming on his side, his face half-submerged, he rapidly overhauled the Shrimp.

The latter, meantime, was learning that for a non-swimmer to keep afloat, lying on his back in deep water, by the seemingly simple expedient of moving hands and feet, is less easy in practice than on paper. Thrice, try as he would to prevent it, he had shipped strangling gulps of lake. And once his head had gone clean under—a mere nothing for a man who can swim, but a moment of delirious horror for one who cannot.

Nevertheless, the century of battling came to an end at last. A hand gripped a wet collar; the immersed head was jerked above the surface, and a laughing yet annoyed face appeared very close to the Shrimp's.

"Alan!" sputtered the Shrimp.

"Don't try to talk, Doc," retorted the big man, speaking in staccato, detached clumps of words. "And, whatever you do, don't grab me around the neck—or I'll have to put you out. Lie straight. Stiff as you can. Hands holding my shoulders. Not too tight. So. Now, keep your head and don't wiggle."

The mighty body started shoreward, with the same long, lazy strokes, the Shrimp bobbing along in tow. The Shrimp obeyed orders, right meekly. He lay stiff and straight along the water, his face stuck upward, turtle fashion; his shaking fingers barely maintaining their grip on the swimmer's shoulders. He felt very sick, very dizzy, very helpless—and, at blurred glimpse of the white clad woman awaiting them on the camp dock, very much ashamed.

And thus rescuer and rescued reached the head of the little pier. The big man raised himself easily over the side of the dock and, stooping, lifted the Shrimp bodily by the scruff of the neck, to the stringpiece.

The Shrimp's knees turned to tallow, as the other placed him none too gently on his feet. He collapsed suddenly to a sitting posture on the boards. There he sat, blinking, gasping, looking up in dazed helplessness at the man and woman above him.

"Alan!" exclaimed the woman again.

And, at something in her tone, the Shrimp's dizzied brain cleared ever so little.

"It's all right, Hera," laughed the big man. "Don't be scared. There wasn't any danger. The boat'll wash in pretty soon. The wind's bringing her along. In ten minutes or so I can wade out and right her."

"But—"

"In the meanwhile," he went on, pointing to the gasping and recumbent Shrimp, "permit me to turn over to you that bright light of the medical profession, your gallant husband. You'll find him rather weather-beaten and a trifle moist in spots. Just at present he's hardly recognizable as the 'Little Giant of Surgery,' as one of the papers, last month, called him. But when you've dried him and ironed him, you'll be amazed to see how nicely he'll freshen up."

The woman looked at the speaker. The morning sun was beating down on his flushed face and drying gold hair; his eyes were blue as a frozen river. The wet silk shirt clung close to his body, outlining its muscular curves, the great sweep of chest and shoulder. He looked like some re-incarnated Norse sea-king newly arisen from the waves—splendid, gloriously strong, perfect in beauty and in youth.

From him the woman's dark eyes roved to the Shrimp. He sat there, on the dock, flattened out, spineless. From his last thinning black hair and limply straggling little mustache and carefully trimmed beard the water trickled. The gay outing suit he had worn to-day for the first time was a grotesque wreck. His big head seemed too heavy just now for the puny neck to support; and it slumped ludicrously above the narrow chest and the thin, bony shoulders. The army of patients who were wont to reverence him as Arbiter of Life and Death, and the world-great doctors who hailed him as peer, would have lost a shred of their idol-worship had they seen him just then.

The Shrimp had summoned all his resources to smile up reassuringly at his wife. And in so doing he had caught both looks that flitted over her daintily bronzed face: the expression that had leaped unbidden into her eyes as they had rested on the hero-form at her side, and the slower, less well-masked aspect wherewith she had gazed down on himself. And the Shrimp's hardly-achieved smile was wiped from his face as by a sponge.

Slowly, painfully, he scrambled to his feet, and stood swaying ever so slightly, in the center of a spreading pool of water.

"You'll catch cold," said the woman in sudden maternal solicitude. "Hurry and change your clothes."

It was to Alan she spoke. Yet it was the Shrimp that made quick answer.

"All right," he said, dully, "I will. And—thanks, Alan. I hope I haven't hurt your little yacht."

"It's a cat-boat, Doc," said Alan, carefully. "Not a yacht. And you haven't done it any harm. Better get a change and a rubdown and a drink, though, or you'll have your rheumatism back with you again."

The Shrimp turned meekly and plodded up the path toward the shack that stood in the little lake-island's center. His soaked, bedraggled appearance as he toiled up the slope was too much for Alan's risibles. He broke into a big laugh, a laugh in which Hera, after an instant's struggle with compunction, joined.

The duet of laughter beating agonizingly in his ears, the Shrimp pursued his way to the shack, not once looking behind him. The sound of the others' mirth lent speed to his lagging feet, as a flung stone might quicken the pace of a dog that has run away from a beating.

Half an hour later, Hera, coming into the shack to make ready for luncheon, found the Shrimp crouching on a camp-stool, his pose suggesting a caricature of Rodin's "The Thinker." He had not taken off his wet clothes, and the deerskin rug beneath the camp-stool was soaked.

With a punctilious observance of minor courtesies that of late always vaguely irritated his wife, he got to his feet as she came in. She halted just within the doorway and surveyed him, her dark straight brows drawn together in a wondering disapproval wherein her husband read contempt as well.

"What a mess!" she exclaimed, with a glance at the rug. "And you haven't even changed your things. What in the world have you been doing all this time?"

"Nothing," he answered, as he struggled to get out of his shrinking coat. "Nothing."

For a moment, she did not speak. Then she said with a sort of weary impatience:

"Nothing? That's what you have done most of the time, since we came here. Isn't it?"

"No," he made categoric reply after a brief interval of thought. "I've done a good deal, I think. I've got a burned hand, trying to make fires. I've infected two of my fingers, pulling fishhooks loose from gills. I cut my foot pretty nastily, last time it was my turn to chop firewood. And to-day—just because I thought I remembered, from a boy, how to sail a cat-boat—I nearly drowned. Yes, on the whole, I've done quite a lot of things since you got me to rent this island."

He did not speak with the remotest accent of complaint, but more like a child who recounts, at command, a list of the schoolday's tasks.

"That is true," she agreed lightly. "In fact, if only you *would* do 'nothing' there would be fewer silly accidents and less to worry all of us."

"I'm sorry I worry you, dear," he said, in genuine regret. "I haven't meant to. The whole thing was done to please you: taking the island, spending my vacation camping here, asking Alan along, and—"

"Alan!" she echoed. "I don't know what we'd have done without him. I never realized, back in Philadelphia, what an Admirable Crichton he was. He has been the salvation of the whole affair."

"Yes," assented the Shrimp, "he has. I've noticed it. You're—you're—you like Alan pretty well, don't you, dear?"

She glanced sharply at him. But the Shrimp was busily wringing out his drenched coat and had no eyes for her look of query-challenge.

"Yes," she said at last, "I do. What woman wouldn't?"

"That's right," he assented, with difficulty loosening his stringy tie and limp rag of collar. "What woman wouldn't? He makes a big hit with women. I've heard men talk about it. A big hit. I wonder why."

His remark did not seem to call for an answer, yet Hera accorded one, speaking quickly and on impulse.

"Why?" she repeated. "Why not? Isn't he everything that women, from childhood, look up to as their ideal in a man? He's a giant, he's handsome, he's unbelievably strong. He knows by instinct how to do everything. Apart from his cleverness and apart from the strain of protectiveness and chivalry that women love so, he is—oh, he's a *man*. A *man*."

"I see," said the Shrimp. "I see. A man. That is true. He's a man. By the way," he broke off, with a rueful little smile of self-deprecation, "do you know what he called me once? A 'shrimp.' I heard him. It was at the club, last—"

Hera's irrepressible laugh broke in on his recital.

"A 'shrimp!'" she cried. "Oh, it was rude, I suppose, abominably rude. But —but it—"

"But it fitted," he finished. "I know. We don't pick out our own bodies beforehand. It's no more my fault, I suppose, that I look so insignificant my own wife laughs when she hears me called 'a shrimp,' than it's to Alan's credit that he's built like a Greek statue. Our bodies are wished on us. And all we can do is to make up for their defects, in other ways, if we can. A fellow wrote about me, once, in a Sunday paper, that 'I hadn't enough body to cover my intellect and that my mind is almost indecently exposed.' A body like mine wouldn't turn into an Apollo Belvidere if I trained and took physical culture for a year. And at the end of that time I'd probably be a more muscular shrimp—but still a shrimp. With the mind, it's different."

"No doubt," she said, with a half-stifled yawn. "No doubt the 'mental strength' you're forever talking about would be a very wonderful thing. And no doubt it's a fine thing to be spoken of as one of the deepest thinkers and most brilliant surgeons in America. But,"—with another glance at the collarless, meager little man—"you'll have to forgive poor frivolous women if they are more interested in watching a glorious figure than in watching the workings of a weighty mind such as yours. Sometimes I get almost sick of hearing praises of your intellect, from people to whom physique is nothing. A Canova gladiator may not be as instructive to gaze on as a twelve-volume encyclopedia, but it is more ornamental—and more thrilling. If Alan had lived in the cave-man days—the days of the Survival of the Fittest—the roomiest cave and the loveliest cave-girl would have been his."

"While I'd have roosted in a tree, and gone a long time without a mate?"

"I didn't say so," she murmured politely, a little ashamed of her outbreak.

"You didn't have to," he replied. "Your eyes saved your lips the work. Even if I'd had a mate, in those days, I suppose— I suppose Alan would have had little trouble in winning her away from me?"

She flushed hotly, opened her lips for a quick speech—whether of denial or rebuke—then closed them again.

"A wilderness camp like this brings people back, more or less, to cave days, doesn't it?" he asked, irrelevantly. "I've thought of it, several times lately. Makes worthless

the things we learn in civilization and scrapes off the veneer. If there's a true cave-man under that veneer he comes out strong. But when a physical weakling, a man of cities, is under it, why, such brain-power as he's been able to acquire doesn't count for much. And he's more or less likely to come out—a shrimp. The fact that he has made good in the World of Brains doesn't help him to shine in this forest World of Bodies."

He wandered shufflingly into the adjoining room for dry clothes, the water in his absurdly small shoes "squattering" drearily as he walked.

But at lunch time he seemed quite to have forgotten his pessimistic chat with Hera. He had lost the half-sullen taciturnity that had marked him during the past few days. He was lively, unwontedly talkative—for him—and he roused Homeric laughter on the part of his wife and Alan by his weird efforts to prepare Beauregard eggs in a way he said he had once seen them cooked at a studio meal.

Lunch over, Hera banished both men while she took her daily hammock siesta.

Alan and the Shrimp strolled off, pipe in mouth, toward the shingle below the rocks.

For a time after they threw themselves down on the sun-warmed beach, they smoked idly and in silence, lazily watching the little blue waves flap against the shore stones and then retreat, drawing a rattling line of pebbles along with them.

It was the Shrimp who broke the silence.

"That fellow you were telling us about, at the fire last night," he began. "The Malay who ran *amok* and came for you with a knife, on the beach at Kata-Kata— were you scared?"

"Scared?" repeated Alan, with manifest effort coming out of a reverie as he answered. "Scared? No. Why should I have been? There wasn't any time. It was touch and go. I had just time enough to duck under his arm, as he lunged for me, and grapple him."

"You broke his back, I think you said?"

"The underhold. Yes. It was a case of me killing him or him killing me."

"You don't believe in showing mercy when it's a life-and-death struggle?"

"Mercy's a fine thing, Doc—in theory. But when it comes to a 'life-and-death,' or any other vital issue, there's only one choice, I should say."

"And you weren't afraid?"

"Of the Malay chap? Not that I noticed."

"No remorse?"

"For killing a rabid beast? Scarcely."

"That's queer," mused the Shrimp. "I'd have lain awake nights brooding over what I'd done. And, as soon as I'd fallen asleep, I'd have waked again with a jump, at the memory of how he had come at me with the knife. Kris, I think you said the name for those Malay knives is, didn't you? Yes, I'd have worn myself to a wreck, between remorse and retrospective scare. I envy you your pluck and your nerve. You've got both. I've seen them tested, often enough. I envy them almost as much as I envy you all that strength of yours and your way of knowing just what to do in a crisis."

"Thanks," replied Alan, somewhat embarrassed by the crass openness of the praise; then shifting the talk from himself, he added in ponderous humor:

"But if remorse for killing one greasy Malay would have kept you awake, I wonder how you ever manage to sleep. You've been a doctor for how long? Fifteen years or so, anyhow. And they say you have performed more operations and more delicate operations than almost any man in America. Your list of slain, by this time, must make *Bluebeard's* collection look like a deserted village."

The Shrimp frowned ever so slightly. The rare deaths among his patients lay ever like millstones about his neck. And whenever his almost matchless skill chanced to be set at naught by Death's wholly matchless power, his grief and shame were poignant.

But his face cleared almost at once. He even forced to his tired eyes one of the dutiful smiles that Hera had lately begun to find so annoying.

"Perhaps," he said meekly. Then, the smile still twisting his lips, he went on, in the same almost deprecatory voice:

"You're in love with my wife, aren't you, Alan?"

The younger man leaped to his feet and stood glaring down, dumfounded, at the little recumbent doctor. The Shrimp had shifted neither pose nor expression.

"Don't get excited, Alan," he reproved gently. "Sit down and let's talk sanely. There's no need for being rattled. I wonder what it is that always makes even the brawniest, pluckiest man so deadly afraid of—of even a Shrimp, when the Shrimp also chances to be a husband, the husband of the—"

"What in blazes are you talking about?" growled Alan, his face red, his eyes ablaze—adding: "And I am not 'scared,' as you call it. It's only that your insulting fool-question took me by surprise. I—I—"

"Sit down. A chap who has faced death, fearlessly, as you have—a dozen times or more, I suppose—ought to be ready for surprises. And he ought to keep up his nerves in better shape. Sit down, won't you? Yes," the Shrimp rambled on, "it's a queer thing, the way the Lover is always in mortal fear of the Husband. It's the law, I suppose. But it's not well that any man should be so afraid of another. I remember, once, at St. Joe, a patient of mine—a husky ex-pugilist he was—ran ki-yi-ing down the street in blue terror; and after him ambled a little one-armed man, with only half a lung, and carrying no weapon. And—"

"I tell you," snarled Alan, "I'm *not* afraid! Not of you or of any other man. And what right have you to hint that Hera—"

"I always put the 'I'm-not-afraid' liar in the same boat with the 'I'm-an-honest-man' thief," observed the Shrimp. "But of course—"

"I was knocked out for a moment to think you could insult Hera so damnably. That was all. If you were only larger—"

"If I were larger," mildly suggested the Shrimp, "we could have had a spectacular cave-man battle here on the beach. But I'm not. It would hardly afford you even a minute of after-lunch exercise. Now, sit down, and try to get your nerves in hand. I—"

"My nerves?" snorted Alan. "I have no nerves. I—"

"No 'nerve,' perhaps? And after that fight at Kata-Kata, too! Sit down, won't you? Let's talk this thing over, quietly. I'm not going to preach. And I'm not going to remind you that you call yourself my friend, and that perhaps you owe part of your start in life to my help. I just want to talk things over, sanely, with you, as I said. Surely, you owe me that much."

"Sanely? I think you're insane," sputtered Alan. "As for your daring to insult Hera as you have—"

He finished the sentence in a rumble. But he forced himself to sit down—at some slight distance from his host.

"That's better," mildly approved the Shrimp. "Now I'll be as brief as I can. You're in love with Hera. She fancies she's in love with you."

"I—"

"She isn't really. Only, she doesn't know it. What she's in love with is an Ideal—an ideal that's a cross between a primordial anthropoid and a collar advertisement. She thinks it's you. I don't blame her."

"Doctor," put in Alan, getting better grip on his self-control and speaking with a very fair semblance of annoyed superiority, "your ducking this morning must have washed away your brains. You're an old friend. I owe a lot to you. And the Missus has been mighty kind to me, besides. So I overlook what you've said. When the guide comes back from the mainland this evening with the launch, I'll start for Philadelphia. For, of course, after this, I can't—"

"Alan," commented the Shrimp, "I heard you make the same brave sounds, once, at the Union, when you were trying to convince three other poker players that your bob-tailed flush was a royal. Drop it."

"Doctor—"

"Hera and I have been pretty happy, the ten years we've been married. She was content with me, even though she's of the Juno type, and I'm physically negligible. It's Nature's law of averages that such marriages are generally happy. We doctors understand that. She was proud of me, too—proud of the scraps of fame I was able to glean. Then, three months ago, I brought you to the house. I think it was about three months ago. Or was it four? No matter. —You were all the things I'm not. And, from the start, you and she were attracted to each other. She didn't know it yet. But I did. She liked to look at you, and she liked to hear your yarns of adventure. You got to calling each other by your first names. And—"

"If you objected to that, why—"

"I didn't. Only to what it meant. I've known cases like yours and Hera's that died a natural death when the man and woman were thrown together all day and every day for a long time. When the woman didn't have a chance to fluff her hair, and when her nose got shiny with sunburn; when she had a view of the man before he'd shaved and when his coffee hadn't routed his morning grouch. That's why I rented this island when she wanted me to. And that's why I asked you to camp here with us. It was a sort of operation. But it worked out the other way. One of my failures. It showed you at your best and me at my worst."

"You're talking rot. She—"

"This morning was the climax. I can read her face as easily as I can read print. She knows now—or *thinks* now—that she cares for you. You are her hero. Her cave-man. She looks at me as though I were a monkey with fleas."

He paused, and with petty precision adjusted and relighted the tobacco in his pipe, his sensitive surgeon-fingers working swiftly and with skill. For a time, Alan did not answer. Then, squaring his shoulders, he met the Shrimp's pleasantly inquiring gaze with eyes in which flashed a new-born resolve.

"Well?" queried the Shrimp.

"Well," echoed Alan, "let it go at that. I'm in love with Hera. You say she cares for me. I'd give my life to believe it. What then?"

"Good," approved the Shrimp. "Now that we're dropping bluff and coming down to facts we can get somewhere."

"I love her," said Alan, almost fiercely. "From the beginning I've loved her. It has been torture to keep my mouth shut. I've tried to remember what I owe to you and that you're my friend. Perhaps I might have succeeded, if you hadn't smashed everything by speaking as you've just done. Now it's too late."

"Yes," agreed the Shrimp, "it's too late."

"Back at home," pursued Alan, "you'd probably order me out of your house. And then I'd probably waylay Hera in the street or else telephone her. Out here, there doesn't seem any set rule to go by. If it were a few hundred æons ago, and you and I were better matched, we'd have fought for her. If we were in France or Italy, even now, we'd settle it with pistols, or—"

"But unluckily we aren't there or in the Cave of Ages or in Philadelphia. As for shooting at each other, the only weapon on the island is Hera's cat-rifle. And I'm afraid, even if we took turns, we'd use up all the ammunition before we did much damage."

"How can you joke about it?"

"If *I* can stand it," said the Shrimp, "can't you? The joke seems to be on me."

"On *you?*" growled Alan, in a flash of rage. "On *you?* No. On *me*. And on every other big and strong man. Once a man's glory was in his strength and size. Strength was the cave-world's aristocracy. But this is the Age of the Little People, the triumph of the mediocre. It began when gunpowder made the cripple's trigger-finger more powerful than all the giant's muscles. And it's been getting worse, every century, since. What's the advantage of size and strength, nowadays?"

"Having neither, I can't say. But—"

"Strength used to rule. Then the Little People conjured up a bugaboo and called it the Law. And it bound Strength, hand and foot. The Law is what's fighting for *you,* to-day, and making me helpless against you. There's no equal ground where we can meet, man to man. I wish to Heaven there were!"

"You are mistaken."

"I am not. There is no—"

"If there were—if there was an 'equal ground' where you could fight me, man to man,—where neither Law nor Strength would be invoked,—would you fight me—for Hera?"

"Would I?" shouted Alan, his eyes aglow with furious eagerness. *"Would* I?"

"That is what I asked you," courteously prompted the Shrimp.

"You know I would. To the death!" cried Alan, unconscious of his own theatrical vehemence.

"I am glad," said the Shrimp, with a smile that now was neither rueful or deprecating.

From his pocket he drew a little oblong, pasteboard box, opened it and produced a flat, folded paper.

"I prepared these before lunch, to-day," he explained. "They are powders, you see. Quite fresh."

He opened the paper he held, revealing a pinch of powder in its center.

"The idea isn't wholly mine," said the Shrimp, "as perhaps you'll recognize. You remember the famous duel between the two Napoleonic officers? They'd tired of the old sword-and-pistol customs, and they resolved to light a duel whose originality should make it the talk of France. It did. They got a chemist to mix five big pills, all alike in looks. Four were made of chalk and gluten. The fifth contained enough poison to kill a half-dozen men. The duelists ate pill after pill, in turn, at five minute intervals, till one fell dead. Now this powder is—"

"If you think I'd enter into a bughouse contest of that sort!" cried Alan, getting to his feet.

"Of course you will," corrected the Shrimp, with perfect friendliness. "It's just what you were clamoring for. A man-to-man fight, on perfectly equal ground, where neither Strength nor Law would count."

"The law—"

"The law will know nothing about it. One of us will be dead, within the next three hours—of heart trouble. There will be no inquest. I've provided against that. No Inquest, no Scandal."

"You're mad! I—"

"No. For the moment, I'm a 'cave-man.' Like yourself. We are in the primeval wilderness, battling for the woman we both love. Doesn't that sound natural? Hera hinted to-day that if we were back in the prehistoric ages, you would have the loveliest girl for a wife, and that I'd have to wait long before I found a mate. Well, I shall have to wait three hours—or less. By that time, I shall have won or lost. She will go to the winner. Come, man! Even a gallant soldier of fortune need not turn up his nose at such a deadly duel. It will need almost as much courage as it took to break that Malay's spine when he ran *amok*."

"Do you think I'll do such a suicidal thing?" yelled Alan, eyeing the powder with all a normal strong man's ignorant horror and dread of drugs. "You're a dangerous maniac, Doctor! Throw that stuff away! Throw it away, do you hear? Throw it away, or I'll take it from you."

Alan made a move as though to fulfill his threat. The Shrimp, with a gesture equally quick, lifted the powder to his own lips and gulped it. Alan stared at him in dumb fear.

"I used two powders," remarked the Shrimp, evenly. "One is perfectly harmless. The other is one of the most powerful drugs known. I've taken mine, as you see. Now—"

Alan, with a gasp of stark fright, tore the little pasteboard box from the Shrimp and hurled it into the lake.

"Thanks," said the Shrimp. "I was just going to do that. It was empty. This powder I took was the only one left in it when I brought it out of my pocket."

"The only one *left* in it? What—"

"Keep cool, friend. Really, you're not at your 'cave-man' best, at this moment. I've taken my powder, and I'm more or less calm about it. Is the hero of the Malay affray going to be less of a man than—a shrimp?"

"What's an antidote for the stuff you've taken? Quick! Tell me!"

"If it's the harmless powder, there's no need for an antidote. If it isn't, there's no antidote for the need. Where are you off to?"

"To call Hera. If—"

"Hold on! You've forgotten about your own powder."

"My own? I told you distinctly I'd have no part in such suicidal craziness!"

"I was afraid you wouldn't," sighed the Shrimp. "I hoped I'd misjudged you. But I was afraid. You're all right when strength can help you. But when it's a matter of true courage—stripped of strength—I had my doubts. So I made certain."

"Made—"

"Made certain. By giving you your powder beforehand."

"It's a lie!" almost screamed Alan. "I haven't taken any medicine in more than a year."

"Oh, yes, you have," smilingly corrected the Shrimp. "So don't call names or get all worked up. You took it. And you didn't like it."

"Didn't like it? Oh, you're mad as a hatter!"

"You *said* you didn't like it. That's all I know about it. You laughed at it, and you said: 'It tastes pretty awful. But I'm hungry enough to eat the shack itself.' So you bolted it."

"*It?* What?"

"The powder. In the Beauregard eggs. Less than an hour ago. When I fixed the eggs for lunch, you'll recall, by the way, that I put yours on your plate myself,—well, I—"

Alan seized him by the throat. But the mighty hands were clammy wet; and the fingers, that meant to crush, merely shook.

"You—you vile little murderer!" babbled Alan.

"Was that what the Malay called *you?*" asked the Shrimp, making no effort to defend himself, and speaking with tolerable ease through the panic-weak grasp on his throat. "This is no murder. It's a fair fight. Cave-man against cave-man. The kind you've just 'wished to Heaven' we might have. On equal terms; and on the only equal terms that would involve no scandal. The duel is on. In a very short time it will be settled in one way or another. We are fighting fair. I give you my word of honor that I took an even chance with you on the powders. Hera need never know how one of the two men who loved her died. No one need know. It will all be quite natural. First a clamminess of the hands, a dryness of the throat, a sense of chill and dizziness, then—"

Alan's sweating hands fell limp to his sides. His lips cracked and his mouth stood open. Of a sudden he turned, with a choked cry, and ran staggeringly up the slope. The Shrimp followed, calling in alarm:

"Surely you aren't going to be cur enough to distress Hera by telling her?"

Alan neither heard nor heeded. Bursting into the clearing beside the shack, where Hera lay reading in her hammock, he panted:

"I'm poisoned! This—this devil has murdered me!"

A single glance at his distorted face and glassy eyes, and Hera was on her feet beside him.

"Alan!" she cried, seizing his arm. "What do you mean?"

He threw off her eager clasp in a rough frenzy.

"Don't stand gaping like a fool!" he cried. "Get his medicine chest. You must know where he keeps it. Get it and find some antidote for—"

"There is no antidote," quietly interposed the Shrimp. "At least, none that I care much about giving."

At the half-hope in the words, Alan wheeled on him:

"For God's sake, Doctor!" he croaked. "For *God's* sake—"

"Alan!" broke in Hera, in stark bewilderment. "What on earth!"

"He's poisoned me!" bellowed Alan. "I can feel the symptoms. All of them. The dry throat, the chilliness—"

"I have not poisoned you," retorted the Shrimp, coldly. "I took an even chance with you. You know that. Man, brace up, can't you, and behave more like a human being and less like a kicked puppy. If it is death, then face it at least as bravely as your Malay—"

"There *is* an antidote?" wailed Alan. "Get it for me. I'll—"

"You will give her up?"

"Yes. Yes, oh, *anything!* Give—"

"Give up what?" demanded Hera.

"Give *you* up," translated the Shrimp. "Alan's in love with you. Aren't you, Alan?

He longed for a chance at cave-man methods, so he could battle on even terms for his mate. So I—"

"It's getting worse!" moaned Alan. "The antidote! I'll do anything—"

"Alan!" demanded Hera, "are you delirious? Tell me what—"

"You see, my dear," went on the Shrimp with the air of a clinic lecturer, "the 'cave-man' you called so glorious and so chivalric, is losing a little of his magnificent poise. But—even in death—he still adores you. He would far, far rather die loving you, than take the antidote and live without you. Eh, Alan?"

"*Give* it to me!" entreated Alan, unhearing, his faculties dulled to words and looks, alike, sensible only of his peril.

"You'll give up Hera if I do?"

"Yes. Yes. I—"

"You don't love her?" persisted the Shrimp, ignoring Hera's indignant protest.

"The antidote! I'm getting faint! It's working up to my brain."

"Alan!" again cried Hera, dumfounded. "What—"

"You wouldn't risk death for her?" persisted the Shrimp. "Hera, try to persuade him."

Alan shrank from the wondering woman as if she had struck him. His knees shaking, he stretched out agonized hands of appeal to the Shrimp.

"Say 'I don't love you, Hera,'" dictated the Shrimp. "Say 'I want to live and I don't want you.'"

"I—" croaked Alan, panic-deaf.

"*Don't!*" begged Hera, wheeling on her husband. "I can't understand this hideous farce. Are you trying to humiliate me? It isn't—isn't like you. It's horrible to see a grown man so abject as he is. I didn't know—I—oh, do what Alan wants you to, whatever it is! And make him stop gibbering so. It's *terrible!* I feel as if I were in a nightmare. Ugh! Take him away, *please!*"

"Just as you wish," said the Shrimp, with a shrug. "But—"

"The antidote!" wailed Alan, drunkenly fixing his faculties on one idea, and deaf and blind to all else. "For God's sake, the antidote!"

"The antidote for what?" asked the Shrimp. "For the powder I put in the Beauregard eggs? It was a subtle and mysterious compound known as 'paprika,' hitherto ignored by science as a mere condiment. I see now, though, that it is a strong cave-man reagent. My own discovery. The only possible antidote I can think of is an allopathic dose of sanity."

Alan, swaying, stared dumbly at him, trying to grasp the meaning of words and tone.

"My own powder," went on the Shrimp, "contained five grains of asperin. I take it for my rheumatism. It was the last powder in the box, but I don't grudge it. A twinge of rheumatism, down there on the rocks, gave me the idea."

"Asperin?" muttered Alan, still dazed. "What's—"

"I told you one of the powders was a deadly drug. Asperin is one of the deadliest on the market—if you take enough of it. Half a pound, or even an ounce. I told you the other powder was harmless. Paprika, until now, was always supposed to be. I told you, too, that we'd fight our duel on grounds where neither Strength nor Law could interfere. You remember that, don't you? Well, we have fought it."

Alan, a gurgle in his throat, vanished into the shack. The Shrimp turned to face Hera. In her face, indignation and bewilderment still battled for mastery. But, looking keenly at her, the Shrimp read more, in the big eyes fixed on his. So it was with a new note in his quiet voice that he asked:

"Should I have had to wait so very long for my mate in the cave-days, Hera? Shall I have to wait *very* long for her—now?"

L IDA REECE was "emergency" on the third floor of the Rayson Department Store. Her duties comprised some of the following tasks:
To "spell" any girl on the floor who might chance to be ill; to take the lunch-hour "time" of fifty-one girls; to "spell" six "lunchers" and to keep mental run of stock and prices for the whole floor—besides helping in the cashier's gallery. Also, because she had taught herself stenography and typewriting, she was allowed now and then to take some of the junior partner's dictation when his regular secretary was otherwise busy or away.

All this avalanche of diversified labor fell on Lida's slender shoulders. And she kept at it nine hours a day, (except in rush seasons, when the nine hours stretched to eleven or twelve). And because she was quick and strong and a dynamo for work and the best "emergency" in the store, she received nine dollars a week.

Nine dollars a week was a fair living wage. The courts had once decided so, and the Working Girls Improvement League had endorsed the decision. And it was more than the bulk of the Rayson girls received. So Lida was as nearly contented as was good for her work.

Lida was not only an efficient worker, but in looks she was well up to the average of most girls who eat and dress and board on nine dollars a week—and on no more—and who work hard for not less than nine twenty-fourths of every six days.

Which does not mean that she was actually pretty. Perhaps not one woman in thirty is. In any case, beauty is seldom intensified by hard work and by an unreinforced nine dollars a week.

She was too busy to think much about her looks. For she had not only energy but grinding ambition. She knew that, as a rule, the more money one deserves, the more money one will receive. So Lida spent the bulk of her evenings in brushing up her stenography and improving her typing speed. Her spare moments—there were no spare "hours"—in the daytime, were devoted to learning and digesting more information about the store's business. And all with the hope of advancement—honest advancement.

As though mere work and sleepless ambition were not a load heavy enough for one tired girl to bear, worry soon added itself to her burdens. Worry—centering about a man: Mr. Haliburton Surles.

Mr. Surles was the junior partner. He was thirty-two, and his hair was beginning to grow thin. But he was impressive looking, had a good figure and dressed divinely. Also, there was a dash and latent energy about him that set two hundred and five girls to re-reading Laura Jean Libbey with a new and personal interest. Lida was not one of the two hundred and five. She was sensible. And her ambitions were all sane, not based on literary trash.

Mr. Surles' office was on the third floor down the corridor marked "Private," just back of the white goods department. And since he had learned that she understood stenography, Lida was summoned thither perhaps three times a week, for a half hour or so of rapid-fire dictation. It was on these occasions that worry set in.

Not that she knew the very faintest idea or desire of winning Mr. Surles' heart and hand, or that she was fool enough to have fallen in love with him. She was a very real-life girl. But Mr. Surles had a Reputation!

He was a *Lothario*, a *Don Juan*, a *Lovelace*, a man-about-town, a fellow who stared in frank and unashamed admiration at any unusually pretty girl he might chance to notice. May Merton had seen him at a cabaret with a front-row show-girl whom, from a gallery seat, May had beheld that same evening in a musical comedy. "Our Mr. Prawle" had twice seen Surles motoring along the Drive with a vaudeville actress whose face was familiar to all faithful students of billboards. And there were other and similar tales.

Lida heard these tales—through no wish of her own—and they distressed her keenly. So did the Junior Partner's occasional glances in her direction. For that reason she had always tried to have her back turned when Surles passed near her in the store. She was a good girl. And she preferred to flee from temptation, rather than to resist it, face to face, at danger of losing her cherished job. She avoided Surles. She had hoped he might not notice her. Then, when he *did* notice her, she hoped she put a wrong construction on his looks. Little by little, she waxed frightened, and very unhappy.

Then, thanks to her ability to take dictation, had come the half-hours in his office. And at such times she could not prevent his looking at her. More than once, as she glanced up, during the dictating of a letter, she had surprised his gaze fixed directly upon her face, and her soul cringed, as at a whip-lash.

After a few of her mandatory visits, Surles took to greeting her advent with a nod and a decidedly familiar smile. One day, when she brought him for signature a batch of letters she had finished in record time, he sickened Lida by patting her jovially on the shoulder and exclaiming:

"Good kid!"

Lida understood her peril. She felt that peril drawing closer and closer to her as the days went on. And of late—there could be no doubt of it—she was sent to Surles' office far more frequently than of old. His secretary, Miss Gaynor, seemed to be absent oftener than formerly. Lida wondered if the girl were sent away on pretext. She dismissed the thought as absurd. But ever it crept back to her. She watched; and her suspicion became a miserable certainty.

TREMBLINGLY, yet trying to feel secure in her own goodness, Lida Reece awaited the inevitable: the scene when Surles would speak plainly. And she worked and studied the harder, to prepare herself for the new job she must then seek. She believed she would find the job—unless he should go so far as to blacklist her. Such things had happened more than once, for various causes. The "blacklist" was no mythical bugaboo.

She had always done her best. She had always led a clean, upright life—not like Zaidee Fraser or Irene Macnair or that girl with the made-up lips in the millinery department.

And Heaven would protect her. She felt that, borne in upon her as a revelation, every time she rose from her prayers. Then stealthily would come black worry to undermine the white ramparts of faith; and the battle would rage again. But, at last, out of the prayer-stilled strife a certain dazed calm emerged.

Armed with this strange calm she went boldly into Surles' office at her next summons thither. Pencil and notebook in hand, she seated herself across the desk from the Junior Partner. For a full hour, this afternoon, with almost no let-up, he dictated. And with her rapidly-increasing skill she kept abreast of his words, scarcely conscious of fatigue, though the end of a long and tiring day was at hand.

At last, Surles pushed back his chair, lighted a cigarette and stretched. Then he looked at his watch.

"Lord!" he exclaimed, "I didn't know it was as late as all this. Run along home. You can transcribe all that stuff in the morning. The letters will be in time if they go off on the ten o'clock mail. I've tired you a lot, I'm afraid. You worked so well that I forgot you weren't as used to this as Miss Gaynor is."

She closed the notebook and got up. Her knees were cramped. So was her hand. Her cheeks, in the glow of the green-shaded electric desk lamp, were pallid.

Surles glanced more closely at her. She felt his eyes preying on her half-averted face, as she busied herself putting away her pencils. And, without looking, she read his expression. Moving a little faster, she thrust the pencils and the notebook under one arm and turned to go.

Surles also had risen.

"Little girl," he said, very gently, "you look all worn out. You're working too hard."

Working too hard! In all the annals of department stores, so far as Lida Reece knew, never had an employer said such a thing to any employee. It could have but one meaning. The blood hammered at Lida's temples and her breath came short. The child was frightened—frightened clear through.

She took a furtive step toward the door. But Surles laid a tenderly detaining hand on her wrist.

"How would you like—?" he began.

He hesitated, then went on, slowly.

"How would you like to be in a position where you would get ever so much more money, and—and have a much easier life?"

Lida gasped. Then, wholesome fury seized her. She doubled the fingers of her free hand, so that the ill-trimmed nails gnawed into the fear-sweated palms. And she measured the distance between his alluringly smiling face and her clenched fist. And then the office door opened and Miss Gaynor came in. As the secretary entered, Surles dropped Lida's wrist with as much suddenness as though it had all at once turned to white-hot iron. At the same time, he took a step backward.

Lida's own fingers unclenched. There was no need now for that indignant fist-blow in the tempter's smiling face.

"That is all, Miss Reece," said Surles loudly. "Good night."

Dropping his voice, as Miss Gaynor crossed to a wardrobe closet in the corner, he added in a rush of whispered words:

"Come in here at ten to-morrow morning. I think we shall be able to arrange something to our mutual advantage."

IN blind horror, Lida found her way, somehow, out of the office—to the dressing room and thence, stumblingly, to the street. It was raining. And the sidewalks were jammed with home-goers.

Lida did not feel the downpour. She did not feel the grind of jostling shoulders or hear the gibes or growls of such pedestrians as she in turn happened to jostle.

Guided only by the homing instinct, her brain numb, her heart dead, her whole system dully nauseated from reaction, she blundered along. Presently,—or perhaps in a century,—she reached her boarding house, let herself in and toiled dizzily up three flights of squeaky stairs to her own hall-room. There, behind a locked door, she sat down very suddenly and very weakly on the white bed-counterpane of figured cotton, and began to cry like a frightened baby that is lost.

Little by little she came to herself. And she forced her sick mind to go over every detail of the scene of dread she had just been through. There was no longer the shadow of doubt, the shadow of hope. She was face to face with the situation—the situation she had so long and so shudderingly forecast, and which thus did not find her all unprepared. Hope and faith were gone. Only terror was left. She wanted her mother.

Lida realized that never again must she set foot in the Rayson store. She must hunt work somewhere else. And that being decided on, she realized that she was faint and that she had eaten nothing since breakfast.

She bathed her face in cold water—the only sort her room afforded—and dabbed her eyes with diluted witch hazel. Arranging her tumbled hair with shaky fingers, she went down to dinner. One must keep one's strength if one would seek a new job. One must eat if one would keep one's strength. And boarding-house dinner-hours wait not on temptation or even on heartbreak.

Lida conscientiously bolted a certain amount of food which, for aught her numbed palate told her, might have been compounded either of cyanide of potassium or of ashes. As she was leaving the table, the evening mail arrived. And with it came Lida's weekly letter from her mother, in Hampden.

Lida had forgotten, in the stress of everything else, that this was the night for the weekly letter. Its presence strengthened and calmed her. It made her feel less hideously alone. She ran upstairs to her room to read it.

It was not a wholly cheering epistle. Here is a brief abstract from its four close-scribbled pages:

A specialist of note had just examined Lida's little sister Martha, who had been a cripple from babyhood. The great man had readily diagnosed her malady and had declared unhesitatingly that he could cure her.

(Lida began to forget her own griefs in this unbelievably wonderful news, for she adored the little deformed girl.)

But, the letter went on, the very lowest price for the operation and all its kindred expenses would be three hundred dollars. The widowed mother's income from her husband's insurance being barely enough to keep herself and Martha alive, this sum was prohibitory. Unless—

Could Lida possibly get an advance of three hundred dollars on her salary? If not—and oh, how crazily happy Martha was, over this chance that she might become like other girls!

"I am making—I *was* making—nine dollars a week," mused Lida aloud; her voice flat and dead. "If I sent every cent of that to them I couldn't raise it all for nearly eight months—even if I didn't have to eat and dress. Besides, no store would advance it. Eight months' pay in a lump—without security! And—and I haven't a job now, anyway. I haven't anything!"

All night, Lida Reece sat there, on the side of her bed, the cheap gas whistling and roaring unheeded and with gross extravagance, in the jet above her. All night she battled. And by daylight, she had conquered—or she had lost. At all events, the path lay clear.

AT precisely ten o'clock next morning, Lida entered the Rayson store. Evading the wrath of her chief for her crime of two hours' tardiness, she made her way straight to Mr. Surles' office—down the third-floor private corridor behind the white goods department.

Without knocking, she went into the office, and across it to the junior partner's desk. There she halted and, without a word or without glancing at Surles, laid her mother's letter, open, on his desk.

He picked it up, wondering at her abrupt entrance, and began to read. When he had finished he looked up in quick sympathy, to confront a pair of eyes whose expression changed to an astonished silence the words he had been about to speak. Before he could recover from the momentary surprise, Lida was talking.

In measured, forced utterance, she began the speech it had taken her three terrible hours to rehearse. Even as she forced her voice to steady cadence, so did she force her gaze to meet and hold Surles'. Both efforts were equally unnatural.

"Mr. Surles," she said, in pathetically stilted diction, "don't think for a moment that I have misunderstood your recent words and actions and looks. I understood them all—too clearly—even before your—your—proposition—of last evening. I—"

She hesitated an instant, confused by the look in the man's eyes. Then she steadied herself and continued.

"From the first, you were tempting me. Every day, I saw it more and more clearly; I didn't want to think so, but I couldn't help it. Until last evening there wasn't anything definite I could resent. Then, when you dared to—"

"I—" began Surles, confusedly; but Lida hurried on.

"If I were alone in this and hadn't anybody but myself to consider, I would never have come near you again. But—but you have just read about my little sister. I've got to have the money to make her well. I've *got* to. No matter what it costs me. Do you understand?"

"Understand?" mumbled Surles, dazedly. "Why, I—"

"I have come this morning," she finished, "to tell you—to tell you—to say I'd a million times rather die; but that I'm going to sacrifice myself for Martha. It's worth it. And it's the only thing in the whole world that is. There! I have told you."

She felt very weak in the knees, very dry in the mouth. She had not been able, toward the last, to meet his eyes. Now she faced toward him again in dizzy defiance. But she saw he had risen and turned his back on her. His shoulders were heaving, as with emotion. And, to her self disgust, a little thrill tingled through the tense horror of the moment.

Then, his face a trifle flushed, but set and grave, Surles turned toward her again.

"Sit down," he ordered, quietly.

She obeyed, her chin trembling, her palms wet. Surles crossed to where she sat, and stood looking down at her.

"Listen to me," said Surles, making no move to touch her. "I am going to waste a few moments—of time that I can't spare—in talking to you. And I want you for your own sake to pay attention to what I say."

"Ye-s," faltered Lida.

"I know," began Surles, "that the vast majority of employers are vile seducers. Nobody can doubt that. But that 'vast majority' is almost wholly recruited from the ranks of fiction. Real-life employers—myself, for example—are usually too busy trying to dodge involuntary bankruptcy to waste the time and the money needed to wreck the lives of their feminine workers. Also, those same women are more desirable and infinitely more useful to them behind their counters than in harems. You won't believe that. I don't expect you to—largely because it is true. If it weren't true, every big business enterprise would be in the hands of receivers and every employer would be in jail."

He spoke carelessly. Lida suspected that he was joking, that the obscure jest was leading up to some declaration.

"You are a splendid worker, Miss Reece," he was saying. "And you are a neat, pleasant-faced girl, the kind our ancestors used to call 'comely.' And you will some day make one of my clerks—or one of another man's clerks—very happy. I hope he will be worthy of you and prove a fairly good husband. But—will you forgive my rudeness if I say you are scarcely the type of woman for whom a man like myself would lose his head and risk disgrace and all sorts of trouble? That is the mildest and kindest way I can put it. You won't believe you aren't a beauty. I don't expect you to. What woman *does* believe it?"

Through the fear-pallor on Lida's cheeks a wholesomely indignant red began to throb. She still did not catch the full drift of his talk, but this latest part of it was as readily understood is it was insolent. He resumed:

"To be still more vulgarly rude, I don't buy chuck steak when I can get *filet-mignon* for the same price. Why should I start an "affair" with a shop girl whose low wages and hard work have made her look as—nine-tenths of my shop girls look? Girls with roughened, reddish hands and badly kept nails and hair that inclines to greasiness and feet whose shape is spoiled by long hours of standing! Girls who don't know how to dress and who mistake garish tawdriness for elegance. Up to the time he is twenty-one, any girl appeals to a man. But when he passes thirty, he grows fastidious!"

"Mr. Surles—"

"I never yet have seen one girl, out of the hundreds I employ," he rumbled on, now caught by his theme, "who could hold a candle to the better-class musical comedy girls, in looks, in daintiness or in any form of fascination. If they were as pretty or as charming, they'd be earning from fifteen dollars, up, on the stage, instead or working their lives out in a store and earning from ten dollars, down—

mostly down. There are pretty shop girls, by the scores—for those who care for that sort of beauty. But there are prettier stage girls by the hundreds. Perhaps now you understand what I meant by my comparison between chuck steak and *filet mignon?*"

"I—I—"

"Don't get the notion for one moment," he added, more gently, "that I am running down the girl who works for a living. She has come to stay. She has proven herself well worthy to stay. And I honor her. But I don't make a sweetheart of her. Neither do most employers. She is far more valuable to them as a worker. And in their hours of loafing they prefer girls who aren't associated with their work."

Lida had half risen.

"I'm not being a beast and trying to hurt your feelings," said Surles. "This is doing you good—as much good as pulling an ulcerated tooth, and probably with as much discomfort. But you need it. And you asked for it."

"I—I never—"

"You and most other girls," continued Surles, unheeding, "get your ideas of life—and especially of men—from books written by people who have no more sense of real experience than yourselves. Until women stop reading books and begin reading human nature, they'll never know any more of the world than the fool, whose books they read, can teach them. For instance, writers, for hundreds of years, have given every woman the idea that she could roll in wealth if she chose to go wrong. Rot! They also give the idea that every girl on earth is in hourly peril. Those are two of the most asinine lies ever coined. Remember that, always.

"Take the average girl—by the average girl, I mean twenty-six out of every fifty girls you meet in stores or on streets or in cars or at shows. Take the average girl: If she behaves herself, she is in about as much real danger from men as a dress-form would be. And whether she behaves herself or not, the wages of sin wouldn't do much more than keep her in shoes and carfare.

"She isn't attractive enough to catch any man who has the wealth to take his pick of all the gloriously temptable and temptingly glorious women he meets. And the men in such girls' own walk of life are generally too broke to spend any big sums in that way. Poor men have a hard enough time to keep from starving. They can't afford to pay highly for their vices. So, where does the average working girl get her glittering temptations? She gets them—*nowhere.* She hasn't any.

"If she keeps straight, she keeps her self respect and other people's respect. But if she doesn't keep straight, she makes less money by following the primrose path than she'd make as an expert laundress.

"It pleases women, a lot, to imagine that they are throwing away vast opportunities for wealth by keeping straight. So let them keep on nursing the silly falsehood. Also, it pleases them to regard all men as possible seducers. I never yet heard of a well behaved girl coming to grief from any normal man. Their dangers are nine-tenths self-imagined. They don't understand that sane men don't buy plate glass at a hundred and fifty dollars a carat.

"I'm not speaking of girls who go crooked through sheer viciousness or folly. Small towns are fuller of those than big cities are. And they aren't recruited from the workers as much as from the class that looks on work as a disgrace. I'm speaking of girls who think the Wages of Sin are Wealth. They're dead wrong in thinking so—as I've tried to show you.

"Now, young lady, I've talked to you boresomely and long-windedly. And, ten to one, it's done no good, because what you read in print, you believe; and what you hear, you don't. That's the way it goes. But if my lecture has been stupid, it's your own fault. Why—what in blazes made you come here to-day with such an insane notion about my intentions toward you? What on earth have I ever said or done to make you—"

LIDA sat dumfounded, her mental foundations rocking. She felt as might a Martyr who, striding into a den of ravening lions, finds himself amid a litter of friendly and frolicsome collie pups. But she still clung to one fact.

"Mr. Surles," she broke in on his queries, "I suppose you expect me to think you are in earnest. Though, I can't see how you can expect it, after what you said last evening."

"Last evening? You've spoken several times about 'last evening.' What do you mean?"

"Since you force me to degrade myself by repeating it," she flared, "I will. Perhaps you were drunk, and don't remember. In this very room, on this very spot, you asked me how I would like more money—'much more money, and an easier life.' Then Miss Gaynor came in and you told me to come back this morning—"

The same emotion that had caused Surles' shoulders to shake now overcame him again. But as, this time, he was facing Lida, she saw he was convulsed with sudden laughter.

"Oh, you poor, over-expectant kid!" he panted. "I'm sorry to ruin your lovely fears. Here is the secret of my vile words of last evening: Miss Gaynor is leaving us next week. She is going to marry Prawle, in the Cloaks and Suits department. And I've been looking for the right kind of successor for her job. I didn't want her to know just yet whom I picked out, for she'd tell Prawle and it would get all over the store. I've watched your work, Miss Reece, and I like it. This was the proposition I wanted to make this morning. Would you care to come in here as my secretary? It's twenty-five dollars a week and—"

The girl broke down. Not by degrees, as is the manner of some overwrought women, but all at once, and pitiably. When she was able to note anything beyond her own hysterical sobbing, Surles was patting her reassuringly on the back and saying:

"As for this little sister of yours, I'll give you a check to-day for the three hundred dollars. You can pay it, ten dollars a week, out of your new salary. And—"

"Mr. Surles!" sobbed Lida, rapturously, gripping his hand in both of hers and trying in a spasm of gratitude to kiss it, "Mr. Surles, you've—you've—oh, Mr. Surles, I—I didn't think *anyone* could be so good!"

"No?" he laughed. "Yet you had no trouble at all in believing that anyone could be so bad. Run on, now, and have your cry out; and then come back for some dictation."

As the sobbing girl ran out into the passageway she heard a sound from the office behind her that made her pause. She was sure it was a short laugh. Then she was sure it was a still shorter oath.

And she fell to wondering which it had been.

"At $32 Per"

THE only fluffy things about Amy French were her name and her hair. Apart from these drawbacks, she was one hundred per cent business woman for nine-twenty-fourths of six days of fifty weeks of every year—holidays deducted.

Hers was a career such as elderly failures love to write about in "Success and Efficiency" periodicals. It had been very edifying, this career. It had served as an example to many a fellow toiler. Here are its high spots in a mere mouthful of words:

Amy's father had been a patrolman. He died just as Amy had entered the Normal College. The three hundred dollar yearly pension, plus his life insurance annuity, had been just enough to keep his widow in comfort; and had left, over and above, nothing that Amy had cared to waste on her own support.

So the girl had switched from the first of her four proposed Normal College years to one double-time year at a business school, and had thence slipped into the battle-line of work-seeking stenographers. Her first job, as a "sub" in the stenographic corps of the big mercantile house of Beardsley & Company, had netted her seven dollars and fifty cents a week.

On this sum she existed, until she could earn enough to live. And as she was a glutton for work and had a so-called "man's brain" for business detail, she rose rapidly.

Now, at twenty-five, she was the envy of every one of Beardsley & Company's three hundred and twelve girl employés. For she was secretary to the junior partner. And her salary was thirty-two dollars a week.

To a man with a fifteen-thousand-dollar income, thirty-two dollars a week is insignificant. To a five-hundred-dollar-a-year worker, it is affluence. As there are more five-hundred-dollar people than fifteen-thousand-dollar folk in the world (and none of the latter in Amy French's world), thirty-two dollars a week is affluence to the majority—especially when it is earned by an unencumbered girl, in a business realm where women's salaries seldom go above twenty dollars.

Amy's world knew of one or two women—buyers, millionaires' private secretaries, and so on—who earned more. But they were of a certain age and most of them were supporting somebody. To have that salary at an age when life runs at its fullest, and to have no one to take care of, with it—this was well nigh unheard of. Beauty, youth, infinite capacity for a good time, and almost infinite money to gratify that capacity—what more could mortal girl want? Wherefore, of her own set, Amy was the plutocrat and the Favored of the Gods.

She had a glorious time in life. She had all the money she really needed, and almost as much as she wanted. She could—and she did—dress well, eat well, lodge well. She had spending money, for theater, for vacation, for anything else. She even had money, occasionally, to swell her account in the Aaron Burr Savings Bank.

THERE was a man. He was on the clerical force of Beardsley & Company. His name was Karl Hunt. His salary was twenty-five dollars a week. He was in love with Amy. And Amy tried harder and harder every day not to be in love with him.

Even as she had conquered business obstacles, she conquered in this new fight, though it was harder than any other she had waged. She had clearly-defined ideas and ideals. And these she lived up to. Hunt's fervid love-making left her outwardly cold. He approached a proposal from every possible angle, dozens of times, during three months of ardent courtship—only to meet on every side a blank wall of discouragement that killed the love words, unborn, on his lips.

And so matters went on—Amy remaining persistently friendly, Hunt hopelessly ardent—until at last, one day in the early spring, courage overcame discouragement, and he spoke.

It was on a Sunday afternoon. He and Amy had been for a walk in the park. And when they returned to the big, airy flat she shared with her mother, they found Mrs. French had gone to see a neighbor. The coast was clear, the time perfect. Some of the languor of the springtime seemed to have got into Amy's ice-clear brain, dulling its usual vigilance. For she failed for once to note the preliminary warnings and to guard against their result.

On their way from the park they had been talking of a rumored reorganization of an unknown nature in Beardsley & Company—one of those rumors, sometimes absurd, sometimes amazingly accurate, that rise no one knows how, and run, like grippe germs, through a storeful of workers.

Hunt had heard the vague gossip and he had spoken to Amy about it. He knew no details. And Amy, better versed than he with the workings of the executive departments, was busy weighing what he had said and trying to decide whether or not a grain of truth might be sifted from the story.

So busy was she with this problem, as she laid aside her hat, on coming into the apartment's living room with Hunt, that she fell silent. Indeed, she failed to catch the drift of several things her guest was saying. All at once she found herself looking at him in blank bewilderment, as her mind belatedly repeated to her the words he had just spoken. Something in their intonation had roused her from her reverie.

"I won't be held off any longer," he was saying, half-defiantly. "I love you and you know I love you, and you've known it all along. A woman always knows, they say. *You* knew, anyhow. And you've kept me from telling you. But you can't, any longer. I love you. And—"

AMY sat down somewhat suddenly in the nearest chair and looked at him with an expression of frank chagrin that checked his impulsive step toward her.

"There!" she exclaimed in despair. "You've done it now! How I happened to let you, I don't know. You've gone and spoiled everything. Oh, dear!"

There was a disappointment in her words and in the interjection that ended them—a disappointment such as one might voice for tearing a new dress or letting the steak burn. It puzzled Hunt.

"What have I spoiled?" he demanded. "I don't understand you at all, Amy. I told you I loved you. How has that 'spoiled' anything? I love—"

"It's spoiled *everything!*" she retorted. "Everything. All our friendship and the good times we've had together, and—"

"'Spoiled' them?" he broke in. "Yes, it's 'spoiled' them the way a bar of gold is spoiled when it's fashioned into a crown. Friendship is mighty well 'spoiled,' when it changes to love. And oh, girl, dear, I *do* love you so! I've been so crazy to tell you, and you'd never give me a chance, till now. Say you care a little bit. *Say* it, sweetheart! I—"

"Oh, *don't!*" she begged, in honest distress. "Don't make it worse, Karl."

"Worse?" he babbled, dumfounded.

"Yes, worse—if it *could* be worse. Can't you see how it smashes our friendship? Can't you forget what you've just said and let us be—as—as we were?"

"Never in ten thousand years!" he declared. "And ten thousand nevers besides that. I've been in misery. And—and now you know I love you. I've been able to say it at last. 'Forget' it? I couldn't if I wanted to. And it's the very last thing I'd want. I can't understand you, dear. Is it so unpleasant to you to be loved the way I love you? Why do you want us to 'forget' it? Can't you care for me at all?"

"Yes," she made answer, meeting with level eyes the eager tenseness of appeal in his. "Yes, I can—only too easily. But"—as he started forward, with a half-uttered cry of joy—"I am not going to. I won't let myself. That's why I asked you to forget it and just be friends again."

"You—you say you *can* learn to care for me? I—"

"And I also say I won't. That is final, Karl."

"Final? It isn't even the beginning."

"It's the end. And of the friendship, too, I'm afraid!" she said, a strain of sadness underlying the usual clear crispness of her voice. "I see that, now. We can't go back to where we were. You'd never be content with it. And I'd always be remembering and be on my guard. No. It will have to be the end of your coming here. And—and I'm so sorry!"

"I don't understand you," he protested in dire perplexity, "I don't understand anything about it. It doesn't make sense. I've told you I loved you. If you didn't want me, it would be simple enough to account for the way you've been talking. But you confess you could learn to care—'only too easily,' you said; so please explain it, won't you?"

THE boyish incoherence of his appeal sent a swift mist across her steady eyes. Then, at once, she was her cool-headed self again.

"Will you be patient and listen to me?" she asked. "I'll try to explain it. I didn't want to explain. Because I know how hard and heartless it must sound. Common sense always does. And it *is* common sense. Will you listen to me, Karl?"

Dumbly, still dizzy with perplexity, he nodded.

"What is your salary?" she asked.

"Twenty-five a week," he answered, dashed by her curt tone.

"Good!" she approved, "—not the salary, but your telling the truth about it. Every man I ever knew, from the errand boy on up to the general manager, lies about the amount of his pay. It seems to be as much a masculine trait as snoring or hating to shave."

"What's that got to do with—?"

"With my not marrying you? It has a great deal to do with it. It is why I won't let myself care. We pay thirty-five dollars a month for this flat, Mother and I. Could you and I afford as nice a flat in as good a neighborhood on twenty-five dollars a week?"

He stared, dazedly, at her, without reply.

"Our grocery and butcher bills last week," she went on, "were eleven dollars and seventeen cents; and it was a light week. Could you afford to pay those bills every week—besides gas and carfare and clothes (this dress cost thirty dollars)—on your salary of twenty-five dollars? Could you take me to the theater every Saturday night—as Mother and I go—and buy me supper afterward? Could you? Could I go to the Islands for two weeks, as I went last year? In short, could I have half the spending money, the clothes, the amusements, the home comforts, the luxuries that I have now? Of course, Mother's pension and the insurance money eke out the expenses of the flat now. But they couldn't, if I were married. What have you to offer in exchange for all I'd have to give up?"

"Myself," he answered unsteadily. "That's all. I'm sorry it isn't enough."

"It isn't enough, Karl! I don't mean to be unkind or nasty, but it *isn't* enough. And I haven't spoken about the chief thing I'd be sacrificing."

She opened a tiny trunk-shaped vanity box that she had laid on the table alongside her hat, and produced from it a brass key.

"That," she said simply.

"That?" he stuttered. "That's just a measly latch-key."

"No," she denied. "It's Independence."

"Oh, I don't understand you at all!" he groaned. "It's like some nightmare. You talk as if you had no heart."

"No," she corrected, gently, "only as if I had a brain, too. And I have."

"You have no heart!" he accused. "I offer you all a man can offer—my love, my future—everything. And you calmly say it isn't enough and that you prefer to keep your own luxuries. Luxuries! I'd work my hands to the bone to get for you. Oh, you're heartless. You are utterly selfish!"

SHE bent her head a little, as though the whirlwind of his invective was a tempest that beat against her. But instantly she rallied.

"I think there is nothing more to be said," she responded, as he paused for breath. "I can't blame you for feeling as you do. And you are right—according to your own ideas."

"No!" he contradicted. "I was wrong. All wrong, dear. It can't be true. It can't. I've known you for months and months. You're white and honest, and clever—not the kind of woman who can mean such things as you've just said. You *don't* mean them."

"I'm afraid I do," she sighed. "And I'm in the right. That's just the trouble, Karl. I started to explain to you, a few minutes age. But somehow we got switched away from it. Do you care to listen while I try again?"

Taking assent for granted, she went on:

"From the beginning of the world, it used to be Woman's one aim in life to get a husband. Marriage was her great goal. Everything was bent toward that one end. For it, she made herself pretty and attractive. For it, she learned to cook and wash and sew—all to catch a husband, to find some one who would permit her to be a general house-servant and a nurse, for the rest of her days, at no wages. It was a gorgeous ambition, wasn't it?"

He made some inarticulate protest. She continued:

"Women used to leave the ease of their well-to-do parents' homes to starve with some worthless man. Women who didn't make legalized slaves of themselves were sneered at as 'old maids.' A man could pick and choose. All a woman asked was the privilege of being his chattel and of drudging for his welfare, till the day of her death. All the payment she asked was one cheap gold ring for her third finger. Women were so afraid the price might drop or the marriage market slump, that they banded together to crucify every woman who dared to undersell their rates and to waive the right of the wedding ring."

"Amy!"

"That's right! Look shocked. Thirty years ago, any unmarried girl who said that would be looked on with horror. For, innocence (that's a polite word for *ignorance*) was part of the pitiful stock-in-trade set forth to catch a husband—part of the allurement a girl offered to induce some man to accept her as an unsalaried drudge."

"This is the crazy feminist screech we read about in the papers!" growled Hunt in crass contempt. "I never thought that *you'd* sink to it."

"I haven't; I've *risen* to it. I am earning thirty-two dollars a week. My mother has about fourteen dollars more. On that, we live beautifully. We lack for nothing. I earn every dollar I get. And I'm entitled to all the pleasure I can get out of every dollar I earn. I suppose," she added, as an afterthought, "you wouldn't expect me to keep on working at Beardsley's after we were married?"

"You know I wouldn't!" he blazed. "I'm no—"

"Yes," she assented, "I knew you wouldn't. So instead of having a reinforced income of thirty-two dollars per, and my freedom and all that both those things mean, I'd have to live on a share of twenty-five dollars a week. I would have to keep house. I'd have to cook and dust and sweep and mend. We couldn't keep a maid, of course. And everything but the washing and the scrubbing would have to be done by me. We'd have money for mighty few amusements. I'd have to make one dress last as long as I make three last, now. I'd have to be at your beck and call. I'd have to save and scrimp and go without things and lie awake nights planning how to make one dollar do the duty of five.

"I've had to work hard to get up to where I am now. And I'm entitled to every atom of fun I can wring out of life. Not one girl in a thousand has such a salary as mine. Why should I throw away that salary and all it brings me? Why should I become a servant, a drudge, and, later, a nurse? Why should I make myself poor and a slave?"

"For love," he answered very simply, all his perplexity and wrath gone. "For love, and to fulfill your destiny."

"Old fashioned drivel!" she scoffed.

"Girl, dear, this hasn't been *you* talking. It has been the mass of feminist stuff you've swallowed and can't digest. The real *you* is a true woman, to the very soul— not a calculating human machine who uses money and not heart as a measure of life. You don't mean what you say. You may think you do, but you don't. What has been right and natural, since the days of Eve, will keep on being right and natural to the end of the chapter. What has gone on for six thousand years is not likely to stop short and change itself, in a single quarter century. Nothing in nature has ever done that."

"Woman has—"

"Woman has been let into the industrial world, during the last few years. She has not 'invaded' that world, as she likes to think she has. She has been invited into it by Man; because a million industries have suddenly expanded and branched out in such a way that more workers are needed. And women have been called on to fill that need."

"Nonsense! The—"

"The old-time store had from one to six clerks. And those clerks were generally men. Then came the department store. It hired hundreds of clerks. And, because the proprietors wanted bigger profits and because women would work more cheaply than men, women were invited to take the jobs. It has been the same in factories; in business offices; in public schools; in every line of endeavor. There was need of more workers at low pay. And women were allowed to fill that need. So, pretty soon they took to declaring that a Woman's Era had dawned. And they shouted—a lot of 'em—that Woman was coming into her heritage at last and that Man's day of supremacy was over. The possession of wages drove them crazy. As it's driven *you* crazy."

"NO," SHE denied, hotly, "it has driven us *sane!* When men held the purse strings, and doled out the pennies to us, we were their slaves—as I should be yours, if I were fool enough to marry you. When we learned to earn our own living, we became free, for the first time in all history. I, for one, mean to stay so, until I can be made as comfortable by marrying."

"Free? No. There is no freedom except in happiness. And the woman who tries to strangle her own heart and to slap Mother Nature in the face is never happy. You think you're happy. You're not. You're only having a good time. That isn't being happy—any more than a shiny new penny is a gold dollar. You will find out the difference when night comes—when the first jolly feeling is gone and you're just a middle-aged, tired, bored, single woman with a nice salary and nothing else. Have you ever seen the look such women give, on the sly, to some poor mother who passes them on the street, with a youngster hanging on to each of her arms and a stupid-faced husband plodding contentedly beside her? Well, I've seen it. And it's brought a lump to my throat."

"That is all sentimental slush!"

"It is the sort of sentimental slush that hardens into a strong enough mortar to hold the whole fabric of the world together. Dear girl of mine, you can't buck against Nature any more than you can hold out against God."

"It—"

"Drop it! I love you. You say you can easily learn to care for me. That means you *do* love me, but that you won't confess it for fear of being poor for a while. It isn't worthy of you, darling. You're turning your back on the most wonderful, God-given happiness in all life. You're doing it, just for the sake of a chance to spend more money than you need to and for an independence that is only another word for uselessness. You're swapping the substance for the shadow. I'm not worthy of a girl like you. I don't pretend to be. And I'm only earning twenty-five dollars per,—as you so carefully remind me, twenty-five per cent less than your own salary. But I sha'n't always be earning so little. With you to work for—"

"You won't be hampered by having me to work for," she raged. "If you were a billionaire and the last man on earth, do you suppose for an instant that I'd marry you?"

"But you said—"

"That was before I knew how you regarded women. I've tried to listen patiently to your ranting, ignorant arraignment of us. And I've fought back the things I wanted to say. But now that I have had a glimpse of your real self, now that I see how you look on us all—how you sneer at our gallant fight for emancipation—"

"Emancipation from what?"

"From the tyranny of the ages."

"The tyranny that has always made a decent man protect a woman with his own life? The tyranny that makes a woman's unsupported word, in court, outweigh all the evidence a man can bring forward? (If you doubt that, ask yourself if in all the history of law there was ever a woman who brought a breach of promise suit, who didn't win her case, no matter how flimsy that case was.) Do you mean the tyranny of laws that make a man responsible for all his wife's debts and that forbid him to disinherit her and that won't even let him sell a dollar's worth of his own property without her signature? Do you mean the tyranny that almost invariably refuses to punish a murderess? The tyranny that says: 'When the majority of women want the vote they will be welcome to it?' Do you?"

"Oh," she interposed, dazedly, "it's useless to try to make you understand! It is enough for me to know that you look down on women, as—"

"Stop!" he ordered. "I can't let you go on getting a wrong idea of me. Women, *as* women, are the most perfect part of this dreary old world. Every man knows it. Look at the men who are slaving their lives out. Are they doing it for their own pleasure? You know they aren't. It's always for some woman. And they glory in doing it. At the end of the day or at the end of the battle or at the end of the world, there's always a woman waiting. Next to God, it is she we worship. It is she who makes life worth while. It is *you* who are some day going to make *my* life worth while, dear heart. It won't be to-day. It won't be to-morrow. But some day the dollar will be spent and all the candy eaten. And then you'll come home—to *me*. And I'll be waiting—waiting, if it's a whole life-time. I won't bother you again till then. Good-by, little girl."

IT TOOK an entire week for Amy French's righteous rage against Hunt to simmer into sulkiness; and another whole week for sulkiness to merge into a pathetic grievance. And by the end of a month she found herself—to her own keen disgust—missing him terribly.

For, since the Sunday when a perfectly good love scene had distorted itself into a furious sex-argument and arraignment, she had not once set eyes on Karl. He called no more at the flat. Hitherto, Karl had made pretexts to pass through her department at Beardsley's, pausing for a chat; now he kept to his own part of the building.

Amy sought to buoy up her sinking balloon of anger by recalling all the abominable things Hunt had said about herself and her fellow-warriors in the Emancipation conflict. But gradually she found it harder and harder to bring back to memory the exact wording of those unforgivable slurs. And at last, all of his tirade she could remember were the phrases: "Sweetheart," "Dear girl of mine," and "I love you."

She was heartily ashamed of herself, but she had a way of being honest—even with herself. And in time she took herself in hand and forced herself to look fairly and squarely into her own heart. And there she read that she loved Karl Hunt, and that the world, without him, was growing to be a very unprofitable and tiresome place—even at thirty-two dollars per.

Because her thoughts were, for the first time in eight years, centered upon something other than her work, Amy missed many minor signs of coming storm, in the office—signs that in former days would have set her to conjecturing. As it was, she went through her days' routine, mechanically, then hurried home at the first possible moment and into her prettiest clothes in the shamed hope that Karl Hunt might call. But he did not.

And then, one morning, she quite lost her last ragged remnant of self-respect. On reaching her desk she scrawled a note and sent it to Hunt by an office boy. She wrote it in a rush and held herself tightly in her chair to keep from hurrying out of the room to call back the messenger. And yet the missive held nothing more incriminating or degrading than the scribbled words:

"Dear Karl: What has become of you?

A. F. "

THAT day, the world came to an end—at least, Amy French's professional world. At ten o'clock the first whisper of an immediate change swept through the employees' ranks. At eleven it was confirmed to Amy by a letter she took at the junior partner's dictation.

Beardsley & Company had not been "reorganized." It had been "taken over." Both partners were retiring, and the whole concern had been bought by the rival firm of Durling & Mickens.

At noon, the story of the long-pending deal was made public.

At one o'clock, the junior partner tactfully told Amy that he "was informed the new proprietors and department chiefs were already supplied with an ample force of secretaries;" and that she might, if she chose, accept two weeks' pay in lieu of a fortnight's notice to quit.

He was very nice about it; and he added something consoling in the form of a hint that this was the slack season and that he hoped Amy had laid by enough money to tide her over, as no job such as she had been occupying seemed to be vacant just then. And he patted her hand—thus invoking a gust of indignation which dried her unshed tears.

Amy French had left home that morning, one of the best paid women workers in the city. She went home that night a working girl out of a job.

She knew that positions such as hers are seldom "filled from the outside." Employees work up to them. A high priced secretary who has lost her job in one business house stands scant chance of receiving the same position in another, without climbing once more the greater part of the steep ladder.

Luckily, her mother was dining with some friends that night. So Amy was able to face the situation alone, unhampered by well-meant sympathy. And so busy was she in the wretched task of readjusting her plans to this cataclysm, that the bell rang twice before she so much as noticed it.

Then, listlessly, she answered the summons. And she opened the flat door, to discover Karl Hunt on the mat. For a moment she gazed at him in stark wonder, wholly forgetting the summons she had sent him. So much had happened that day, she had not yet tried to "place" Karl in the new scheme of things; and all day she had remembered him only subconsciously—as she had of late been doing, unwittingly, day and night. His advent, just now, took her at a grossly unfair disadvantage.

Amy tried to say something. So did he. Neither succeeded. Then Amy tried once more. What she intended to say, she could never remember. It was something that was polite without sounding too cordial. To her horror, she heard her treacherous voice murmuring, through no volition of her own, the following idiotic words:

"The—the dollar's all spent. And I—I—oh, I want to come *home!*"

In His Wife's Name

THE perennial Trusted Employee—in the day's news and in Wall Street fiction—has a sad trick of speculating with the firm's funds. Playing a straight tip or backing his own more or less ripened judgment, he makes the stock market plunge which is to scare away forever the bogy of a poverty-ridden old age and insure luxurious ease. His tip or his judgment goes awry. And then comes publicity—followed by jail or suicide or some such deterrent to other venturous Trusted Employees.

The news sheets bristle with such cases, have bristled with them, and will bristle with them, so long as a few employees forget that "trusted" and "trustworthy" should mean the same thing; so long as men who handle millions are not content to live on hundreds; so long as a short-cut holds more lure than a rutted hill-road.

But the world hears only of the men who are caught—the losers. If no gambler had ever cashed a bet on a horse race or at a roulette wheel, wheat and weeds would be waving over every circular track, and gaming paraphernalia would be as dead as the Pterodactyl. A Trusted Employee loses—and is pilloried. A Trusted Employee wins—and keeps his mouth shut. So, we hear only of the loser. Men do not care to brag:

"I stole five thousand dollars from my employer, played the market, pulled out with fifty thousand, put back what I had taken and cleared up forty-five thousand on the deal."

It is one form of boasting that is not done. But there is many a clerk who has discovered with mild envy that the thirty-dollar-a-week man at the next desk has fallen heir to a heaven-sent legacy which has let him buy a ten-thousand-dollar house and salt down another twenty thousand or so.

All of which leads up to the story of a man who staked what was not his and who won.

Saul Beiser was fifty-five. He was cashier for the bond house of Retz, Mason & Arnheim. His salary was fifty-five dollars a week.

Beiser was not a genius. He was competent; but he was merely competent. When he went to work for Retz, Mason & Arnheim, thirty-five years earlier, the finance world was thirty-five years younger. Beiser learned the methods of that other day. He had been a protégé of the elder and bygone Retz. Wherefore, the present Retz kept him on as a cashier, not wholly under protest, but quite without enthusiasm. Beiser's death or resignation would not have wrecked the firm. Indeed, either event would have given an excuse for installing certain changes which, while desirable, could wait on sentiment a while longer.

Beiser realized all this dimly. Fifty-five is a splendidly mellow age for an employer. For an employee it begins to savor of over-ripeness. Beiser, like all men who near the dead-line, knew this too. He had come to the time when vagrom failure-shadows, which now and then blot a younger man's day after a bad night or a piece of black news, are ever-present realizations. He had lived to the age when he knew that life would never, under normal conditions, mean more to him than the following hodgepodge of items:

A fifty-dollar flat for fifty weeks a year and a growingly uninspired summer hotel or camp sojourn for the remaining fourteen days; two new modest-priced suits per year; a sparing outlay for fresh ties and linen; self-shaving; sparsely scattered evenings of watery amusement; household bills that must not exceed seventy dollars a month; one general-housework servant; a wardrobe and a list of pleasures for his wife just meager enough to keep discontent alive and sub-acute.

That for the present. For the days to come:

The grim surety of superannuation within a decade, and an almost equal assurance that no pension would lighten the Day of Doom. There were a few— pitifully few—dollars salted by. And there was his "trial size" insurance. Those were the only buffers—and they would fend off the old-age problem about as effectively as a dipper of water would stem a prairie-blaze.

Beiser could look forward, no longer morbidly but with jaw-stiffening nearness, to the time when he must remember to hold his shoulders back and his head up and to force solidifying joints to an ambling spryness—yes, and secretly carry home the work that his dulling faculties could no longer dispose of in the daily eight hours. All this as prelude to the End: the End that is Nothing; the End that is the average wage-getter's.

He had seen it all so often! He knew, from observation, every move of the descent. At best, he could not hope to be better off than he now was. At worst, or rather, in the normal course of events—

TEMPTATION came to Beiser—much as the temptation of a flung rope or a floating spar to the drowning. And—he was ever supermethodical—he set about yielding to temptation in a way whose lack of thrill bade fair to turn his Recording Angel's tear-stained page into a mere day-book debit sheet.

As to his procedure—there is no need in going into a mathematical wealth of detail which would set outsiders a-yawn, and would start amateur Wall Street *cognoscenti* to figuring with envelope-back and pencil in search of technical or arithmetical errors, and finding them. Briefly and non-technically, this is how, three months before his fifty-sixth birthday, Saul Beiser undertook to guard against a leaden future:

He took from the Retz, Mason & Arnheim vaults a sheaf of unregistered Morris & Essex bonds, left there for safe-keeping by a customer who was wintering in California. These securities he deposited with the brokerage firm of Horgan & Sons, in Boston, and proceeded to trade against them.

One of the favorite and, perforce, harmless occupations of Wall Street's elderly mediocres is to follow breathlessly—and cashlessly—the fortunes of various so-called "gambling stocks," watching their rockety rises and swooping slumps with a trained wisdom which does not follow, but prophesies, every shift. These prophecies, through long practice, are wont to be surprisingly accurate. One imagines that such prophets, in childhood, courted the double amusement of biting on a sore tooth and of imagining themselves the heroes of the dime novels they were reading.

Beiser was an expert at this futile if tantalizing form of gambling. Again and again, his mind-bets had been pyramided and brilliantly manipulated into netting him imaginary quarter-millions. Seldom had his mental plunges gone amiss. He had specialized mentally, for the past five years, in a highly erratic stock for which C. G. & X. is as good a name as any. He had conned its zigzag courses until he felt he knew the lightest mental processes of the cliques which alternately inflated it and wrung it dry. And upon depositing those bonds he sold C. G. & X. short. In seven weeks he cleared up a trifle more than $125,000.

Then, unsuspected, he replaced the Morris & Essex bonds in the vaults of Retz, Mason & Arnheim. He deposited his winnings, temporarily, in the Chemical National Bank. He deposited them in his wife's name, to give a feminine twist to the inevitable "legacy" story, as well as to guard against loss in case of detection.

BEISER, in his normal dry-as-dust state, would have known he had blocked detection or even suspicion. The bonds were safely tucked away where they belonged, in the Retz, Mason & Arnheim vaults. There was nothing whereof to accuse their temporary borrower. But Beiser, just then, was in a decidedly abnormal condition.

It is no light thing for a man in the mid-fifties to rip to pieces all at once the close-knit fabric of his life, to blaspheme the business religion of thirty-five years, to cast down and smash his self-reared idols. In fact, for a man in the mid-fifties it is no light thing to depart suddenly and violently from any mode of life wherein the years have molded and hardened him.

Add to this the tense watchfulness, the biting suspense, the unremitting nerve-rack of a seven-weeks' battle between prosperity and prison. Superimpose these on a man whose age is nearly fifty-six, whose height is six feet, whose chest measure is thirty-five inches and whose daily lunch is crackers-and-milk, and "cracking under the strain" takes on a new meaning. After an eight-hour day at the office and a tediously uninspiring home evening, Beiser had taken to lying awake for several hours, calculating to a month his possible prison sentence, weighing the exact percentage of chances for and against discovery before the closing of the deal. These modes of whiling away the sick hours of darkness did not tend to his physical uplift.

When, at last, his money was won and he had moved, unscathed, out of the danger zone, Beiser was a wreck.

His next step was to sever his connection with the bond house of Retz, Mason & Arnheim. This called for the cleverest work of all. And with his last flash of shrewdness, he met the situation and conquered it. A few carefully planned errors in an important detail of his office work brought down upon his graying head an oversharp rebuke from the junior partner, Arnheim, who had never liked him.

Beiser, with a splendid imitation of the turning worm, answered back. The encounter suddenly took on the proportions of a noisy quarrel, in the presence of six ecstatic clerks and four lazily interested bond salesmen.

Beiser quite lost his head. He told Mr. Arnheim exactly what he thought of him, of the value of his services to the firm, of his private character, even of his personal appearance. Arnheim, young and hot-headed, retorted in kind. Whereat, Beiser went to the two other partners, declared he had been grossly affronted, pleaded his long and faithful years of work, and demanded that Arnheim be forced to apologize.

The most favorable terms he could secure were a gentle reprimand and a promise that in view of those same faithful years of work the incident would be overlooked. And Beiser, volubly heart-broken at such ingratitude from the men in whose employ he had grown gray, resigned his position.

It was a beautiful bit of work—this outburst of cranky rage on the part of an old watch-dog whose temper had sharpened as his yellowed fangs had blunted. There was not a shadow of suspicion. And Saul Beiser was free.

He was free; he was rich; he was only a little over fifty-five; and—he was very, very sick. He had won a marvelous victory. And now he wanted to go away somewhere and rest—rest for a long time.

BEISER'S wife—they had no children—was large and blonde and gentle, with a face that was still slackly pretty, and doughy arms, and a fondness for double Canfield and kid-curlers. Her breath always savored just a little of lukewarm tea with much milk—not cream—in it. She was a good woman, a very good woman; and a good wife. Her first name was Luella.

She and Beiser had been married for seventeen years. In that time they had never quarreled. Happy is the married couple, as is the nation, that has no history. And the Beisers—as a couple—had none. Their home life had been smugly eventless, and Luella knew and cared as little about her husband's life downtown, his real life, as he knew and cared about her delight in wandering with amiable aimlessness through the big shops or deliriously playing auction bridge twice a week for a tenth of a cent a point.

Yet they loved each other, and they had no idea that they were strangers. Luella had noticed that the statement, "Mr. Beiser is in Wall Street," evoked admiring interest in other women. She said it often, and was proud of her husband. Saul had observed that on their rare outings, Luella would now and again receive glances of approval from men of the type who used to frequent the "Blonde Burlesque" shows. This pleased him, and he would urge Luella to spend all she could afford on evening dresses.

When Beiser won his fortune, he had no trouble in eluding any suspicion from Luella. Her perfect and all-embracing ignorance of matters financial was his bulwark of safety. To her, dishonesty in business was ever linked with dark lanterns, safe-blowing, policemen, handcuffs and the Forged Will and other moving-picture accessories. Had Beiser told her in detail just what he had done to acquire the $125,000, she would not at all have understood. But, with the parrot-like memory that served her in the stead of brains, she might readily have reeled off the whole tale verbatim to some one who would understand. Wherefore, Beiser sought to confuse the trail further. And, as his head was oddly tired, he did it far too elaborately.

He came home at noon, dizzy, his eyes aching horribly, one side pocket padded with get-rich-quick prospectuses that he had gleaned for the purpose from a fly-by-night firm on Nassau Street.

Luella was so astonished at his return a whole five hours ahead of his usual schedule, that she did not see how desperately ill he looked. Observation was not her forte.

"Dear," he began abruptly, as he entered the dining-room where she sat at lunch, "I have great news for you—*great* news."

With the expectant joy of a child whose bachelor namesake-uncle approaches with one hand held significantly behind his back, Luella jumped solidly to her feet and hurried to meet her spouse.

"What is it?" she demanded, breathless; then: "Oh, I know. It's another raise!" (The last had come fourteen years earlier.) "Now we can get that—"

"Guess again," he coaxed, with a nauseated effort at playfulness. "But you'd never guess," he added. "So I'm going to tell you. Prepare yourself for the surprise of your life. I have left Retz, Mason & Arnheim. And now I—"

"Oh, Saul!" she wailed, the smile twisted ludicrously from her face, "you're not *discharged?*"

"I said 'great' news," he corrected patiently. "I have not been discharged. In fact, I have discharged the firm. I—"

"Oh, I don't understand you!"

"Listen, then," he pursued, drawing from his pocket the handful of pamphlets as he spoke. "It is a secret, and you must promise not to tell. We are—well, not exactly rich, as the term goes nowadays—but our income will be about double what it used to be. And I won't have to work for it."

"O-h!" she sighed in ecstasy, continuing after an instant of rapt thought: "And we can have an elevator apartment. And another maid. And perhaps my allowance can be bigger, too."

"Yes," he agreed vaguely. "Of course."

It was all so easy—even easier than he had dared to hope. The tidings had had but one meaning to her. The actual miracle of the new-got wealth had, for the time, passed her by untouched. Beiser hurried on—talking as to a mental defective:

"It is a secret. You see, being on the Street day after day, year after year, I am in a position to know the right kind of investment when one crops up. And you remember how I have been insisting, always, on putting a few dollars every month in bank. I saved a good many thousand dollars that way, in all. And it gave me the means to invest when the time should come. And at last it came. I invested my capital, and now we have enough to live on for the rest of our days."

"But," she protested, "isn't—isn't that what they call 'speculating?' I read once—or was it in the movies?—about a man on Wall Street who—"

"Yes, yes, I know," he interrupted, crossly. "But this wasn't speculating. It was an investment. The two are different. I invested in Orinoco Bullion Consolidated. You must have heard of the concern. If you haven't, here is some of its literature I've brought home for you to read when you get time. You will see it practically insures its investors of from four hundred and fifty to five hundred and twenty per cent a year on their money. I invested. And to-day I sold out."

"But why did you sell out?" she asked. "If they give you that much—or is it that many?—per cent a year, why didn't you keep on investing in it, till you got a great deal more money?"

"Because," he said, trying to lie convincingly, with a brain that ached and throbbed like an ulcerated tooth, "because the Orinoco people thought I was making too much. They said it wasn't fair to the other investors. They made me withdraw my capital. If—if they had let me keep it there another six months, it would have brought me a million dollars or more. But let's try to be content with what we have. I—I had to promise the president of the Orinoco Company," he went on, striving not to speak thickly, "I had to promise him we wouldn't tell we'd made so much money out of the concern. He'd be swamped with applications. You'll remember, won't you, not to tell a soul? Not a soul. Just say I've left Retz, Mason & Arnheim, and that I'm looking around a bit before I accept another position. Can you remember that?"

"Remember it? Of course I can remember it," she said, indignant. "And I won't say anything to anybody, since you've promised the president of the What-you-may-call-it Company that we won't. But I'm sorry you had to go and make such a silly promise, Saul. It would be nice to—"

"You are mistaken, dear. It wouldn't. Just be content at having so much more money to spend, and don't worry over not being able to brag about it. Now, if you've finished your lunch, I want you to come downtown with me. I'm going to open an account in your name at the Chemical National. That's a bank. I've made arrangements to open an account there. The money will all be in your name until I get a good chance to re-invest it. It's—it's a compliment to you."

The next hour was a meaningless kaleidoscope of stupid happenings to Mrs. Beiser. Sudden immersion in the business world had much the same effect on her intellect as would a souse into a bucket of cold water on a setting hen. Dully, and ever prompted by her husband, she answered questions, wrote her sprawly signature in a book and did other senseless things. And, on the way home, she tried with honest eagerness to grasp what Saul told her about the banking system of which she was now a unit.

All she clearly understood was that while the money was nominally hers, she must not spend it, and that only on checks made out and signed by her could it be drawn. She might have gleaned more from Saul's homily had the lecture been delivered less disjointedly.

NOW that the long ordeal was past and every last detail safely arranged, Beiser's whole being was suffering from reaction. He was desperately sick. And he could not think clearly. It was only by a hurty effort that he forced his mind and tongue to brief spurts of coherence.

The moment he reached home he announced that he had a sick headache— he often had them—and that he was going to bed. Mrs. Beiser, who had been planning a gaudy evening's celebration of their good luck, meekly sidetracked her golden plans and devoted the rest of her day to preparing mustard footbaths and cold head-compresses and other helpful horrors for the sick man.

At nightfall, Beiser fell into a fever-drugged sleep. At dawn he awoke from it and burst into a ribald song. Luella remonstrated. The singer thereupon proceeded to weep, in a wheezing, creaky fashion.

Luella routed out the janitor and sent that half-asleep and wholly disgruntled functionary for the nearest doctor. An hour later she heard the verdict: Saul Beiser was in the grip of a somewhat far-advanced attack of cerebral typhoid. For days, doubtless, he had had the malady in its "walking" form; had Mrs. Beiser heard him complain at all of feeling badly? She had not; but now that she thought of it, she remembered he had eaten hardly anything, lately, and he had got into a way of tossing about at night and muttering. These phenomena had not alarmed her, because Beiser had never had a day's illness since their marriage.

Ensued four weeks wherein the smugly, stupidly peaceful Beiser home became a foreign place to its mistress—a place ruled by a regent with a white cap and professionally gentle face, and by an overlord with a black bag and a brown beard, who called from once to thrice daily.

The maid—better known as the "girl"—had left on the first day of the ordeal. Thus Mrs. Beiser was the only remaining member of her own tiny house-world. For assuredly that moaning, swearing, growling, muttering Thing lying in the first bedroom was a stranger to her. He was no more like her dry, precise, domesticated husband, than the bedroom, in its glaring new whiteness and bottle-array, and with its sub-reek of medicine and disinfectant, was like the cosy, tastelessly furnished, pot-pourri-perfumed little shrine that Luella had fitted up and loved.

The nurse speedily discovered that Mrs. Beiser was absolutely no use in a sick-room, and that her habit of dissolving unexpectedly into tearful sniffs was annoying to the patient. So, very kindly and with training-school tact, the wife was banished from what had been her own dear bedroom and from the presence of what had been her own and even dearer husband. She spent the bulk of her waiting hours sitting, cramped, in a low chair just outside the half-open sickroom door, crying as silently as she could learn to, praying, remembering how good and friendly and companionable Saul had always been. Why, he had never once, in all those seventeen years, spoken a harsh word to her, never had lost his colorless temper! Where and how and when he had picked up the vocabulary his tired, hoarse voice was nowadays airing was a mystery—a revolting mystery—to Luella.

Still more was she mystified that this

raging, struggling, fiercely dissatisfied soul could have found unsuspected hiding-room for so many years under the correct gray nature she had thought she knew so well. And little by little, as she sat out the long days in the dusk of the stuffy hall,—her usual placid little vocations gone, her flaccid mind turned inward upon herself,—she grew to be ashamed that she had lived so long with this man and had never sought to understand him better or to enter into any but the outer chambers of his life.

His disjointed talk nowadays was almost wholly of the Street: of margins, of bond issues, of puts and calls, of similar things whose very names were Greek to her. He babbled of broken hopes, of financial triumphs that could never be his, of aspirations she had never dreamed he harbored.

And, woman-like, Luella forgot that she had made his home comfortable for him and had loved him and had filled his life as best she knew how. She realized only that she had been remiss, that she had taken no pains to enter into his dreams, his longings, to understand and inspire and help him.

Then and there, slipping blowsily from the low chair to her plump knees, she vowed that should he be spared to her, she would make herself worthy of him; that she would be his life-partner and not merely the sharer of his flat; that if possible she would redeem herself in his eyes and show that she could be a helper instead of only a helpmeet.

Then, as ever, with unwilling fascination, she fell to listening to the eternal rumbling whisper of the worn-out voice in the room beyond. And listening, day by day, she found that the dreams, the longings he voiced, were all of wealth. Money was the keynote of his discordantly endless solo. In delirium, he was back at the office, surrounded by countless chances for wealth, and able to take advantages of none of them; handling millions and permitted to retain for himself only a yearly $2,860, out of the treasure-heap that ran through his bony fingers.

Money! That was his never-ceasing refrain. Millions! That was the word oftenest on his cracked, black lips. The chance to make millions, to rise to glowing wealth. Millions!

AFTER a century or more, came a day when the doctor ventured to tell Luella that her husband had a fighting chance—later, that there was every prospect he would get well. After another eon she was allowed in the sick-room.

A right unsightly skeleton filled the whole length, and a ridiculously narrow width, of the bed—a skeleton with putty-colored skin stretched over jutting bones, with a grizzled and straggling growth of hair from nostrils to throat, with hollowly staring eyes several sizes too big for the shrunken face, with hands like powerless and fleshless claws.

For nearly a solid hour before she was allowed to see Beiser, both doctor and nurse had impressed on Luella the urgent need for repression and for cheerfulness during her brief visit to the convalescent. Therefore she battled back her desire to break into the hysterical keening wail of her species. She stood silent for a full half-minute, gaping fish-like at the strange little skeleton-face that smiled wanly up at her from its miles of white pillow. Then she sputtered her rehearsed speech:

"How—how well and strong you're—you're looking to-day, Saul—Saul darling!" She bolted to the uttermost end of the flat, where she sobbed uncontrollably until the exasperated nurse put her hartshorn under her nose.

But her next visit to Beiser was more of a success. And so were the next and the next and many others. The patient, having had scant strength to lose and a spare frame wherein to lose it, convalesced with a gratifying speed. And now Luella could spend hours at a time at his bedside. He rather liked to have her there. He had grown to miss her, as life and sanity had crept back to him. There was something very restful in her ample and bovine presence, when she was not crying or making awful faces to keep back the tears.

These days of drowsy convalescence were the happiest Saul Beiser had ever known. As the exhausted swimmer, safe ashore, lies in blissful laziness on the warm beach, so Beiser lay. His battle was fought and won. His peril was passed. His work was over. Comfort and freedom were henceforth to be his. No more need he dread the onset of old age, nor worry over petty expenditures. No longer need he be civil to folk he disliked.

For the first time since he could remember, he was resting, both in mind and in body. For thirty-five years he had labored and scrimped—and feared. Now he had entered into his reward. He was very weak. But he was very content. More than once he caught himself muttering a quotation he had heard at the elder Retz's funeral:

> Peace after war, port after stormy seas,
> Rest after toil—

And one bright morning in the early spring, Luella and the nurse lifted him out of bed—he weighed little more than the bedclothes—and put him in a big pillow-lined chair in the sunshine by a window. As he sat there, dreamily glad of everything on earth, he became aware that Luella was talking to him.

Ordinarily, of late, he listened to her talk as to the plash of water or the patter of summer rain: something vaguely pleasant but not at all necessary to translate into words. But now, a phrase she used brought his happily straying thoughts back to her.

"And so," she was saying, "I made up my mind I *would* be a help to you and that I'd show my poor sick boy I could understand the things that interested him. So, after you got out of danger, and before they'd let me be with you, I read up on financial things and—"

His amused, kindly smile added to her self-assurance, and she went on:

"I didn't know what books to ask for at the library. But I came across those funny little pamphlets you brought home to me the day you fell sick. Do you remember? The ones about the Orinoco Bullion Consolidated Company? You'd asked me to read them, you know. So I did. I was afraid at first they'd be hard to understand. But they weren't a bit."

The kindly smile took on a sardonic tinge. Beiser very well knew that the literature put out by such companies as the Orinoco Bullion Consolidated (shortened to "O Bull Con!" by some Wall Street jester) was not "hard to understand." He knew it was shaped to meet the intellectual limitations and to tickle the imagination of just Luella's type of investor. Indeed, this was the chief reason he had brought home that particular breed of pamphlets.

"And then," she prattled on, "my wonderful idea came to me. You know you said you had to draw out all your money from the Orinoco Company, because the president thought you were making so much it wasn't fair to the other investors. And you said if you had left your money there, it would have brought you a million dollars or more."

The smile was not even sardonic now. Indeed, it had vanished, leaving worried blankness in its place.

"And, all the while you were delirious, you had been talking about wanting to make more money," she said, with a little shudder of reminiscence. "So I saw my chance to help, to surprise you, to show I was good for something. I went to the address on the pamphlets and I asked for the president and I told him how sick you'd been and how happy it would make you if only he'd let you invest in the Orinoco Bullion Consolidated for just a little while longer—till you'd made, perhaps, a single million dollars."

A wordless, throaty sound interrupted her. But she was too eager in breaking the good news to hear it.

"He is a splendid man," she said with enthusiasm, "—so sympathetic and deep-hearted. He told me he understood just how things were, and because you were such an old customer of his, he'd make an exception and let me invest our $125,000 in Bullion Consolidated once more. He even showed me how to write out the check to get the money from the bank. And," she finished in thrilling triumph, "there, down in the space under my bottom bureau drawer where I keep the gold-tray, you know, I've got all the stock-certificates. He told me to be very careful of them. Aren't you glad, dear? And I *am* worth while, aren't I, after all? And now I'll get them and show them to you."

But she didn't.

The doctor said it was heart-failure.

The Other Man

DEAR old Renwick: Do you remember a silly promise we made each other, once? Back in '99 it was, on June 16. I never forgot the date, because it was Commencement Day, the day when College turned us loose on the world, with a sheepskin apiece and about as much real equipment for the fight as a roly-poly collie pup that is planning to investigate its first cat. But we felt wiser and more important and a million years older than we ever can, again.

We had gone through the delights of class day, of the Prom, of the ivy-planting, of the sing-song and all the rest, during that last week. Then, when we were already fed up on thrills, came Commencement and the bonfire, and the good-by class supper at the Inn.

It was about 3 A. M., I think, when the supper crowd broke up, after meteoric and tearful speeches, and songs that got to sounding solemn and choky.

You and I had both eaten more than we wanted and drunk more than we needed. So we waxed sentimental over leaving the good old place. We were crossing the campus to our room, I remember, when it occurred to us, as a sublime wind-up, to sit on the chapel steps and wait to see the sun rise, for the last time, over Dormitory Hill.

So we sat there, like two youthful owls, blinking into the pink east. We were smoking those black class-pipes of ours and trying in our talk to make each other believe we were sophisticated men of the world and that the parting next noon was all in the day's work. But there was a lump in my throat as I realized I was getting out of the only world I knew and into a world I didn't know, and that I was saying good-by to the chap who had been my room-mate and chum for four years.

People form their real friendships before they're twenty-five,—generally, before they are twenty,—I think. Up to that time we're trustful and hideously disinterested; and after that age we get to liking people for the amount of amusement or profit or inspiration we can drag from them. But, up to then, it's friendship because—well, just because it's friendship. That's the way it was with us, anyhow.

As we sat there, in the dawn, we spoke pretty confidently of licking the whole universe into shape and of carving success for ourselves out of the rock wall. Then, as the supper—or the drink—or the sunrise—or the strong tobacco—got hold of us, we fell to talking about what good friends we'd been and how we were going to keep in touch with each other always and always.

And (I, don't know which of us suggested it, but I do know we both promised very, very earnestly) we agreed that if life ever threw us far apart from each other for any great length of time, we'd write and tell just what we had been doing and all the really big things that had befallen us. In that way we'd keep from growing out of each other's memory. And when we should meet again, we'd be up-to-date in mutual history. We were to keep in touch with each other, always, by means of periodic letters telling the most important things that had happened to us—the "big things," we said.

I don't need to remind you that neither of us kept that pledge after the first three years or so—and with growing gaps between our letters, even up to that time. I don't know which of us stopped writing—which of us owes the other a letter accounting for himself and his history.

But to-night I'm settling up a lot of old debts, with the dying of the year, so that I can start to-morrow with a clean slate.

And it flashed into my mind a little while ago, that I owed you the keeping of my long-lapsed promise. A promise seems to me the most pressing of all possible debts of honor. So I'm paying my debt to you to-night. The last debt it is, by the way, that I owe on earth. I was reminded of it by reading an item about you in one of the metropolitan papers. It gave your address, too.

LET me see—I told you about my work and all that sort of thing, didn't I, when I wrote the last time, a decade or more ago? Did I tell you about my marriage? I think that came after my last letter. As that is the biggest thing—the one big thing—in my career, I'd like to write you something about it.

I married Mildred Kerr, a girl I had loved for years—and who hadn't loved me. That was ten years ago, to-morrow.

I was madly in love with her. I still am. And she was not in love with me. She was in love with Clive Ruyter, a man with twice my good looks and twelve times my money. In fact, she was engaged to him. They had a terrible quarrel over something or other. He went to Europe. And she married me.

I knew she did not care, not as I cared. And in morbid moments I told myself she had married me out of pique.

But what did that matter? She *did* marry me. And I knew—I was sure—I could make her happy, that I could make her care, even as I cared. I had a whole lifetime to do it. And, from the very first, I succeeded.

Day by day, I could see she was more and more fond of me. When two people—or two draft mules, for that matter—are thrown into each other's society, day and night, for months and years, they either grow tremendously attached or they grow to hate. It was my life-aim to see that Mildred should learn to love me. And I accomplished it, little by little. She began to be fond of me, as one grows to love a home.

It was not the mad, ardent love such as I've read about and that I used to long for. I see, now, there are better things than that. A prairie fire soon burns itself out, and it destroys a lot of innocent things in its path. But the earth that is warmed gradually by the sun, *stays* warm, and in time it blossoms into loveliness.

That was the kind of love I tried to bring into existence, and I did it... I was unbelievably happy. And Mildred was becoming happy, too, more and more. The goal was in sight. I could see, at last, when I came home from work, the light creep into her dear eyes. And the kiss she met me with held affection, now, instead of mere duty. The myriad little things she did for me, around the house, were coming to be labors of love, not matters of routine. I felt like a sculptor who is slowly and painfully fashioning the ice-cold block of marble into an angel.

Then Clive Ruyter came back.

He had been gone for nearly two years. I had half forgotten him. I thought Mildred had, too; but I wanted to make sure. So when I met him on the street, I asked him to come and see us. They had to meet, some day, you know, he and she. And I wanted to put it to the test, without delay, and have it over with.

Not that I had any fear of the result. They had quarreled and they had separated. If they had really loved each other, wouldn't that love have brought them together again, in a day, at most? What quarrel could have stood out against such a love as mine, for instance?

And, because they had let a quarrel part them, I was certain they had not loved but had merely been blindly infatuated, for the time, one with the other.

I am petty, at heart, I'm afraid—because there was another reason why I asked Ruyter to call. I was small-souled enough to want him to see us together in our own home, Mildred and me; to see how happy we were, together; to see that soft light in her eyes when she met me at the door; to see how pretty and dainty she had made our home. I wanted him to know—not what he had lost, but what I had won. I wanted everybody to know.

Well, he came to see us. It was not a brilliant success, that call. Mildred treated him as she would have treated any other friend of mine. But she was rather quiet; and he could not have seen that light in her clear eyes, because she never once looked at me while he was there.

I tried to cover up her lack of vivacity as best I could, by making Ruyter feel at home and by telling him all about our life and about Mildred's success in our tiny social world and our jolly plans for the future.

Ruyter bore himself splendidly. There was not a hint of embarrassment and he didn't seem to notice Mildred's dearth of cordiality. He admired everything in our top-floor flat and

he listened with the keenest interest to all I told him about us.

When he went away, I was so jubilant over my experiment that I couldn't keep my joy to myself. I came back from seeing him to the door and walked up to where Mildred still stood, in the middle of the living-room.

"Well, little girl," I said, drawing her to me, "did you like meeting him again? I was proud as *Punch* to have him see you looking so beautiful, and to see what a marvelous home you've made for me. I'll bet he's cursing his luck, all the way down the street, at losing such a treasure."

Then I stopped short, for she was crying. I'd never seen her cry, before, and I didn't know what to make of it. I tried to get her to tell me what was the matter; but she just clung close to me and sobbed all the harder and kept saying:

"I love you, Miles, dear. Oh, I *do* love you!"

It was the first time she had ever told me that, of her own accord. And it swept through me like the breath of God. That was the very happiest night of all my life.

FROM that time, she seemed to have lost the last shreds of her old-time indifference toward me. She took to planning little things for my comfort. She used to kiss me without being asked to. She would follow me with her eyes wherever I went, in a sort of appealing way that made me want to cry.

I could see she was growing to care for me, at last, just the same way I cared for her; to want to be with me all the time; to think more of making me comfortable; trying to study my wants and to fulfill them before they were really formed.

There was something about her like a little child that yearns to be forgiven and loved. I could see she was sorry for not having cared enough, before, and that she was seeking to make up to me for it.

Ruyter's visit seemed to have opened her eyes. I had been almost afraid that the sight of him would make her wish she hadn't thrown him over. You see, he was so much cleverer and better looking than I. And he had a manner—a way with him— that I never could learn to imitate.

Yet, in spite of all that, it appeared she never knew how clearly she had come to love me till she saw us both together.

I grew to grudging the nine hours a day I had to spend downtown at work. The earliest minute I could leave the store I would rush home as if I were a boy going to meet his first sweetheart. And Mildred was always at the door waiting for me. It made up for the honeymoon we'd never had. I used to tell her that I wished Ruyter and I could change jobs, because he was never at his office for more than three hours a day, and I could have spent those extra six hours so blissfully at home.

Then one night I came back to the flat in a thundering bad temper. One of our traveling men, Dick Corson, had fallen sick and I had been told to take his place on the road for a week. I had just time to get dinner and pack my suit-case, and then to bolt for the eight-twenty train. How I grudged that week away from Mildred!

But if I was sore at having to leave her, she was a hundred times unhappier to have me go. The poor girl broke down and begged me to stay. I explained to her that if I made a hit on the week's work, it probably meant a raise. But she wouldn't be comforted. At last she pulled herself together and tried to smile, and she insisted on packing my suit-case for me. But I could see her hands shaking as though she had a chill.

Well, I got away at last. And she waved at me, out of the window, as I went down the street. I got to the station, still seeing things rather mistily. And the first man I ran into, near the ticket window, was Dick Corson, the fellow whose route I had been told to take.

He'd gotten to feeling better, and he had 'phoned the boss that he was able to go. So there he was, ticket bought, waiting to send me back home. I suppose he'd been afraid I'd make good on the road, and that his job might be rendered shaky by any success I might score. Job-fear is a wonderful curative for sick workers.

I was as glad to see Dick as if he'd been Old Man Good-Luck, himself. No, I didn't even stop to think, for a single second, of the chance for promotion I might be losing by giving up the trip. All I could think of was that I wouldn't have to be away from Mildred. I nearly shook poor old Dick's flabby hand off. Then I started home.

Halfway to the flat a bright idea came to me: I wanted to make this surprise as delightful for my wife as I could. If I showed up at home less than half an hour after I'd left, it wouldn't mean as much as if I waited another hour.

By that time she'd have begun to be really lonely, and to realize that I was gone, and to miss me. The flat would seem empty and silent and desolate to her. And then, all of a sudden, I'd walk in. And that would make up for everything. She'd have had just enough taste of loneliness to make her all the more glad at seeing me.

A fool idea? Maybe so. But most love-ideas are fool ideas, if you try the acid test of logic on them. That doesn't make them any less wonderful, does it?

Well, I loafed around for a solid hour. I spent part of the time buying her a big bunch of carnations and a box of candy, a couple of pounds of it—the kind she liked best. That hour was the slowest ever. But it crawled by, somehow or other; and at the end of it I went home.

I let myself into the flat as quietly as a second-story man, and I set the suit-case down by the hat-rack and shut the flat door after me without making a sound.

There was a light in the living-room at the end of the hallway. I took the carnations in one hand and the candy in the other, and I tiptoed down the hall. It was all I could do to keep from laughing out loud, to think of her face when she'd look up and see me standing in the doorway in front of her.

I was so taken up with walking on tiptoe and trying not to snicker, that I hadn't ears for anything except the chance of a creaking board under my feet. It wasn't till I was within two steps of the threshold that I heard any voices. Then I just stood there. I didn't mean to. I didn't mean to eavesdrop. I just did it because my body stopped, and my mind with it. Ruyter was saying:

"It isn't. It's Fate. It's Hegger's own lookout. He brought us together again. He is away all day long, and how can he blame you if I have tried to make the time pass less drearily for you? He goes away, now, for a week, and—it's Fate, I tell you, sweetheart. And Fate is too strong for two mortals to fight against."

Then her voice broke in, and she was sobbing.

"It *isn't* Fate!" she declared. "There isn't such a thing as Fate. Let's be honest enough not to blame our own wickedness on Destiny. I've tried so hard—so hard! And I'm too weak—too bad—too worthless—to win such a battle. I knew I was lost, as soon as you came here that first evening. I knew all the prayers and the strivings of the past two years had gone for nothing and that I had never stopped loving you—that I never *could* stop loving you—"

"Girl of my heart! I—"

"And," she went on, in that same choked, stifled voice, "even while I knew there wasn't any hope for me, I fought on. I tried to make up to him for what I knew he must lose. He is so good, so gentle, so patient, and he loves me so, Clive. He *loves* me so! He is just the type of man that heaven generally curses with a wife like me. I tried to make it up to him, to make him content. I tried to make you stop coming here in the mornings. And all the time I knew I couldn't have the courage to keep you away or the honesty to confess to him that you were dropping in here all the time. He—why, he thinks the sight of our happiness—his and mine—and your memory of our home—are keeping you from coming to see us. He told me so!"

Ruyter's laugh was as genuine as if he had heard a brand-new joke.

"The memory of *this* home?" he said. "Why, sweetheart, the thought of you, mured up in this stuffy hole of a tenement, turned me sick. It was like the Kohinoor in a mud-puddle. And as for your happiness—a blind man could have seen how heartsick you were. The poor, grinning idiot!"

"Stop!" she ordered. "You sha'n't speak so of him. And you sha'n't speak so of the home he thinks is so marvelous. Isn't it enough that you have stolen the one woman of all his life, without making fun of him?"

"I have not 'stolen' you," he made answer. "I have told you I love you. I have asked you to let me atone for my crazy folly of two years ago by making you happy, by taking you away from all this and giving you the life you crave."

"I don't crave it!" she flashed. "Or—or I didn't, till you came back. Oh, I'm not myself when I'm with you, Clive! You are so strong, so invincible! You sweep me off my feet. You make me think and speak as you dictate. I feel as if I were in a hypnotic trance when I'm with you. And—I was growing to love Miles—really to love him—and to be happy with him. Then—oh, you have changed all the world for me!"

"I *will* change all the world for you, my darling," he promised, his big voice vibrating like an organ-chord, "if you will let me."

"I can't!" she wailed. "Oh, I can't!"

"You must," he said, and there was a queer note of power in his words. "Dear, we aren't children. We must look the truth square in the face. I have humored you in everything. Perhaps you think it has been easy to keep from so much as kissing your lips! But the hour has come. Hegger is away. We have a whole week before us. The world lies ahead, beckoning to us—the World of golden sunshine and happiness—and *love!*"

"No, no! I—"

"Mildred, my own sweetheart, you are coming away from this hovel of a place—from this sordid, wretched life that cramps your youth and your glorious loveliness. You are coming away—with *me,* out into the future that is ours—the future that Love has given us."

"No! Miles will—"

"Miles will be as unhappy as his half-pint soul will permit—for a handful of days. Then he will become justly enraged, in true *bourgeois* fashion. And he will divorce you or let you divorce him. Then—then we can make up for all we have lost; and I can claim you openly for my wife—even as I claim you now in the sight of heaven."

"No, in the sight of hell!" she corrected him. "Can't we be honest in this sin you are urging me into? Must we take heaven's name in vain? Miles will he heartbroken, crushed! He—"

"Is such paltry unhappiness as a clod like Hegger can feel, to wreck the lives of us both? Mildred!"

There was an appeal in his magnetic voice that would have drawn the heart from an ice-maiden. The thrill of it must have reached into her innermost soul, and it dashed away the last fragments of resistance. He held out his arms.

"Kiss me," he said, very quietly, but with that same organ-chord vibrating in his throat.

Mildred took a faltering step toward him. Then she halted.

"Kiss me!" he said again.

And, like a woman in a dream, she moved forward.

It was at that moment a board creaked dismally under my inert weight. Mildred whirled about, almost in the shelter of Ruyter's arms, and saw me standing in the doorway—still with that foolish grin frozen on my sick face, still holding out those pitiful flowers and the box of sweets.

I DON'T know, at all, how long we all three stood there, just like that. It was Mildred who spoke first. She must have understood that I had been there long enough to hear.

"You can kill me if you want to," she whispered, staring blankly at me with those big, hopeless eyes of hers.

And then, at sight of her mortal terror, I found my own voice. And by a miracle, all the reason and the coolness I ever possessed rushed back into my dead brain.

"Why should I kill you?" I asked, speaking as if she were a child and as if I were a stranger. "Why should I kill you, dear? You have done *me* no harm. It is yourself, not me, you are damning. Just because you choose to shatter all your ideals by throwing away decency, is that any reason why I should throw away mine, too, by forgetting I am a man and killing you as a beast might kill a mate that proved faithless? You haven't anything to fear from me. Please don't be frightened. I hate to see you look like that. There's nothing for you to be afraid of."

She tried to speak, but she couldn't. She turned, instinctively, toward Ruyter, who hadn't stirred and who kept glaring dully at me. Then came my inspiration—the inspiration I gleaned from the look in his eyes, the inspiration I verily believe God sent me.

I went up to Ruyter, slowly, my face a mask, my gaze fixed on his. And as I came close to him, I reached out and took Mildred's hand. It was as cold as ice. Without shifting my eyes from Ruyter's, I said to her:

"No, you need never be afraid, wife of mine, so far as I am concerned. I could not harm you if I would. I would not if I could. With this man it is different."

Ruyter's mouth opened, but no word came. I noted that his lips were pallid. "With this man," I went on, in the same slow, even voice, "with this man it is different. Mildred, this hero of yours—this Paladin of story-book seducers—is *afraid*. He is sick with fear. He would not dare meet my eyes, if he were not still more afraid to look away from me. He is half a head taller than I and thirty pounds heavier, and he is an athlete, while I am not. Yet he is more afraid of me at this moment than a clean man could be of anything on earth. The pitiful coward!"

"You—you lie!" croaked Ruyter, but there was no conviction behind his denial.

"He is afraid of me," I went on, "because, to an animal of his species, I am that most terrifying creature extant—a husband. In *me* he sees the law, the punishment of the law, the ostracism of Society, the smear on his name that will last all his days. He sees more: he sees the one man in the world who can shoot him dead, at will, and whom no jury will punish for the deed. He is a wild beast for whom the 'open season' is any season *I* may dictate. I and I alone hold his worthless life in the hollow of my hand. I can kill him as I would kill a cat that has fits—and with no greater legal penalty. He knows it. And his courage has turned to water within him."

"I—" babbled Ruyter; but I continued without stopping to heed him.

"No burglar, no murderer, caught red handed," I said, "is one-tenth so horror-stricken as is the home-wrecker when the husband breaks in upon his work. This man fears not only the law I may evoke and the law I may take into my own hands, but he fears something still worse. He fears that, through me, Society may force him to regard as serious something he intended as a mere pastime. He is afraid he may be forced to marry you. He also fears I may mulct him for ruinously heavy money-indemnity. Why, if I chose to demand them at this very instant, he would cheerfully hand over to me his watch and rings and money—as a price for escape. And he would send me a four-figure check the first thing in the morning. Wouldn't you, Mr. Clive Ruyter? And did you think it was just by chance I happened to be at home this evening, when my wife told you I had left town?"

"W—what's this?" blustered Ruyter, his teeth a-chatter. "A frame-up between you two? A badger game?"

I heard Mildred gasp, and she flinched from him as in mortal pain.

"It is anything you choose to call it, my friend," I answered cheerily, "though it's hardly kind or courteous of you to make such a charge against a woman whom you were just offering to lead forth into the 'golden sunshine'— 'into the future that Love has given you.'"

"You knew he was here all the time?" Ruyter panted, accusingly, to Mildred. "You knew it and—"

"Your simple trust in the woman you love is really touching, Mr. Ruyter," I broke in, before she could answer. "But let her reply for herself. Mildred, tell him you are innocent of plotting against him—against *any* living man except your husband."

She did not speak. Ruyter darted his panic gaze toward her. Then drawn by the attraction of stark fear, his eyes returned to mine.

"Mildred," I said, "I want to show you one more odd phase of human nature. Look!"

I stepped forward and struck the man lightly across the face with my open palm. My hand came away sticky with the fright-sweat that smeared his forehead. He did not redden; he made no move to resent the blow. I doubt if he realized I had struck him.

"You see, dear," I explained to Mildred, "there is your hero, your invincible, all-compelling King among men; the demigod whose magnetic power has won you away from your poor, timid, commonplace husband. And now for the final and most painful scene: Mr. Ruyter, I am minded to hasten your departure with the toe of my boot. In another ten seconds the impulse will be much too strong for me to resist. Get out!"

Through the mist of fear, he evidently grasped the fact that he was free to go. And galvanized into sudden life, he bolted.

NO, the man was not a coward, at least not that I know of. But he was a Lover, and I was Husband. Some people might not see the point or understand his helpless fright. But many others would—only too clearly. For your own self-esteem's sake, old friend, I hope you belong to the former class.

When he was gone, I turned for the first time to Mildred. Her face was ghastly. Yet it was the ghastliness of convalescence. And with a great throb at my heart, I knew I had conquered.

It is a wondrous thing to find oneself a hero to one's wife, if but for a moment.

Somebody once told me that most men are heroes to their wives for only two months—the month before marriage and the month after death. But here was I, acclaimed a victor and a superman in the very midtide of wedded life!

Not that Mildred's ashen lips spoke words of adulation. But her wide eyes, upraised to mine, told me volumes. At last, she summoned courage to plead brokenly:

"Miles—oh, my dear, my *dear*—won't you take me back?"

And in the ecstasy of my joy, I gathered her closely, tenderly to me, and made reply:

"Take you *back,* my wife? Why, I have never let you go from me!"

HAVE I bored you, my former chum, with this long-winded letter? I have written it as I told you, because I promised to let you know of the "big things" in my life. And this is the biggest thing that has ever come into it.

Since that night, everything has smiled on me—Fortune, Love, Peace, Health—all have become mine in incredibly ample measure. The flat that Ruyter called a "stuffy hole" has given place to a roomy house of my own building. And I no longer have to restrict myself to cheap flowers and bonbons when I wish to give Mildred a homecoming present.

She has crowned my life, she and the three blessed boys who, as I write, are asleep in their cribs in the nursery up-stairs...

I had written thus far when two clear cool hands were laid across my tired eyes, and Mildred leaned over me to say: "Bedtime, busy boy!" And as her will is law, I must end this letter, here and now.

With all the good wishes of the happiest, luckiest man on earth,

MILES HEGGER.

The Unbaited Trap

JOAN and Hugh Vedder had been married eight years—ever since she was twenty and he was thirty. Happy the nation—tenfold happier the wedded couple—that has no history. And the Vedders had been very happy indeed.

There had been no struggle to make both ends meet. From the first, the Wolf and the Door had never been within a mile of each other. Vedder was a good business man, a good husband, a good comrade. Joan was more than satisfied with her quiet, home-loving mate, and with the quiet home he loved.

If there were no thrills in their lives, neither were there any heartaches. They loved each other; they suited each other. A placidly sweet engagement merged very naturally into a sweetly placid married life. Their friends were of their own sort—pleasant, ultra-respectable folk, fairly well-to-do, simple in tastes, clean. If they were not very inspiring, none of them knew it.

All this was in New York, mind you—in the actual New York, not the New York of fiction or of visitors' tales; the real New York, which holds more quiet, steady, home-loving people than any other city in America. New York is merely Pompton, New Jersey, or Grayling, Michigan, seen through a magnifying glass. Everything (except human nature and the average apartment) is on a gigantic scale; that is all. There is no greater number of social strata; there is nothing to differentiate the metropolis from any other village, except that it is infinitely larger.

And the Vedders had lived for eight years in New York as though New York were Springfield, Massachusetts.

THEN a man whom Vedder knew in business—Archer Dunne—became associated with Hugh in a real-estate deal. Their wives met. And the Vedders were asked to dine with the Dunnes.

That started it. Right around the corner from their own apartment, the Vedders walked in on a new world: a world of jolly liveliness that was only a shade too lively and too jolly, a world that sparkled and was professionally gay. To the home-staying Vedders, there was nothing tawdry in the sparkle, nothing forced or fevered in the gayety. It was all spontaneous and novel and delightful.

As the bread-and-butter child might revel in its first course-dinner, so did the Vedders revel in this glitter-world into which they had blundered. There was something thoroughly likable about Joan and Hugh, a unique something that attracted the clique of people they met through the Dunnes. The "something" was wholesomeness, though neither they nor their new friends realized it. It was a novelty to the Dunnes' set, a novelty that made its two possessors very welcome among the home-haters.

The Dunne set can be found in a village as well as in Gotham. In the village its membership scarce reaches into the dozens. It swells far into the thousands in New York, but only because New York is that many times larger. In the village it is made up of women who would rather board than do their own cooking and who dawdle away precious baking-day afternoons in gossiping and in playing progressive euchre or putting on their best clothes and walking down to see the five-fifteen train come in. Its men would rather make five dollars on a semi-doubtful horse swap than earn ten dollars at the factory. They dress better than their neighbors; and they have the rare gift of getting perpetual credit, on no security, at the grocer's.

In New York, the women of the Dunne set plead the servant-problem bugaboo as an excuse for living at hotels instead of keeping house. Their men, once wooed from the old-fashioned home idea, abet them in this. These same men are in New York merely because they can make more money with less work there than anywhere else, and because so-called good times are to be had in all sizes, varieties and locations.

Both the men and the women, being divorced from home ties, have plenty of time to get into mischief. They keep open the doors of the flashier dining places, the after-theater restaurants and certain types of theaters; and they keep the taxicab companies from bankruptcy. Time, to them, is like deer to a sportsman: something to be killed as quickly, as excitingly and as frequently as possible.

It is a dreary, dreary routine, this life of the home-haters, whether on Main Street, Yaphank, or on Broadway, Manhattan.

Yet, to the visiting Vedders, it was a grown-ups' fairyland. To them, restaurant dinners still had the charm of brilliant novelty. Cabaret brass was virgin gold. A theater evening was an exception, not a rule. Butterfly people were a marvel and a joy to these staid home-dwellers.

Once or twice, just at first, they both noticed and wondered at a certain queer freedom of speech, at jokes and discussions on themes their old friends had always avoided.

But they told themselves and each other that they must not be provincial or prudish, and that they had probably become too narrow-minded from long lack of friction with up-to-date people. And, in an amazingly short time, the feeling of embarrassment died a natural death.

Into this gay new world the two stay-at-homes launched themselves with all the blended zeal of explorers and proselytes. And daily they learned more and more of its astounding ways.

For example, Hugh found that a man who likes to spend all his evenings at home with his own wife is in danger of becoming a fossil. Worse still, he is in peril of ridicule from wiser folk. Mrs. Dunne herself told him this—this and a hundred other interesting things. She told him in such a pretty, tactful way, and so convincingly, that he began to look back on the old life as a new-hatched millionaire remembers his dinner-pail and his one shirt a week.

Women learn anything and everything far more quickly than do men. Their powers of adaptation are positively uncanny. While a lucky-strike miner is still trying to learn not to eat with his knife, his once-calicoed wife already can go through the complete litany of afternoon tea or dinner etiquette.

So it was with Joan. Before Hugh had fairly begun to realize his new surroundings, those surroundings fitted her like a made-to-order glove. She learned to laugh prettily, instead of showing blank dismay, when the women around her spoke openly of flirting with other women's husbands. She learned not to shudder—even inwardly—when folk talked of the liaisons of seemingly respectable men, as of everyday matters.

She scoffed daintily at old fogies of both sexes who were tied bovinely and complacently to marital apron-strings. She looked back with amused self-contempt to the prehistoric days when she had deemed it "fast" for a woman to smoke a cigarette or drink a cocktail, and when the sight of even a mildly drunken man had filled her with sick horror.

True, she could never learn to smoke without choking, and cocktails always tasted like hair-oil and made her sick. And she could not bring herself to adopt, personally, the loose-moraled conditions that had once shocked and now amused her. But she was no spoil-sport. And the Dunne set adopted her without question.

JOAN was mentally adapting herself to her new sphere to an extent she had not counted on. For example, she unconsciously found herself beginning to compare Hugh with the men around him, and her own uneventful wedded life with their wives'. And at last she saw she had been deprived of something.

Hugh was a dear, faithful old chap. But he was not inspiring. She recognized that, now. And her love-life, by contrast to some of her present friends', had been a stagnant mill-pond compared to a cataract. Yes, she had missed much.

Fate had robbed her of the one "grand passion" that is every woman's right, had shackled her to conventionality, when the right man might have swept her off her feet and set her thrilling. She had never thrilled. She yearned to.

And bit by bit, merciless self-analysis told her she had never loved Hugh, did not love Hugh, never could love Hugh—in the mad, reckless "world-well-lost-for-love" fashion that she felt her nature could rise to under the proper incentive—or improper incentive, as the case might be.

No, her affection for poor old Hugh was more maternal than marital. She felt a tender devotion for him, a desire to make his road smooth, a keen motherly interest in his success, a worried solicitude for his welfare. That was all. He could not appreciate her. He never had appreciated her. Wild, all-encompassing sex-love had passed her by. And she rebelled. It was not fair that she should go through life cheated out of the one Great Love.

Joan Vedder was quite certain that she arrived at all these sorry conclusions without one atom of outside help. If she had been told that they were the direct result of a score or more of fragmentary talks with Archer Dunne, she would have denied it vehemently and honestly.

True, she liked Dunne, admired him and enjoyed hearing him talk. He knew so much of life, of love. He had such rare insight into feminine nature. He understood her as no man had ever understood her. His tired dark eyes seemed to look down into the very soul of her, to read all her heart-emptiness, her capabilities for sublime love, the strangely elusive charm that made her so different from all other women. He said so himself. And she knew it was true.

IT was coming home from Shanley's that Dunne told Joan about the "elusive charm" and her unlikeness to other women. Ten of them had gone to the theater and to supper. That left two over, after two taxies were filled for the homeward ride. And she and Dunne chanced to be the two. Hence the tête-à-tête in a third taxicab.

"I never understood why men could rave about the subtle mystery and the miracle of women," he was saying, "until I met you. Till then, all women had seemed to me pretty much alike, and not at all mysterious. And then I met *you*—my Lady of Mystery. Tell me what it is that makes you so different—so unforgettable."

"Why," she laughed, embarrassed, "I'm a very ordinary mortal, I'm afraid."

"The man who lets you think so deserved a 'very ordinary mortal' for a wife," said Dunne, savagely. "And he is about the only man of my acquaintance who hasn't got one."

Vaguely, she felt she ought to rebuke him for the implied slur on Hugh. But the impulse was not strong enough to rise all the way to her lips. Besides, she found it inexplicably sweet to listen to such unwonted praise of herself.

How this man understood her! How he read her! It was—it was almost supernatural. How different from Hugh's boorish compliments, which usually took the form of a bear-pat on the shoulder and some such coarse words as "Old girl, you're all to the good!"

"I'll be a better man—I'll be a happier man—always and always," Dunne was murmuring, "for having known the One Woman. You don't know what it means to me, Lady of Mystery."

His hand closed softly over hers. There was nothing of flirtation in the gesture. So tender, so reverent it was, that Joan had not the heart to draw her hand away.

"I am glad," she said, shyly. "I'm glad if I've—helped."

"Helped?" he echoed. "Why, you've made 'a new heaven and a new earth' for me. Oh, if I could tell you all it had meant—all it will mean—forever, till I am dust! Will you let me tell you, darling?"

His free hand was stealing about her waist. And even Joan could read nothing of reverence in this new gesture.

"Don't, please," she said, moving forward. "You mustn't."

"Forgive me!" he cried, all contrition. "But if only you knew! You *must* know, Joan!"

And, all at once, Joan knew. This man loved her. And something told her it was the Great Love—the wild, adoring, suicidal love that her life had missed. The thought thrilled her to the soul. It surged through her, setting her warm blood atingle, her brain awhirl.

"I—I mustn't listen to you," she said feebly.

"You must!" he urged with really beautiful abandon, his body trembling from head to foot. "You *must,* my sweetheart. Heaven has brought you to me, from all the world. I can't lose you! I *won't* lose you."

The taxi lurched around a corner. Joan forced herself to turn from the man's imploringly hypnotic eyes and to look out of the window. By the delicatessen store with the gilded boar's head on a blue platter in the window, she saw the cab was turning into her own street. In another two minutes she would be at home. Dunne also saw where they were.

"Listen, dear heart," he said adoringly, "I must leave you in a minute or so. When can I see you again—*alone?* I must see you, to-morrow. Say I may."

She hesitated, her mind still in a delicious turmoil.

"Do you know the Prince Crœsus Hotel?" he went on. "The tea-room is so cozy and dim-lit and secluded. Will you meet me there—say, at five—tomorrow afternoon? Tell me you will! I *must* see you."

"Y-es," she heard herself answer faintly, through no volition of her own.

"Thank you ten million times!" he exclaimed, fervently.

As she timidly eluded his effort to kiss her, he added more prosaically:

"I'm certain I can make it by five. I've a big directors' meeting at three. But it ought to be over in time for me to get to the Prince Crœsus before five o'clock. If I'm detained, I'll telephone you. But I'll move heaven and earth to get there."

"You—you *can't* telephone me," she faltered. "How can you? If I go there to meet you, it wouldn't do to have a page shouting my name all over the room. Don't you see it wouldn't?"

"H'm!" he meditated. "That's so! But—"

"I have it," she broke in. "If you find you must telephone, ask for 'Mrs. Senoj.'"

"'Senoj?'" he repeated, puzzled. "How did you ever happen to think of such a queer name as that? Is it a real name, or did you make it up? How do you spell it?"

"*S-e-n-o-j,*" she answered. "It's *Jones* backward. I—"

The taxi halted with a jerk, in front of the Vedder apartment. Hugh was on the steps, waiting for them. So was Mrs. Dunne. A departing taxicab had just disgorged them. There were voluble farewells. Hugh and his wife went indoors, together, both phenomenally silent, for once in their lives.

THE Prince Crœsus Hotel is a half-block off Broadway. It runs through from one numbered street to another. It is one hotel in a hundred. And the other ninety-nine are precisely like it—except for the tea-room.

The Prince Crœsus tea-room is an institution. It is known to lovers from

Greenwich village to the Bronx. Also it is wholly respectable.

A huge room, it is, fully one hundred and fifty by ninety feet in area—a room of magnificent distances. The distances are rendered greater by the subdued light that bathes the place in a soft, warm dimness through which the solitary little pink light on every table shines like a misted star. Coming in from the bright foyer, one's first impression is of a twilight blur, spotted here and there by tiny table lamps that glow but do not illumine.

The walls and ceilings are in somber colors, arabesqued and frescoed and latticed in neutral tints that absorb light without reflecting it. There is no regular arrangement of tables. Practically all of them hug closely the four walls or snuggle in half-niches. At the tables are low fauteuils and lower chairs—wicker and upholstered in gray. The room's center is given up to the big pillars, to a table or two sheltered by them, and to a writing desk and a lounge.

It is an odd place, this tea-room of the Prince Crœsus, a place devoted to low lights, to lower voices, to tender silences. It is as far removed from New York's life and racket and rush as any hidden valley in the Lotos Land.

Into the tea-room, at five the next afternoon, came Joan Vedder. She paused for an instant in the curtain-hung doorway to accustom her eyes to the soft gloom. At first she could distinguish nothing. Then, gradually, her eyes began to take in vague details. Two white-capped maids and a waiter or so were moving about silently. But no one came forward to usher her to a table.

As she stood there, hoping that Dunne would appear out of the dim-lit spaces to guide her to her place, a man and woman just beside her rose to their feet and (after various athletic feats with a tight overcoat and with a wrap which insisted on holding itself up-side down) departed, whispering. Joan sat down at the table they had vacated.

By this time her eyes had focused themselves to the half-light. She could see, for instance, that every other table within her range of vision was occupied. And at all the tables but one, were a man and a woman, alone together. Sometimes the couple sat in the big, low wicker chairs; oftener on one of the very narrow fauteuils, side by side. And at least three such pairs were semi-openly "holding hands."

The one table, forming the exception to this rule, was the gathering point of three old ladies, a young woman, a six-year-old child and a thoroughly uncomfortable looking man with lonely whiskers. The group were as out of place as a wheelbarrow in a temple of Venus. And they evidently knew it.

At the other tables some of the couples were drinking highballs or cocktails. A very few were sipping tea and nibbling at English muffins. One fat and bald-headed old man with a bilious visage had just ordered for his opulent-figured companion a bottle of champagne. The beverage was long in arriving, and the wine-opener was fretfully rapping on the table with his thick finger-tips and inquiring of the head waiter:

"Can't I get a little service here?"

Joan presently lost interest in what was going on around her. She sat where she could see the doorway, and toward the doorway she looked, far more in fear than in hope, waiting to see Archer Dunne's trim figure appear there, waiting to hear his tenderly contrite apologies for being late.

(It chanced that Archer Dunne, at that moment, was neither contrite nor tender. He was fuming in blasphemous impotence, as a subway rush-hour "block" held him in a stuffily smelly subway train, stalled midway between Twenty-third and Twenty-eighth streets.)

The day had not been wholly pleasant for Joan. On the preceding night, the excitement of what she had gone through and the dazzling revelation of Dunne's love for her had kept her buoyed and strangely exultant. She had felt like a heroine in a popular novel.

The sound of Hugh's tranquil snores in the next room had sickened her at thought of his material grossness. She wished he would sleep more quietly and leave her in peace to her new golden dreams.

But the morning had dawned rainy and raw, as the next morning has a cynical way of doing. And reaction had set in. First of all, oddly enough, she had regretted repeating the idiotic name "Senoj" to Archer Dunne. Not because it was idiotic, but because, to her, it had once been half sacred—although she had not thought of it for many months, until it had popped unbidden into her mind when the question of a telephonic name came up.

When she and Hugh had been engaged—oh, a century or more ago, when she was in her late teens—she used to telephone to him every day at his office. And as the engagement was not yet announced, she did not want to telephone so often under her own name for fear the office people might talk (which they did).

Thus, after one of the long conspiracy-conferences so dear to true lovers, she and Hugh had evolved "Jones" as a pseudonym to throw the others off the track. She would henceforth announce herself to the office telephone-girl as "Miss Jones." Then it had occurred to Hugh that "Jones" was such a terribly plain name that the operator might suspect it was not genuine. Whereat, in real inspiration, Joan had suggested that they pronounce it backward. And, for months thereafter, the demure telephone-girl had called daily to Hugh:

"Mr. Vedder, Miss—er—Senoj is on the wire."

And *that* was the name she had been so disloyal as to give to Archer Dunne to use!

Joan felt as if she had shown one of Hugh's love-letters to a stranger. She did not see how she could have been so base as to take the holy name of Senoj in vain. Well, it was done! and anyhow, the chances were fifty to one that Archer would be at the tea-room ahead of her. So she felt at liberty to pass on to the next worry.

Underneath the jolly veneer of the past few months, her older principles began to stir. It was one thing to realize that she did not love her husband except in a maternal way, and that she had an inalienable right to at least one Great Love in her life. It was quite another thing to listen, unrebuking, to the love-vows of another woman's husband, to arrange to meet him clandestinely. And her lately deadened Puritan conscience throbbed uncomfortably.

She had forced back the moss-covered old scruples that threatened to engulf her new ideas of freedom. She had forced them back, after an all-day battle. And now she was here—here in this dim-lit Lovers' Lane of a tea-room, waiting to hear Archer Dunne tell her again that he loved her; that she was the One Woman; that she was a Wonder Girl; that she was his adored Lady of Mystery.

And now, after all, he was not here to tell her these glorious things. The anti-climax of the situation jarred upon Joan's taut nerves.

A man parted the curtains and came uncertainly into the room, silhouetted for a

moment against the glare of light from the foyer. At sight of his blackly outlined figure, Joan was certain he was Dunne. To her amaze, she was aware of a little pang of sick terror, something perilously akin to disgust—not at all the joyous thrill she expected.

Then the man moved forward, and she saw he was not Dunne at all, but one of the ten thousand other New Yorkers cast in the same general mold and clad after the same sartorial pattern. And she felt a sudden glad relief, a relief that bewildered her.

The man glanced about him. A stunningly pretty woman, far down the room, raised a white-gloved arm in signal, and he hastened eagerly toward her.

Joan did not note his progress. She was too much absorbed in wondering at her own unexpected change of mind. From her unbidden emotions at first glimpse of the newcomer, she realized with a shock that she did not at all want to meet Archer Dunne, that she was not in the very least in love with him, that she did not even want to hear him say again that he loved her or call her his Lady of Mystery.

She could not think why she had come here at all. She had not wanted to come. She knew that, now. It was abominable that Dunne should have dared to suggest such a thing, that he should have insulted her by telling of his love.

A wave of righteous indignation against the man and against herself swept over Joan. What had she done, what had she said,—she, a happy wife,—to make *any* man think he had a right to regard her as the type of woman to whom he could make love, whom he could meet, like this, in secret?

With charming dearth of logic, Joan raged against the man she had come to meet. Unsparingly she told herself how vile she was, how ungrateful and disloyal to the dearest husband in all the world.

BY comparison with Dunne, Hugh stood out as a Galahad. This clean-minded, honorable husband of hers at whom she had lately scoffed was worth fifty Archer Dunnes—she realized that now, even if Hugh did snore sometimes. She *liked* to hear him snore. It was normal. It was wholesome. And that was more than anyone could say of a man who tried to steal other men's wives and who tried to disgust those wives with their own husbands—while accepting the husbands' friendship and hospitality.

Inch by inch (her eyes ever furtively upon the curtained doorway), Joan Vedder forced herself to go over the last few months' happenings. And with a belated clearness of view she saw the line of blunders that had led her to the brink where now she stood. So, they say, a criminal, after conviction, looks back with clarified vision at the path he trod so blindly.

With a gush of love and repentance, Joan's heart went out to Hugh Vedder.

On quick impulse she gathered up her wraps and got to her feet. She was going home. And what was more, she was going to tell her husband the whole nasty, horrible story and ask him if he would forgive her. She knew he would. And she wanted to get out before Archer Dunne could arrive. It would avert an unpleasant scene.

HALFWAY to the door, Joan saw the curtains part. A woman came in. At the first brief glimpse of her, Joan shrank back and crouched against the wall, flattening her slender body as much as she could, to avoid notice. For she recognized the newcomer.

It was Archer Dunne's wife.

Mrs. Dunne was alone. Her eyes still unused to the dimness, she passed close by Joan without seeing her and went on toward the lower end of the long room.

Here were tragedy and complication and French farce, all rolled into one! Suppose Archer Dunne had arrived five minutes sooner? Joan turned sick at the thought. This woman would have caught her and Dunne together—and *here*, of all places on earth!

Dizzy at thought of her own miraculous escape, Joan tottered out through the doorway and into the foyer. There were several men and women loitering about.

Down the foyer, and moving toward the tea-room, a bell-boy was shuffling.

As the bell-boy advanced, he intoned nasally, at ten-second intervals:

"Mrs. Senoj, please!—*Mrs. Senoj, please!*—Mrs. Senoj, please!"

Joan was minded to flee past him. Then natural pluck came to her aid. Soon or late, she must tell Archer Dunne that she wanted nothing more to do with him. It would be easier to say it over the telephone than face to face—and far safer than by letter. She halted the chanting bell-boy.

That worthy hireling checked his eternal drone of "Mrs. Senoj, please!" and graciously told her to what telephone booth to go.

Once inside the booth, Joan once more took hold of her slipping courage and picked up the receiver. But her quavered "Hello" sounded hoarse and unnatural, even to herself. Nervousness had turned her throat and mouth into desert dryness.

"Hello," came the man's answer, in somewhat faltering tones—tones, however, which gradually gained in strength and steadiness as, without waiting for further word from the suddenly trembling Joan, he went on speaking:

"You will probably think I am a cur or a milksop," he began. "And perhaps I am. But I can't meet you there, to-day, or any other day. I thought I could. I thought I wanted to. But I can't. And I find I don't want to. Please don't think I'm trying to be rude. I'm not. But it's got to be said, once and for all."

Joan gasped. Then she listened open-mouthed, breathless, as he continued:

"I've been thinking it over, all day, all last night. I haven't been able to think of anything else. And the more I've thought, the more clearly I've seen I can't do it. You are laughing at me for a fool. I don't blame you. But my ways aren't your ways. And now I see they never can be. I—I love my own wife. I love her with all my heart and soul. I love her so much that I can't enjoy even a harmless little flirtation with any other woman. I love her so much that I can't dishonor her by meeting any other woman and taking tea with her alone, at such a place as the Prince Crœsus. I can't. I'm sorry. I tried to. I tried to make myself think it was all right, that even such an innocent affair with you would be a delightful adventure. But it's no use.

"I know what you are thinking of me. I know how a woman of the world regards such things and how you will look down on me for a milk-and-water Puritan. But I can't help it. There are still such things as right and wrong, even here in New York. To you, such a thing would be all right. To me, it would be wrong—hideously wrong. I would despise myself, forever, and I wouldn't dare look my sweet-souled wife in the face again. I suppose you won't want to see me any more. I think it would he wiser and happier for all of us, in the circumstances, to let the whole pleasant acquaintanceship drop, here and now. I'll arrange it with my wife without giving any reason. I can do it. And you can say whatever you think best to Mr. Dunne. Good-by."

Joan listened in dumbly horrified fascination—even to the faint click as her husband, at the wire's far end, hung up the receiver.

Lucrezia Borgia: The Much-Married Siren

IN the matter of marriages, she ran Henry VIII a close second. She married early and often. But not early enough or often enough to avert dozens of extra-marital affairs—or to debar her from scores of unions that never came through the customhouse.

For centuries she was branded as one of history's archfiends and most adroit poisoners. Of late years, certain apologists have tried to whitewash her character—with about the success that might attend the same operation on a coal mine. This whitewashing process, by the way, has been tried lately on Nero, on Richard III, and on Henry VIII But I have not heard that any of them have been canonized as a result of this treatment.

So, if you don't mind, I'll stick to the story of Lucrezia Borgia in the form that seems to me likeliest to be true; the form followed by historians who lived nearest to her own gaudy time.

There is about as much chance of pumping up sympathy for Lucrezia as for a Gila monster; so I shall not put on the *vox-humana* stop, but give as fair a picture as I can of the woman's hideous career. Many of its details cannot be written or even hinted at. Accept in advance my apologies for these omissions. If you are a prurient Seeker after the Truth, you will find the unexpurgated facts set down in full in Dumas' "Celebrated Crimes." But only in the original French. The English version has, wisely, been denatured.

SHE was gloriously lovely—with Titian coloring; with a vivid mind and body; with a serpentine charm that dragged her lovers into perils that a blind drunkard might easily have recognized and avoided; and with only the debit side of her moral ledger written up.

Her father was Cardinal Rodrigo Borgia; her mother was a noted and notorious Italian beauty—Rosa Vanozza. This unwed couple had several children, chief of whom were Lucrezia and Cesare. Rodrigo had but two life aims—money and the papal throne. He used Lucrezia's beauty as stepping-stones to both.

When the girl was only eleven, he married her to a young Spanish grandee, Don Cherubin de Centelles. It was a mere marriage of name, little more than a formal betrothal. Presently Rodrigo had reason to think that he could make a better match for his child. So the Centelles union was declared off, and Rodrigo looked for a still more powerful family wherewith to ally himself. He decided on another Spanish noble—Don Gasparo de Procida.

The twice-married girl of twelve might have been expected to remain the wife of Procida for at least a year or two; but she was not merely a girl—she was also a checker piece in a huge game. And almost at once Rodrigo saw a chance to advance her one square nearer to the king row.

So the Procida marriage was annulled, and Lucrezia was duly wedded to Giovanni Sforza, scion of one of the strongest houses in all Italy.

This was in 1492. A lot of things happened that year.

For one, an expatriate Italian tried to reach the East by sailing west. He had but one idea, and that a wrong one. Sailing as far westward as he could, in his quest of India, he bumped into land—and died still believing that the land was India and its natives Indians; as possibly you may have heard. I believe the story has been printed somewhere.

That same year—which just now concerns us more—Rodrigo Borgia was elected pope. He had been a cardinal for that purpose alone; and when the election was held, his money-annexing methods had made him quite ready for it. He bought the holy office by means of unbelievably large bribes.

To one wavering member of the College of Cardinals he sent six mule loads of silver; to another, a treasure chest; and so on, every man according to his price; and he carried the election by a big majority; thereupon taking office as Pope Alexander VI., with the usual *"Homo Est"* ceremonials—entirely needless in his case—and all the rest of it.

Thereupon, the horrible Borgia dynasty began to flourish in real earnest.

Let me pause here a moment—won't you?—to say that what I must write of Alexander VI. and his times carries absolutely no reflection upon the holy church he misrepresented, or upon the still holier name of religion. The church had for the moment fallen into the hands of men who should have been in jail instead of in the Vatican. Presently it emerged from their clutches, as pure, as exalted, as ever.

A Jew journeyed to Rome during Alexander's pontificate, to study the vile social conditions there. He came back converted to Christianity, explaining to his friends:

"If that religion were not divine, it would have been wrecked long ago by the Borgias."

Rodrigo—or Alexander VI; let's keep on calling him Rodrigo—reigned supreme, and his lieutenants were his two sons. He made the eldest a duke—the Duke of Gandia; he made Cesare—still in his teens—a cardinal. He also quarreled with the

Sforzas, and decided to find a new and even more exalted husband for Lucrezia.

But this time his checker-game methods did not work out as smoothly as before. Young Giovanni Sforza had fallen crazily in love with his beautiful girl wife, and had no intention whatever of giving her up. Nor, on the other hand, did he care to be stabbed or poisoned, as people had a way of being when they interfered with the Borgia plans.

So, taking Lucrezia along, he fled by night from Rome, and he did not pause in his flight until he was far beyond the reach of Rodrigo's long arm. He settled among devoted friends, where a dose of poison or a dagger thrust stood a slim chance of reaching him.

There he was happy and safe. The fact that Lucrezia enslaved the hearts of his friends did not trouble Giovanni. He looked on their adoration as tribute to his own good luck, and he could trust his wife; or, if he could not, he did not know it. Which, for the time, perhaps amounts to the same thing.

But Lucrezia grew tired of exile. Here she was nothing but Giovanni Sforza's pretty wife; at Rome she had been a princess, the daughter of the pope himself, the beloved of the world's greatest nobles. She secretly began to correspond with her saintly father, and between them they cooked up a very pretty scheme.

Early in December, Rodrigo wrote to Giovanni, saying in effect:

"Let bygones be bygones. I repent my injustice to you, and I beg for a chance to atone for it. I am an old man. I want all my children around me at Christmas time. Bring my daughter to me for that blessed season."

Giovanni was inclined to doubt the good faith of the humble plea; but Lucrezia told him that she knew her dear father much better than any one else could, and that the pope's repentance was sincere. She implored her husband to accept the overtures of peace and to come back with her to Rome for Christmas. She wept, she entreated, she fell ill and said that only the air of Rome could cure her. What could Giovanni do, being young and foolishly in love?

Back to Rome they went, Lucrezia and her spouse. The pope received them with tearful delight. So did the Duke of Gandia. So did Cesare. In all the annals of domestic life, this was one of the few family reunions that had nothing in common with a cat fight.

There was a splendid reconciliation feast at the Vatican. The pope sat in state upon his throne. Lucrezia cuddled on a cushion at her father's feet. Her husband and her two brothers caroused with the other guests of both sexes. It was a red-light scene. Says Tomassi:

"By the appearance of the assembly, and the general conversation and manners, one might rather have imagined himself present at the splendid and voluptuous audience of a king of Assyria than at the severe consistory of a Roman pontiff."

After the reunion, Rodrigo kept Lucrezia a willing prisoner at the Vatican. He drove Giovanni away by force of arms and under fear of death. Then, by power of his pontifical office, he proceeded to annul the marriage.

So much for Giovanni Sforza. He "got off light." I wonder if he appreciated his own rare good luck. As for Lucrezia's share in the matter, why, compared with some of her other exploits, her connivance in Sforza's dismissal was almost noble.

I am going to touch somewhat lightly on these same "other exploits." I would much rather skip them altogether, but that would de-Hamletize Hamlet.

Restored to her loving family, after Sforza had been disposed of, Lucrezia spent the interval between this marriage and her next in a whirl of mad debauchery, which is described, with startling detail, in "Celebrated Crimes," and which I shall not describe at all. Her brothers, her father, her mother, and a choice assortment of Italian nobles, were her fellow revelers. Here is a pen picture of her, drawn by Dumas in his account of this stage of her career:

"She was immoral from environment and inclination; impious from natural impulse; ambitious from calculation. She panted after pleasure, flattery, honors, rank, gold, jewels, rich dresses, and courtly palaces. A Spaniard under her light hair, a courtezan under her open, guileless manner, she had the features of one of Raphael's Madonnas and the heart of Messalina. She was thus doubly dear to her father, who saw in her the reflection of his own passions and vices."

She joined not only in the debaucheries, but in the political intrigues, of the papal court; and many historians openly declare—as did many people of her own day—that she not only helped her father and brothers in putting away several political foes, but that she made use of "the Borgia sugar" to gratify personal hates. "The Borgia sugar," by the way, was a sweet white powder, supposed by modern scientists to have been arsenic.

A single case of Lucrezia's murderous proclivities is all we need to cite here:

Two of her reputed lovers were Prospero and Giacomo Gaetasi, brothers, and bitter rivals for her fickle favor. She cared for neither of them, but she clearly loved the city and province of Sermoneta, which they owned. Giacomo died very suddenly of arsenic poisoning. Prospero—on his way to visit Lucrezia, in reply to an urgent message from her—was overpowered by ruffians and strangled.

The Sermoneta province became at once the property of the church, and, by Rodrigo's command, the Apostolic Chamber sold it to Lucrezia for eighty thousand crowns. Lucrezia paid the money to the last copper coin, and next day it was secretly paid back to her by order of the pope. Family finance flourished under the Borgias as never has "frenzied finance."

Soon Rodrigo decided it was time for another move in the matrimonial checker game. He was eager to cement by family ties his new alliance with the King of Naples. So he arranged a marriage between Lucrezia and the Neapolitan monarch's natural son, Alfonso of Aragon, Duke of Bisceglie.

This time there was trouble from the very start. Alfonso knew of Lucrezia's reputation as a poisoner; also her history in the left-handed courts of love. He flatly refused to marry such a woman, ungallantly declaring that he would sooner take a cobra to his arms. His family were as fiercely opposed to the match as was he, and for a while deadlock reigned.

The King of Naples was able to put enough pressure on the youth's relatives to win their shuddering consent, but Alfonso himself stuck to his refusal. Then Lucrezia took a hand in the game.

She arranged a meeting with the reluctant swain, and proceeded to tear the heart out of him by her glorious beauty and by the serpent charm that no man could withstand. In less than a week Alfonso was her helpless worshiper, clamoring for the marriage as vehemently as he had once opposed it.

When a grown man weeps childishly for a chance to ruin his life, there is seldom any one to spank him and stand him in a corner. Fate has a prompt way of pacemaking such idiots in their race to hell, and Alfonso of Aragon was not an exception to the rule.

He and Lucrezia were married in 1498. Thus she celebrated her fourth wedding while she was still a few months under eighteen; and for a time the luckless bridegroom dwelt in a fool's paradise.

Then Rodrigo allied himself with the King of France, Naples' enemy, and broke with the King of Naples. Alfonso was no longer necessary to his plans. Indeed, the young man was a drawback, besides standing in the way of a more advantageous match for Lucrezia. Wherefore, Rodrigo began to talk significantly of poison and of hired ruffians.

If horses always ran true to form, grass would soon grow on every race track in the world. If stocks ran true to form, the Stock Exchange would be used for storing furniture instead of storing life tragedies. If women ran true to form, one love story would read just like another—only stupider. One of the joys—and griefs—of an otherwise monotonous world is that horses and stocks and women almost never run true to form; and, for once, even Lucrezia Borgia failed to.

Hitherto, she had always assumed a filial "just-as-you-say-daddy-dear" attitude when Rodrigo had suggested that she would look better with a newer husband; but when, now, he mentioned the plan, she balked.

And all because—wonder of wonders—she had fallen head over heels in love with this fourth bridegroom of hers. Perhaps she loved him because he had been so hard to win; perhaps because she liked the way his hair grew at the back of his neck. Who knows?

But love him she assuredly did, and she would not give him up. She was far too wise to say all this to her father, or to Cesare. Instead, she told Alfonso of his danger, and husband and wife eloped together from Rome. According to one account, he went alone and she joined him later.

Away, into exile for the second time, and with the second imperiled husband, fled Lucrezia. Her brother Cesare, who hated Alfonso for personal reasons, as well as for causes of statecraft, is said to have fallen in a fit, from sheer blind rage, when he learned of the escape.

Speaking of Cesare, Rodrigo still kept him a mere cardinal, while his elder brother was a duke. Cesare wanted to be a duke, also. His father thought one duke in the family was quite enough. He said so. Cesare agreed with him, and decided to be the family's one duke himself.

He took counsel with his favorite assassin, one Michelotto. As a result, the Duke of Gandia was ambushed on the way from a banquet to his sweetheart's home, one moonlight night, and was hacked to death. Then his body was flung into the Tiber.

His father mourned him dutifully, but readily forgave the murderer—who was ever the best loved of his children—and wound up by giving Cesare the coveted dukedom.

This incident is just a side light on the old "honor-among-thieves" maxim; and so back to Lucrezia.

Rodrigo's wiles deceived even the daughter who knew him so well. He actually led her to believe—at long range—that she might be able to induce him to let Alfonso remain her husband.

Back to Rome she hurried, leaving Alfonso, and promising to send for him at once if she could persuade Rodrigo to give up his scheme to marry her to some one else. If she should fail, she would return at once to their place of happy exile.

She exerted all her powers of persuasion on Rodrigo, and she found him surprisingly easy to convince. Then, together, they sought to allay Cesare's hatred of Alfonso. This, too, proved easier than Lucrezia had dared to expect.

She wrote to Alfonso that all was forgiven, and that he could return home. Home he came. There were revels to celebrate his return. There was a bull-fight, among other pastimes. Alfonso and Cesare had a bull-killing contest. Then in the arena they publicly embraced, while Lucrezia wept for joy at the spectacular patching up of their ancient feud.

For a clever woman, she seems to have been remarkably easy to hoodwink; or else her memory was too faulty for her to compare this scene with the family reunion at which Giovanni Sforza had been the guest of honor. It is suggested that her sublime faith in her own powers of coaxing made her think that the present reconciliation was the real thing. If so, she was not fated to be left long in ignorance.

Alfonso was bidden to a medieval stag party at the Vatican. Lucrezia, in their palace by the Tiber, with her newborn son, awaited his home-coming; and home he came—with a half dozen dagger wounds in his body.

He had been attacked at the doorway of his own home by a gang of Cesare's bravos, and had been left there for dead. Love had given him strength to crawl to the threshold of his wife's bedroom door. At sight of him the arch-murderess swooned.

Alfonso grievously disappointed Rodrigo and Cesare by refusing to die of his wounds. Under Lucrezia's skillful care, he even began to get well. In a month he was able to leave his bed. Lucrezia, meantime, would not speak to or see her father and brother.

On the morning of August 18, 1500, just after Alfonso had been reported out of danger, Cesare called on him. Lucrezia drove her brother from the house.

Presently he returned, with his pet assassin, Michelotto, at his heels. They forced their way into the sick room, overpowered the feeble Alfonso, and strangled him to death.

Cesare, at Lucrezia's frenzied demand, was brought to trial. He admitted the murder, but said that he had killed Alfonso in self-defense; and this truly remarkable plea served to acquit him. Lucrezia was helpless.

She might reasonably have been expected to wreak vengeance on Alfonso's murderers. Instead—perhaps realizing the hopelessness of warring against such men as Cesare and Rodrigo—she merely went for a while into seclusion, and then submissively took up her old life at the Vatican.

"It would be wrong to blame this unfortunate woman," says Gregorovius, "because at the fateful moment of her life she did not rise to avenge the husband she loved, and make herself the subject of a tragedy. Of a truth, she appears weak and characterless. She was always subject to the will of others. This woman, regarded by posterity as a Medea or passionately loathsome creature, probably never experienced any real feeling. Perhaps she did assail her brother with hysterical recrimination and weak tears."

At the Vatican, she rose to high power, presiding over all secular consistories, consulted on matters of state—which she did not at all understand—and ever the petted and spoiled-child companion of the pope and Cesare.

Presently, when her grief for Alfonso was somewhat dulled, her father set to work arranging a fifth marriage for her. It is not on record that she objected, but the man who was picked out as her new consort made up for that by objections of the loudest and most uncomplimentary sort.

He was also an Alfonso—Alfonso of Este—son and heir of the aged Duke of Ferrara. The old duke declined to let his son marry such a woman. The son declined still more forcibly; and they proceeded to make public the reasons for their refusal.

They stated—among other reasons against the marriage—that Lucrezia was the illegitimate daughter of a priest—which was perfectly true; that her personal character had little in common with the Madonna; that she was shameless, a murderess, and worse; that she was party to the vilest crimes proven against the Borgia family.

If you want a list of the faults wherewith they charged her, I refer you to Maturizzo, Attilius Alexis, Marius, Petrus Mustyr, Machiavelli, and Guicciardini— none of whose works you have read, or ever will read, and only one of whom is familiar to you even by name. Most of the facts concerning Lucrezia's sin life are gleaned from these sources.

By using his boundless influence, and by squandering his cherished wealth in the right directions, Rodrigo at last smashed the old duke's opposition, and

Lucrezia, as in the case of the other Alfonso, managed to exert her fascinations on the young man, to the extent of making him forget prudence and sanity and consent to marry her.

I think Lucrezia's conquest of the two prejudiced Alfonsos speaks more eloquently of the power of her super-woman charm than could a thousand pages of eulogy.

Alfonso of Ferrara took his wife from home to the Duchy of Ferrara to live; and, as the Borgias could secure no loftier husband for her, they graciously permitted this fifth consort of hers to remain alive.

The wedding took place at the Vatican, on December 30, 1501, soon after the bride's twenty-first birthday. Thus she had averaged one husband every four and one-fifth years of her brief life. Alfonso of Ferrara was her last.

The marriage procession and pageants surpassed in splendor anything in medieval history. A veritable mountain of jewels from foreign potentates and local dignitaries formed the nucleus of the wedding gifts, and, with the blessings of his holiness, the happy young couple set off for Ferrara, where the paternal duke conveniently and somewhat suddenly died, to make way for his son and to make Lucrezia the Duchess of Ferrara.

This is as good a time as any to dispose of those two noble kinsmen, Cesare and Rodrigo Borgia. They invited several cardinals to dine, and prepared a flask of poisoned wine for one of the guests. A servant accidentally filled the cups of the pope and Cesare from this flask. Rodrigo died at once, in fearful agony. Cesare was terribly ill, but recovered; recovered to find the Borgia dynasty forever at an end. He was thrown into prison, escaped, and soon afterward was killed in battle.

Now as to Lucrezia, Duchess of Ferrara:

She seems to have turned over the frayed and thumb-marked "new leaf" when she came into her duchy. She settled down to the duties of wife and mother and chatelaine. Her people grew to love her devotedly. Her husband, it appears, loved her, too, though to the last he always kept her on the suspected list. Strangely enough, some men are like that—always delving into ancient history which the history's heroine or hero is placidly willing to forget.

But Alfonso de Ferrara seems to have had ample cause for using such memories as a guide to the future, for he was an eminently matter-of-fact personage, and there were plenty of men in the Ferrara court who weren't, as Lucrezia took the trouble to find out. For instance:

Pietro Bembo, poet and mystic, was the duke's honored, if not honorable, guest. He fell in love with Lucrezia, and she flirted outrageously with him. That the affair was not of the type to which Plato would have affixed his O. K., is amply proven by the letters, still preserved, that the duchess and the poet wrote to each other. In one of these is tender mention of a lock of hair Lucrezia sent her adorer.

At last, guarded though the lovers were, the duke learned the truth. Bembo left the Ferrara court in great haste, a very few laps ahead of marital justice. He later became a cardinal.

How Lucrezia turned from herself the wrath of her husband is not known; but the charm that enslaved every one was still potent, and soon the couple were reconciled. But the experience taught the wife nothing, for before long she was in the thick of another intrigue.

The hero of this affair was also a poet—Ercole Strozzi.

Poets, painters, story writers, inventors, minstrels, all the disciples of the arts, had a way of flocking to royal and ducal courts, seeking patrons in the local rulers. In return for such patronage they cringed and fawned and flattered and did odd jobs, and—in such rare instances as Dante's, Ariosto's, Galileo's, Columbus', and so forth—cast deathless radiance on the memories of princelings who, but for them, would have been forgotten centuries ago. Ferdinand and Isabella—to cite one instance out of hundreds—live in history, not because of their Moorish conquests and bloody religious wars, but solely because they consented to act as patrons for an obscure Genoese theorist.

Ercole Strozzi was Lucrezia's last recorded lover. Theirs was a white-flame liaison while it endured, and into it Lucrezia seems to have thrown herself heart and soul.

Strozzi came to the court of Ferrara with strong letters of introduction. He is said to have looked enough like Lucrezia's husband to have been the latter's twin brother. When Ercole had his first audience at court, the duke commented on this likeness, saying, with the quaintly refined wit of the Middle Ages:

"Messire Strozzi, you and I are as alike as two peas. Did your mother, some thirty years ago, happen to visit the court of my late father?"

"No, your grace," answered Strozzi; adding demurely, "But my father did."

Which passed for high-grade repartee in those good old days.

Strozzi's flaming love for Lucrezia at last burned itself out. He made the tragic blunder of ceasing to love her before she grew tired of him. He was the first of her admirers to commit this breach of amateur etiquette. He aggravated the offense by falling in love with another woman—one Barbara Torelli—and marrying her.

Now this was rank treason. All the court—with the barely possible exception of the duke—knew that Strozzi had been Lucrezia's lover, and all the court, therefore, knew that he had jilted her. Such crimes were not on the free list— when their victim was a Borgia.

Strozzi married Barbara Torelli on May Day, 1508. At dawn on May 14th, he was found murdered. Twenty-two ghastly wounds adorned his graceful body. The curled and perfumed love-locks framing his handsome face had been torn out by the roots. He had been mutilated in a way to wring a grunt of approval from a Sioux war chief.

No, most decidedly it was *not* a safe pastime to jilt a Borgia—not even a Borgia who had settled down to smug respectability, as had Lucrezia.

The rest of Lucrezia's life is uneventful, and seems to have been as nearly blameless as a Borgian life could hope to be. She founded a hospital and a convent and a "refuge." Two hundred beggars were fed at her door every day.

She died on June 22, 1519, mourned by every one; even by her own husband, who said in a letter to a condoling kinsman:

"I cannot write without tears, knowing myself to be deprived of such a dear and sweet companion. Her exemplary conduct and our mutual love made her wondrous precious to me."

Be that her epitaph. It is quite as truthful as is many another.

The Fear of the Job

ANNE LEIGH was the kind of stenographer one reads and hears about—but that one seldom sees in real life.

Anne had the rare, Heaven-sent gift of doing just what she was told to do, and doing it quickly; of taking dictation with flawless accuracy; of being neither a machine nor a butterfly, nor even a cross between the two. And she had a positively uncanny sense of punctuation.

As she was totally reliable, she received fourteen dollars a week—and not a cent more. (Reliability is a precious gem. It is always paid, but never by any chance overpaid. The strictly reliable person will always have a job. And it's equally safe to say, the strictly reliable person will always need one.)

Reliability was Anne's strong suit. Not only was she on the job during every working hour of every working day, but, whether she were typing a three-line note or a fifty-page report, there was no need to scan her work for inaccuracies. There was none. There *are* such stenographers.

Anne Leigh found time, moreover, amid all her manifold duties, to fall in love, to fall very, very much in love with Arthur Wayne, the head clerk.

Wayne was a good chap: clean, efficient, normal. And he was just as deeply in love with Anne Leigh as she was with him—not because she was a paragon stenographer, but because she was very pretty and had soft hair and softer eyes, and because, out of office hours, she was jolly and irresponsible and altogether adorable.

Anne and Wayne walked home together one night, after a movie show. It was a brute of a night, wet, windy and slimy. And they had no umbrella. But to them it was a night for the gods— because it was during that soggy walk that Wayne got up courage to tell Anne how wonderful she was and how idioti- cally and all-consumingly he loved her; and because Anne told him he was the first man for whom she had ever been able to care a snap of her finger, and that she really believed she had begun to care about him, just a little bit, the very day she met him.

They reached her boarding-house and stood on the steps in the *dear* pattering rain for the best part of an hour, talking—just talking. His face was all wet and cold from the running rain-drops when he kissed her good night. But it was a marvelous kiss. She didn't tell him he was the first man who had kissed her, because it was so true it didn't need telling. He didn't tell her she was the first girl he had kissed, because it wasn't true, and he felt too holy just then to smirch with a lie the mouth she had just kissed.

And the very next day good luck began to dawn for them both, which proved to them that Providence was directly guiding their joint destiny. Anne said so.

On that morning they went to work, to find that an interdepartment shake-up had just lifted the Assistant Manager, Horace Raeburn, to the rank of Manager, and that he had chosen Wayne as his private secretary and Anne Leigh as his personal stenographer. This meant a ten-dollar raise for Wayne and a four-dollar raise for Anne. They looked on the whole thing as a miracle.

It wasn't a miracle. It was not even a coincidence. Raeburn picked Wayne for secretary because the young fellow chanced to be by far the best man at hand for the job. And Anne Leigh was the best and most reliable stenographer in the place. Raeburn was merely taking the cream of the concern for his own private office.

Anne, too, was pretty, very pretty. And Raeburn, like George Washington, "had ever an eye for a fine woman." But at that point all resemblance between Mr. Horace Raeburn and the Father of his Country came to a startlingly abrupt end.

The new jobs meant also easier work and shorter hours for the two lovers. This, too, Anne pointed out as providential, since it gave them longer time to be together. On the salary Wayne was now drawing they could readily marry, although they would, of course, have to live simply. All they were waiting for was for Wayne to lay by enough money to start housekeeping, and for Anne to save up toward a little trousseau. Six months, at most, they had figured, would be enough for both prospects.

BEFORE two of the probationary six months had passed, Anne's first radiant happiness began to cloud—not that she loved Wayne less, or that he had ceased to adore her, or that she did not look forward as day-dreamfully to the roseate future: but a cloud was there, none the less.

Anne was as level-headed and as free from prudishness or unhealthy imagination as any woman alive. Therefore the cloud had begun to gather long before she was aware. And even when it came at last between her and the sun, she would not at once admit that it existed.

The first unmistakable sign of its presence came one day when she crossed to Horace Raeburn's desk with three letters for his signature. As she handed him the letters, he caught her hand in his and gave it a decided and non-platonic squeeze. Then he glanced nervously over to where Arthur Wayne sat, his back to them.

Anne drew her hand away with great suddenness and returned to her own desk. She sat down, adjusted a sheet of paper in her typewriting machine, and began, with unhesitant fingers, to transcribe from her notes the next letter of the morning batch. That was the advantage of being reliable. She worked by instinct. Another advantage was that she could think, detachedly, while she typed. This was a dangerous practice and one to which she seldom yielded. But just now her mind was awhirl, and her thoughts had absolutely no connection with the work she was doing.

The cloud existed. She could no longer doubt it. And the matter called for thought.

Anne Leigh was twenty-five. Ever since she was eighteen she had been a stenographer. She had worked for all sorts and conditions of employers. She had talked with hundreds of working-girls. Her experience had taught her much.

It had taught her, among other things, that ninety-nine business men out of a hundred are far too much engrossed in the task of making money to bother about flirting with the girls in their employ. She had learned that the stories of a working-girl's perils are as a rule nothing but lurid moonshine, and that a self-respecting girl generally is as safe in a business office as in church.

Often she had heard other girls—vain, superimaginative, or frankly mendacious—tell of advances made by their employers. And she had learned to discount such stories. She knew that most business men regard their women clerks and stenographers as mere trade assets and have absolutely no personal feeling toward them.

Nevertheless there were exceptions to the rule. No one would deny that. And now she realized fully, for the first time, that Horace Raeburn and herself formed one of those exceptions. The man palpably was trying to flirt with her. There had been lesser indications for weeks. But up to now she had not allowed herself to give them a second thought.

However, the period was past for giving Raeburn the benefit of the doubt. Men do not grab and squeeze girls' hands by accident, and then look furtively across the room to see if they have been observed.

ANNE'S first eager impulse was to tell Arthur Wayne all about it, as he and she lunched together that noon. But, with her wonted sanity, she fought back the desire. She did not want to make him miserable. She did not want him to give Raeburn a thrashing—as she was morally certain he would. That would mean the loss of Arthur's position and her own.

For herself, the idea of losing her job did not frighten her. In a very few months she was going to give up office work forever, anyway. But for Wayne—it would mean the smashing of his whole future. He would lose his position if he resented anything Raeburn might do. The season was slack. And even if it were not, an applicant is not welcomed by many concerns if one of his qualifications is that he thrashed his last boss. Moreover, as Anne well knew, the commercial "black-list" is no myth.

Decidedly she must handle the situation alone. And she must handle it with genius, if Wayne were not to lose his job. Loss of job, four months before one's wedding, is a guaranteed cure for roseate day-dreams. And Anne had no desire to lose them.

That afternoon, half an hour before going-home time, Raeburn called across the room to Wayne:

"Take these invoices over to the branch office and compare them with theirs, and give me the report in the morning. You needn't come back again to-day."

Wayne set off on his mission. For a few minutes longer Raeburn bent over the papers on his desk; then he turned to Anne, who was on the last page of a circular letter.

"Miss Leigh," he said, jocularly, "you're a mighty good worker, for such a pretty kid."

She did not answer, but typed a trifle faster and more loudly than before. "I'm going to boost your pay, a couple of dollars, next week, little girl," went on Raeburn.

"Thank you very much," said Anne primly, her hands still moving fast above the keys, her eyes on the copy she was transcribing.

"How about a little celebration of your raise?" queried Raeburn presently.

She did not hear. The machine was making too much noise. Indeed, Raeburn had never before noted what a horribly rackety typewriter it was. He cleared his throat, and smiled roguishly.

"Drop that for a minute, please," he ordered, raising his voice above the clatter.

Reluctantly, Anne paused, her fingers still hovering above the keyboard.

"Take dictation, please," ordered Raeburn.

Anne smothered a sigh of relief at the command, picked up her pad and pencil and took her usual chair at the far side of Raeburn's desk. The man rose, ponderously, came around to where she sat, and stood over her, leaning against the desk-corner.

"This is a private letter," he said. "Ready?"

"Yes sir."

"Go ahead, then: 'You are the—'"

"Excuse me," she interrupted. "You haven't given me the name and address. Or is it a circular letter, and shall I begin it 'Dear Sir' or 'Gentlemen?'"

"It's a private letter, I told you," he chuckled, his little eyes twinkling as at some delicious secret jest. "And you can fill in the name and address afterward. Start in."

He cleared his voice again; then he began dictating:

"'You are the dearest, daintiest, prettiest little girl I ever saw, and you've sure put the Indian Sign on me!'—Got that?—'I've been getting fonder and fonder of you for a couple of months. And you know it, too, for all you're so demure and proper. I am writing this to let you know that I know you know, and to tell you I want you to have dinner with me this evening, and go to a show somewhere with me, afterward. You'll never be sorry you happened to make the hit of my life with me. I'll call for you in a taxi at seven.'—There! that's about all," he added, leaning farther down toward Anne. "How does that strike you, Miss Leigh?"

"Does the dictation end at 'seven,' or at 'That's about all?'" she said evenly.

"At 'seven'," he answered, momentarily put out; then, "How does that strike you?" he repeated.

"Shall I address it to Mrs. Raeburn, sir?" she asked, looking up at him, her voice and her eyes empty of everything save a polite inquiry.

His face reddened. His smirk changed to a glower; then, at closer study of her impassive eyes, he grinned again.

"No. It is not for my wife. You see, little girl, my wife doesn't understand me. She doesn't care for me. She has made my home unhappy. It is a sore subject, and I never care to speak of it. You couldn't understand. No one can. But I am very miserable and lonely at home. That is why I want to get just one little gleam of sunshine in the darkness. That's why I wrote this letter. Can't you be just a bit sorry for a lonely old fellow like me?"

"Shall I type this now, sir?" she asked, unheeding.

"Not till I give you the name and address. Yes, I am a lonely old fellow—and not so old as I look, either. But I get terribly lonely. If it weren't for my mother, down South, I believe I'd kill myself, just to end the dreary boredom of it all."

Patiently, the pencil poised above the pad, Anne waited, as though for the address. Her dearth of emotion stirred Raeburn to annoyance.

"Don't pretend you're ignorant," he snapped. "You know very well *you* are the girl I was talking to in that letter. Why should you hedge? There's mighty few girls in your position, I can tell you, that I'd bother myself to fall in love with."

He checked himself, changed his tone to one intended as wheedling, and went on:

"There! The truth is out at last. I'm awfully fond of you, little girl. Can you learn to care just a mite for me?"

Anne had risen, shut the pad-book and started over to her desk. He followed her, puzzled, talking as he went.

"If there's no more work," she said, "I'll finish the circular—I've only two lines more—and then go home. It's five o'clock."

"You haven't answered me," he persisted, coming alongside and trying to slip a fat arm around her.

"There isn't any answer, Mr. Raeburn," she said quietly, "unless you want my resignation."

"Resignation?" he echoed. "Who in blazes is talking about resignations? I'm going to boost your salary, I told you—not two dollars a week, either, but four dollars, if—"

"There isn't any 'if,' Mr. Raeburn. Can't you see that, even now? I've tried to make it clear."

"Why?" he stormed. "Why? Tell me that. I'm giving you a chance that any girl in the place ought to be glad to jump at. If it's a question of money—"

"It isn't," she said, putting mighty restraint on her nerves and temper.

"Then what is it?" he coaxed, trying to take both her hands. "Why do you throw me down like this?"

"If you must know," she said, stepping back and putting her desk between them, "I'll tell you. I might say it is because I am decent. I might say it is because, even if I weren't, I wouldn't rob another woman of her husband. Both those reasons are true. But I'm afraid both of them mean very little to you, and that if I gave them, you'd only argue and try to make me see things differently. So, I'll give you a reason that even *you* can appreciate. I am in love with some one else, and we are going to be married in April."

"Huh!" grunted Raeburn, with a sound not unlike that evoked by a sudden blow in the solar plexus; then: "Man around here? Some one working for us? Or a fellow you met outside?"

"That doesn't concern you at all," she said. "I spoke of it only to—"

"Oh, ashamed of him, eh?" he sneered. "Like to keep his name dark!"

"I'm not ashamed of him!" she flashed, thrown for the first time off her hard-kept poise. "It's Arthur Wayne."

"Wayne? The devil you say! It's been going on right under my nose, has it?—while you were both supposed to be working. Well, Miss Leigh, I won't interfere with any true lovers. In fact, I'm going to fix it so you can both of you have all the time you want, for billing and cooing. After this week, neither of you need waste your precious hours in this office."

She had closed her desk and had taken her hat and jacket from the niche at one side of the room. At Raeburn's last words she turned and came slowly back to him, hat and coat in hand.

"Do you mean," she asked, "that we are discharged—he and I?"

"I'll make it plainer by putting it in writing, to-morrow," he replied. "This office is no lover's lane."

"No? What were *you* trying to make of it, five minutes ago? Mr. Raeburn, as I understand it, I am discharged because I refused without thanks the beastly offer you made me. As I understand it, too, Arthur Wayne is thrown out of work because he is so unlucky as to be engaged to me. For the pretext that we neglected our work because we were engaged is too silly to speak of. You know neither of us has neglected our work for one minute. You told your assistant, in my hearing, not three days ago, that Arthur is a perfect private secretary, and that you were lucky to have picked him out. You've often spoken well of my own work. You are discharging us because you are furious that Arthur Wayne possesses what *you* have no right to and have no chance for. You are punishing him for no fault of his. It is unjust. It is abominably unjust!"

"It goes," he said.

"Do you want it known that you discharged a woman because she was decent and that you discharged a man because she loved him?"

"It won't be known," he said lightly. "Do you suppose anybody pays attention to the lies of discharged employees?"

SHE was silent for a moment, staring at him in a helplessness that almost touched him, it was so utterly childlike and appealing.

"Come, now," he urged, less truculently. "Be a sensible kid. You're fond of Wayne. Well, go ahead and be fond of him, if you like. I've no kick—so long as you'll be just a little fond of me, too. Let him keep his job, if—"

"It's not fair!" she blazed, beside herself with hot rebellion. "Oh, it's not *fair!* We people who work for others have a hard enough time of it at best. It's slave, slave, slave from morning till night, from childhood to old age, through all the sunshine hours of the day and all the sunshine years of life. And all for what? To make a bare living and to help our employers grow richer. To earn a few dollars, to eat—that we may have strength to work harder. To earn a place to sleep—so that the sleep may refresh us for another day's work. And all for somebody else! And then—"

"You'll have it a lot softer than that, if you'll—"

"And then," she raged on, "to have the Fear of the Job held over us like a nightmare. Not the hope that we may better ourselves, but the horrible haunting fear that unless we do, better and better for the man who employs us, we'll be deprived of the chance of working ourselves to death for him; that we'll be discharged, and have to look for some other slave-driver to give us a chance to wear out our youth and strength for him. And the Fear of the Job makes us servile and cringing, and makes us swallow insults and come back for more—for fear we won't be allowed to work ourselves to nervous wrecks for just enough money to keep us alive. The Fear of the Job! It drives many a girl to do what I've just lost my job for refusing to do. It drives many a man to turn crooked, at his employer's order, when his conscience tells him to stay honest. Oh, it isn't fair! It *isn't* fair!"

"You're quite a Socialist, little girl," exclaimed Raeburn, highly amused at his usually demure stenographer's flare of temper.

"I'm not a Socialist," she cried hysterically. "I don't know just what a Socialist is. But I'm not one. I'm a girl whose sweetheart must lose his job and his hopes of marrying me, because I won't be wicked. If we lost our positions because we were lazy or weren't competent, I wouldn't complain. But we've worked so hard and so well! And to have all our beautiful future smashed like this—"

She broke into a passion of weeping that swept away speech and strangled her with fierce, wrenching sobs.

"Say," consoled Raeburn, uncomfortably, patting her on the back, "don't go all to pieces like that. Be sensible, can't you? There's no need of heroics. There's no need to take on so. Think it over, and maybe you'll find it isn't such a bad bargain I'm offering you, after all. Brace up."

Presently, as he spoke, she choked back her sobs. Her shoulders slumped pathetically. Her face, behind her clenching hands, worked convulsively. Her head drooped. The fight seemed to be all taken out of her.

HORACE RAEBURN had not risen to his present station by mere luck. Among a score of other winning qualities, he was a shrewd judge of character. He read, unerringly, the girl's attitude of hopeless defeat. And he pressed his advantage.

"There, now," he rumbled, slipping an arm around her. "Don't you go getting

unhappy. Brace up. It'll be all right. I'm not such a fossil old chap as you think. I'll show you a mighty good time, and—"

"And—and Arthur can stay on here?" she sobbed.

"Bless your dear heart, yes!" boomed Raeburn, in delight. "Till doomsday, if he wants to."

She slipped away from his grasp, went shakily over to her desk and opened it again. Then, dabbing at her eyes with one hand, she sat down and opened her pad-book.

"What are you doing?" asked Raeburn, close behind her, and looking over her heaving shoulder as she fitted a sheet of paper into place and began to play nervously on the keys.

"I'm—I'm surrendering," she whispered, bashfully averting her head.

Raeburn, over her shoulder, watched—at first in perplexity, then with a grin of appreciation—as she wrote her own name and address and proceeded to transcribe from her notes the mock letter he had dictated fifteen minutes earlier.

"*Miss A. J. Leigh, 999 Blankton Street,*'" he read aloud slowly, repeating each word as her flying fingers pounded it on the page. "*You are the dearest, daintiest, prettiest little girl I ever saw, and you've sure put the Indian Sign on me! I've been getting fonder and fonder of you for a couple of months. And you know it, too, for all you're so demure and proper. I am writing this to let you know that I know you know, and to tell you I want you to have dinner with me this evening, and go to a show somewhere with me, afterward. You'll never be sorry you happened to make the hit of my life with me. I'll call for you in a taxi at seven.*'"

She drew the sheet from the machine and laid it on the drawn-out extension-flap of her desk. Then, dipping a pen in the ink, she said, with a sorry little attempt of mimicking her usual office manner:

"Ready for signature, sir."

Horace Raeburn burst into a laugh of appreciation. The wit of the thing, the delicate way of showing him she was his, tickled him mightily. Her quaintly original manner of yielding made him ten-fold infatuated with her.

"Signature, eh?" he laughed, delightedly, entering into the spirit of the thing, and fondly patting her on the shoulders as he leaned over her. "You bet! I only wish I could sign such a letter every day."

He sprawled his name across the foot of the page.

"I'll keep that forever as a souvenir of the daintiest kid on earth!" he chuckled.

"Wait!" she suggested, ever methodical. "The ink's still wet. You'll smear it. I'll get a blotter."

She took the letter daintily by one corner, holding it far away from her, and crossed to his desk for a blotter. She wavered as she walked. He threw out an arm to support her.

"I want a kiss, first," he said.

But she lurched, dizzily, and thrust forward her free hand against the desk, to steady herself. Her trained fingers struck against five of the electric buttons there, and pressed them hard.

"A kiss, I said," repeated Raeburn, unobservant.

Playfully, she eluded him, running around the desk. He made as though to follow. Then the door flew open. His office-boy stood on the threshold.

"What the deuce do you want?" roared the Manager. "Get out!"

"Yes sir. You rang, sir," faltered the boy.

"I didn't. Get out."

The boy stepped backward, colliding with a porter, who in turn was followed close by a clerk and a messenger. A special officer formed the intruders' rear guard. The discipline, long since inculcated into the staff by Mr. Horace Raeburn, in the matter of swift response to bell-summonses, was excellent.

"What's the matter?" bellowed Raeburn at sight of the small army. "Is there a fire?"

"A fire?" shrieked Anne Leigh, and dashed terrified from the room before she could be stopped.

But she came back.

BY the time Raeburn had explained right blasphemously for the fourth time that he had not pushed any of the buttons, and by the time the invading host had jointly and severally and repeatedly declared that each and all of their indicators had flashed the signal, "Manager's Office," the besiegers and the besieged came to a mutual agreement that the electric wires were out of order. And the visiting quintet departed.

Then it was that Anne Leigh came into the room again. Her panic was quite cured. She was actually smiling at her foolish fears, as she picked up her hat and prepared to spear it into place.

So pretty did she look as she smiled that Raeburn advanced upon her, fat arms outstretched, a smirk of adulation on his face.

He bore down upon her like a charging elephant. And he

shrank back from her at almost the same instant, with a dolorous howl of pain and amaze, nursing a pudgy wrist into which a quarter-inch of hatpin had just penetrated.

"You she-devil!"

"Mr. Raeburn," said Anne, as primly as an Elsie Dinsmore heroine, "you forget yourself."

"You—you stabbed me! I believe you did it on purpose!"

"I most surely did," she returned cheerily. "And if ever you try to lay one of your fingers on me again, I'll drive the pin full length into you. I hope you won't make me do it; it's a good pin, and I'd hate to have to throw it away."

He stood gasping. Adjusting her hat carefully, in a vanity-box mirror she had just propped up on her desk, Anne took advantage of the man's brief dumbness to say:

"I'm sorry I was so frightened just now, about the fire. I couldn't help running. But I didn't run far—only into the clerks' room. I happened to see an envelope and fountain pen and a stamp there. So I enveloped that letter of yours and addressed it to myself, in a friend's care, and dropped it down the mail-chute in the hall. Wasn't it a nice way to dispose of the disgusting thing?"

Again she smiled up at the purple and gasping Manager.

"You see," she confided, almost cooingly, "I'm going to have it photographed. And I'm going to address one of the photo's to the head of the firm here, and another to your poor wife, and another to the editor of *City Gossipings*."

Raeburn made a wordless sound, after the manner of one who seeks, through a set of swollen tonsils, to gobble like a very sick turkey.

"Oh, don't be worried," she soothed. "I'm only going to *address* the photo's to those people. I'm not going to *send* them. That is," she added, with conscientious effort at accuracy, "I'm not going to send any of them unless Arthur Wayne should happen to lose his job during the next few years—or should have the job made so unpleasant for him as to make him resign—or shouldn't be promoted as fast as he deserves. In such cases as those, of course, I'd feel it was my duty to—"

"Blackmail!" he coughed, apoplectically.

"Oh, what an ugly, *ugly* word!" she reproved him. "Good night, Mr. Raeburn. I'm going home now. I'm afraid I'll be an hour or so late in the morning. I've got to stop, on the way here, to get that letter photographed. But I'll be as quick as I can. Would you like one of the copies? I'm sorry I can't give you the original. I'm going to leave that in my brother's charge. He's a lawyer, you know. And—and thank you *so* much for lifting the Fear of the job, *forever and forever*, from Arthur Wayne and me. It's *dear* of you!"

"A WHOLE armful of tremendous things have happened to-day," announced Wayne, in joyous excitement, when he called at Anne's boarding-house one evening just a week before the wedding and just a week after she had left the firm's employ. "I'm going to tell them to you in their order. All ready?"

"Ready and trying to wait in meek patience," said Anne.

"Mr. Raeburn's a brick," began Wayne. "I told him about our engagement to-day. I told him you wanted me to. And he was so surprised and delighted! He said I could have an extra week off for a wedding trip, and—don't faint!—he offered of his own accord to give me a ten-dollar raise, beginning next month. Of his own accord, mind you? It's a joy to work for such a man."

"It is, indeed," solemnly agreed Anne.

"And I honestly believe, from something he said," went on Arthur joyously, "that he means to give us a wedding present."

"If he does," answered the girl, "I'll throw it into the river with my own hands." But she wisely neglected to say it aloud. Instead, she asked demurely:

"Is that the whole 'armful' of things that happened, or is—"

"No," he answered gayly. "I told you I was going to repeat them in their order. There's one left—the biggest; I've kept it hidden, up my sleeve. You know Dick Hyland, of the Curtis-Bayne Company? He asked me to lunch with him to-day. And when I got to the restaurant, who do you think was at the table with Dick?"

"President Wilson!" she said promptly.

"If you're going to be flippant," he replied with terrible severity, "I'll shove this wonderful piece of news back in my sleeve and—"

"I'm sorry," she said humbly. "And I'll try not to be disappointed if the mysterious Other Man at the table wasn't anybody but Mr. Bryan."

"If I had a home," proclaimed Wayne, sternly, "I should leave you at once and go to it. I shouldn't waste any more time talking to such a frivolous young person. I shouldn't even stop here long enough to tell you that the man with Dick Hyland was Ahasuerus T. Curtis, senior member of Curtis-Bayne. I shouldn't bother to mention to you that he offered me fifteen dollars a week more than Raeburn's paying me, and that I've accepted it and that I'm going to work for him the day we get back from our honeymoon. This is the chance of a lifetime for me. Aren't you glad?"

"Glad?" she murmured, almost in awe. "Glad? Of course I'm glad. Gladder than I can say, or than you'd understand. It's—it's providential, Arthur."

The War Bridegroom

*T*HE whole thing started with a dollar cigar. "Corona-Corona" was the brand. Its label was not nearly so garish as that on Jim Hunter's average cigar. The cigar itself was no larger, and it cost only ninety-five cents more.

Cigars of any sort were an event in Jim's life. On thirty dollars a week, a head clerk with a wife cannot smoke even five cents' worth of tobacco at one sitting without feeling the pinch.

Jim Hunter was head clerk for Cawthorpe & Watts. He had been working for the firm ever since he left grammar-school at thirteen. And his rise from errand-boy to head-clerkship had consumed the seventeen most glorious years of life.

He was a good, honest, conscientious worker. He deserved every penny of salary he received. But he did not much more than deserve it. For he belonged to the non-commissioned majority—the majority that does the task set for it and does it well—and does no more; because Nature has withheld from it the curse of imagination and the blessing of initiative.

At twenty-five Jim had married Molly Mercer. Her father was a broken-down clergyman, living on a pension that a secular firm would have been ashamed to give an old employee. And from childhood, her knowledge of practical economy had been of the post-graduate order. When her father died and she married Jim, the bridegroom's salary seemed positive affluence to her—just at first. Soon she knew better; and life became to her what it usually becomes to the careful wife of a New York clerk. Still, they were moderately happy. Also, there were windfalls. In fat years there was an extra week's pay at Christmas. And there was always a fortnight's vacation with pay in summer.

Then came a year when there was no extra thirty dollars on Christmas week —when, instead, four men were discharged; and there was an office rumor that salaries were to be shaved. Over on the other side of the world certain monarchs and statesmen, whose names sounded like excerpts from a wine-list, had decreed to turn Europe into an armed camp. Three thousand miles of open water had served as a splendid conductor for the war-shock. And it smote and paralyzed American business.

JIM was not one of the four luckless employees of Cawthorpe & Watts who joined several million other employerless employees in celebrating the Yuletide by a search for new jobs. Nor was he one of the twelve other men whom his firm "let go" during the next year. But all this meant a tremendous access of extra work for him; and he did it tremendously hard—all the harder when Turner, next in succession to him, announced loudly one day (to nobody in particular and standing as close as could be to the glass partition of the junior partner's office) that he stood ready, in case of emergency, to do Hunter's work, and do it well, for ten dollars a week less than the head clerk was receiving.

Worry began to do grotesque things to Jim's eyes and hair. And he was pitifully grateful that he had sternly denied himself luxuries in the better years, in order to lay by a little money for just such a crisis as this.

Two thousand dollars or so in bank, at a time like that, means all the difference between bearable worry and insomnia-torture.

There was no vacation that summer for any of the overworked handful of wage-earners who now kept the Cawthorpe & Watts business alive. In the early winter old man Cawthorpe died, and Hutchins Watts, the junior partner, took sole command.

As a horse feels the change of drivers, so did the staff. The old steady touch on the reins was changed to a jerky, spasmodic tugging. Watts drove his men hard and himself harder. He even lowered the pay-roll by another cut or two; and he let his nerves and temper go to wreck along with those of his workers.

But he had one safety-valve that was denied them. He could—and frequently did—take the razor-edge off his troubles by drinking. And not a soul in his employ dared do that.

But with the dawn of summer, Watts relaxed his savage slave-driving. The wrinkles began to smooth out from his forehead. His manner gained back some of its old jauntiness. Drink now made him jolly instead of ferocious. No more men were fired. Indeed, two extra clerks were taken on. Business was picking up. But it was picking up far too slowly to justify the change in Watts.

Which brings us by tedious stages to the dollar cigar.

HUNTER went into the private office with a batch of papers to be signed. Watts had been out at lunch for an unconscionably long time, that day. And a blind man with a fairly good sense of smell could have told that he had not visited a temperance restaurant.

He was swinging back and forth in his swivel chair, a newly opened box of cigars in front of him, a smile of calm bliss on his plump face. He greeted Jim with positive effusion, signed the papers with a curlycue flourish, and as the head clerk was departing, called after him:

"Hey, have a cigar, Hunter. These are the real thing. First of the kind I've had the nerve to buy, in God knows when. In famine times a man hasn't got the nerve to pay twenty-five dollars a box for smokes."

Hunter gazed at the box in respectful wonder. He usually bought cigars singly—never more than five at a time. And this box held twenty-five. That meant the cigars cost a dollar apiece. It did not seem possible.

He would have lavished still more amazement on the display of wealth had not Watts' manner embarrassed him and made him want to get back to his own desk.

But Watts had caught up the box and was thrusting it, a little shakily, toward Jim.

"Have one," he invited cordially. "Smoke it after dinner. Don't go wasting a Corona-Corona on an empty stomach. Want you to take it, to celebrate with me. This is an occasion—a real he-occasion. It's custom to hand round cigars when man becomes a husb'nd."

"Husband?" repeated Hunter. "I congratulate you, sir; I didn't know."

"Didn' know I was married? Well, I am. I'm the newly wed husb'nd of—of whole fam'ly of war-brides. Whole harem of 'em. Some of 'em have brought me nice big dowry. The rest are going to. Have a cigar. Oh, you've had one. That's so. My mistake. That's the way to make up for hard times, Hunter—by buying war-brides, I've lost a lot of cash in this leaky ol' concern, this past year. But I'm getting it back an' then some."

"Really, sir? You're fortunate to—"

"Cleaned up more'n two hundred an' twelve thous'nd this past four months. Going to make a bigger killing yet, on Standard Munitions. Got the tip at lunch to-day. Got it from right man. Had to get him lit up to do it; but I landed it all right, an' I placed my order, 'Standard Munitions.' Grabbed a thousand at fifteen. That little stock's going to two hundred, sure as blazes. Then watch me. Have a—Oh, you've got one. Well, I—"

One of the lightning-quick psychic changes of phase that are an unexplained part of drunkenness came over him, in mid-sentence. The babbling mood shifted, to cranky suspicion. Watts seemed vaguely aware he had said too much. He glared in peevish uncertainty at Jim, his flushed face creasing into lines of displeasure.

"That will do, Hunter," he said with lofty severity. "This is a business office. Not place to jabber. I'll hear the rest of your story 'nother time."

Majestically he turned about to face the desk. Jim Hunter, dollar cigar in hand, went back to his work.

THAT evening, after dinner, he drew forth from his vest pocket the cigar, and gingerly lighted it. Presently Molly, clearing away the dishes, stopped for a moment beside his chair.

"What a long ash!" she exclaimed. "It's half as long as the cigar itself. Is that the same kind of cigar you generally smoke?"

"Yes," returned Jim. "The very same kind—plus about two thousand per cent. It is a gift from my revered employer. It is part of the dowry of his war-bride."

"His—*what?*"

"War-bride. That's a slang name they have on the Street for stocks that boom on account of the war. Ammunition and copper and steel and all sorts of things like that. It seems Mr. Watts has been recouping his business losses that way. His latest houri is Standard Munitions. He says he's just bought a block of it at fifteen and he's going to hold it for two hundred."

"That means he will make a great deal of money, doesn't it, Jim?"

"Of course. He says he's cleared up several hundred thousand dollars this past few months. And I dare say he has."

"Why don't you do it, too?" she asked wistfully.

"Oh, for several fairly good reasons: First, I'm not a born fool enough to risk all my little handful of coin on one throw. Second, because it takes capital to make capital, and we've got barely twenty-four hundred dollars on earth. It took me seventeen years to save that, and I don't care to lose it in a week. Third, because I don't have the good luck to travel in a crowd that can give me such tips as Watts gets. Then—"

"But," she urged, "you just got a tip."

"This dollar cigar? That isn't the kind of tip I'm talking about. I mean—"

"I know. I know. But this 'Standard Ammunition,' or whatever the name is—the stock he told you he's just bought—isn't *that* a tip?"

Jim Hunter stared dully at his wife.

As a matter of fact, he had so long and so earnestly taught himself that his only means of wealth was by hoarding his salary that he actually had not, until that minute, realized the possibilities for himself in Watts' half-drunken burst of confidence.

"A tip?" he echoed with stupid solemnity.

"Isn't it?" she persisted.

"Why—why, yes! Of course it is. I—never thought of that."

"And here you're in Wall Street every day!" she laughed. "You've been brought up and educated there. Yet it takes your silly stay-at-home wife to tell you what a tip is!"

"I've seen so many good men go to smash that way," he answered, "that I've always kept as far as possible away from such things. Whenever one of the clerks blabs about a stock-rumor he's heard, I always walk away. It's the only safety. That's the sort of thing that leads to the bread-line or to jail or—"

"Or to a bigger flat," supplemented Molly, "and a maid and new clothes and a whole new set of dining-room furniture and a chance to entertain, and seats at the opera sometimes, and—"

"Don't, old girl!" he begged. "You know I'd do all that for you if I could—all that and a lot more. But playing wildcat tips isn't the way to get them."

"What is the way, then?" she asked, a tinge of bitterness creeping into her voice. "Working along at thirty dollars a week, and scrimping and pinching over every penny we have to spend, and wondering how soon we'll be fired?"

"I'm sorry!" he said stiffly. "And I do the very best I can for you. It isn't my fault I'm a dub. I'd be a Malefactor of Great Wealth, if I knew how. If you'd married a live chap—Lord!" He broke off, slamming the cigar-butt to the floor. "The measly thing burned my thumb!"

She was all sympathy, at once, and insisted on inspecting the burn and then on kissing it to make it well.

Thus the cigar both began and ended their mild quarrel.

But memory did not die with the dying end of the dollar perfecto. Instead, though no more was said by either of them about speculating, the magic words "Standard Munitions" danced maddeningly before Jim's mental vision all night.

Next morning he did not speak to Molly about the tantalizing stock. But on the way to work and all forenoon he said a great deal about it to himself.

This was no clerk's-rumor tip. It was from on high. By playing just such tips from just such sources, Watts had raked in a fortune in an unbelievably short while. And he, Jim Hunter, with the key to freedom in his own hands, must forever go on drudging and grubbing for a pittance from the man who had inadvertently put wealth within his reach.

It was the chance of a lifetime. Standard Munitions was selling at fifteen. Or, rather, it *had* been selling at fifteen, the day before. Perhaps, by now— Jim unobtrusively pawed over a tangle of ticker tape.

Standard Munitions—16⅛.

AT lunch-time Jim Hunter went at top speed to the savings bank, where his twenty-four-hundred-dollar hoard was industriously, if slowly, increasing itself at the rate of three per cent a year. He drew out all except a few odd dollars, and made for a brokerage house of the less pretentious type which had a reputation for square dealing and whose proprietor he knew.

He had no intention of securing the stock outright. That was a safe but much too petty process for him in his new rôle of plunger. The art of marginal buying and of pyramiding was as familiar to Jim Hunter, through long observation, as though this were not the first time in his thirty years that he himself had put his knowledge to active use. His campaign was already laid out, step by step.

He had asked Watts for two hours' leave of absence from the office that noon, on plea of sickness. When he returned to his desk, he looked still sicker. He had bought Standard Munitions—on a margin so narrow that the memory of it froze his hands and feet. He went home early and straight to bed. He told Molly he had a chill. He had.

That sleepless night preceded many another. But he was following out his carefully arranged campaign—pyramiding wisely, brooding over the stock as though it were a dying child. All that remained now was for Standard Munitions to keep on living up to his hopes.

And Standard Munitions proceeded to do it.

Though every dollar withdrawn from the investment implied the loss of many more dollars in future, yet from time to time, as the Standard Munitions rocketed, Jim drew out sums varying from fifty to three hundred dollars, and turned them over to Molly for household use. Moreover, he no longer religiously put aside the usual percentage of his salary for the savings bank, but gave that to her too. He had told her of his speculation, and she had rejoiced mightily. She rejoiced a thousandfold more as the driblets of spending-money came in.

It was the first cash she had ever in her life possessed to do with as she chose. Its possession went to her unaccustomed head like strong drink. At first, it was rapture to buy the things she and Jim had so long needed—the new furniture, the extra glass and china that the apartment had lacked. These and more needs were easily supplied. And still the golden stream was not exhausted.

Next she launched out in the things she had always craved but had never hoped to own—the pretty clothes, the maid, the occasional taxicab rides, the Broadway theaters.

People were beginning to be so nice to her, too. Heretofore, she had had rather few friends. But now, at the merest hint of Jim's new prosperity, these friends had begotten new friends until she had a large and fast-growing list of acquaintances.

These later acquaintances, some of them, were charmingly gay people. They were forever on the go, and they took her with them. The men she met at the places to which her new friends introduced her were a revelation to Molly. Jim had always been so tired and logy when he came home from work; and his clothes were anything but fashionable. But these men seemed never tired and had all the leisure time they wanted; and with them dress was a fine art.

Molly was pretty. They told her so. They also told her she danced divinely. They told her a lot of equally charming things—things poor plodding Jim had long since forgotten to say to her. She was seldom at home now. She had never dreamed New York held so many wonderful places to go to; and she looked back in frank amaze to the pleasure she had once taken in a rare gallery-seat show with Jim, or a reading-aloud evening at the flat or a penurious jaunt to Coney Island. She seemed to have been born anew into an undreamed-of and glorious world.

As for Jim, his body remained at his work—from seventeen years' force of habit; but his mind was eternally busy with Standard Munitions. Up, up and up soared his war-bride. And the war-bridegroom—between his now-detested office labors and his worry over the stock-market—was fit for nothing, when he reached home at night, but to bolt his dinner and tumble into bed. Molly could not lure him into going out with her. So she went out alone—or with some group of newly acquired intimates.

One morning, as Jim sat down at his desk, he was summoned to Watts' private office. He went in, listlessly. Gone were the days when a call to the firm-head's presence could thrill him with hope or dread. A man was leaving the office as he entered. Watts pointed to a chair. Jim sat down.

"Did you see that man who just went out?" Watts began. "That was an expert accountant. He and I have been here since seven o'clock this morning going over your books together."

He paused and looked keenly at Jim. Hunter bore the gaze, carelessly. He had scarcely noted what his employer had said.

"We've been going over your books," repeated Watts. "In a job like yours, there's always a chance for a clever chap to steal—not that you're particularly clever."

Vaguely, Jim realized Watts was insulting him. And, vaguely, he resented it.

"My books," he said sullenly, "are—"

"Your books are all right," Watts cut in. "And that's what surprises me. I made sure it was a case of another good man gone wrong—trusted employee, and all that—with a striped-suit sequel. But it isn't. I can't make it out."

He sat thinking, his plump face a-pucker with perplexity. Jim watched him in amazement. The man was not drunk. But what was he driving at? Suddenly Watts looked up.

"Hunter," he asked, fairly shooting the question at his head clerk, "what's the opening quotation on Standard Munitions to-day?"

Jim snapped out the answer without a second's hesitation. His careless demeanor was gone. He was whip awake and tensely interested now.

"H'm!" mused Watts. "So that's it. I blabbed about it to you when I was lit up, one afternoon. I remembered it afterward. I wasn't too far gone for that. But I didn't think you'd take it up. It isn't your way. And that's where it comes from, is it?"

"Where *what* comes from?" queried Jim crossly, with a feeling that he was somehow caught in a trap. "What do you mean?"

Watts did not answer, at once. He seemed to be marshaling his words with great care.

"You know the firm's rule against speculating, of course?" he said at last.

"I know you've set us the example of doing it!" flared Jim. "But if you want my resignation, because I followed a tip that you yourself gave me, why, go ahead and fire me."

"I'm not going to fire you," said Watts with no show of resentment, "—partly because you'll need your job pretty badly when you go broke on the Street, but mostly because I'm interested in you."

"That's good of you," sneered Jim.

"Yes," assented Watts in perfect seriousness. "It is. I'm interested in you. You've been here longer than anyone else we've got. And you've plugged away, hard and faithfully. And my old partner was fond of you. I don't go in for sentiment very much—not in office hours. But I am interested in you and I like you. That's why I kept you on, at thirty dollars in the hard times, when your assistant could have done your work just as well for twenty dollars. That's why I fired him for trying to get your job. That's why I felt as if I'd been kicked in the face when I thought you'd turned crooked. That's why I feel bad to think you've fallen for the stock-ticker game. You're not the man to play it. You're bound to lose."

Jim did not answer. The sharp retort that jumped to his lips died into nothingness at the older man's crude expression of friendliness. He sat dumb and frowning, while Watts went on:

"That's why I'm going to waste my time and your time and the office time by handing out a bit of talk to you. You don't have to listen if you don't want to. You've plunged on Standard Munitions. You've broken your lifetime resolutions and turned from worker to gambler. What's it brought you? Some spare cash that you don't know how to enjoy. What's it taken away from you? About twenty pounds of flesh, the power of snoring eight hours a night, the zest you used to have for your work. It's made you sour and nervous and lazy, and it's started you on the toboggan. Is it worth it?"

"*You've* seemed to find it so."

"Yes, I have. It's my own game. It isn't yours. I know how to play it, when to play it and where to stop. You don't. Speculating won't harm me. It will kill you."

"I'll take my chances," was Jim's surly answer; and he added, a little less ungraciously: "Thanks, just the same."

He rose to go, but the other man waved him to his chair.

"Just a minute," said Watts; "I want to tell you something. Or rather, I don't want to, but I've got to. And it'll explain how I found out about all this. Ever hear of the St. Crœsus Cabaret?"

"No."

"No, you wouldn't be likely to. It's a place where decent family men and their wives aren't to be found. I go there sometimes; I went there last night. There was the usual mixed crowd of social gangsters and men of doubtful character and women whose characters left no room for doubt. There was a nasty little cuss there, named Knox Hinkle. Ever hear of him?"

"No. We don't go to such places; we leave that for—"

"For your disreputable employer? Well, Knox Hinkle is a youth who achieved fame as a society blackmailer and then as a forger. He went to Sing Sing—got pardoned through a pull, and came back to Broadway. He makes a living out of chorus girls and the like. A good looker, in his own slimy way, and a dandy dancer."

"Well?" prompted Jim in undisguised boredom, as Watts paused.

"Well," resumed Watts, "last night when I got there I happened to notice him, among fifty other dancers who were shuffling and wabbling, out on the floor. He was dancing with a mighty pretty little woman. I didn't recognize her, though I know most of the place's 'regulars' by sight. So I asked a man who she was. He told me she was a newcomer and Hinkle had frozen onto her. It's his game to fascinate well-to-do simpletons and then scare them into giving him cash, on threat to squeal to their husbands or fathers. And she was getting fascinated, all right. The man I was with said she had a husband who had just come into a lot of cash."

Watts cleared his throat and looked apprehensively at the politely bored Hunter. Then he continued:

"Some rapid people had taken her up, my friend said, and were planning how to bleed her, when Hinkle got her away from them, so as to grab the lion's share of the loot. I asked some more questions. It seems her husband is a clerk, downtown, who has struck it rich all of a sudden, and she's launching out. That got me to thinking—but not till I heard her name."

Again he ceased speaking, and looked almost imploringly at Jim. But Hunter was very evidently letting his attention wander. Indeed, he was having some trouble in strangling a yawn.

"You fool!" blazed Watts in sudden irritation at such denseness. "It was your own wife!"

Slowly, very slowly, Jim Hunter got to his feet. In his eyes was the glazed stare of a sleep-walker's. He stood thus for a moment, open-mouthed, blank-faced. Then, with a yell, he hurled himself bodily across the desk at Watts.

His employer stopped the maniac charge with a big hand that caught Jim fast by the throat and held him helpless. Hunter writhed, beating in futile fury at the big man's body, which he could not reach, and mouthing wildly incoherent blasphemy and insult.

Presently the paroxysm passed, leaving Jim faint and dizzy. He collapsed panting into a chair, and rocked to and fro—muttering, gasping, choking back a hysteria of sobs. But little by little he grew calmer. From far off, he heard Watts' deep voice saying:

"It was rotten medicine, lad. But it's cured you—or if it hasn't, you'll never be cured."

"I'm—I'm cured," muttered Jim dazedly, as he got to his feet. "I'm going home," he added.

Leaning heavily on the desk-edge until the mists began to clear, he lurched out of the room and on into the street.

A half-hour's aimless wandering in the cold air brought him to his senses. He found himself murmuring stupidly, over and over:

"I'm cured—I'm cured—I'm cured."

Then the power of thought came back to him. Inch by inch he reviewed everything. And to his own amaze, he could feel nothing in his heart for Molly but an infinite pity.

With cold logic he reviewed everything. She was not to blame. It was he who had given her the poison that was destroying her—he who loved her and would blithely have died to make her happy. He forced himself to remember their dear life together, of other days—the sweetly eventless life, when his homecoming had been the day's great event, and when they two had lived for each other alone. She was so lovable, so helpless, so young! And he, by his money-avalanche, had crushed out the good in her and had wrecked the happiness God had given them.

It was the money.

And with a momentary return of his Berserk fury, he cursed it. Then, with returning coolness of mind, came the solution—the one and only solution. He crossed the street to a telegraph office and scrawled a line or two to Watts:

> Thank you for what you have done for me. And forgive me for speaking and acting as I did. I shall take you at your word and keep my job. But first I must have a few days' leave of absence to adjust things. I'll come back as soon as I can. Thank you again.

He enveloped and sealed the note and ordered it delivered. Then he went to his broker's. A glance at the ticker showed him that Standard Munitions was still merrily rocketing. Calling the broker aside, he said tersely:

"Go short a thousand shares on S. M."

Vale, the broker, grunted as though he had been kicked amidships by a mule.

"You're in fun, aren't you?" he asked feebly.

"I don't joke in business hours."

"If you're not joking, you're stark crazy," said Vale. "S. M. is at 100⅛ this morning. In a week or so, at this rate, it'll be at one hundred fifty. This order you've just given me will wipe you out before the stock gets to one hundred forty. D' you understand, Mr. Hunter?" he insisted, speaking as to a defective child. "You'll be cleaned out—broke!"

"That's my lookout."

"It's your clean-out!"

"Either way you like. The order goes."

"It's suicide!" fumed the broker.

"It's resurrection," contradicted Jim; and he walked out.

MOLLY was not at home when her husband reached the flat. On the few times, in the old days, when he had chanced to come back from work and found she was out, the place had had a dead and homeless look that had stricken him to the heart. But now he was glad of the chance to sit there alone, with his own soul for ghostly adviser, through the long hours until her return.

At dusk he heard her key in the lock and her step in the hall. He was ready to meet her now. The hours had brought him counsel. He rose and went to meet her, drawing her into the dimly lighted living-room.

"Have you anything to do this evening, dear?" he asked.

"Why, yes," she made answer. "We're going to the Casino and afterward to the St. Crœsus Cabaret for a dance and some supper. Want to come along?"

"No, thanks. I've a bit of a headache, and I'm sleepy too. You say 'we' are going. Who are 'we?'"

"Blanche Dunby and her husband and the Hutches and Knox Hinkle and I."

"Hinkle? Who is he?"

"He's one of the most interesting men I ever met!" she gushed, "and the very best dancer. He used to be something or other on Wall Street, I believe. But he has retired. He—Jim, do you *have* to yawn in my face, or do you do it as a parlor-stunt?" she broke off.

But it was not a yawn she heard, there in the dusk. It was a sigh of utter relief. Women of Molly's stamp do not refer to men they secretly love, in the way Molly had just spoken of Hinkle. And the knowledge gave Jim his first throb of happiness for many weeks. He was in time! His money was well lost.

"I've bad news for you, little girl," he said gently. "The market has taken an ugly turn. Our 'Aladdin fortune' is gone."

"Gone!" she shrilled.

"We're back where we were," he continued, "—minus our savings. I'm sorry, dear. Try to be brave! I—"

He got no farther. Her soft arms were flung around his neck. Her cool face was pressed to his hot cheek.

"Oh, my poor, *poor* boy!" she wailed. "And it means so much to you! So *much* to you! And the savings you worked so long to lay by! Please, *please* try not to be too unhappy about it. I'll help, all I can. Honestly, I will. And we'll stand it, together. That will make it ever so much easier than if you had to face it all by yourself. Oh, my darling, I wish I could do something to make it easier for you!"

Hot tears, for which he felt no shame, came unbidden into Jim's eyes, there in the darkness. He was happier than ever he had been. His wife was not lost to him. The real Molly—not the frivolous girl whose head had been turned by a handful of bank-notes—was loyal and loving and self-forgetting. Her first thought—her only thought—was for him and to ease the blow that had fallen upon him.

He felt an absurd yearning to kneel down and kiss the hem of her skirt. But he steadied his voice and said:

"I want you to do something for me, dear. I want you to go out, this evening, just the same. I—"

"No!" she refused fiercely. "No! No! What do you think I am, to leave you like this, when—"

"To please me," he urged. "I mean it. I want you to go, Molly. I'll explain afterward. It's necessary. I can't tell you why till afterward. But it is. You must go. And I want you to tell your friends of our bad luck. It's only fair they should know."

Despite her tearful pleadings, he remained firm. So, heavy-hearted and wondering, she at last consented. She would have consented to anything, just then, to please him.

Jim prepared for six or seven hours of loneliness. But before ten o'clock Molly came back. Her eyes were very bright; her face was very pale. She was not inclined to talk. A single furtive glance at her told Jim the story. But he wanted it in words. So he asked, in excellent surprise:

"What in blazes brings you back at this hour? The theater isn't out yet. And you said you were going to a cabaret afterward. Didn't—"

"I didn't want to stay," she said briefly. "I couldn't stay, after—"

"Did you tell them we are broke?"

"Yes—after the first act, I told them all about it. That's why I couldn't stay longer."

"Because you were ashamed of my losing our money?"

"No," she sobbed, all at once breaking down, "—because I was ashamed of them—and of myself for having been fooled by them as I'd been. Oh, Jim, I don't want to talk about it, yet! I never knew there were such people! You couldn't believe—"

"Perhaps I could," he interposed, drawing her to him. "Perhaps that's why I wanted you to go there, to-night."

"Jim!"

"I think we're both cured now, little sweetheart," he told her. "And I've a scrap of good news for you. Mr. Watts has given me a vacation. It began to-day. We're going to run away somewhere, you and I, for a honeymoon. By the time we get back, we'll be all adjusted to our dear old-time life here."

TWO weeks later they came home—tanned, clear-eyed, gloriously rested, from their country sojourn. A little sheaf of mail was waiting for them. Most of it was in the form of circulars and bills. But one envelope, forwarded from the office, bore the imprint of Jim's broker.

Hunter idly tore open the envelope—half-smiling as he forecasted the politely sympathetic notice that his account was wiped out. But his faintly amused expression melted into blank wonder as he read Vale's informal scrawl:

> Dear Hunter:
> I don't know how in Sam Hill you ever got the hunch, two days ahead of time, that the Standard Munitions plant was going to be blown sky-high and that Standard Munition stock was going to be blown just as far in the other direction. I've been trying for a week to get hold of you. And when S. M. hit the 60 mark and seemed inclined to start on the upward crawl again, I acted on my own responsibility and sold you out. It's lucky I did. For she's up to 62½ to-day. I enclose our account.

You'll see by it that I hold, to your order, $79,894.50 of yours.

"And one week from to-day," yelled Jim deliriously, "twenty-seven savings banks are going to hold it. I'm cured of Wall Street, all right. But money's a grand thing to have—after people have learned how not to use it. Come on, sweetheart, let's celebrate—at the very best movie we can find!"

The Cheat

MARK RIKER had been everything from a Texas Ranger to a Cripple Creek faro-lookout, up to the time he took over the fickle Molly Mercer copper mine in payment of a bad debt. Three years later he was worth two hundred and sixty-three thousand dollars.

He found a strong and permanent seven-per-cent investment for his money, and then went to Chicago to live—he and his wife. The wife was a Chicago girl who had taught district school for two terms near Cripple Creek, before Mark Riker—then working for the local Bottom Dollar temple of chance—married her.

Little Mrs. Riker had shared poverty and all sorts of frontier vicissitudes with her husband, and she had thriven on unadulterated hard luck. But, even as some species of African rock-mountain cattle sicken and die if they are driven to the rich grass of the lowland pastures, Mary Riker did not seem able to stand the placid ease of her new life.

Perhaps that was why she grew weak and languid and fleshless within six months after her pretty Michigan Boulevard home was furnished and ready for occupancy. Or perhaps no woman can stand more than a certain amount of privation; and she had had her full life-quota of it out there among the plains and hills in the days when food was scarce and danger was not. In any case, her thread of life raveled more and more, day by day.

Very gently, very steadily, very uncomplainingly, she drifted toward the Open Sea. Then one evening her husband started up guiltily from a doze of exhaustion in his chair beside her bed to find that, though her wasted hand still clasped his in that timidly trustful pressure he loved, she had drifted forever beyond his call.

THROUGH the hell of his first anguish, one thing and one alone remorselessly knouted him back from trying to follow by force the trail of the woman who had been his whole little world. This sole obstacle to the suicide-idea which so starkly lured him was his twelve-year-old daughter Gracia.

She was a spindling child with a snub nose and freckles and fiery red hair. She had a temper that sometimes made her pigtailed tresses seem pallid in contrast.

Gracia Riker at twelve was as unpromising a brat, both in looks and disposition, as a day's search through Chicago could have unearthed. If she inherited any of her mother's patient sweetness or any of her father's gentle strength, assuredly neither trait had yet peeped into sight above her bristling hedge of faults.

Yet Mark clung to her with pathetic tenderness. She was all of Mary that remained to him. And because the child needed him, he took up again for her sake the sickening burden of life—took it up calmly, without whimper—as, in earlier years, he had at various times taken a faro-table knife-thrust; as he had once taken a death-sentence for a man killed by him in self-defense; as he had taken the news that his herd of beef cattle, which represented the savings of ten years, had been rustled across into Mexico.

He hunted up Mary's aunt, a decayed and recently impoverished gentlewoman of fairly good family and tolerable social connections. He persuaded her, by means of a heavy salary, to make her home in the Michigan Avenue house, there to bully him and misapply the household expense-fund and, incidentally, to bring up Gracia.

It was a wise move, for the old lady had really excellent ideas as to the upbringing of children.

And at the age when hair goes up and skirts go down, the motherless girl was the object of one of Nature's most uncanny and most blessed miracles: she bourgeoned into a startlingly beautiful woman.

When Gracia was twenty, her great-aunt died. And the girl then became her father's housekeeper and close companion.

Mark Riker was more nearly happy than ever he had dreamed he could be again. He was idiotically proud of his lovely daughter, and he lavished on her all that was left of his smashed heart, centering about her his entire interest in life. And Gracia loved him—loved him dearly. Oddly enough, too, they had a thousand interests in common; that all of these thousand interests were Gracia's, and not Mark's, did not lessen the bond.

Mark did not expect enough from happiness to fool himself with the hope that it could continue to be his. He knew well that a girl of Gracia's beauty and queer, elusive charm would not be allowed overlong to remain single. Dozens of youths were forever calling on her; and Mark tried to teach himself to look forward with a certain pitiful cheerfulness to the day when he should have to face loneliness once more. For he was too wise to plan the hideous farce of living on as supercargo in a married daughter's home.

Self-sacrifice was perhaps not a monopoly with Riker, but it had long ago become a fixed habit. With no complaint, spoken or mental, he awaited the day that should give him second place in his daughter's heart and life.

When Phil Garrett began to call three times a week instead of once a month, and when Gracia took to scolding the youth for extravagance if he brought her flowers or candy in wholesale quantities, Mark saw the inevitable day was at hand.

And he wondered that its prospect brought him so little foreboding.

Phil Garrett was the son of Mark's one intimate friend, a chum of the old rough-and-tumble days who, like Riker himself, had struck moderate wealth out in the Rockies and had followed his comrade to Chicago.

The families had been near neighbors in the word's true sense for a decade or more. Phil and Gracia had grown up together. Mark knew the boy's every shade of character, and he would have been well content to have so clean and strong a son of his very own. So, looking on the eventlessly pretty love-affair from afar, he was glad—quietly, whole-souledly glad.

THE one bit of acting in all Mark Riker's career—a poor but conscientious bit of acting at that—was the dramatic amazement wherewith he hailed Gracia's rapturous confession that she and Phil were engaged.

Three months later Mark was punished right sharply for this one deception by learning from Gracia that she had broken her engagement.

He was aware of a thrill of disloyal joy that his little girl was to remain his little girl awhile longer. But the thrill was quickly submerged under the knowledge that Phil must be horribly unhappy, and that Gracia herself was wrapped in a sort of melancholy daze.

"No," she told Mark wearily, "we didn't quarrel. We didn't quarrel at all. We've never quarreled, even when we were little. I just found out lately that I had been all wrong when I thought I loved him well enough to spend my whole life with him. I know it's a horrible way to treat him, but it would be a great deal horribler to marry him when I don't care enough for him, any more."

That was all she would say. Mark did not ask questions. Yet he saw that while she was unhappy, she appeared more perplexed than miserable. It was as though she were passing through a land—or phase—new to her, altogether at variance with anything she had known or been taught to expect. So Mark finally sought out Phil Garrett to offer awkward and almost mute sympathy, and to glean, if he might, some real information. Phil was not at all reticent to this man he had known and revered from babyhood.

"She's not to blame, sir," he said at once. "It isn't her fault. All girls of her age are easy to dazzle. I felt, from the time he started in, that I hadn't a show against him. It's the same old story of the amateur having no chance against the profes-sional."

"What—what are you driving at, son?" asked Mark Riker, to whom most of the young man's blurted explanation was pure Doric Greek. "I don't get you. Who's 'he'?"

"Didn't she say?" exclaimed Phil in genuine surprise.

Mark shook his head, bewildered.

"I didn't ask her," he said. "Is it some one else who's courtin' her, or—?"

"She didn't make any secret of it to me," replied Phil, "and I don't see why I should to you. If she hasn't told you, she will, of course. But I supposed you'd have noticed before now, for Dorrance is there nearly every day, and it's funny you haven't—"

"Dorrance? Who's Dorrance?"

"You must have met him often enough at your own home. I—"

"Maybe I did. Gracia's always havin' me into the settin'-room to meet her fellows. But they all look alike to me. I never notice much about 'em. I steer clear when I can. Who's Dorrance?"

"He's the son of Hamilton Dorrance of the Twelfth National," said Garrett. "I'm sure you must have—"

"Son of old Ham Dorrance, hey? Then he must be a younger brother of the Cuyler Dorrance there was all that fuss about in the papers last year—the sweet-scented cuss who gave the monkey dinner that ended up in a police court, the fellow whose wife divorced him because he—"

"No," said Garrett, uncomfortably, "Cuyler Dorrance hasn't any brothers… But the newspaper reports probably made things out a good deal worse than they were."

"Well, the divorce-court records didn't," drawled Mark. "An' the papers printed the records pretty near straight, I guess, as much of 'em as *could* be printed. But if Cuyler Dorrance ain't got any brothers, then how—? Phil," he broke off, with as near an approach to excitement as any living soul had ever seen him show, "—Phil Garrett, you don't mean it's *that* Dorrance who's been comin' to my house? Speak up."

"I supposed you knew," stammered Phil.

"S'posed I knew, hey? S'posed I'd 'a' stood by an' let my little girl—? Phil, why in hell did you let him come round? Why didn't you tell her? Why didn't you tell *me?*"

"I thought you knew," repeated Garrett miserably. "And as for telling her—why, Mr. Riker, a man can't do that. He can't knock another fellow who's interested in the same girl as himself. At least, a white man can't. All I could do was to try to hold my own with her against him. I had about as much chance, after he settled down to work," Phil went on, still more bitterly, "as a featherweight drug-clerk would have against Jess Willard. Love-making's been an exact science with Dorrance since the days when I was a kid in rompers. It isn't a science with me. I never cared for any other girl but Gracia, and I don't know the moves a man must make to keep from being cut out."

"And Gracia was ninny enough to—?"

"It's not her fault!" declared Phil. "I told you that before, sir. He's good looking; he's clever; he's got plenty of money; he's got a way with women. They say no woman he really wants can resist him. And Gracia's so young, sir, and—and I'm a dub. I don't blame her. I didn't cut much of a figure alongside of him. She did her best, her very level best. I could see how hard she fought to keep on caring for me and not to get interested in him. She—she was fine about it. It wasn't till she found she couldn't help liking him better—"

"I see," mused Mark, "I see. An' I see now why she shied at tellin' me 'bout Dorrance. She knows plenty well what I think of men whose wives divorce 'em on the grounds that got Mrs. Dorrance her divorce. She's probably waitin' till she gets reg'larly engaged to him before she springs it on me. She'd rather we'd have a quick, hot scrap about it than a long battle. Yet," he sighed, helplessly, "if she's made up her mind to marry him, she'll do it whether I say yes or no. That's Gracia's style. Lord!"

"Perhaps," suggested Phil, with a wretched attempt at optimism, "—perhaps he'll make her happier than I could. She loves him, you see; and many a man's been put on his feet by a woman's love. A reformed rake, they say, makes the best husband—"

"Not for *my* daughter he don't," gravely corrected Mark; "nor yet any other kind of a rake don't. I—I s'pose," he added, apologetically, his leathery face coloring, "—I s'pose it's dead certain he *is* aimin' to marry her."

"If I thought he wasn't," growled Phil in sudden fury, "—if I thought for one second that he wasn't, I'd—"

"No, you wouldn't, son," drawled Mark, rising to go. "That's *my* job."

FROM Phil Garrett's home, Mark slouched across-town to a private detective bureau run by a former Cripple Creek marshal who was under heavy old-time obligations to him.

In two days he called again on his friend the detective and was handed a typewritten report several pages long.

"There's all we've been able to dig up so far," explained the detective. "Most of it's old stuff we got out of the records and the newspaper files, mostly from the files. If there had been anything very libelous in it, there would have been record of a damage suit; and there isn't. You'll see that about all the up-to-date information, since his divorce, is that an actress is making common-law claims on him, and that he's supposed to be engaged to a New York widow who has nearly four million dollars in her own right. The cash will come in handy. He's blown most of the fortune his father left him."

"Can you verify that thing about the rich widow?" asked Mark with no great show of interest in his perpetual drawl. "If you can, I'd like you to, in a rush. I'll pay for extra speed. If your bureau's got an agent in New York, wire him to whirl in on it and to report by tel'graph. Let me know as soon as you hear, won't you? It's kind of important."

ONE evening three days later Mark Riker let himself into his own house at about ten o'clock, and walked slowly down the hall to the little library at the rear where his daughter usually entertained the more intimate of her callers.

Gracia heard him coming and advanced to the library door to meet him. He stooped as usual to kiss her; then, instead of passing to his own room, he followed her back into the library. She glanced at him in some astonishment and in no great pleasure, as he slouched uninvited into the room. It was not his habit.

But Mark did not notice her look. His washed-out light-blue eyes were staring past her.

Near the fireplace, in front of a chair from which he had just risen, stood a well-dressed man. He was perhaps thirty-eight years old, heavy of build and something above middle height. In a certain way, he was decidedly good looking, though a physiognomist would have looked twice—as now did Mark Riker—at the dark skin under the eyes and at certain lines around the full-lipped mouth.

"Dad," said Gracia, none too much at ease, "you remember Mr. Dorrance?"

"Yes," said Mark awkwardly, in his embarrassment failing to see the shapely hand the guest extended toward him or to listen to his word of pleasant greeting. "Yes, I remember him. I've read quite a lot in the papers about him, one time and another. Pleased to meet you, Mr. Dorrance. Sit down. I thought I'd drop in for a little chat. I'll smoke, I guess. Gracia don't mind."

AFTER this speech —quite the longest his daughter had ever heard him make to any caller of hers— Mark carefully drew a cigar from the worn leather case he carried in his side pocket, and proceeded with great deliberation to light it; then he dropped the case back into his pocket.

"Perhaps Mr. Dorrance will have a cigar, Dad," suggested Gracia.

But Mark did not hear. He was singularly absent-minded to-night. Dropping clum-

sily into an easy rocking chair, he leaned back thoughtfully.

"You've been comin' here to see Gracia quite a spell, now, haven't you, Mr. Dorrance?" he asked conversationally, adding, before the visitor could reply: "I'm sorry I didn't have the good manners to get acquainted sooner. But maybe you'll let me make up for lost time by visitin' a bit with you and my daughter here this evenin'."

He blew a second smoke-cloud and beamed from Gracia to Dorrance. Both had seated themselves. Gracia's momentary displeasure at the interruption was gone. With not the slightest feeling of shame at her father's uncouthness, she was glad that he should show so much interest in this particular guest of hers.

"Yes," pursued Mark hospitably, "let's get acquainted, you an' me, Mr. Dorrance. I know some few things about you, from the newspapers, but—"

"I hope, Mr. Riker, you won't let the yellow journals be my judge with you," said Dorrance in kindly patronage.

"But," continued Mark, so unresponsively that Dorrance began to wonder if his host was deaf, "—but I guess you haven't heard as much about *me*. You see, I ain't what you'd call a celebrity. I'm just an ex-flannel-shirter. Why,"—in garrulous reminiscence,—"once I wasn't even as big a toad in the puddle as I am now. I used to help run a faro-layout in Cripple Creek in the boom days."

"Really?" ejaculated Dorrance, trying to pump up a show of courteous interest. "That must have been—"

"It was. Mighty interestin'. Yes, I helped run a faro game. I ain't ashamed of it. It was a square game—as square a game as any in camp. Cheatin' was always the one thing I couldn't an' wouldn't stand for, then or now."

Dorrance suppressed a yawn, vexedly wondering how long this windy old vulgarian would continue to interrupt his *tête-à-tête* with Gracia.

"Never could stand for cheatin' or for a cheat," rambled on Mark. "I remember, once, out there at the Creek, a feller tried to palm a phony double-eagle on our game to pay for his chips."

"Did he succeed?" asked Dorrance in acute boredom, as Mark paused.

"Succeed?" echoed Riker. "Not him. I told him he was a cheat, an' I told him our game didn't want him. Then he called me a liar an' he pulled a gun on me."

Mark paused again. His evil-smelling cigar had gone out. He groped in his vest for a match, found one, struck it on the broad sole of his boot and relighted the cigar.

"And what did you do?" asked Dorrance, with weary politeness.

"Who? Me?" queried Mark, as if puzzled at so needless a question. "Why, I'm still on deck, ain't I? I drilled him, of course—drilled him clean."

"Drilled?" repeated Dorrance.

"Dad means he had to shoot him, in self-defense, you know," Gracia interposed, not a little nervous as to Dorrance's reception of such a tale, but still pleased that her father should have taken so unwonted an interest in her guest. "You see, he had no choice. The man had drawn a gun against him. He had to—"

"No, girl," gently contradicted Mark, "I didn't have to. I could 'a' shot the gun outer his hand, or I could 'a' chipped the point of his elbow to put him out of business. I'd done that before. I used to be able to plant my shots pretty much where I liked. I still can, I guess, for all I'm fifty-three next week. But this feller was a cheat. He had it comin' to him. So I drilled him, through the lung. If he hadn't 'a' pulled through after a couple of months in bed, it's likely I'd 'a' had a lawsuit on my hands for downin' him. You see, the law was beginnin' to find its way around at the Creek even then."

Dorrance made no comment. He looked in new interest at the odd little man, as at some strange specimen. Gracia wondered at Riker's unheard-of garrulity. Already, this evening, he had wasted what was to him an ordinary month's supply of talk.

"So I was lucky," rambled on Mark, "—lucky that he didn't cash in like that tin-horn down to Andalusia did. I was new to Andalusia at the time. The mayor of the town was Baldy Arden. He ran the only gambling-joint in town, and he ran it so crooked it could 'a' hid behind a corkscrew. Why, a cow-man blew in there one day an' lost all his dough. As he was comin' out, dead broke, I says to him, 'That joint's crooked.' 'I knew it was,' says he, grinnin' sheepish-like, 'but I had to play there 'cause it's the only gamblin'-house in town.' Baldy Arden heard I'd called his place crooked; so he came gunnin' for me. An'—like the cheat at Cripple Creek, I told you about—I downed him. Not because he was after me, but because he was a cheat. An' he never happened to cheat again."

"It reformed him, eh?" suggested Dorrance. "It taught him a lesson?"

"It reformed him," said Mark solemnly, "the only way a cheat can ever be reformed—by killin' him."

"Dad!" exclaimed Gracia, to whom the story was new.

Horrified, she glanced covertly at Dorrance to study the effect of the story on him. Dorrance missed the look. His big, luminous eyes that women found so hypnotic were fixed in questioning scrutiny on Mark. He was disposed, offhand, to regard the older man as a braggart liar. But there was something in the lined face and the steady drawling voice that spoke neither of falsehood nor of braggadocio. A terrible sincerity seemed to pulse through Riker's quaint words.

"That was the time," added Mark, "that they sentenced me to swing—Baldy bein' the big man of the town, an' me a rank outsider. But it was worth it for the priv'lege of sendin' a cheat where he belonged. Some of the boys caved in one side of the 'dobe calaboose just before sunrise an' turned me loose."

Again the smelly cigar had gone out. Again he slowly and laboriously lighted it.

"Those must have been stirring times in the West," commented Dorrance. "I almost envy you your experiences there."

"You needn't," Mark gravely assured him. "You needn't envy me, 'cause the same experiences are on foot right here in Chicago this very day, just as much as

ever they was in the West. Cheats are cheats, the same here as out there. An',"—
with a glint of cold steel in the softly drawling voice—"they're due for exac'ly
the same line of punishment if any of 'em tries to double-cross me—or mine."

"Luckily, the gambling-houses are pretty well closed during this administration,"
laughed Dorrance. "All except the few that—"

"Yes," chimed in Gracia lightly, trying to mask her repulsion at what she had just
heard and to gloss over her father's admissions. "Isn't it lucky, though? Otherwise,
dear old Dad might feel it his duty to draw that huge six-shooter he always insists
on carrying for old times' sake, and wander forth to cleanse Chicago of dishonest
gamblers."

"There ain't much danger," drawled Mark, "—not much danger of my meetin'
up with any p'fessional gamblers nowadays. I don't care for such folks, and I
never go where they're li'ble to be found. If I did, though, I bet I could spot
the first crooked move of their cards. I've had enough experience as lookout to
get onto all the phony card deals there is. I know 'em all. I can work 'em all, just
from seein' 'em so often. When Gracia was gettin' over that appendix-operation
of hers, I used to amuse her, by teachin' her such tricks. Some day you must get
Gracia to show you what she can do with the cards, Mr. Dorrance. She's even
better at it than I am, when it comes to makin' the pasteboards do queer stunts.
Only, I don't need to tell you neither of us would soil our hands by usin' the
things we know, in any reg'lar game."

"And you really go armed?" asked Dorrance, harking back to what Gracia had
said, "—even here in Chicago?"

For answer Mark raised one of the bottom flaps of his loose black vest,
revealing the scarred butt of a service revolver that showed above the waistband
of his trousers.

"Just for old times' sake," he said deprecatingly.

"But—"

"Speakin' of cheats," Riker meandered on, aimlessly, "it's just like I was tellin'
you. There's as many here as there was there. Only here they mostly cheat for
worse things than card-money. An' they deserve a heap less mercy. F'r instance,
here's a case I heard about not so long ago."

He flipped his cigar-butt into the grate fire, cleared his dry voice and proceeded:

"There's a young lady livin' here in Chicago. She was keepin' steady company
with a feller she'd known since they was kids. She loved him. He just worshiped
the floor her cunnin' little foot trod on. He was a good white feller, too. Didn't
have none of the bag o' tricks that a man has who's makin' a business of gettin'
women to fall in love with him. They was terrible happy, those two; an' everything
was framed for a happy life together all the way to the finish. Just then along
comes a chap that I'm flatterin' a whole lot when I call him a skunk. He thought
it would be kind of amusin' to get this pretty little girl stuck on him. An' he starts
in to do it. It was a cinch—thanks to his experience an' the way he had with

women. He stole the girl from the feller who loved her, an' he cheated that feller out of the love he had won fair an' square. That's what *I* call a pretty filthy sort of cheat—don't you, Mr. Dorrance?"

"Oh," said Dorrance, uneasily, "all's fair in love and war, they say. And—"

"An' they lie when they say it," interrupted Mark sternly. "That's a maxim for blacklegs, not for white men. Now, if that kind of cheat was to come my way—f'r instance, if I happened to be the father, say, of the young lady who—"

"Dad!" broke in Gracia again in sudden terror, as Mark very deliberately got to his feet and walked up to Dorrance.

Her father's face had not changed from its wonted slack gentleness, except that something lurid seemed to smolder far behind the tired, washed-out eyes. Dorrance saw the smolder, and involuntarily his own gaze darted to the protuberance under Mark's right vest-flap.

"Mr. Dorrance," said Mark quietly, "you stole my girl from the man she was going to marry—stole her as crooked as a bum steals money from a blind man's cup. You're the rottenest breed of cheat I've met up with yet. And I've met up with a whole passel of 'em, soon or late."

"Dad!" cried Gracia, aghast. "How can you—how *dare* you—say such things? Cuyler,"—turning to Dorrance, —"I'm so sorry! So *sorry!* I—"

"Please don't be distressed on my account," said Dorrance tenderly. "I will say good night to you now, if I may. I don't want to cause a scene that will make you unhappy. So I'd rather overlook the whole thing, because he is your father—because—"

"Because I carry a forty-five gun in my waistband," supplemented Mark with no emotion whatever, "an' because you know if I shot you dead, here an' now, I could tell a story that would make any jury in Cook County acquit me without so much as leavin' the box; because I hold your life just where I want it; an' because if you stir six inches without my leave, you're as good as dead."

"*Oh!*" gasped the girl, half choked with dismay. Then, recovering herself, she flared:

"You are drunk! Or else you have gone stark crazy. Whichever it is, you have insulted me *vilely*, by insulting my guest. I'll never forgive you. I want you to leave this room. Do you hear me?"

"Gracia," said Mark softly, turning his smoldering eyes full on hers with a look no woman had ever before seen in them, a look that made the brave girl, of a sudden, sick with nameless terror, "Gracia, be quiet. An' sit down."

Marveling at her own undreamed-of cowardice, she dazedly obeyed.

"Mr. Dorrance," went on the drawling voice, "you are just where I want you. Your life, accordin' to my ol'-fashioned idees, b'longs more or less to me. Well, I'm goin' to dispose of it for you."

Dorrance's career for two decades had not been of the kind to strengthen his nerve for dire emergencies.

"I warn you," he blustered, a crack in his deep, musical voice, his eyes ever straying in helpless fascination toward the bulge made by the pistol-butt, "—I warn you that any violence toward me will cost you dearly. My family is influential in Chicago, and—"

"I know it is," politely agreed Mark. "Your family's all right, except, like a potato plant, the best part of it is underground. Still, it's a good fam'ly as fam'lies go. That's why I'm thinkin' of lettin' my girl join it."

"You mean," stuttered Dorrance, whitening a little, "—you mean that you—?"

"I mean this: Out in my own neck of the woods, I'd 'a' done one of two things to a swine like you, Mr. Cuyler Dorrance: either I'd 'a' plugged you at sight or else I'd 'a' made you fight me. Well, that last is what I'm goin' to do now."

"Dad!" cried Gracia.

And in the same breath Dorrance essayed to regain a fragment of his self-possession by saying scoffingly:

"This is Chicago, not a mining-camp. Decent men don't fight pistol duels here."

"Who said anything about pistol duels?" retorted Mark. "Mr. Dorrance, you an' I are goin' to fight in a diff'rent way—a way that won't make me dirty my hands with a cur's blood. Here's my proposition: If I win this fight, you're to git out o' Chicago by the first train to-morrow mornin'. Where you go to, I don't care. If all I've heard is true, you'll likely head for New York. But—I'm goin' to pay out good money to have you follered an' watched. An' if ever you set foot within five hundred miles of Chicago again, I'll shoot you. An' when I tell why, no jury'll punish me; an' you know they won't. That's what happens to you if *I* win this fight of ours."

Mark's right hand, from old custom, rested lightly above the pistol-butt as he resumed:

"If *you* win the fight, you're to marry Gracia. An' you're to treat her right— under the same penalty. There are my terms, Mr. Dorrance. They aren't yours to take or leave as you choose. They're yours to accept whether you want to or not. If I win, you leave Chicago for good. If you win, you marry Gracia. Is that clear?"

Dorrance's gaze was shifting like a cornered rat's. He tried to speak, but his lips were kiln-dry.

Mark put his left hand behind him, his half-shut eyes never leaving Dorrance's face, and took something from a little table that stood near the fire-place.

"Here are the weapons we're goin' to fight with," he announced, tossing on the table a morocco case that held a pack of cards.

"I—I don't understand," mumbled Dorrance.

"Gracia and I play euchre in here, sometimes, of a rainy afternoon," replied Mark. "The deck's a square one. Examine it for yourself if you like. Gracia, get up an' take these cards. Mr. Dorrance, draw up that chair and sit across the table from me. So! Gracia, deal us each a poker hand. Prefer a cold hand or a draw, Mr. Dorrance?"

Dorrance did not answer. He was staring at the cards in Gracia's shaking hand.

"No choice, hey?" went on Mark. "We'll make it a draw, Gracia. Gives us more run for our money. *The stakes are understood, ain't they?* If I win, you git out an' you stay out. If you win, you marry Gracia. All ready, dealer."

He pulled out the shiny old cigar-case and peered into it for another cigar. Had his eyes not left Dorrance and his daughter, he could scarce have failed to notice the sudden change that had come over each.

Without so much as a mutual glance, they both seemed possessed by the same exhilarating thought. Dorrance's lost self-possession returned to him as by magic. Gracia's hand no longer shook as she held the cards. Her eyes were glowing, and a faint flush throbbed across her pale face. With dextrous motions she ran the cards lightly through her fingers as she riffled the deck.

"It is agreed," said Dorrance, his voice once more resonant and musical, "that in case I lose, I will leave town and not come back. If I win, I am to be permitted to marry Gracia. I suppose I can trust you to keep your word, sir?"

"You sure can," Mark assented cheerfully; "an' I can trust myself to see that you keep your share of either bargain. Deal 'em out, daughter."

Again he busied himself with the slow process of finding a match and lighting his new cigar. While his eyes were upon the engrossing task, Gracia dealt. Her white fingers manipulated the cards with unbelievable speed. By the time the cigar was at last alight, five cards lay on the table before each of the two men.

Mark gathered up his, looked them over, puckered his thin lips thoughtfully and said:

"Three, here."

He discarded three of his cards and took the trio Gracia dealt in their place. She glanced inquiringly at Dorrance. His handsome face set in a perfect poker mask, the man answered the look by saying:

"One card, please. And—oh, wish me luck, Gracia!"

"Aimin' to jack up a flush or a straight?" queried Mark, jocularly, as his opponent threw a pasteboard into the discard, and took up the card Gracia dealt him. "Or holdin' up a maverick for a kicker?"

Then, leisurely, the speaker read his own hand.

"If you've anything better'n a measly pair of treys, you win!" sighed Mark, laying down his cards, face up. "I didn't better myself none on the draw. This sure isn't my lucky night. I remember once at Leadville, I—"

"It is the unluckiest night of all *my* life," interrupted Dorrance, his rich voice quivering with suppressed grief. "I haven't even a pair."

He flung his cards face downward on the table and rose to his feet. His face infinitely mournful and hopeless, he looked down at Mark's sprawling figure, across the table from him.

"I suppose, sir," he said hesitatingly and yet with a world of appeal, "I suppose there is no chance that you will relent?"

"You lose!" answered Mark tersely. "Git!"

Cuyler Dorrance turned toward Gracia, his dark eyes anguished and brimming. The girl was standing, statue-still, staring straight ahead of her. Her face was dead white; her hands were clasped tight together above her breast.

"Good-by—oh, *good-by!*" murmured Dorrance, a sob in his beautiful voice.

He wheeled and strode from the room. Presently the front door closed behind him.

Then for the first time Mark Riker spoke. Looking quizzically up at Gracia, who still stood moveless and ghastly as though petrified with horror, he asked:

"What did you deal him, little girl?"

And, speaking against her will, she made halting answer:

"F-four aces."

"I figured it'd be suthin' like that," he commented, nodding approval. "An' I knew I could count on his losin'. A cheat'll pretty near always run true to form."

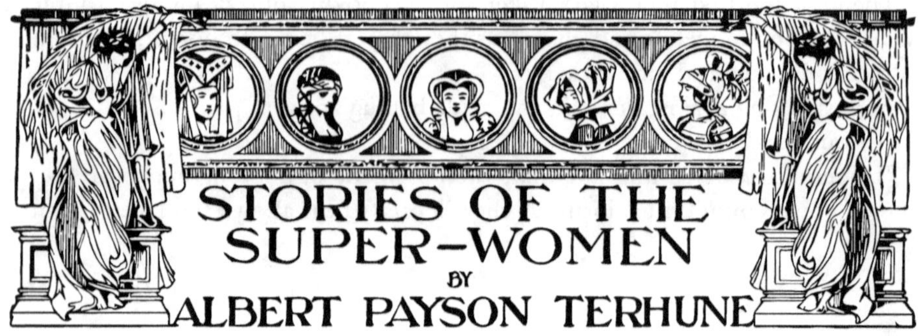

Eugénie, Empress Of The French

AGAIN and again, during the past twenty years, a bent old woman in deep mourning has driven through the streets of Paris, stopping her hired carriage now and then, as she looked sadly out at some landmark or descended to enter a shop.

Other folk in other carriages gave her not a glance. The people in the street scarce noticed the slender, increasingly feeble figure that moved so slowly across the pavement from curb to shop door. She was, to them, merely a white-haired grandam whose old-ivory coloring and dainty features hinted at earlier beauty.

She was really nothing of the sort. She was a ghost.

She was the ghost of empire, of supreme feminine power, of a fame and a charm that had swayed half the world. No disembodied spirit, returning to its earthly haunts, would find itself more forgotten, more invisible, amid the scenes of its former glories than did she.

The busy Parisians did not see her as she moved among them. Yet, a few years earlier, these same busy Parisians had clamored for the privilege of rending her limb from limb. And a few years earlier than that, they had sprained their throats cheering her and their bank accounts in heaping gifts on her. They had been swept off their feet by her super-woman loveliness. Their wives had slavishly acclaimed her the whole world's arbiter of fashion.

The fragile old lady in black was Eugénia Maria Ignace Augustina de Montijo Bonaparte, once Empress of the French.

Incidentally, she is the only one of my super-women who is still living, in 1916. Perhaps this may make her story more real, more vivid, though her career was exciting enough without such help. She is credited, among other things, with having originated crinoline and the Franco-Prussian War—two noteworthy monuments to the memory of any one mortal woman. Also—at the risk of turning away any information-loving reader at the very outset—she is almost the only super-woman against whom no scandal was ever proven.

She was born at Granada, Spain, May 5, 1826. Her grandfather, William Kirkpatrick, was a Scotch wine merchant, who did much of his business in New York, and whose beautiful eldest daughter, Maria, married a yellow-faced, one-eyed, crippled veteran of the Napoleonic wars—Don Cipriano Guzmán de Palafot y-Porto Carrero, Count de Teba, and son of the Count de Montijo, grandee of Spain.

When Maria Kirkpatrick married Don Cipriano Guzmán de Palafot y-Porto Carrero, the King of Spain would not let her be presented at his court until proofs of her nobility of ancestry could be shown. Whereat, Maria produced a family tree that included in its branches such choice blossoms as King Robert Bruce, of Scotland, and Fin M'Cual, the ancient Fenian chieftain. The Spanish king wept with laughter over the parchment of pedigree, and allowed the much-descended Maria to be presented.

This was in 1819. Seven years later—on the fifth anniversary of Napoleon Bonaparte's death—Maria's daughter, Eugénia—but let's call her by her French name, "Eugénie"—was born. She was born during an earthquake that was thickly sprinkled with thunderstorms. It was beastly weather to be born in.

They named her Eugénia Maria Ignace Augustina. At that, she was still a lap or two behind her crippled father in the matter of names.

Eugénie's mother belonged to the tribe of home haters. She spent most of her time at court. So the girl's chief companion was her saffron-faced, one-eyed father, Don Cipriano Guzmán, etc., Count of Teba. The count used to tell her of his campaigns under the great Napoleon, of the emperor's unbelievable prowess and glory, until the half-grown girl's brain was a riot of empire and of Napoleonism.

Teba succeeded to the title of "Count de Montijo." Soon afterward a civil war in Spain scattered the family. Old Kirkpatrick sailed for America, where he made a new fortune in lead mines. The count stuck to his post of duty at Madrid, where presently he died. The countess and her two daughters, Eugénie and Francesca, fled to Paris to live.

At the French capital, Maria engaged in a lively flirtation with Prosper Mérimee, the novelist. And she gave him the plot of a story that she herself had once intended to write. The story made Mérimee immortal. It was "Carmen."

Mérimee superintended Eugénie's education; a task that was cut short when her father's death sent the widow and daughters hurrying back to Spain.

Eugénie was growing to young womanhood, and in Madrid she began to win and to wreck men's hearts. Here is a description of her:

"Unlike Francesca, who was as dark as any of her father's people, Eugénie was dazzlingly fair, with hair of burnished red-gold—a throwback to her Scotch ancestors—with magnificent violet eyes, divinely molded shoulders, tiny feet and hands, and a tall and pliant figure. Her voice was sweet to hear and her manner was of a regal and radiant graciousness."

Such a girl, despite her lack of fortune and the drawback of an over-gay mother, was bound to be the center of whatever society she sought. And, for some years, Eugénie was the belle of the Spanish capital. Among her suitors was the Duke of Alba, who, failing to win her, married her brunet sister.

Eugénie, for some reason best known to herself, refused offers that would have seemed glittering life goals to most girls in her station. She refused, quite as coolly and far more decidedly, several tempting morganatic alliances with royalty. She was saving herself for—she alone knew what.

A drastic reform government cleared Spain's court of many persons supposedly dangerous to the morals or the welfare of the state. Marie and Eugénie went to England. Thence, they moved to France. They timed their arrival at Paris very fortunately; so fortunately, indeed, that people afterward declared it was part of Eugénie's campaign.

France was in upheaval—an upheaval that was, in a little while, to carry Eugénie to the summit of her ambition. Be patient with me, please, for just a minute or so, while I dip into history. It is needful to the understanding of this story. And I will be as brief and as unprosy as I can.

Napoleon Bonaparte had won many thousand Frenchmen to his belief that it is better to be an ancestor than a descendant; that King Stork will give his people more action than will King Log; and that a plebeian upstart with brains will make a better ruler than will an aristocratic doodlewit with centuries of kingly forebears at his back.

So Napoleon, acting on that theory, had stood old-fashioned Europe on its head, and had kept it in that humiliating position for twenty years. Then Europe had combined against him and bundled him off to St. Helena, where, on his bleak sea rock, the broken-winged eagle proceeded to eat his heart out, and make life miserable for his professionally faithful attendants, and coin epigrams, and fight against the treacherous inroads of fat upon his waistline, until he died.

His only son was brought up in the Austrian court, as a mollycoddle, and is said to have dribbled away his useless young life at the twinkling feet of Fanny Ellsler, who was a professional dancer and several other things.

That left no direct heir to Napoleon the Great. But there were a swarm of nephews and cousins and so forth. And the next in line was the son of Napoleon's younger brother, Louis, who had married his own stepniece-in-law, Hortense Beauharnais. This son was Prince Louis Bonaparte, the surviving head of the Napoleon dynasty.

He was a crook, a mountebank, a poseur, an inspired liar, an all-around cheap blackguard. He had all his mighty uncle's fierce ambition, dearth of conscience, and genius for trickery, with no more than a shred of his inspired genius. He was the fox that follows the lion.

He yearned to be Emperor of the French, like his uncle. But the majority of Frenchmen had just then had about all the Napoleonism they could hold, and were content to plod along for a while longer under the dull rule of the old line of French kings, who had been restored to power when Napoleon fell. So the public at large paid little heed to Louis' requests that the monarchy be overthrown, and that the Napoleonic empire be restored, with him at its head.

When Louis grew more than usually obstreperous in these requests, the authorities had a habit of banishing him or putting him in jail. Once he sailed to France, calling on the nation to rise to his support. As he landed from the ship, a giant eagle swooped down from the sky and perched on his head.

"It is an omen!" gasped a few trained onlookers.

But it wasn't. The eagle was a tame one that had been taught, during the voyage, to light on Louis' head and eat a scrap of meat fastened there. The nation yawningly refused to rise in its might. And Louis was thrown into prison—whence he duly escaped to England.

Dead broke most of the time, he served as special constable in London, and, crossing to America, taught school in New Jersey. He was waiting his time, patiently watching for the psychological moment when the restless French should tire of their stodgy Bourbon king and want a change of government. That would be his cue for a triumphal entry upon the political stage. He had already mistaken several other lines for his cue, and had dashed prematurely onto the stage, only to be shooed off again. But at last he gauged his entrance correctly.

Louis Philippe, King of France, was deposed in 1848. A republic was proclaimed, and Louis Napoleon was elected "prince president" of France. By the most solemn oath, Louis bound himself to uphold the republic. At the first possible moment, he broke his oath, overthrew the republic, and, amid bloodshed and riot, had himself proclaimed "Napoleon III., Emperor of the French."

So much for historic biography, and back again to the story of Eugénie.

She and her mother found Paris in a hideously tangled social condition. The old-line nobility recoiled in disgust from associating with the upstart emperor. Throngs of mushroom aristocrats, from millionaire plumbers to soldiers of fortune, flocked to his court. Nobody knew exactly who was who.

But everybody knew who and what Madame and Mademoiselle de Montijo were. Paris looked on them as brilliant and beautiful adventuresses; which, indeed, they were. Mother and daughter lived by their wits, ever wriggling upward in a desperate climb toward their goal.

In other days, they would have had no earthly chance of coming within a million miles of the French court, or of meeting the French emperor except clandestinely. But in the new hodgepodge that just then made up French society, they had no great trouble in attaching themselves to the court of Napoleon III.

And, from the very first, Louis found himself desperately and hopelessly enslaved by the glorious Eugénie de Montijo. He made violent love to her, and his courtiers prepared themselves to enjoy the resultant scandal. But no scandal followed.

Eugénie kept her head most admirably. All her life she had been trained for this very crisis. And now that the crisis had come, her equipment was perfect. She did not lose one single trick in the daring game.

The emperor vainly pleaded his love, and offered to bury her pretty body under avalanches of jewels and titles. She replied very definitely that she would not accept his jewels; that her love was worth nothing to him without his hand as well; and that the only title she craved was that of Empress of the French.

"Always magnificently dressed," writes Fitzgerald Molloy, "supreme in her loveliness, and experienced in the arts of fascination, she roused a storm of passion in the heart of an admirer whose susceptibility was illimitable, and who was unwilling to tolerate any hindrance to his desires. But always discreet, conscious of power, practical, notwithstanding a strain of romanticism, mistress of herself because of a preservative coldness of temperament that expressed itself in the hardness of her voice, strong willed and brimming with ambition—she disdained all proposals that refused her the highest position it was in his power to give her. When, selecting for his mission the Comte de Morny, Napoleon sent her a paper bearing his signature, above which she was desired to name her own terms as the reward of her submission, it was returned to him with but one word dashed across its page: 'Marriage.'"

Now, it is one thing for an ambitious new emperor to be in love with one of his own subjects. It is quite another thing for him to make her his wife. No one knew better than Napoleon III. how much his throne needed strengthening, nor how perilously a marriage with Eugénie might weaken it. And he was not enough in love to take this mad chance—yet.

He scoured Europe for a royal wife—some princess whose marriage to him would make firm his position and give him a valuable alliance with a neighboring kingdom. But not one princess in all the world would listen to his suit; not one kingly house failed to deny the proffered honor with unflattering promptness. Napoleon III. was very plainly given to understand that his fellow rulers looked on him as a low-bred demagogue, and that they considered it a gross insult for him to aspire to marry any of their daughters.

And all the time, Eugénie watched and waited, ever tightening the glamour web in which she had enmeshed her victim.

More and more vehemently, the emperor urged his suit for Eugénie's love. And ever she kept him at arm's length, her shrewd old mother coaching her every play from the side lines. As one princess after another refused the emperor's hand, Eugénie made him think less and less of the dangers of marrying a mere courtesy countess like herself. Marriage was her fixed price. She would listen to no compromise rates.

One day, the emperor rode past the Montijo house. Eugénie was standing on a balcony. The emperor threw the reins to his groom and dismounted. He looked about him for the nearest door that would lead to the balcony. Seeing none, he called to her:

"Mademoiselle de Montijo, by what door may I get to you?"

"Only through the door of the church, sire," she made quick answer.

"Well played, mademoiselle! Well played!" applauded a foreign diplomat who was riding with the emperor.

It *was* well played, but not well enough. The emperor still hesitated. And Eugénie tried another angle of attack.

Naturally, women of the court looked on in tigerish rage at the royal game of hide and seek. Especially did the emperor's Bonaparte relatives hate the thought of his marrying this Spanish woman. And they formed a cabal against Eugénie. This made her miserably unhappy—or she said it did, which amounted to the same thing—and she took her troubles to the emperor.

Now perhaps there is a man, somewhere, who has the mingled wit and heroism to mix successfully into a quarrel between two women. But Napoleon III. was not that man. If he had been, he would probably have ruled the universe, and not merely France. So all he could do was to feel helplessly sorry for Eugénie, and helplessly furious at her enemies.

At a Tuileries ball on New Year's Eve, 1852, the climax came. The emperor entered the ballroom and almost collided with Eugénie—who, by the merest chance, had chosen that moment to rush out. Her face was flushed. There were tears in her eyes. The emperor, full of loverly solicitude, asked what was the matter.

"I am going home, sire!" she sobbed. "And I shall never set foot in this palace again! I have been insulted—by *those!*" waving her hand toward a group of women. "Let me pass, please!"

Instead, the emperor caught her hand and led her forcibly back into the ballroom. "After to-morrow," he said, "no one will dare to insult you!"

For once in his crafty life, he had been driven into acting upon an honest impulse. Eugénie's hand still clasped in his pudgy fist, the emperor made the round of the rooms, formally announcing his engagement to her. Three weeks later, he published for the benefit of all France this strange document:

> I accede to the wish so often manifested by the nation, in announcing my marriage to you. The union which I am about to contract is not in harmony with old political traditions, and in this lies its advantage. France, by her successive revolutions, has been widely sundered from the rest of Europe. A wise government should so rule as to bring her back within the circle of the ancient monarchies. But this result will more readily be obtained by a frank and straightforward policy, by a loyal intercourse, than by royal alliances which only create a false security and substitute family for national interests.
>
> She who is become the object of my choice is of lofty birth. French in heart, by education, by the memory of the blood shed by her father in the cause of the emperor, she has, as a Spaniard, the advantage of not having a family in France to whom it will be necessary to give honors and dignities. Gifted with every quality of the heart, she will be an ornament to the throne; as in the hour of danger she would be one of its most courageous defenders.

All the world may not love a lover—but all the world loves a love story. And here was a love story worthy of Laura Jean Libby. The romantic French went wild with delight. The city of Paris was given over to fêtes. Medallions and portraits of Eugénie were sold on every street corner. Eugénie herself was cheered to the echoes whenever she appeared abroad. (Yes, the same woman who, black-clad and withered, now visits Paris unrecognized.)

The municipal court voted her a wedding present of one hundred and twenty thousand dollars. She at once turned the money over to a foundling asylum for girls. A wedding present of fifty thousand dollars from the emperor she divided between two Paris hospitals.

And the man in the street cheered himself hoarse.

For the journey to Notre Dame Cathedral, where the religious ceremony was to be performed—the civil ceremony was at the Tuileries—the same state coach was used in which the first Napoleon and Marie Louise of Austria had driven to their ill-fated wedding. During the drive, the imperial crown surmounting the coach crashed to the ground. The same ominous accident had befallen, under just the same conditions, during the first Napoleon's trip to Notre Dame with Marie Louise—same carriage, same crown, and all.

Now dawned for France a brief golden age. European powers recognized the new government; stocks boomed; unexampled prosperity set in; public revenues rose to an unprecedented height; every branch of industry flourished; narrow old streets gave way to wide boulevards. The hungry were fed. There was work, with good pay, for more people than ever before. To the Empress Eugénie went the praise of the nation.

She was adored as a goddess, this once penniless Spanish girl, who had at last wheedled an ex-Jersey schoolmaster into making her his wife. Her power and fame had reached the zenith. And for years they remained there. Napoleon III. was at last actually popular. But his popularity, like a bankrupt's fortune, was chiefly in his wife's name.

Cholera broke out in the army. Eugénie insisted on visiting the cholera war hospitals. When doctors pointed out the risk, she answered quietly:

"It is the only way a woman can go under fire."

At the height of the emperor's greatness, a certain astrologer named Morrison croaked, as follows, in "Zadkiel's Almanac":

> But let him not dream of lasting honor, power, or prosperity. He shall found no dynasty, he shall wear no durable crown; but, in the midst of deeds of blood and slaughter, with affrighted Europe trembling beneath the weight of his daring martial hosts, he shall descend beneath the heavy hand of Fate and fall to rise no more.

The position of Napoleon III. and Eugénie was one of splendid loneliness. All other sovereigns regarded them as parvenus, upstarts, and declined to visit them or receive them—all except Great Britain's queen.

Eugénie won the admiring friendship of Queen Victoria, and did more to knit a friendship between France and England than had any one since the Norman conquest. She was a welcome guest at London and Windsor, and even won there a welcome for her husband. The emperor could be interesting when he chose—he had the most delightful manners in the world—and, urged by Eugénie, he exerted himself to make a hit with England's sovereign. Queen Victoria wrote of Napoleon III. and his wife:

> There is something fascinating, melancholy, and engaging which draws you to him in spite of any prevention you may have against him, and certainly without the assistance of any outward advantages of appearance. He undoubtedly has a most extraordinary power of attracting people to him.
>
> The empress, too, has great charm, and we are all very fond of her. She is full of courage and spirit. And yet so gentle, with such innocence and *"enjouement"* that the ensemble is most charming. With all her great loveliness, she has the prettiest and most modest manner.

Thus began a sincere fondness between the two women, to last until the day of Queen Victoria's death, forty-six years later.

Meantime, Eugénie was acknowledged to be the most beautiful and the best-dressed woman in Europe. She set the fashions for five continents. Her lightest sartorial whim was fashion's law.

For example, before the birth of her only child, she adopted a style of costume known as "the crinoline," to improve the appearance of her figure. At once, women short and women tall, women fat and women lean, women young and women old, women married and women still in doubt—all adopted crinoline. On those of them that didn't need its aid, it was hideous, but the Empress Eugénie had ordained it. That was enough for the world of dressmakers.

The French court was a riot of wit, fashion, splendor, and jeweled indecency. In all these qualities, save the last, the empress led the way. She spent money—the nation's money—in double handfuls. She boasted that she never wore the same dress twice—she who in girlhood had made an art of dodging dressmakers' bills and of refurbishing her old gowns.

When, in 1856, her son was born, Paris once more went dutifully insane with joy. There was at last an heir to the imperial throne—a scion of the Napoleonic dynasty. The parents saddled the luckless infant with the name Napoleon Eugéne Louis Jean Joseph, and created him "prince imperial."

But presently the French began to grow tired of cheering. The empress' extravagance had not bothered them, but now she was beginning to meddle in politics, and the people did not like it; not only because she was a woman, but because she had no more natural aptitude for politics than has a peacock for typesetting. She made costly political blunders, and the knot of politicians who used her as a tool blithely led her from one folly of statesmanship to another.

Errors in foreign policy were also sapping the emperor's popularity, especially when these errors were caused by the empress' jogging his elbow. An Italian made an industrious effort to assassinate Napoleon III. and Eugénie with a bomb one night, as they drove to the opera. They escaped unhurt, and Napoleon III. took occasion to say loudly:

"Man is immortal, till his work is done!"

Then came the Franco-Prussian War, a conflict urged along and insisted on by Eugénie, who playfully referred to it as "my little war."

You know how it turned out, this "little war" of Eugénie's. Napoleon III. left her installed in Paris as regent, when he went to the front. He was desperately ill at the time, and very tired and old. And he rouged his cheeks and waxed his straggly mustache to make the soldiers think he was in good health.

The French were routed in battle after battle. At Sedan's surrender, the emperor himself was captured. When this news reached Paris, the empire was overthrown and a republic was declared. And a mob set out for the palace to revenge the country's shame by killing Eugénie; the same mob that used to cheer her and that, in still later years, did not know her by sight.

Some one had suggested to the empress that she might stem the tide of hatred by riding through Paris clad in deep black, but among all her hundreds of dresses, there was not a single black one. The poor woman has worn no other color for the past thirty years.

In thousands, the mob surged through the streets, howling:

"Down with the empress! Death to the Spanish woman! To the guillotine with her! Long live the guillotine!"

As the crowd neared the palace, Eugénie's advisers begged her to flee.

"It would be as cowardly for me to desert my post," she cried, deadly pale, but unflinching, "as for a captain to desert his ship threatened by a storm."

In vain Buffet, her secretary, pleaded with her; in vain De Lesseps urged; in vain Baron de Pier implored her to escape before she should be caught in the grip of a revolution more dreadful than France had ever known. News was brought to her that the chamber of deputies had been raided, its president dragged from his chair, the deputies dispersed. She heard the dull roar of the throng outside the palace, headed by brazen women with streaming hair and uplifted arms, who waved blood-red flags and squalled:

"A bas l'impératrice! A la guillotine! Vive la Republique!"

Word came that the portraits of the emperor and empress had just been torn from the walls of the Hotel de Ville and slashed to pieces. The imperial eagles had everywhere been hauled down and smashed. The troops were joining in the mob's bellowed chorus of the "Marseillaise." The empress stood like a statue in the center of the audience room.

"I know how to die," she said, over and over.

Several equerries drew their swords and prepared to defend her.

"No blood must be shed to save me," she commanded.

"Is it your majesty's wish to cause a general massacre of your attendants?" babbled Pietri, the helpless prefect of police.

After a pause, during which the lives of those around her still hung in the balance, she answered in calm, even tones:

"I will go. But all of you bear witness that I have done my duty to the last."

In a few words she bade good-by to her household. The mob was breaking into the gardens of the palace. The empress went to her own room. There she put on a plain straw hat and a waterproof cloak, and covered her beautiful face with a heavy veil.

Entering the corridor, where several ambassadors awaited her, she took Prince Metternich's arm. Followed by Chevalier Negra and Madame le Breton, her lady in waiting, she was rushed through a side wing of the Tuileries and entered a gallery connecting it with the Louvre. A crashing, of glass and of wood, the falling of a door, and a roar of voices, told her that the crowd had broken into the palace.

"It is too late," said the empress, pausing to listen. "Leave me!"

Metternich dragged her forward, almost by main strength, until they reached the door leading to the Louvre. On turning the handle, this was found locked. As the fugitives stared at one another in dumb despair, a servant ran forward with a key and let them out into the Apollo Gallery of the Louvre.

Hurrying through this and to a door opening on the Place St. Germain l'Auxerrois, they reached the street and, unnoticed, mingled with a backwater of the mob. The empress was calm.

"You are holding my arm," she said to Negra. "Does it tremble?"

Astonished, he answered:

"Not at all."

A street urchin, with the impudence of his kind, peered up under Eugénie's veil. *"Voilà l'impératrice!"*—"See the empress!"—he shrilled.

Negra sent the boy reeling into the gutter with a box on the ear, snarling at him:

"You little beast, I'll teach you not to yell, *'Vive les Prusses!'*"

Those who stood nearest heard the clever retort. Some of them believed what they heard. A few others believed merely what they saw. But they let her go, unbetrayed—this empress who was no longer an empress.

By offer of triple fare, her escorts secured a cab. They drove Eugénie to the house of Doctor Evans, an American dentist, on the Avenue Bois de Boulogne. Evans sheltered her for the night; then decided to take her, in his own carriage, to Deauville, where he hoped to be able to get passage for her to England.

As they reached the guarded gateway by which they must leave Paris, the officers stationed there called a halt. Evans explained that he was taking an insane patient to an asylum at Neuilly, and begged that she might not be disturbed or excited. The request was granted.

At every wayside inn, the same precaution was taken, of representing Eugénie as insane. The journey lasted twenty-four hours.

At Deauville, where Mrs. Evans, the dentist's wife, was staying, they found safe shelter. At nightfall, thanks to Evans' arrangements, they boarded the yacht of Sir John Burgoyne, which chanced to be lying offshore. A terrific storm sprang up. The sailors demurred at setting sail in such weather. Sir John explained the dire need of haste, and told who the veiled woman was. The sailors shouted:

"We'll see her majesty through!"

And out into the hurricane the yacht reeled.

At Chislehurst, a quiet English country place, Eugénie and her son were joined by the fallen emperor, when the Germans set him free. A huge British crowd greeted his landing at Dover with cries of:

"Long live the emperor! Long live the empress! We ought to have helped you!"

Soon afterward, the emperor died. A little later, during an expedition in Zululand, the young prince imperial was killed.

Widowed, childless, her wealth gone, Eugénie has ever since lived on in retirement at Chislehurst. But every now and then she goes for a few days to Paris—the saddest pilgrimage such a woman could make.

She stood at a Paris window, in early August, 1914. In the street below, bands were playing the "Marseillaise," and people were waving flags. The rhythmic tramp of thousands of feet echoed from wall to wall of the highway. France's army was setting forth to war against the invading German hosts. The aged woman pointed a trembling forefinger at the endless lines of marching soldiers and cried in hysterical triumph:

"This shall be my revenge!"

The
Unknown

By Albert
Payson Terhune

ILLUSTRATED BY
WILLIAM OBERHARDT

WHEN the tiny tourist steamship *Aloha* puffed through the Golden Gate in late November of 1900 for a wintertime loiter in the South Seas, she carried one hundred and seven first-class passengers who had more time than business, or else more money than health.

When the *Aloha* was creeping with blind-man caution, one fog-cursed night late in December, through a reef-starred stretch of remote ocean far southward of the travel-lanes, her captain chose that festal occasion—it was Christmas Eve—to accept a single small glass of punch brewed by a passenger who was one of the line's foremost officials.

This mild potation would not have turned the head of a ten-year-old child. Its very mildness was the captain's excuse for drinking it—that and the fact that the magnate who brewed it and who pressed the glass upon him was the arbiter of his financial destinies.

There was perhaps a teaspoonful of whisky among the other ingredients in that one glass of punch.

It was Captain Stilsen's first taste of liquor since a drastic three-month drink-cure course at a sanitarium eight years earlier had given him strength to change from a periodic drunkard to a smartly reliable navigator.

Stilsen went back at once to the bridge. There all the torments of hades racked his very soul. Presently, turning over the command to his first officer on plea of sudden illness, he went to his cabin.

Thither he summoned a wondering steward, who presently brought him two quart bottles of Scotch whisky, a siphon and a bowl of cracked ice.

An hour later it occurred to Captain Stilsen that the night was very foggy, that reefs were unpleasantly numerous in that stretch of sea and that a captain's place, in such a crisis, was on his bridge. This idea took such complete possession of him that he strode back to his post of duty and resumed command.

Within half an hour the *Aloha's* starboard quarter was the nesting place of a shark-tooth reef.

Stilsen did the two things that remained for a man in his circumstances to do. First he got all his passengers and crew safely into the boats before the slow-settling *Aloha's* weight tore her, inch by inch, from the upholding tooth of rock. Then he went calmly back to his own sharply listing cabin, locked its door behind him and uncorked the second quart of whisky. He was having a very pleasant time indeed when the increasing water-pressure burst inward his locked door and pushed a shower of porthole-glass into the cabin.

OF the *Aloha's* boats all but one was sooner or later picked up. All her passengers but three were rescued, in better or worse condition.

The exception, in the roster of boats, was a little naphtha launch, a mere toy. The three human absentees were:

HENRICUS VAN DUYNE (A. B., A. M., Ph. D., F. R. S.), aged forty-five, Professor of Applied Science at Coromandal University.

MARK BURLEIGH, aged fifteen, a "prep"-school boy, who had been making the voyage as the guest of his maiden aunt, Miss Susan Burleigh, of New York.

MARGUERITE CRAIG, aged fourteen, whose parents, Dr. and Mrs. Bruce Craig (also of New York), were saved by a copra-schooner and reached home at the end of twelve incommodious weeks.

A naphtha launch, a man of forty-five, a boy of fifteen, a girl of fourteen—these were the *Aloha's* missing. The captain did not count. There was no mystery as to his fate.

The launch (which had been stowed on deck, for the benefit of a "way" passenger who owned it and who was to have debarked three days later) had contained fuel and by Stilsen's orders had been provisioned and lowered with the other boats. Who had manned or occupied it, nobody seemed to recall.

The night had been black and foggy. The drink-dulled Stilsen had automatically—and autocratically—assigned the various passenger groups to the different boats. And without panic, but with dazed, sheeplike obedience, they had followed his commands. One boat had upset, spilling its load into the calm water, but everyone—supposedly—had been hauled aboard again when it was righted.

For weeks the tale of new-landed survivors was continued. For months Miss Susan Burleigh and the Craigs and Professor Van Duyne's invalid wife clung piteously to hope. Then, when a year had passed, they schooled themselves to face their losses.

Two insurance companies duly paid Van Duyne's widow seven thousand, five hundred dollars apiece. A dual memorial service was arranged by Miss Burleigh and the Craigs, as belated obsequies for Mark and for Marguerite. And life went on—as life has a way of doing.

But eight months after the year's lapse, a whaler, touching at Sable Island, left there a very dirty and very unkempt man of middle age who promptly introduced himself to the local authorities as Henricus Van Duyne, A. B., A. M., Ph. D., F. R. S., etc., recent Professor of Applied Science at Coromandal University—who demanded instant passage to New York.

The Craigs and Miss Burleigh read the cabled account of Van Duyne's reappearance. And all three of them traveled as far north as Halifax to meet him on his southward journey. But they had their trip and their reawakened hope-pangs all for nothing. Professor Van Duyne could give them no tidings whatever of the missing boy and girl.

THE story Van Duyne told was simple to a degree. He and two sailors, he said, had been assigned to the naphtha launch on Stilsen's learning that he understood the working of motor-craft.

The two sailors—ignorant Lascars—had trusted neither the efficiency of such a newfangled boat nor the guidance of a landsman. Wherefore they had at once slid over the side and had swum across, under cover of the fog, to an undermanned lifeboat fifty feet away and had climbed aboard.

Left alone, Van Duyne had tried to follow the general course of the boats ahead of him, but had lost his bearings in the fog. He had chugged along by guesswork, until daylight lifted the mist. Then all around him the ocean had showed no sign of any other craft. Taking bearings by the new-risen sun, the Professor had continued along the course the *Aloha* had been steering. His supply of fuel gave out before he could sight land. Then a gale had caught his boat astern and had driven it on—while he alternately prayed and bailed—for another forty-eight hours.

At last, with the falling of the wind, the exhausted man had sighted a hilly island

blazing green in the blue glare of the sea and girt with snow-bright sand. Thither, by rigging his shirt on the launch's boat-hook, he had beaten his way more dead than alive and had beached his boat.

On that South Sea island, for six long months, he had lived. Except for lonely hopelessness, he had not fared ill. From fish to breadfruit, from trappable game to edible roots, there was natural food enough on those twenty square miles of fertile land to sustain fifty men.

There were indications aplenty of former human occupancy. A Polynesian tribe had doubtless lived there, but many, many years ago. Some pestilence had probably wiped out or at least decimated the islanders, and the place had since been shunned in terror by all other natives.

Six months later the Professor's signal was seen by a whaler cruising to the island in quest of water. The whaler's captain had been in haste to get well out beyond the reef-fringed coast before the coming of a threatened typhoon, but had stopped long enough to fill a few casks and to take the marooned professor aboard. The captain, however, had refused to leave his course to carry Van Duyne to any port whence he could reach home. Thus the Professor had perforce remained on board, reluctantly working his passage, until toward the end of the cruise, when he was dropped at Sable Island.

The Professor's story was interesting enough, as stories go. But it ceased to interest the Craigs and Miss Burleigh as soon as they found he knew nothing about the fate of Mark and Marguerite. And again hope died.

The mourners remembered the overturning of one of the lifeboats, the spilling of its human freight into the sea, the righting of the boat and the hauling of dripping swimmers over its sides. There had been no "counting of heads," after the capsized passengers were fished aboard again. And, since the launch was now accounted for, there was no longer any mystery as to the fate of the boy and girl.

THE *Aloha* sank on' Christmas Eve, 1900. On New Year's Eve, 1915, Mr. Bruce Craig received by mail a long envelope containing a brief note and a pair of typewritten sheets. The note ran:

> Bruce Craig, Esq.:
> Dear Sir:
> The enclosed is a copy I made to-day of one of the papers I found in the safe-deposit box of the late Henricus Van Duyne of this city. As Professor Van Duyne's next of kin, I was searching his effects for a will when I came upon this statement. I recall the whole case, very vividly. And it occurred to me that you have the right to see this statement at once. So I have herewith copied it. It needs no comment from me.
> Very truly,
> Rufus K. Van Duyne.

Puzzled, Bruce Craig unfolded the sheets of typed paper and read:

> I, HENRICUS VAN DUYNE, being as nearly in my right mind as ever again I can hope to be, have decided to add the following facts and corrections to the statement I made to the press, upon my arrival at Sable Island in August of this year (1902).
> For obvious reasons I cannot make known these facts, while I am still living. But

if I die within the next twenty years, it may not be too late to atone in part for what I have done—and for what God will perhaps forgive me, when He remembers that He gave me the soul of a coward.

My statement to the press was in the main correct—so far as it went. The only actual falsehood I told was concerning the two sailors assigned to the launch with me.

The two persons entrusted by Captain Stilsen to my care, in the launch, were not sailors. They were a boy and a girl—Mark Burleigh and Marguerite Craig.

Nor did they jump overboard, as I said the sailors did. They remained with me through those three days of torture and fear, and they landed with me upon the island that for six months was my prison. There, through my small scientific knowledge, I taught them what plants to use or to avoid, for food. I also taught them how to weave fish-lines from fiber and to shape fishhooks from tuna-bone and how to set game-snares.

One day they two went to the western end of the island for shellfish. They started at dawn and were to return by moonlight, as it was a nine-mile journey each way. An hour after they set forth I sighted the whaler at anchor off shore; its longboat was already rowing toward me, laden with water-casks.

The captain—so the mate in charge of the boat told me—had ordered the casks filled as hastily as possible from the nearest spring, as the glass gave warning of a gale and he wished to get out into deep water. There is no safe anchorage at the island. He bade me be ready to accompany the boat as soon as the casks should be filled—or else to stay where I was.

In vain I begged him to wait until night, so that my two companions might return. He refused. When the casks were filled, I put off to the whaler with him, and there I repeated to the captain my plea for delay.

He brutally refused, telling me I might swim ashore again if I chose, and that he would not risk a hurricane among those reefs, to rescue a whole orphan-asylum.

What was there for me to do? If I went back to that accursed island, a lifetime might elapse before the next ship would touch there—for it is far off the lines of ocean travel, and the whaler merely neared it because blown far out of her course by a storm.

How could I have benefited Craig and the girl by returning? My first duty was my wife—and to the world of science. Also—I realize it, now—I was a coward.

In brief, I made up my mind. I told the captain and mate that I had no companions on shore and that I had mentioned them only in hope of gaining time to go back to my hut, across the island, for some scientific specimens I wished to save.

The captain kicked me for lying to him; and he set me to work scraping blubber—a horrible occupation.

I had time, in the months that ensued, to realize the figure I should cut in the eyes of my friends and of the world at large should I confess I had gained my own freedom and had left my two young comrades to end their days there on the island.

I dared not face the contempt of the public. I should never have been able to live down the cowardice. It would have broken my wife's heart with shame. It would have meant my expulsion from the University—the belittling of my life work. So I framed the story I told on my arrival.

May God forgive me! May those who loved Marguerite Craig and Mark Burleigh forgive me! Perhaps, when I am dead, it will not yet be too late to rescue the two children I deserted.

And yet—if much time shall have elapsed—let those who love the two think twice before seeking to rescue them. Many years ago I read a strange book—"The Blue Lagoon," I think, was the name. It told of a boy and a girl thus cast away on such an island; the thing has happened before now, in fact as well as in fiction. And I advise the castaways' parents or guardians to read that book.

But this latter is no affair of mine. Again I implore forgiveness—my wife's above all.

Henricus Van Duyne.

CRAIG read the confession through a second and a third time. Then he read it to his wife. Then they both went to the gloomy old Stuyvesant Square house of Miss Susan Burleigh. And there Craig read the confession aloud.

He had to read the last half of it to Miss Burleigh a second time, for in the middle of his first reading she fainted.

Then followed much more talk, interrupted now and then by a flood of hysterical tears from both women.

"What is to be done?" demanded Mr. Craig at last, his brain recovering some of its wonted working-power.

"Done?" echoed his wife, amazed. *Done?* What do you mean, Bruce? Surely there's only one thing to—"

"*Done?*" babbled Susan Burleigh, tearfully indignant at the question. "Why, man alive, there's *everything* to be done! What's the matter with you? Don't you understand? The two babies that we've mourned as dead for fifteen years are alive! *Alive!* There on that awful island, in the South Seas! Alive—and waiting for us to bring them home. How soon can we start? It's too late to-night, I suppose. But—"

"Yes," grimly agreed Craig, "it is *too* late, to-night. I'm afraid the last car for the South Seas has gone."

"Bruce!" gasped his wife. "How can you joke, at such—at such a sacred time? The joy has made him light-headed," she explained to Miss Burleigh.

"No," he denied, "it has made me level-headed. Some one must be. That is why I asked 'What is to be done?' You see, I once read 'The Blue Lagoon' —that book Van Duyne speaks about."

"What's that got to do with it?" shrilly challenged Miss Burleigh. "This isn't a time to talk about books."

"We can start for San Francisco, first thing to-morrow morning," declared Mrs. Craig. "And from there—"

"Yes," interposed her husband, "from there—*where?*"

"To the island, of course—by the first ship we can charter. By the—"

"Where?" doggedly insisted Craig. "Where is the island? The South Seas are fairly aswarm with islands—thousands and thousands of them, big and little. That's what *Polynesia* means. It's Greek for *Many Islands. Polloi* means *many,* and *nesos* means—"

"But Professor Van Duyne lived there six months. Surely, he—"

"How could he know?" asked Craig. "He had no instruments, no chart. He himself said that he had no means of guessing except in the most general way, where he was. He traveled three days from the spot where the *Aloha* went down. But in what direction and at what speed? There are probably fifty islands in a two-hundred-mile circle from the place where the *Aloha* sank. And we've only a vague knowledge as to where she sank. The wreck was never located, and the ship's log wasn't saved."

"But the whaler!" cried Mrs. Craig in triumph, "the whaler that picked up Professor Van Duyne! Surely the—"

"The whaler was an old ship fifteen years ago," countered her husband. "She's probably been broken up or gone to the bottom years ago. And her captain would be impossible to locate, even if he is still alive. He was an elderly man, Van Duyne told us. And that was in 1901. The crew are scattered, of course. And probably the ship's log could never be found now—even if the log made record of the exact latitude and longitude of an island, off the regular track, where the ship was blown by a gale and where she watered. They're notoriously careless, those whaling men, in recording anything except catches and deaths and accidents—"

"Mr. Craig!" broke in Miss Burleigh, "I am a fairly well-to-do woman, as you may know. I don't spend one-fifth of my income—because I don't need to. And I am going to spend every cent of money I have in the world, if I have to, to find my boy. I'm going to charter a ship—not *one* ship—a dozen ships. I'm going to have the South Seas combed with a fine-tooth comb. I'm going to offer a reward of fifty thousand dollars—"

"A reward!" eagerly chimed in Mrs. Craig. "That's it! We'll both offer a reward—a reward big enough to set every Pacific skipper to hunting for them. Oh, we'll find them, that way. Something tells me we shall! And we'll charter a ship, too—and—"

"One minute!" said Craig gravely. "Do you realize what this means? Do you realize—"

"I realize I want my little girl—my only baby!" flamed Mrs. Craig.

"And I want my boy!" sobbed Miss Burleigh, "—the splendid little boy who never knew any mother but me. He was only my nephew. But no mother could have—"

"You don't understand me," intervened Craig. "Let me put it as kindly as I can."

HE paused to collect his words in the order he desired. Then he continued:

"You say you want your children. Miss Burleigh, your 'little boy' was fifteen when you lost him. Our little girl was fourteen. That was fifteen years ago, last week. If they are living, Mark is thirty. Marguerite is twenty-nine. Does that mean nothing to you? Think it over."

"It means that they have grown up, of course," said Miss Burleigh. "But we can make up to them for all their years of exile there, and—"

"*Can we?*"

Craig fairly shot the question at her.

"*Can* we make it up to them? If they are alive, they have lived since childhood the lives of savages—with no books, no advice, no civilized surroundings, no teachings—except Nature's. They have fished, hunted, eaten, drunk, slept. They have lived for more than half their lives as young savages might live. No,"—forestalling an interruption from his wife,—"not as young savages, but as animals. For young savages would have tribal customs and traditions and folklore and the experience of their elders to guide them. These two children had not even that. If that cur Van Duyne had stayed there with them, it would have been different. But he stayed only long enough to teach them how to sustain life—not how to *live* life. They would be dragged back here—two savages, nothing better! Perhaps something worse! Is it fair to them? Is it fair to *us?*

"Have you any idea," persisted Craig, "in how brief a time a whole civilized community can revert to barbarism, if it's left to itself? Then how about two children who grow up as ours have—if they've lived to grow up at all? How about clothes? How about mental exercises? How about—"

"Then we must make up to them, all the more, for what they have missed," purred Miss Burleigh benevolently.

With a groan Bruce Craig gave up the battle.

"All right!" he agreed drearily. "Have it your own way! I'll do all I can. I'll do all any mortal can do. I promise that. Only, I insist that you leave the whole matter in my hands for the present. I'll arrange for offering the reward and for chartering a boat and everything. And I'll use all the speed and all the skill that money can supply.

Only, I want you not to take any steps until I've succeeded or failed. Will you agree?"

In the end, because he was a man and she a spinster, Miss Burleigh agreed. And because she had a way of obeying when she saw that queer, set look around his mouth, Mrs. Craig assented too.

And that night as he lay awake and hot-eyed beside his slumbering wife, Bruce Craig whispered over and over to himself in agony of soul:

"My little girl! Dad's own, *own* baby girl! God in His mercy grant that you're safely dead! God grant you died while you were still my baby girl!"

IN the morning Craig was quite grumpy and businesslike at breakfast, and he seemed to have forgotten all about the tidings of the night before until Mrs. Craig recalled the matter to his mind. And before the meal was fairly finished, he left the house.

He did not go, as usual, to his office, but instead to the Public Library. There, consulting newspaper files of August, 1902, he found the story of Van Duyne's rescue. The account gave the name of the whaler and of its captain—also the shipping firm that owned the vessel. It was a New York firm.

Craig jotted down the firm's address and went thither. Two hours later he was climbing the front steps of a jerry-built New Jersey cottage. He was the bearer of a strong note of introduction from the whaling firm, to the whaler's ex-captain, Hiram H. Rance—who had for five years been on the retired list and who was ending his days here in a suburban dry-dock.

Like many another seafaring man who is an unholy terror on his own quarterdeck, Captain Hiram H. Rance, ashore, proved to be a mild-mannered and deprecatory old chap, with watery blue eyes and a lonesome-looking, white patch of chin beard.

He received Craig, non-committally, in the cottage's atrocious sitting-room, and very carefully read the firm's note of introduction. Then he read it again. After that he visibly threw aside the reserve so proper to a sailor who is approached by a prosperous-looking landsman and placed himself wholly at his guest's service. "Owners' Orders" are shipmasters' Ten Commandments.

Craig told his story succinctly, yet in a way that made Rance understand the terrible problem that faced his guest and to do mental homage to the speaker's self-control. Then Craig began to ask questions. And Captain Hiram H. Rance gave full and careful replies.

Yes, Rance had perfect recollection of the island and of Van Duyne's rescue. The matter had not only been entered in the whaler's log but in the private diary which the Captain had religiously kept since boyhood (and which, after brief rummaging, he now produced from a sea-chest in the attic).

Here was the entry—six lines in all. And here, of course, were the latitude and longitude of the island.

Yes, and Captain Hiram distinctly remembered the professorial castaway's story of two fellow-refugees. He had believed Van Duyne's later assertion that there were no such refugees. He had believed it, and in his heart he had been glad, for he had been irked at the need of leaving two white people there for the sake of his ship's safety. He had believed the story, until—until—

"You see, sir, it's this way: That island, now—she's off the beaten track. She's far-an'-away off the trade-routes an' travel-lanes. I knew her, because when I was mate on the *Annie S.* (out o' Gloucester, you know) back in 1887, we touched there for water. That's why I tried to water there when we were blowed out of our course the time we picked up your professor. I don't believe there's a craft of any kind sights that island twice in ten years—let alone stops there. An' for some queer reason, the natives steer clear of it. It isn't even charted."

"Well?" asked Craig impatiently as the narrator's rambling talk trailed away.

"Well,"—Captain Hiram took up his seemingly aimless tale,—"I was retired, back in Jan'ry, nineteen-eleven. My last voy'ge ended a week before that. A three-year cruise it was."

Again he paused, cleared his throat, and looked uncomfortable.

"In St. John's, it was, on the homestretch," he added, "that I met up with Cap'n Boyd of the *Speed an' Follow*. (He went down with his ship an' all hands, off Sable, in nineteen-twelve.) Him an' me got to chinning about this an' that. An' he said he'd read in a newspaper about me picking up Professor Van Duyne at that island, in nineteen-two. He asked me a lot about the location."

"Well?" again interrupted Craig, to whom these devious reminiscences were a growing annoyance.

"Well," said Captain Hiram more briskly, as if nettled by the other's impatience, "I couldn't make out what he was driving at, till pretty soon he tells me he sighted that island early in nineteen-ten,—that's 'bout five years back, now, you see,—being blowed off his course by one o' those mussy little tropic typhoons, same as I was. He passed the island five miles to south'ard. An' he gave it what my grandson calls 'the once-over' with his glasses. He'd heard it wasn't inhabited. But—on the beach he saw—he saw—two natives."

"*What?*" cried Bruce Craig in sudden tense interest. "Two natives?"

"Two natives. At least—at least, he thought they must be natives. An'—an' he *thought* there was only two of them. He couldn't be sure. The day wasn't bright, an'—"

Again his voice trailed away. Craig jumped to his feet, walked heavily to the window and stared out for a long time into the slushy suburban highway. Over and over to himself, through no volition of his, he found himself repeating the Captain's words:

"He thought they must be natives. He *thought* there was only two of them!"

Suddenly Craig turned back into the room.

"Captain Rance!" he said sharply. "You spoke just now of your grandson. Have you a daughter?"

"No sir," answered Rance in surprise. Then, his voice softening, he added:

"Not now. Three sons and the grandson. I hadn't but one daughter, ever. She was took to heaven when she was twelve—summer complaint. I was on a cruise at the time. I call to mind, I brought her home a toy theayter from Frisco, that trip, an' a necklace of abalone. An' she'd been dead pretty near a month when I got to shore. She'd of been—she'd of been thirty-one, this next March—eighth of March. The parson told me at the time that I'd stop grieving for her, by an' by, an' get reconciled to her being took. An' maybe I will. But I don't seem to make very much progress. It's queer how much fonder a man is of his little girl than he is of his big, noisy sons, an' how much harder it is to forget her. Little girls are so cute an' loving an' gentle, an' all that. Why did you ask about Tillie?"

"I asked," said Craig, "because I want your advice—and then your help. I'll *pay* liberally for the help. But the advice must come as a gift from one stricken father to another."

"I don't seem to get your drift, sir."

"Then I'll ask the advice, first," returned Craig. "Captain, look me square in the eyes, and answer me, man to man. Knowing the circumstances as you do, would you change places with me?"

"How d' you mean?" queried Captain Hiram, puzzled.

"I mean," pursued Craig, "would you rather know your little girl had died before the world could lay its dirty claws on her—would you rather know she is happy with the Savior of little children—or to know she might still be alive, under the same conditions that *my* little girl is alive—if my little girl is really alive?"

"Why—why, what a queer question that is, now!" sputtered Captain Hiram.

"It's a fair question," insisted Craig, "and it calls for a fair answer. If you could have your choice: to know your daughter is where she is and *as* she is, or that she is as *my* daughter is—which would you choose?"

"I—I—" began the Captain; but Craig went on:

"And if your daughter were still alive and had been living as *my* daughter has, for the past fifteen years, would you bring her back to civilization? Not for your own sake, but for *hers?* Would you uproot her from the life that an unguided Nature has taught her to lead, and transplant her in twentieth-century New York? Would it—or wouldn't it—be fair to her?"

FOR a long minute, Captain Hiram made no reply. Then he said, with seeming irrelevance:

"I come of New England stock. My folks was among the first Deerfield settlers. You've read, in the hist'ry-books, about the Deerfield mass'cre? Well, a baby girl— one of my fam'ly's children—was carried off by the Injuns during that mass'cre. She was brought up a savage, an' she married a savage. Twenty years later her folks got news about her, and they brought her back to civ'lization an' to their own home in Deerfield. She was a savage, an' her ways was the ways of a savage. She pined for the Injuns. An' as soon as she could, she ran away, back to the Injuns. An'—her folks was glad enough to let her go. That's a true story. You'll find it in the hist'ry-books. Maybe it has some bearing on your question. An', again, maybe it hasn't."

"It comes as near to answering it as I'm likely to get," said Craig after a moment's hesitation. "And as near to it as I have any right to expect. So much for the advice. Now for the help I spoke of. Captain Rance, will a bonus of five thousand dollars, and all expenses paid, induce you to charter a ship and go to the island with me to bring back my daughter and Mark Burleigh?"

"Hey?" grunted the astonished seaman.

"Remember," added Craig, "I foot every bill. And you get not only master's pay from the minute you sign on, but a five-thousand-dollar bonus—half of it in advance."

"But—but Mr. Craig," faltered Captain Hiram, his brain buzzing with the temptation to add so much easy money to his meager savings. "But why *me?* There's scores of younger men—"

"You are the man I want," said Craig tensely. "I've decided that, since I've been here. You are the man I want, because you *understand.* To the ordinary shipmaster, it would be only a job. Will you do it?"

In the end, Captain Hiram consented.

NEXT morning Captain Hiram and Bruce Craig started together for San Francisco. Craig, by superhuman eloquence and argument and bulldozing, prevailed on the two women to remain in New York until his cable from Honolulu, on the return trip, should apprise them whether or not there was need for them to come out to California to meet him.

Six days later, on the slippery docks of San Francisco, Craig fell, breaking his right leg in two places—one of the breaks being a compound fracture.

Two months in the hospital was the very best the local surgeon could promise the sufferer. And Captain Hiram perforce chartered a ship and set sail without him. On the eve of sailing the Captain came to the hospital for final orders.

"I'm doubly glad I chose you for this job instead of any other man," said Craig, who was reclining with his plaster-cast leg thrust grotesquely out in front of him, "doubly glad. Because on this quest, you've got to be not only Captain Hiram H. Rance but Bruce Craig as well. Do you understand me? You've got to use not only your own judgment, but mine as well. I—I can't speak any more plainly. I have no right to—not even to myself. But—but keep on thinking of your own little girl when you go to look for mine. Just imagine you're Bruce Craig, in search of Hiram Rance's lost daughter. I—I—"

"I guess I catch your signals," said Rance gruffly, blinking very fast. "Good-by, Mr. Craig. I don't mind telling you I'd rather do a month in irons in the booby hatch, than tote the load you've just crowded onto my shoulders. I'll have to act as the Good Man gives me light to. That's the best anyone can do."

EIGHT weeks later Bruce Craig, supported by a crutch and a cane, hobbled forward to greet Captain Hiram H. Rance as the latter entered the hotel room whither Craig had been removed from the hospital two days earlier.

"Your 'No-one-alive-on-island' cable from Honolulu kept me from boarding the first liner and coming out to meet you," said Craig as the Captain silently shook hands with him. "You've nothing to add to that?"

"I'm glad you're on your legs again," replied the Captain, finding his voice with some effort and speaking with unwonted effusion. "You're looking better'n I expected to see you, after such a lay-by. I'm sorry you've had to pay out so much good money, too, on a fool's errand. I—"

"Tell me about it! Sit down and tell me about it—everything. You found the island without any trouble?"

"Found it?" repeated Captain Hiram with fine scorn. "Why wouldn't I find it? Give me the latitood and longitood of a place, an' I'll find it as easy as you'd find a house-number. Any navigator can. I—"

"Captain," interposed Craig, "I want you to tell me what you found there. And—it's only a detail, of course—I wish you would humor a sick man's whim by looking at *me* instead of at the floor. You got to the island. Well? What then?"

"We searched three days high an' low," said Rance glibly, like one who repeats a well-learned lesson. "Not a living soul there—not anywhere. We stumbled onto an old thatch, at last. It was overgrown with jungle an' looked like a landsman had built it—Van Duyne, most likely. An'—brace yourself, take it brave, sir—in sep'rate corners of the shack we come upon two skel'tons—of a boy an' girl, it looked like—about fifteen years old, I should say. I take it they'd died of hunger or something when Van Duyne wasn't there any longer to teach 'em what to eat. That man had ought to have been hanged, for leaving them. We buried the bones, an' I read a service over 'em. Then we provisioned with a lot of fresh fruits an' fish an' the like, an' we came back."

"You were able to provision your ship there," commented Craig, "and yet you say they died of starvation? After Van Duyne had taught them how to fish and to trap and to—"

"I didn't say they starved," growled Rance crossly. "I only said I s'posed so. All I know is that I found their—"

"And there were no natives on the island?"

"Not a one. Not a sign of any living person, native *or* white."

"Yet your friend told you he saw two people—at least two people there, five years ago. Marguerite and Mark would have been twenty-four and twenty-five years old at that time. The skeletons, you say, were of a boy and girl of about fifteen?"

"Look here, Mr. Craig!" bellowed Rance in sudden rage, "I ain't used to having my word questioned—"

"Did you ever study physiognomy, Captain Rance?" asked Craig very quietly. "I ask because a study of physiognomy has taught me two things: one is that a thoroughly angry or indignant man always looks straight into the other fellow's eyes. The other is that an amateur liar always clenches his fists when he's telling his most important lies."

"What's all that got to do with—"

"With the fact that you've been looking everywhere except at me?" broke in Craig's dead voice, "and that your fists are so tightly clenched that the knuckles are bone-white? I don't know, I'm sure. We'll start back for New York, this evening, you and I. You've earned your pay, if ever a man did. You're a good fellow, Rance. And a—a good father!"

When the Devil Was Sick

*T*HIS is not a story of the Eternal Triangle, but of a Temporary Pentagon. It would simplify matters—in this as in all stories—if one might follow the theatrical plan and start out with a printed cast. The cast, in this particular story, would also contain the five angles of the Pentagon. It would read:

DICK RAGNAR—*The Man.*
THETIS RAGNAR—*The Woman.*
MAXIMILIAN VAN SCHAICK, M. D.—*The Doctor.*
IRIS THORP—*The Other Woman.*
ROLF HELLMAN—*The Other Man.*

As a matter of fact, though, *The Other Man* and *The Other Woman*, in the following pages, serve chiefly as pegs whereon to hang the plot. On the stage they would be represented by the directions: *"Confused Sound Without"* or *"Enter Courier."*

Dick Ragnar and his wife, Thetis, had been married for seven years—ever since she was twenty and he twenty-five. They had been outrageously in love with each other—which had been their one excuse for marriage, since neither of them had a cent in cash or a dollar in prospects.

Dick had been graduated from the law-school one week before the wedding. Thetis had learned, at a cooking class, to make Scotch woodcock and angel food and golden buck.

The two lovers had pooled their life-equipment and had been married. Dick had got a job in a law-office at fifteen dollars a week, and Thetis had learned practical housekeeping in a two-room-and-kitchenette dovecote that stood five elevatorless floors above the street-level.

According to all precedent, they ought to have been excessively miserable, after the first golden mania ran its course. Dick should have been morose and down-at-heel; Thetis should have waxed snappy and slatternly.

Instead they had been gloriously happy. They had adapted themselves by magic to the cramped new conditions. Poverty had not oppressed them. They had become jollily drunk with it.

As a surreptitious feast of stale cucumbers has been known to cure cholera—as a nervous shock has cured nervous prostration—so these young idiots' challenge to common sense and their blithe defiance of the grim law of probability had attracted Fortune's whimsical favor.

Inside of a year Dick's puny income had doubled. Inside of two years he had a little law-office of his own. Inside of three he had won a spectacular forlorn-hope case that sent his fame and his fees a-rocketing.

He caught the notice of a big corporation—then of another. Within five years after he and Thetis committed financial suicide by marrying on nothing a year, he had dazedly realized that he was a successful lawyer and that he stood in line for wealth and for possible judgeship.

The first boosts of fortune had been hailed by the two lovers with clamorous delight, as implying new good times together and as verifying the lofty opinion they had both formed of Dick's ability. Then, before either of them quite realized it, a bogy-man named "Success" invaded their adorably happy life and began to shoulder them apart.

HE came in various forms, this success-bogy—in the form of more work for Dick and more social obligations for Thetis—in the guise of a troop of friends of both sexes, in fifty other ways such as encompass newly successful people.

With poverty had come home-life, sweet companionship, solitude from distracting outside interests. Success rudely flung open the home-doors, letting in the world with its flood of outsiders, of pressing society-engagements, of extraneous interests. And bit by bit the home ceased to be a home. The lovers, unrealizing, ceased to be lovers.

When a fifteen-cent bunch of carnations had been an event, Thetis had rejoiced at their advent and had rapturously hugged the giver. But she accepted huge drifts of orchids, now, in a far less emotional fashion.

When Thetis had surreptitiously saved enough pennies out of the housekeeping-fund to buy Dick a box of his favorite (but too costly) cigarettes, he had smoked them as a joyous ceremonial, with the giver superintending the rite from a perch on his knee. Now there was no ceremony and little thrill in the oft-purchased big boxes of Corona-Corona or Hoyo cigars.

Home evenings had been a delight. Now they were so rare that they had lost their savor. Yawns, at such times, were more plentiful than kisses.

The Ragnars had made few friends in the early days, being too poor to entertain, and too happy to want to. The only member of their former tiny coterie who went with them from the old life to the new was Doctor Maximilian Van Schaick, a queer old medical genius who had brought Thetis into the world and whose influence had secured for Dick the latter's first law-case.

Van Schaick alone of their friends grumpily refused to congratulate the Ragnars on their changed fortunes. He told them, gruffly, and more than once, that they were much better off as they had been. They both laughed at the cranky old chap for saying so absurd a thing; and as they could not win his approval, they more or less lost sight of him in the rush of other interests.

IT was at about this time that Dick met Iris Thorp. She was a widow and she put her business affairs into Dick's charge. She was under thirty, intensely pretty and with a gay charm that men found irresistible. Dick, perforce, had to see much of Mrs. Thorp in connection with the managing of her money and in regard to several estate suits. And somehow she arranged that he should see still more of her than actual business called for.

All at once Dick Ragnar woke to a knowledge that he was thinking altogether too much and too often about Iris. At first, the realization gave him a jarring little shock. Then, manlike, he began to look about him for excuses.

And he found them. In nothing else is the Biblical promise, "Seek and ye shall find!" more amply verified than in the matter of excuses.

For example: Dick noted that Thetis was seldom at home nowadays when he chanced to get back from the office earlier than usual. (Of old these had been gala times.) Or if she was at home, there were a lot of silly people who had dropped in to tea. When there weren't a lot, there was fairly certain to be one. And that "one" had a way of being Rolf Hellman.

Moreover, when Dick and she did chance to be alone together, she was full of other interests and either yawned dumbly in his face or else chattered about people or things that did not concern him at all. He was not jealous of Hellman,—a decent enough fellow, of his sort,—but he did not like the way the chap was trying to install himself as tame cat in the Ragnar home. If Thetis was going to crowd her own husband out of her life, for such people as Hellman and the rest—why, she had herself to blame if Dick sought amusement elsewhere.

And with this salve to his conscience, Dick no longer bothered to resist the impulse to drop in at Mrs. Thorp's pretty apartment for a cup of tea, on the way home from the office.

A kindly solicitous friend, who once met him there, felt it her duty to mention the call to Thetis. Thetis joked Dick about it. He retorted in jocular phrase that Hellman took up so much room in the Ragnar house that its master was crowded out. To which Thetis gayly answered that it was lucky there was a cozy refuge for the exiled husband in Mrs. Thorp's apartment.

Whereat the subject dropped, with a mutual laugh. But the laugh had a razor-edge; and it clove still deeper the ever-deepening chasm between them.

THEN, one sloppy March morning, Dick started for the office ten minutes late and in such a hurry that he forgot his rubbers. Two years earlier, Thetis would no more have let him go rubberless into the slush than she would have let him start downtown without his trousers. But of late, such foolish little details had slipped her mind. Besides, she was breakfasting in bed this morning—as the aftermath of a dinner dance of the preceding night.

To mere man, a breakfast in bed is a thing of horror, something to look back on with loathing. To the average woman it represents the pinnacle of blissful luxury. Thetis breakfasted in bed more and more often nowadays, leaving Dick with no cheerier companion than his morning paper to share with him the first meal of the day.

Dick had a drivingly busy forenoon. At lunch-time he discovered he was not hungry, and that invisible ice-rivulets were doing funny things up and down his spine—also that some one had poured a ton or so of hot lead into his brains, and that his knees and elbows were stuffed with aching nerves.

He got through the busy afternoon somehow, and left the office as early as he could—for he had promised to call on Iris Thorp on the way home. But to his surprise, as he came out into the street, he found he did not want to call on anyone, not even on Iris. He was sick; his head throbbed; his tongue and lips were dry; when he did not flush all over with heat, he shook with chill. He wanted to go home and go to bed.

He telephoned Mrs. Thorp that he would be detained at the office too late to pay his promised call. Then he hurried off to his own house.

He remembered what a jolly and intimate time together he and Thetis had had, several years ago, during the one brief illness of his married life, and how prettily she had nursed him and prepared wonderful invalid dishes and read aloud to him and sung him the old songs he loved. It would be like this now—perhaps. And he wondered why the prospect did not make him happier.

BUT it was not like the old times at all. When he reached home, Thetis was not there. And he remembered, belatedly, that she had planned to set out at noon for a six-day house-party at a friend's country-place. The proposed parting had not much interested Dick when she had told him of it. Indeed, now he remembered he had planned to use at least one evening of his six-day freedom to take Iris Thorp to dinner and to the theater.

The house was dreary and dim and altogether cheerless. Dick announced to the uninterested servants that he had grippe and that he wanted all the hot whisky and lemonade that he could drink—also a hot-water bag. With this latter Abishag-consoler, he crawled into bed and spent the night in a confused series of efforts to try cases before judges who slept and juries that sang.

When Thetis came back, nearly a week later, Dick was up and around the house once more but very shaky and weak and listless and unshaven. The grippe itself had departed, but it had left him limp and worn out.

Thetis was courteously remorseful for leaving him untended, and she asked in real concern why he had not sent word to her of his illness. As there was no logical answer to this query, she went on to ask if Dr. Van Schaick thought he was wholly out of danger. Then the fact developed that, like most men, he had not troubled to send for the doctor at all, but had dosed the fever out of himself with hot Scotch, starvation and quinine.

Dick added the news that he hoped to be well enough to get back to the office by the next day.

His unromantically bloodshot eyes and unshaven jaw sent a shiver of momentary disgust through Thetis, as she contrasted them with the well-groomed aspect of Hellman and the other bachelors at the house-party. But instantly her dormant maternal instinct awoke—to the extent of telephoning Dr. Van Schaick to drop around at once for a look at the convalescent.

VAN SCHAICK spent two minutes in questioning the sulkily reluctant Dick, and the best part of a half-hour in examining him.

"Look here, Doc!" crossly protested the tired patient at last, "if you keep your confounded ear to my left side much longer, it'll take root there and we'll be Siamese Twins. What's the matter, anyhow? Are you getting too deaf to hear my heart beat?"

"No," said Van Schaick very gravely as he lifted his head and looked with strange intentness into Dick's glowering eyes. "No, my boy, I'm not deaf. And I can hear your heart beat very plainly. But I want to hear it still better. So, if you'll let me use your 'phone, I'll send around for my stethoscope and for one or two other instruments that I—"

"Go ahead and send for a whole set of gardening tools, for all I care," vouchsafed Dick crankily. "I suppose you pill-jugglers have to go through that sort of hocus-pocus to impress your patients with your importance. If you just said to me: 'You are a bit weak from grippe and you'd better take a bottle of tonic,' that would be too simple and truthful to fit your profession."

"Yes," gently assented Van Schaick as he went to the telephone, "that would be too simple—far too simple, in your case."

"What do you mean, Doctor?" demanded Thetis worriedly. "Is there something really the matter with him?"

The Doctor called up his office and gave his directions before answering her. Then, to her repeated question, he answered in what both his hearers could see was a very patent evasion:

"My dear girl, there is 'something really the matter' with all of us. We absorb germs of fatal diseases every day. Our delicate organisms are always on the brink of collapse. Don't you remember the old Sunday-school hymn:

> Our life contains a thousand springs
>   And dies if one goes wrong.
>   Strange that a harp of thousand strings
>   Should stay in tune so long!

"Isaac Watts knew what he was writing about, even if he was a parson instead of a practitioner. You see, we doctors—"

"I WANT to know if there's really anything wrong with Dick!" insisted Thetis, heatedly breaking in on the old man's homily. "Tell me!"

"Rot!" growled Dick. "Don't you see he's only living up to his measly profession? Why, once when I was a kid, a doctor told me I had an 'exacerbated hyperæmia of the cornea.' And I was scared stiff, till I found it just meant the whites of my eyes were bloodshot. He—"

"Doctor," again demanded Thetis, "I want to know why you listened so long to the beating of Dick's heart, and why you've sent for those instruments."

"Grippe almost always leaves the heart rather wabbly for a few days," explained Dick impatiently. "That's the idea, isn't it, Doc?"

"Yes," said Van Schaick, "that is the idea. By the way, up to the time you fell ill, had you been feeling pretty well?"

"Not especially," answered Dick, after a moment of thought. "Now that I remember, I've been in rather rotten shape nearly all winter. Nothing to write home about or call out the guards for. Just too much work and too much food and too little sleep and no exercise. I dare say I've felt as three busy men out of five feel during a rush winter. I'll be all right when spring comes."

"M-m-m," commented the Doctor. "And this attack of grippe was just like all the others you've ever had?"

"No two attacks of grippe were ever alike," said Dick. "Even a doctor ought to know that. But they're all like grippe."

"Perhaps this one was not," ventured Van Schaick.

"What—what do you mean?" cried Thetis.

"Oh, here come my instruments," exclaimed the Doctor in very evident relief. "Now, lad, if you'll unfasten your vest again and loosen your collar—better take off your coat too."

HE was no longer the elderly and prosy friend, but the wholly professional and incisive physician. He applied the rubber-coiled stethoscope; he bent the grudging Dick's body from one angle to another; he thumped here and tapped there; always he listened.

Dick, with bad grace, suffered the prolonged examination. Thetis in growing alarm watched the old man at his mysterious work. When the instruments were at last laid aside, she hazarded a tremulous:

"Well?"

Van Schaick did not answer. He was looking down; and his fingers were playing a tattoo on the table-edge. Presently he spoke—with a jerky nervousness that astonished them.

"Know Erdheim?" he snapped. "Ever meet him? Ever see him? Ever hear of him?"

"Dr. Max Erdheim?" asked Thetis, wondering. "Isn't he the great heart-specialist? The man who was called in when President—"

"Yes. He's the best—the best of a big lot. Ever meet him, either of you?" he asked, looking frowningly from one to the other.

Dick shook his head.

"No," said Thetis. "What about him? And what has he to do with—"

"With Dick?" supplemented Van Schaick. "Nothing, yet. But I want him to. I'll call him up as soon as I get home. I'll make an appointment, if I can, for him to be here with me at ten to-morrow morning."

"I've got to be at my office before ten to-morrow morning," protested Dick. "I—"

"You will be here, to-morrow at ten," denied Van Schaick. "And you will stay here until that time—preferably in bed."

He spoke as though reproving some querulous child; and yet there was an undertone of something akin to solemnity in his dry old voice.

Thetis and Dick looked at each other—Dick perplexed, Thetis in terror.

"Hello, there!" protested Dick as Van Schaick clicked shut his ugly black bag and made for the door. "You're not going without telling me what's the trouble, are you? That isn't playing the game."

"I never 'play' the game," returned the Doctor, without stopping in his ponderous doorward progress. "I fight it. Good day. At ten, sharp, tomorrow—unless I 'phone you that Erdheim is busy."

"Doctor!" pleaded Thetis frantically, catching up with him in the hall, "what is it? You *must* tell me!"

"My little girl," said the old fellow tenderly, patting her shoulder as he spoke, "I will tell you everything about it, because you have a right to know what you are facing. I will tell you—just as soon as Erdheim has seen him."

"No! No!" she ordered, fierce with anxiety. "Tell me *now!*"

"My child," soothed Van Schaick, "I have no right to tell you until some better man endorses my opinion. That is why I want Erdheim. He is the best. There is no appeal from him."

Pityingly he brushed away the clasp of her detaining hands and jogged out of the house. Thetis ran back to her husband, who stood in the center of the living-room, blinking bewilderedly and trying not to look scared.

"Oh, Dick," she sobbed. "Dick!"

She put her arms about him as might a mother who longs to shield her little child from harm. In an anguish of dread she clasped him to her.

"They sha'n't hurt you, dear," she murmured idiotically, over and over again. "They *sha'n't*. I'm right here."

He said nothing—partly because there was nothing to say—partly because he dared not trust the steadiness of his voice. But he smoothed her shimmering hair—and stooped to kiss her reassuringly.

The years were rolling back. The success-bogy was hiding his home-smashing presence from them. Husband and wife were closer together in body and in spirit than for many a long day.

NEXT morning, promptly at ten, Dr. Van Schaick reappeared. With him was a frowsier and older man than himself, whom he treated with exaggerated respect and who spoke not one word throughout the visit.

Once more Van Schaick pounded and tapped the patient's torso. The stranger did the same, and they both listened long and breathlessly into the ear-plates at the end of their instruments' rubber tubes.

To Thetis' eager questioning they made no reply at all. Dick, his lips very tight-set, asked no questions. He answered, as curtly as could be, various queries which Van Schaick put to him for Erdheim's benefit.

By and by the two doctors went into another room to consult. Ten minutes later the front door shut and Van Schaick came back into the living-room alone. He found Dick and Thetis standing extremely close together and covertly holding each other's hands.

"Erdheim has gone," he told them brusquely. "He left me to tell you. Said it was no part of his work. Softhearted for such a big man. He—"

"Tell me!" pleaded Thetis, her feminine intuition showing her that the doctor was nervously seeking to postpone whatever sentence he had to pronounce.

Dr. Van Schaick cleared his throat, winked very rapidly as though to rid his spectacled eyes of unbidden mist, and turned to Dick.

"My boy," he said kindly, "it's a blow. And you must stand it as God meant brave men to stand such things."

"Fire away!" commanded Dick, his throat husky, his shoulders unconsciously squaring.

"It is the heart—as I feared," said Van Schaick awkwardly, fumbling with his watch-chain as he talked, and avoiding his hearers' eyes. "I won't go into details; that you couldn't understand, anyhow. You have heard of aneurisms, perhaps? When one attaches itself to the heart—especially to the left ventricle—"

"Well?" rasped Dick.

"It—such a case is incurable, lad," went on the Doctor hesitatingly. "With every care, and with freedom from work and worry and excitement, you may—you may—"

"He may get well," eagerly finished Thetis.

"He may live—for three months at most," corrected Van Schaick, his dry voice heavy with sorrow.

Dick's teeth set, with an audible snap. But he kept his head high; and he looked his judge square in the face. Thetis cowered as from a whiplash, and once more her arms crept shieldingly about her doomed husband.

"That is Erdheim's opinion too?" asked Dick steadily.

"He agrees with me in every detail," said the Doctor.

"Then," decided Dick, "there's no use frittering away precious time on other specialists, since you say he is the best. And the time that remains is precious. Three months is the outside limit?"

"Come to my office two months from to-day—if you are able to," replied Van Schaick. "I'll look you over once more then and tell you, just as frankly as I've told you, to-day, how much time is left. But remember, I said three months *at most*. There is nothing I can do for you," he continued, speaking briskly, to hide his emotion. "You will not suffer. That is the one blessing of your malady. You can take up normal life—in a careful way, of course—for most of the period. To all intents and purposes you will feel almost as well as usual. It is very merciful, this ailment of yours. Even toward the end—"

A FLOOD of weeping broke on his words. Thetis' gallantly preserved self-control had gone to pieces. She clung to her fated husband, sobbing as if her heart would burst, holding him tight—tight—*tight*—to her heaving breast. Dr. Van Schaick nodded gravely and left them alone together.

It was Dick who broke the awful silence that brooded over them, there in their solitude.

"The luck has run strong, this past year or so," he said dispassionately. "Everything succeeded. And now I see why. The investments I've made, and this house, and my share in the firm—all those will keep you comfortably. Those and the insurance—"

"Oh, stop!" she wailed. "*Stop!* How can you think of such things, when—when—"

"It would be a pretty poor kind of cuss who wouldn't think of just those things, first of all, at a time like this," answered Dick. "You see, girl—you're all that really counts—you and your welfare."

"No!" she denied miserably, and making no effort to stem her tears. "I'm not! I'm *not!* I'm not worth a single thought from you, my darling. Why, you don't even know how worthless I am. Listen: Only yesterday, on the train coming home, I got to thinking how far apart we had grown, you and I. And I wondered if we hadn't made a mistake and if we had really loved each other; and if we weren't mismarried and wouldn't be happier, separated. I did. I honestly did, Dick! Oh, I've been crazy. And now that it's too late, I'm all sane again. I love you so! And now I know I've always loved you, and that nothing and no one ever mattered except just *you!* Oh, I've been so vile, in my heart! So wicked and—and—untrue! Why, sometimes, I've even wondered if I didn't care for Rolf Hellman! And—and I've almost let him make love to me. And—I—*liked* it. I must have been insane, Dick. Won't you forgive me? I—"

SHE got no further. Dick's hand was over her mouth. Her husband was soothing her hysterical outbreak and calling her the dear, silly, secret love names that once had meant so much to them both. Then presently he answered her.

"If you've been crazy, little sweetheart," he told her, "then I've been crazy and drunk too. For I got sick of our home and impatient at you and wondering why we ever married. And I did worse. I fancied I didn't care about you any more—and that you didn't care about me either—and that we'd be better off traveling separate roads. I—I went so far as to think—to think I cared a lot about another woman.

"I can tell you all this, now, just as I'd tell you about a bad dream—because it isn't true. The second I heard I must die in three months, I knew there wasn't anybody on earth for me, but you. It all came to me as clear as God's own voice. And everything else rotted and fell away and left me free and—and *clean*. The petty struggle for success, the—the other woman; the money and the reputation and everything! I saw that none of them count for anything. There's only—you!"

"It meant the same thing to me, Dick," she breathed, fighting her sobs. "And I see now how worthless it all is. God gave us to each other, darling, because we were the only man and woman on earth for each other. We've been blinded by the things the world has thrown into our eyes. But we see, now, dear. We *see*. And it's too late!"

"It's not too late," he whispered, his lips close to hers. "Can't you understand, Baby, that this moment of clear vision is worth dying for? It's brought us close together again—forever and ever. And we have three months—three glorious golden months—to say good-by in and to make up for what we've done. Few people are as lucky as that. I'm going to wind up things at the office, to-morrow. Next day we're going to Bermuda, you and I, on a honeymoon—on an eight-week honeymoon. We'll get back two months from to-day, and I'll report to Van Schaick as he told me to. It'll be time enough then to think of sadder things. We're going on a honeymoon; you and I."

"Oh, it will be wonderful!" she panted, infected by the strange exaltation that had possessed him. "Just you and I! Do you remember, sweetheart, that weird old problem-story we read, once—about the people who were asked with whom they would spend the last day of their lives if they could have their choice, and if nothing they did could affect their salvation? Well, that problem is ours now. And we've solved it. It is the supreme test of love. It proves we love each other, and that—that—"

"That love is stronger than death," he concluded, with solemn happiness.

THE next eight weeks fulfilled Dick's promise for them. The stricken man and wife who adored him went south together to the land of spring. There, beside a summer sea, they began a miraculous honeymoon. They could not bear to be away from each other for five minutes at a time. Each strove to forestall and gratify the other's slightest whim. In the heart-depths of each was a yearning to store up beautiful memories for solace in the dark days to come.

Dick's one thought was to make his wife remember him at his best, that she might be comforted in future years by magic thoughts of this last sweet space of time together. Thetis longed to atone for her blind neglect of the past two years by making her worshiped husband's last months divinely happy.

Each had no thought but for the other. By tacit consent they did not speak of the impending separation.

If Dick, in the long night hours, sometimes reached out to lay his hand on the head of his slumbering wife, in an agony of yearning for longer life with her, she knew nothing of it. If Thetis, when her husband was sound asleep, sobbed and prayed softly in the darkness, in a mad yearning to be taken from life with him when he must go, her smile next morning gave Dick no hint of her torture.

Their love for each other illuminated their faces with an actual light from within. People who looked at them would turn away with a smile. But it was not the derisive smile which an ultra-sane world accords to mushy honeymooners. It was rather a smile with which a child might greet the splendor of the rising sun—a smile of amazement at such sublime love and happiness.

JUST two months from the day when sentence of death had been pronounced, Dick and Thetis were back in their own city. And together—always together now— they went to Dr. Van Schaick's office as Dick had arranged. The physician met them cordially. And now both of them saw him as in their early wedded days—not as a cranky and ill-dressed bore, but as the warmhearted old friend of their childhood.

"Before you begin any examination of me," Dick said to him, on impulse, "I want to tell you something. It's only fair to you. A couple of years ago you warned us that success was pulling us apart from each other, and that love like ours was too beautiful a thing for us to throw wantonly away. We both laughed at you, and we thought you were an old fogy. I'm sorry, but we did. Well, you weren't. You were dead right. If we'd had the sense to listen to you then, we'd have had two years of paradise together instead of only two months. But those two months have been worth all they're going to cost. They're worth an eternity of hell."

"There is no hell," murmured Thetis, her hand stealing into his, "except the memory of what we threw away when—when we didn't know."

"That's nine-tenths of the trouble in life," philosophized Van Schaick. "'We didn't know!' If we could get a second lease of life, after we *do* know—"

"I think," interposed Thetis, "I think that would be heaven."

"It would certainly be all the heaven *I'd* ask—here or hereafter," smiled Dick. "I've had more than my share of it in those two wonderful months. I didn't know there was so much happiness in all the world. But we're wasting your time. Shall we begin the examination?"

"No," replied Van Schaick brusquely, "we shall not. Why should I examine you?

You're fit as a fiddle. With decent care you ought to have fifty years of life ahead of you. You too, Thetis, girl."

"With an aneurism?" cried Dick. "Surely you must have forgotten—"

"Who ever said you had an aneurism?" snapped the Doctor. "*I* never did; I made a few incoherent remarks about the danger of an aneurism on the left ventricle. But I didn't say you had one. I never lie—unless I need to. When I said you *might* live three months at most, by taking care of yourself, I meant it. For no one but the Almighty can say surely that *anybody* is going to live for any specified time."

"But—if—why—Dr. Erdheim!" sputtered Dick, thunder-stricken, while Thetis gasped, speechless.

"Erdheim!" scoffed the Doctor. "Neither of you ever set eyes on Erdheim. He's been in Germany for the past year. The Erdheim I brought to see are you is generally called Mulcahy; and at present you can see him without charge, out there in my garden, planting nasturtiums. He's my man-of-all-work. He—"

"What in blue blazes does this mean?" roared Dick incredulously.

"It means," answered Van Schaick, "that I am foolish enough to be fond of you children. Your love for each other used to come near to reconciling me with humanity. Then you got money and position and flirtations and a lot of other useless assets, that were killing your love. That kind of love was worth too much to be killed. So I set out to save it. The only way to bring you two together again was to shovel aside the mountain of unreal things that had risen between you. The best way to scare off unreal things is to put real things in their place. And the realest thing ever invented is death. So I put the fear of it into you. And it saved you. Now get out and leave me alone. I'm busy. There are six *genuine* patients waiting in the anteroom. Scat!"

SIDE by side, Dick and Thetis left the Doctor's house. On the front steps they paused a moment, still dazed and shaken. A woman in white, passing along the other side of the street, looked across at them and bowed.

With a start, Dick Ragnar came to life. He raised his hat in response to the bow and his smile flashed brightly. Thetis noticed that it was not the dreamily sweet smile of the past two months:

"Wasn't that Mrs. Thorp?" she asked.

"Why—yes, I believe it was," he made sheepish answer. "Jove, but she's looking fit, isn't she? She's taken off her mourning, too."

He glanced at his watch.

"I must hustle down to the office," he announced. "There'll be an awful lot of work piled up for me. Don't worry if I'm late getting home."

"I won't," she promised with a little laugh. "In fact, you'd better arrange to dine downtown. I've been in the wilds so long, I've forgotten what a roof-garden is like. I think I'll call up Rolf Hellman, and ask him to take me to one."

The Girl of the NIGHT-COURT

by Albert Payson Terhune

WHEN Titus Gerry came to New York, four times a year, things insisted on happening. He came, ostensibly, to see a Nassau Street lawyer about the rent and repairs on three Bayard Street houses which he had inherited from his great-uncle and which formed the background to his worldly capital. This legal business occupied Titus for the best part of thirty minutes on each of his trimonthly visits to New York. The remainder of his week in town was given over to acquiring a past.

Throughout the bulk of the year, Titus Gerry lived at Haveridge, where he conducted that pleasant hamlet's single general store. Titus said his store was up to date—but he neglected to mention the date. The Village Welfare League put it roughly at 1832. For the rest, Titus was muscular and not ill to look upon. He had once modestly referred to himself as "a he-man." The aforesaid Village Welfare League had branded him "a sot."

Titus Gerry's half-hour talk with his lawyer had occurred on the first morning of his present visit to New York. For the three succeeding days he had been gleaning a personal insight into the city's life, taking no one's word for anything, but doing his own testing.

As a result he roamed down the lower East Side at ten o'clock one evening, with a dulled power of enjoyment and a mild craving to sit down somewhere for a quiet drink and a quieter smoke—somewhere that would not be lonely or too slow, where he could see and hear things and yet not be called on to take too sprightly an interest in them.

A bunch of electric lights fringing a sign set into the wall above a door informed him that Aliger's Cabaret was still doing business. Titus had known the place in the prehistoric days before it had changed—without in any way altering its character— from Aliger's Dance-hall to Auger's Cabaret.

He had vaguely pleasant memories thereof. So he drifted in through the rattan swing-doors, strolled past the bar and thence into a big and smelly room beyond.

THE hour was not yet twelve—or not yet midnight, as folk in Haveridge would have termed it. (Midnight and twelve o'clock have distinctly different meanings; Titus himself could have told you so.) The smoky room, therefore, was still somnolent and but half filled. The "professor" was whanging cruelly at the tortured upright piano, his cigarette adding a thousandth burned spot to the myriad on the keyboard ledge. A brown pint-flask was deftly propped into place on the musicless music rack in front of him.

Five or six bored-looking couples were drearily dancing to a super-rhythmic and sub-melodic tune as devoid of real music as was the professor's music rack itself.

Thirty or forty men and women were scattered among the four ranks of tables that flanked the dance-quadrangle at the center of the room. They were sipping uninspiredly at their glasses or talking to their table-mates with no great show of interest.

Truly, for so notorious a resort, little glamour clung to-night to Aliger's. It was anything but the gilded haunt of iniquity which the new reform mayor had that day described to the equally new and equally reform police-commissioner—a description the latter had dutifully passed on to the anything-but-new and totally unreformable precinct captain.

Tom Aliger waddled uninterestedly from point to point in the quadruple stockade of tables, favoring one habitué with a grin of welcome, another with a noncommittal grunt and a third with a glazed stare of curiosity.

Titus Gerry's frumpily ill-kept store back in Haveridge would have been gayer than this besotted hole. Yet in his present humor he decided it was the very best spot he could have chosen for his meditative glass and smoke.

HE chose an empty table, and was not in the least mystified at the miracle which caused an ambulant waiter to pause beside him at that identical moment. He ordered a long glass of dark domestic beer and—forever losing caste in his urban hearer's eyes—asked almost timidly:

"I don't suppose you keep 'Rose of the Valley' plug, do you?"

"Come again," suggested the puzzled waiter.

"'Rose of the Valley' plug," repeated Titus. "It's chewing tobacco—the best brand there is. I'd kind of like a chew, this evening. I feel just like it—and I left mine in my other coat."

"We don't keep eating tobacco," was the cold retort. "Our city patrons prefer pie. If you don't like beer without tobacco-juice, there's a cigar joint on the corner below, where they'll maybe have it in stock. Ten cents for the beer, friend—not forgetting the handsome waiter."

Left alone, Titus mused morosely over the silly disrepute wherein tobacco-chewing had fallen in select New York society. Then, as a solace, he drew out a blond and bloated cigar and lighted it. He tasted his beer, found it to be what he might have expected at Aliger's and sank back into bovine contemplation of the dancers.

But he was not allowed to follow his mood of peaceful meditation. Some one had threaded the labyrinth of chairs and tables from a far end of the room and was sitting down beside him.

Titus glowered at the intruder in surly rebuff. As he had foreseen, it was a woman.

"Good evening," she said listlessly.

"Nothing doing," he returned with exquisite courtesy.

He buried his nose in his beer-schooner, as a delicate hint that the interview was quite at an end. But the woman stayed where she was. Titus glowered annoyedly at her. She did not move. She did not even smile.

He had scarce had the optimism to hope that a single rebuff would drive her away, to let him go on ruminating in peace. But he had confidently expected her to smile the pitiful smile of the cowed, or else the bluffing grimace of the brazen. Instead, she sat grave-faced and unperturbed. Titus therefore looked at her in more interest.

SHE was dressed with a simplicity that stood out from the gaudiness of her she-neighbors like a bird-call above the wheeze of a hurdy-gurdy. Her make-up was almost artistic in its tenuousness. She was not beautiful—scarcely even pretty. But she had a square jaw, a startlingly direct glance and a pair of brown eyes that God had surely meant for an honest face. Her mouth was firm, without being thin-lipped. She herself was thin, yet not angular. And what struck Titus most forcibly was that she was looking at him as a man might have looked at another.

"I don't think you want to dance," she said with a half-glance at his bulge-toed Haveridge boots. "I'm glad, because I don't, either. Will you buy me a drink?"

"Why?" asked Titus, vaguely wondering at himself for so absurd a question, yet wondering far more at her for the dearth of coaxing in her request.

"Why?" she repeated as if not wholly understanding.

"Yes," he repeated crossly. "Why should I buy you a drink? I've bought myself one. That pays my admission here. I've told you I don't want you around. Why should I stake you to booze?"

"Because," she answered with the same odd directness that had begun to catch his languid interest, "because I need the money. And I need it badly."

"The money?" he queried, puzzled. "You asked for a drink."

"It's the same thing," she told him. "Aliger gives us twenty-five per cent off all the drinks that are bought for us. They do it at most of these places. If you order a twenty-five-cent drink for me and another for yourself, I'll get ten cents."

"But why should I?" he pursued, the born countryman's suspicion looming up. "Why did you pick me out for a mark?"

"I didn't," she said frankly. "Aliger gave me the sign to come over to your table. If I hadn't done it, I couldn't have gotten in here again. And he'd likely have blacklisted me all the way down the line. I had to."

"You do a lot for ten cents," he scoffed, beginning to enjoy this odd conversation.

"It isn't only for the ten cents," she answered, "though I could surely use any members of the ten-cent family that come my way. If I'd been as lucky as some of the girls, I'd have gotten up and quit you when you told me there was nothing doing. But I can't afford to."

"Why not?"

"I haven't much knack in separating men from their cash," she said. "Aliger told me so when I came back here to-night. He says he doesn't care much for chair-warmers. That's a hint that I must get more men to buy drinks or else clear out. Will you buy?"

"Yes," he said, amused, "I'll buy. What'll it be? A little of the stuff that killed Father, or one of the fancy drinks?"

"It's all the same to me," she answered. "I won't drink it, anyhow."

"Why not? They sell rotten stuff here, of course. But it's better than going dry."

"I don't know whether it's 'rotten' or not," said the girl. "I don't know the difference between good booze and bad. You see, I don't use it."

"That's funny!" he commented, adding sardonically and with a sudden expression of throwing himself on guard: "I suppose you promised your dying mother, you'd never touch a drop, and through all your hard luck you've stuck to that one sacred pledge, hey?"

"No," she said, quite unruffled by the sneer, "that isn't how it happened. I never promised my mother anything. She died before I was old enough."

"Too bad!" he commented.

"Too bad I can't remember her?" queried the girl. "Oh, I don't know. From the little I heard of her, I don't think I missed much. You hear a lot about—about my sort of girls breaking their old mothers' hearts. Maybe they do—sometimes. But not often. You see, a good mother generally has a good daughter—and the other way around. That's not in story-books, perhaps, but it's in real life. I guess there aren't many mothers of the right kind who are crying for lost daughters."

TITUS blinked at her in surprise, as one who hears a joke and cannot wholly grasp its point. His invariable experience with her type of woman had led him to expect certain well-defined varieties of lies. He was at a loss to tabulate this new specimen; it aroused not only his curiosity but also a vague resolve to verify his former knowledge. Failing on the dear-old-mother line, he shifted back to the subject of liquor.

"So you never drink?" he resumed. "And it isn't because you promised not to. Why, then?"

"I don't like the taste of it," said the girl. "And it makes my head ache, and it costs too much. Besides, I've seen what it does to other girls. What they get from it isn't worth what it gets from them. It—"

"The handsome waiter is among you," nasally intoned the greasy drink-dispensner, halting again at their table. "Whassit goin' to be?"

"A bottle of native champagne that you've soaked the label off of and replaced with the label of some brand that can't be got till the war's over," ordered Titus. "And bring one glass with it."

The waiter sped on his mission, revising and exalting his former opinion of the tobacco-chewing countryman. The girl turned in astonishment to Titus.

"Why," she exclaimed, "that will cost you six dollars! What made you do it?"

"On the level," he confessed sheepishly, "I don't know. It was—a hunch."

"It was a silly waste of good money," she accused.

"It was a nice rake-off of a dollar-fifty for you," he said sulkily, defending himself. "Perhaps it'll give you a new boost with Aliger. Look!"

The waiter was returning, in record time, with the champagne. Behind him trailed Tom Aliger himself, to nod civilly to the surly rustic and to beam in positive radiance upon the girl.

With almost reverent ceremony the waiter poured out a glassful of wine. It creamed and sizzed into the doubtfully clean glass, establishing at once the usual mysterious geyser from the bottom of the goblet's hollow stem.

"Looks good," said Titus as the waiter (duly paid and unduly tipped) left the girl and himself alone together once more. "Better change your mind and have some."

"No, thanks," she declined.

"H'm!" grunted Titus. "You don't drink, and you didn't have a gray-haired mother. Next you'll be telling me your father wasn't a fine old Southern gentleman."

"He may have been, for all I know," admitted the girl. "I never knew who he was."

"D'ye mean to say," demanded Titus in genuine interest, "d'ye mean to say he wasn't a fine old Virginia aristocrat who cast you off? Aren't you even going to tell me that if I heard your real family name I'd hardly believe it?"

"You'd believe it as much as I would," said she. "I don't know what my real name was. My mother called herself Mary Mercer. So the asylum named me *Hulda Mercer.*"

"*Hulda Mercer?*" he echoed in dismay. "*Hulda?* You sure don't keep on using a home-brewed monicker like *Hulda,* do you, in this trade? Why, you *can't!* Aren't you *Gladys* or *May* or even *Aggie?*"

"My name is *Hulda,*" she answered quietly. "I'm sorry if you don't like it."

"I do," he told her. "Only—only it don't seem to belong. It's like—like absinthe with griddle cakes, or like a tidy on the back of a faro-lookout's chair. It don't fit. Now,"—resuming desperately his air of banter—"won't you put me on the right track again by telling me about the Harvard man? Or was it a crool employer with a black mustache?"

SHE stared at him, perplexed. There was no doubt as to the real bewilderment in her face.

"The chap who started you in this game," he prompted her. "He's generally a Harvard man, maybe because *Harvard* is an easier name to remember than *University of Wisconsin* or—"

"No," she said, understanding at last, "there wasn't any Harvard man. If you're trying to guy me, go ahead. You've paid for the right to. I'm sorry I didn't get your meaning, at first."

"So that's why you're civil to me, hey?" he grinned. "Earning your one-fifty?"

"Yes," she assented. "That is why."

"You're honest, anyhow," he said with grudging approval. "Say! I can't dope you up, at all. You aren't like the rest I've met. What ails you? You don't belong in this game, any more than your name does."

As he spoke, he was fumbling in his vest pocket. Now, by a brilliantly executed maneuver, he tugged at his watch, yanking it out with such force that a two-dollar bill came from the pocket with it.

The bill fluttered to the floor almost at the girl's feet. Titus, with elaborate care, was studying the dial of his watch, turning his back on Hulda to get a better view of the time.

He was recalled to memory of her presence by a touch on his arm. She was leaning across the table, the two-dollar bill in her gloved hand.

"This fell out of your pocket," she said, "when you took out your watch."

Dumbly he took the money. Dumbly he stared at the girl. Very much he wanted to swear aloud, in sheer astonishment. Some undefined impulse checked the lurid words. He wondered at his own restraint.

"What in blue blazes *are* you, anyhow?" he stammered, presently.

"I think you know," she said. "Of course, you know. If I was a nun or a trained nurse, I wouldn't be hanging out at Aliger's. What's the use of asking such a question?"

"There's a whole lot of use in it," he declared vehemently. "How long have you been—been like this? And how did you happen to be?"

For the first time she laughed. It was a short, barking laugh, and not wholly pleasant to hear. It was bitter, self-disgusted. But in it there was none of the timbre of the street-girl giggle. Also it gave a momentary flash of a decidedly good set of teeth, slightly under-shot. And the steady brown eyes flickered prettily.

"If you're looking for the good old story that reformers like to lick their chops over," she replied, "I'm afraid you'd better tackle one of the girls that knows it better than I do. I'm not very good at sob-stuff. I didn't have a nice, story-book tumble."

"Tell me," he said curtly.

He had leaned forward, both arms on the table; his eyes fixed oddly on hers. His amused curiosity had fled, as had the earlier mood for sodden meditation. He was stirred—queerly stirred. And he half resented the feeling he could not combat.

"Tell me," he said again.

"There isn't anything interesting to tell," she returned, seeming to wonder at his new intentness. "I was sent from the Asylum—'Home' was what some funny-man called it—when I was fourteen. I got a job as cash-girl, and I held it till I was sixteen. Then I went to work in a laundry. After a year I got scalded in a boiler blow-up there. When I got out of the hospital, they'd got some one else in my place. I went to work for a while in the stock-room of a department-store. It was two floors underground, and the damp got into my lungs."

"Two floors underground?" he broke in, catching at the possible flaw in her spiritless recital. "In a department store?"

"Not in the part of a department store the customers see," she explained wearily. "A theater isn't all footlights and orchestra. And a department-store isn't all pretty goods and electric lights and bright glass counters... It got into my lungs. The store doctor said I'd better get out, before it gave me T. B. So I went. I worked for a while in a garment-factory on Houston Street—'sweatshop' is the French name for it. Then came the garment-workers' strike. I was in it. In fact, I helped stir it up. For we were certainly treated a lot worse than the public ever knew. I did more than any other girl to organize our branch of that strike.

"One of the papers printed a picture of me," she continued, with sorry pride, "and called me the sewing-machine Joan of Arc. It isn't on the free list to be a member of the Arc family, I guess. For when the other girls got back, I was frozen out. There wasn't another job open for me. That was the hard-times season, anyway—the season that sent a whole army of girls to parading down Queer Street. It was a year ago, pretty near. That's all. Have you got your dollar-fifty's worth yet?"

"Don't talk that way!" he protested hotly, stung by the cynicism of her question. "Just forget about the dollar-fifty, can't you? Listen here!"

"Well?" she said as he paused.

BUT he did not say what he had intended to. For a moment, he said nothing at all, but sat frowning at her and irresolutely chewing his under-lip. He felt he was in some kind of a whirling maze, from which he could not extricate himself. He had never been this way before.

He wanted time to think. He did not like being swept off his feet.

"Say!" he suggested, rising from the table, "I do better thinking when I've got a bite of tobacco between my jaws. They don't keep it here. The waiter says there's a tobacco-shop at the next corner. I'm going there to buy a chew. Will you wait here for me?"

A half-smile, that had no mirth at all in it, twisted one corner of the girl's firm mouth.

"Good-by," she said briefly. "I'm sorry it's been so slow for you."

"Will you wait here for me?" he repeated, ignoring her inference.

"Good-by," she said again. "I'm sorry—"

"Will you wait here for me?" he asked, speaking very incisively, his eyes on hers.

She met the glance with a piteous derision that gradually merged into wonder.

"Yes," she said at last, "I'll wait."

Titus made his way through the smoke-reek, past the sloppy bar and out into the street. He was dazed. Even out in the comparatively clean air, he could not think consecutively.

He found the corner tobacco-shop, asked for a plug of "Rose of the Valley" and waited with fuming impatience for a full five minutes while the clerk sought and found a box of the commodity from somewhere "in stock." Then Titus started back again toward Aliger's.

The street had been all but deserted when he had left the cabaret. Now it was choked with people. The crowd was ragged-edged, but it thickened well nigh to impassability at its center. And its center was the front door of Tom Aliger's place.

Titus, with the countryman's instant thought of a fire, bored his way through the outlying sections of the crowd and pushed onward until the press of human bodies brought him to a final halt, six feet from the doorway.

Here, as his height enabled him to see, a police-lane had been formed and was maintained by night-stick butts. One end of the lane was at the front door, the other at the sidewalk curb. Backed up to the curb was a patrol wagon.

Three more vehicles of the same dismal brand were passaging through the crowd, to take their turns at the sidewalk-edge. A half-dozen patrolmen were passing in and out of the cabaret's grimly garish entrance.

"Place on fire?" Titus asked a brown-derbied man at his side.

"Fire, nothin'," replied the other. "It's pulled."

TRULY, the reform mayor's talk with the reform commissioner and the latter's oration to the unreformable precinct captain had borne early fruit! Titus understood. For an instant he stood, an amused onlooker, at the too-common night scene. Then he remembered Hulda Mercer. And only the prod of a night-stick in his meridian checked his rush toward the entrance.

Now more policemen appeared from within the cabaret, a sprinkling of plain-clothes men among them. They were herding a right disreputable assortment of prisoners. Some were sullen; some were joking loudly; a few women were sniveling. One girl in a flaring hat was attracting undue notice to herself and away from her fellow-unfortunates by a screeching fit of hysterics.

First of all came Tom Aliger himself, followed by three of his waiters. They were packed into the front of the patrol-wagon, taking their disgrace with a cold stoicism that would have won Titus Gerry's admiration if he had had time or thought of anything but Hulda.

Then came the guests. And between doorway and patrol-wagon these were duly sorted and separated by the police. The men prisoners were shoved roughly to freedom into the ranks of the snickering crowd, with gruff injunctions to "beat it." The women were led or propelled into the waiting patrol-wagons.

Titus had only a fleeting look at Hulda as she walked wagon-ward, in a group of four or five other girls. Her companions held their heads high, even those who were blubbering. One of them was shrilly exhorting the rest to note the features of the plain-clothes men for the profit of future recognition.

But Hulda's head was bowed—not in tears or in terror, but as one might avert one's face from the intrusive wooing of a street camera.

Titus pressed forward again—once more to receive the blow of a night-stick's end in his short ribs, and a blasphemous command to keep back from the human lane.

Before he could recover his breath, the wagon into which Hulda had been hustled had made up its toll of criminal freight and had clattered off. The clang of its departing bell roused Titus Gerry to frenzy. Wheeling on the brown-derbied youth, he demanded:

"Where are they going? What station-house?"

"Oak Street," was the laconic response.

"How do I get there?" asked Titus excitedly.

The youth looked up at him in pleased interest.

"Girl of yours in the bunch?" he inquired.

"How do I get there?" fiercely repeated Titus. "Which way is it?"

"No use in your going there at all," said the interested youth. "Before you could make it on foot, they'd be away again."

"You mean they'll be set free?"

"That parcel of Janes?" sneered the youth. "Not much. It's the night-court for theirs. And if you want to get in touch with any of 'em, there's where you'd better hotfoot it. The Women's Night-Court—up to Jefferson Market. Magistrate Meagley's sittin' to-night, and he's easy—dead easy. You're in luck."

PAUL DURANT had once written, for *The World,* what is known to managing editors as "a human-interest story" and what the staff usually names "slush." It had been the story of a pathetic happening at the Women's Night-Court. He had received a five-dollar bonus, and the story had been pinned, for a week, to the soft-pine bulletin-board in the city room, together with a violet-ink mention of the award.

The five dollars had been spent in an evening; the glory had been wiped out by the next editorial call-down. The story itself had long been forgotten. But the curse remained. In other words, on slack evenings, the city editor had a habit of sending Durant up to the Night-Court to browse around for another human-interest story. Nineteen times out of twenty the resultant yarn was a flivver or a fake. Twenty times out of twenty it was uninspiring, and it reflected its author's distaste for the assignment. But the city editor continued to hope—hope being the only treasure left in the oft-rifled Pandora box which reposes under every city desk.

To-night was slack. And to-night Durant was wandering drearily about the half-empty Night-Court, hopelessly trying to evolve human interest out of a straggling collection of drunks, disorderlies, petty thieves, frail damsels and neighborhood pests. It was an unpromising lot, this evening's catch of the police-net. Glumly, Durant yearned for the presence of some resuscitated victim of a suicide pact. He even craved the lesser delights of a beery father visiting the court to plead for an unruly son.

He had loafed about the inclosure for a full hour, listening to the tragically brief trials that mean jail or freedom to their victims—scanning the docket, chatting with returned patrol-men.

He had stepped back to the corridor to speak with the door-man when on his return, inclosure-ward, he was accosted by a large and florid-faced visitor.

"Say!" began the florid stranger, "I've tried to get these cops and fresh attendants to listen to me, and they won't. You look as if you had sense. Will you let me talk to you a minute? I'll make it worth your while."

DURANT understood the blunder. As the reporter carried no hat, the big man had mistaken him for an official of the Night-Court. He was about to explain and back away, when the stranger went on in feverish haste:

"My name's Titus Gerry. I run the Occidental store at Haveridge. Here's my business card. I'm interested in a case here. A girl was caught in a raid down at Aliger's, awhile ago—she and a lot of others. They'll be coming up for trial in a few minutes now, a cop told me."

"I'm not a lawyer—" protested Durant.

"Then tell me how to get hold of a good one, at this time of night!" begged Titus, "—soon enough to have her acquitted. Man, don't go edging away like you wasn't interested!" he continued, his voice shaking. "I can pay you for your trouble. This means—this means a terrible lot to me."

The trail of the human-interest story was struck at last! Henceforward Durant stood without tying.

"Who is she?" he demanded. "Your sister, or—"

"She's not anything to me," replied Titus. "That's the trouble. She's just a girl I happened to meet. But say! Her eyes are the squarest, cleanest eyes I ever saw. And she's honest, and she tells the truth. And there's something about her that sort of won't get out of my mind. What'll they do to her?"

"Probably give her thirty days," said Durant. "That's the usual sentence. But a girl such as you describe isn't caught in a raid. She's probably fooled you into thinking she was better than she was. It's an old trick of the Daughters of Rahab. You can offer to go bail for her, of course. But she'd jump her bail and leave you in the lurch.

Take my advice. Sober up and go back to Haveridge and forget her. She'll have forgotten you by this time to-morrow. All men look alike to these girls."

"I tell you," retorted Titus stubbornly, "I tell you I'm going to get her out of this. If you can help me, you can have all the cash I've got left in my clothes. If you can't, point out a good lawyer to me, and I'll—"

"I'm doing more to help you, by steering you away from her," said Durant, "than if I could get her acquitted. You've been drinking. You've been drinking for days. I know the signs. Every newspaper man does. You're not drunk. But the accumulated booze has made you sentimental. Sentiment is thrown away on these women. Save it for the kind of girl a man can marry."

"Marry?" repeated Titus ruminatively, a fantastic idea all at once obsessing him. *"Marry?"*

Durant was turning away when Titus aroused himself from his brief stupor of cogitation and barred the reporter's path.

"Look here, Mr. Court Officer!" he said eagerly, "you go to your boss, the Judge, and tell him if he'll let Hulda Mercer go, I'll marry her and take her home to Haveridge with me and be responsible for her. I mean it. Now go tell him. And here's something for yourself."

He tried to slip a creased and limp ten-dollar bill into Durant's hand. For a second or more the reporter was too dumfounded to thrust it back upon the donor.

Here was human interest, with a vengeance! The hound-keen newspaper instinct swept away the last trace of altruistic desire to save a fellow-man from playing the fool.

"Do you mean that?" he gasped, incredulous. "Do you mean you'll actually *marry* her?"

"I sure do," stoutly affirmed Titus, adding: "That is, if she'll have me. You can tell the judge so."

"Sit here!" croaked the tremblingly eager hunter of human-interest stories, forcibly pushing Titus into a seat. "Sit here, and don't stir till I come back to you. Oh, keep your measly ten dollars! *I* don't want it."

FIVE minutes of tedious waiting ensued. During that time Titus Gerry inhaled the indescribably horrible air of a police-court, and seventy times he told himself he was a fool. But seventy-one times, something idiotic, inside of him, bade Common Sense to hold its babbling tongue.

At the end of the five minutes Durant was back, walking fast, his eyes agleam.

"Come along!" he bade the questioning Titus. "Magistrate Meagley will talk with you in his private room."

Up the aisle, through the inclosure gateway, around the bench and through the brown door in the wainscot of the rear wall Titus plodded in the wake of his guide. At length he stood in a bare little room, in the presence of a plump man who was so bald that his ruddy complexion extended unbrokenly all the way back to the nape of his neck.

"Judge Meagley," said Durant, "this is the man. He's approximately sober, and he seems sane. You can figure out the rest for yourself."

The bald man looked appraisingly at Titus. Then, not at all in his court-room voice, he began to fire questions at him. Presently he nodded to a court attendant who lounged in the doorway.

The attendant wriggled out of sight, coming back in a few minutes with Hulda Mercer. The girl stood blinking in the strong light. Her direct brown eyes strayed from the attendant to the magistrate—from the magistrate to Durant, from Durant, at last, to Titus Gerry.

Her face lighted strangely as her gaze met Titus'. Oblivious of the others' presence, she exclaimed:

"It wasn't my fault I didn't keep my promise to wait there till you came back! I never broke a promise till then. But they—"

"Young woman!" broke in Meagley, "how many times have you been arrested before this?"

"Not at all," she answered, her direct gaze challenging his. "I have been lucky, up to now."

"No," admitted the magistrate, "I've never seen you here before. Have you?" he asked the attendant.

"No, Your Honor," reluctantly admitted the blue-coat, "not that I remember. And I've got a pretty good memory for faces. I'm here about every night, too; for the past two years and—"

"Hulda," went on the magistrate abruptly, "if you had a fair start, could you travel straight?"

"What other business is open to me?" she asked listlessly.

"You're in the oldest business on earth," he replied; "and the next-to-the-oldest business is open to you. Want to marry?"

"Sir?" she stammered, doubtingly.

"Here's a man who is willing to marry you if I'll set you free," said Meagley. "Go into that corner, you two, and talk it over. Durant, hang around here, will you, and let me know what they decide."

He popped from the room, like a plump cuckoo, through a door in the wall that led to the court room.

Hesitatingly, Titus Gerry walked up to the corner where the utterly bewildered girl stood. Durant withdrew to the opposite end of the room and began to scribble madly on a doubled wad of copy-paper he drew from his side pocket.

FOR an instant Titus and the girl stared at each other in stupid silence. It was Gerry who spoke first. Clearing his voice, he began huskily:

"You—you heard what the Judge said? Well, it's all true. Will—will you marry me, Hulda?"

"But why?" she panted, aghast. *"Why?"*

"I don't quite know why you should," he answered, dashed by her manner. "I'm no great catch for any girl, I guess. But I'm better'n jail, aren't I? Or *am* I?"

"You don't understand!" she cried, her hand on his arm. "I didn't mean it that way. I meant why should *you* marry *me?*"

"I don't quite know why," he said again. "But I want to, if you'll let me. Will you?"

"But I don't—I—why, you *can't* want to marry me!"

"Why can't I? If you mean because you haven't been what folks call straight—well, I haven't been any blooming St. Anthony myself. And from a snap judgment, I should say you've got about all the virtues—except maybe the single one that all the rest of them take their name from. No, I don't know why I want to marry you, girl. But I do. And I haven't ever wanted to marry anyone before. Marrying wasn't exactly in my line. Will you marry me?"

"To save myself from going to jail?" she flashed, in a momentary gust of indignation. "I'm not coward enough to—"

"No," he contradicted, driven on by the odd impulse that had now taken entire control of him, "not to save yourself from going to jail. To save me from going back home—without you."

"But," she insisted, flushing, "you don't love me. Why, you *can't* love me! And I'm just a—"

"Maybe I can," he made slow reply. "And then again maybe I can't. And whether I do or not, I honest don't know. But I'm going to find out. Sha'n't we let it go at that?"

"I—I—"

"If it comes to loving," he pursued, "you can't very well love *me* either, can you?"

"I—I don't know," she faltered, her direct gaze for once wavering, her face's set mask breaking up into a score of unsuspected dimples and tearful smiles and a surge of fiery blushes. "I—I don't know. Oh, I'm not fit to!"

"What's one man's misfit," he expounded oracularly, "is another guy's paper-on-the-wall custom-made suit. I can stand it if you can. Is it a go, Hulda, girl? Say so, dear!"

THE WORLD'S several hundred readers, next morning, scanned Durant's first-page human-interest story of the Magdalen's Marriage. Its gifted author, incidentally, received a ten dollar bonus for the "beat" and a second brief spurt of bulletin-board fame. And he was condemned for another eternal period, to Night-Court duty.

The story aroused a good deal of talk. The evening papers took it up. (Their reporters searched in vain for the bride and groom—who had left town on an early morning train.) One paper even commented editorially on the sordid little romance, the editorial's final paragraph running thus cynically:

This is one of the real-life tales that each reader must finish for himself—which is fiction's chief advantage over real life. Will the rescued bride make the best of the strange deliverance that has come to her? Will she grasp her heaven-sent chance? Or when the first glow of gratitude has ebbed, will old habit reassert itself—as in the case of St. Peter's dog—and send her back to her former mode of life? Will she follow the immemorial custom of her kind? In every reader's mind will remain the unanswered, unanswerable query: "What Happened Afterward?"

WHAT happened afterward? Nothing that either cynic or sentimentalist had foreseen. Titus had merely found a master.

The first change was in the conduct of the store. In less than six months the grimily back-number emporium shone like new paint and was full of customers who were drawn thither by the new regime as much as by the attractive new stock. A bright efficiency reigned, and profits were quick to follow. Hulda was pushing her dazed husband into an undreamed-of prosperity. The woman of the streets was teaching Gerry the cash advantages of respectability.

Titus writhed fumingly at times, but her grip on his will-power was as inexorable as it was habitually gentle. The clash came when—growing placidly accustomed to what had lately been a delightful novelty—his spirit began to crave one of his periodical visits to New York. He broached the subject to Hulda—casually telling her that he must run down to the city on business, the first of the following week.

"I'm afraid we can't arrange for that quite so soon, dear," she answered sweetly. "The white-goods sale is for Tuesday, you know. And on Thursday we have the furniture opening. Wait till the next week. Then perhaps we'll be able to get away for a day."

"*We?*" he sputtered wrathfully. "Who said anything about *we?* I'm going on business. You'll have to stay and look after things here while I'm gone."

"On business?" she smilingly took him up. "I know—to see your lawyer. A letter to him, or a phone call, will do just as well, old boy. And you know it will."

"I'm going!" he roared, writhing in the meshes of her kindly spoken words like a bear in a net. "I'm going! And that's all there is to it!"

"No, Titus," she corrected him in the same measured calm, "that's not all there is to it. There is a great deal more. If you go, you won't find me here when you come back."

"Now, what d'ye mean by that?" he demanded.

"I mean," she said very slowly, "I mean, Titus, that I know how you used to spend those business trips. You remember, I met you on one of them. That was the last one. Not the latest one, but the *last*—the very last. Let that be understood. If there is to be another, then I am going on one myself, *and with whatever companion I choose!*"

"HULDA!" he grunted, like a fighter who has failed to guard against a stomach-blow.

"I mean it," she said evenly. "If you had married some sweet young girl, you could have fooled her, to the limit. She wouldn't have known. If she *had* known, she wouldn't have understood. But *I* know, and I understand, because I've been there."

"Don't talk about that! I—"

"If you'd married the average girl," resumed Hulda, "she wouldn't have owed you anything. *I* owe you everything. You saved me and put me on my feet. I'm going to save you and put you on *your* feet. I've been doing it, for months. And I began to think I was paying my debt. It made me happy—because I hate to be in debt. That's why I wasn't happy till we'd cleared off all that nasty pile of outstanding money you owed here in Haveridge. But I—"

"I've a right to—"

"But I don't mean to be fool enough to help a man who won't be helped," she continued, unheeding. "I'm not wearing old clothes and lying awake nights planning to make you rich—just to have you throw away our money on drink and on such people as you'd meet in Aliger's. Understand that."

"It's my own money!" he snorted rebelliously. "Now, see here, what'd you be—"

"Without you?" she asked. "I'd be what I was before I met you. And that's what I am going to be, if you slip back to what you were before you met *me*. I love you, Titus," she went on, a rare note of tenderness in her voice. "I love you, dear. And I've felt that if I could make a man of you—a clean, prosperous white man,—it might redeem—might make up for—for—"

"Don't!" he protested, realizing sulkily that he was beaten. "I—"

"But if I can't do that," she said, "then I'm throwing away my time by living with you. What is the use of my staying as clean as I *am,* if you are going to be as worthless as I *was?* If you are going to waste your money with women who are—are what I used to be, then I'm here under false pretenses. When you come back, I'll be gone. Now go, if you like."

"Go?" repeated Titus, slack-jawed surrender lost in an odd exaltation that stirred him to the soul. "Like hell, I'll go! I'm going to keep right where I am, and watch *you."*

"Watch me?" she asked with a thrill of resentment.

"You bet I am!" declared Titus. "When a man's whole fortune and future and happiness and everything else are tied up in one investment, I guess he'd better stay on the job and look after it. Especially, if that investment's got a bulldog jaw and a mouth that can kiss almost as well as it can scold. To blazes with going to New York! *Now* are you satisfied?"

Money Thrown Away

LOIS MADDEN was happy, very, very happy—until some one told her she was not.

Happiness is a mystic bud that a single breath can wake into riotous bloom or wither to a shrivel. And it has no existence except in its possessor's heart. That is why a breath, laden with a few silly cynicisms from a wise fool, was able to do all sorts of things to Lois Madden's gladness. Here is the story:

When Hugh Madden married Lois, she did not think he was the most wonderful man in the whole world: she *knew* it. And the knowledge only deepened and strengthened, during the next six years. It was Hugh's wonderfulness that made Lois so happy.

She rejoiced in his cleverness, his clean good-looks, his popularity, his fast-growing business success. Most she rejoiced in the miracle that had made such a man choose her for a wife.

This last-named reason for rejoicing abides with many a woman, for at least two months in her life—for a month before marriage and for a month after her husband's death. To Lois Madden it had been given to feel like that for six beautiful years—which was a blessing to her husband and a still greater blessing to herself.

The Maddens led a jolly, uneventful little life together—at first in an elevatorless fifth-floor flat. Lois used to explain gayly to apoplectic and panting callers that her only excuse for living on the fifth floor was that there was no sixth.

Then, as business waxed better and better, Hugh and Lois moved by easy steps into more luxurious and more accessible quarters; and cigars and dollar-a-pound candy became everyday occurrences rather than events.

Hugh was doing splendid work, and he was drawing a splendid salary. Yet the couple were as devoted as when a raise from forty dollars a week to forty-five dollars had been a godsend. True, there were fewer early home-comings from the office nowadays, because extra pay meant extra work of a sort that could not be shelved. And there were occasional evenings when Lois sat alone or dined with her parents, because Hugh had to stick at his desk until midnight. But longer summer vacations together made up for these home-time losses.

Yes, Lois was so happy that sometimes it frightened her. And then, one idle day, she read the book.

THE book was four hundred and twelve pages long. Its title was: "Dead Sea Fruit." It was written by Marcia Kibbe Klaw, the literary genius whose name is adoringly revered by the elect of two continents.

There is no more merciless mental vivisector unhanged than Marcia Kibbe
Klaw. Compared to her ice-bright scalpel, Balzac and Thackeray wielded wands
of whipped-cream and swans-down. She sweeps away pretty human shams and
conventions as with a sand-blast, revealing the crass rottenness of the core. (All
this information is for the benefit of the several hundred million men and women
who stupidly prefer to take their reading as a recreation instead of as a visit to a
dissecting-room, and who therefore are not conversant with the deathless literature
penned by Marcia Kibbe Klaw.)

Lois saw "Dead Sea Fruit" most favorably mentioned in a publisher's
advertisement in a newspaper. The next week she heard three of the women at the
Friday Afternoon Bridge Club hotly and avidly discussing it. As the three were at the
same table with herself, Lois felt woefully ignorant and ill read.

On the way home from the Club she stopped at the circulating library to leave
an order for the book. To her surprise she did not have to wait her turn. "Dead
Sea Fruit" was on the library's shelves, and there were no orders ahead of Lois'.
Perhaps the class of people who read Marcia Kibbe Klaw do not infest circulating
libraries. At any rate, Lois Madden walked proudly home with the numbered and
paper-jacketed volume under her arm.

NEXT morning dawned rainy and raw—one of those days nobody wants. As

soon as Hugh had been invested in raincoat and rubbers and had been waved to, from the bay window, as he set forth officeward into the sloppy street, Lois curled up on a couch and began the great book.

At lunch-time she was still reading it—not because it thrilled and uplifted her as she had expected, but for the reason that makes one listen, with disgusted interest, to a liar.

"Dead Sea Fruit," to Lois' uninitiated mind, was a stupendous lie from cover to cover—a nasty lie, at that! Its plot could have been told, in full, and with all due and overdue ramifications, within the scope of thirty pages. The remaining three hundred and eighty-two pages were taken up with the gifted author's personal preachments and with the hectically heartbroken musings of the heroine.

In brief, "Dead Sea Fruit" told of a sheltered-life woman who at the outset knew little of the seamy side of life and who cared about it even less—a woman whose god was her husband and who, on learning that her god was only a mortal, lost faith in all men. This apparently was what Mrs. Marcia Kibbe Klaw herself had long since done and what she sought, verbosely, to argue her feminine readers into doing.

"I've been reading a perfectly horrible book to-day, Hughie," announced Lois as she and her husband loitered over dinner that evening, "—a perfectly disgusting book. And not one vile word of it is true. Not one!"

"H'm!" vaguely responded Hugh, looking up from lighting a cigarette. "'Horrible' book, eh? There's a lot of them, these days. I wonder how they get away with it. Why, when I was a kid, women—nice women—never even got a chance to read that sort of book, But now they're right on open sale—"

"No, no," hastily corrected Lois, "this wasn't 'that sort of book'—not the sort you mean. At least—well, some of it was vulgar enough, goodness knows, but when I said it was horrible, I meant because it told such stories—"

"Stories?" queried Hugh with mild interest. "Pretty raw stories in it, eh? What's its name?"

"Not 'raw,' as you call them," she set him right. "And not stories, at all, in that sense. I meant it tells such falsehoods about—about husbands and wives. Marcia Kibbe Klaw must have had a horrid married life. And I suppose she thinks all men are like that—just as her heroine does. But it's a shame to let other people read such stuff—single people, young girls—and let them get such an outrageous idea of marriage. Don't you think so?"

"Sure," agreed Hugh, furtively looking at his watch. "It's too bad. Who wrote it?"

"I just told you," said Lois. "Marcia Kibbe Klaw. She's tremendously famous. I—"

"Not in *my* poor brain," denied Hugh. "No, she's a novelty to me. I never heard of her."

"I'm so glad," declared Lois, "—because I hadn't either. But everybody else seems to know all about her. Isn't it nice we're both ignorant about the same things? She takes up a whole thick book just in trying to prove that men are beasts and that they aren't true to their wives. She says: 'All men are polygamists and all women—'"

"The old fool!" snorted Hugh fervently. "Why do you read such drivel, baby?"

"I don't," she replied. "I never did before. And I'm never going to again. It's sickening. Honestly, it is. Why do you keep looking at your watch?" she broke off as Hugh once more fumbled in his waistcoat pocket. "We aren't going anywhere."

"*I* am, worse luck!" he made rueful answer. "I wish I wasn't. I've got to run back to the office for two or three hours this evening. That—"

"Oh, Hugh!" she exclaimed in keen disappointment. "It's so rainy! And I've been alone all day! I couldn't get out, even to—"

"That Cleveland order is giving us a lot of bother," he went on. "I promised Lowndes I'd meet him at the office at eight-thirty, sharp, and go over the correspondence with him. I'm sorry, kid, mighty sorry. It's a shame to leave you alone like this. But it's a case of must. I'll be back as early as I can."

THE wind-driven rain slithered and slapped crossly against the living-room windows. It was a snugly pleasant night to be indoors—with one's own. Left alone, Lois grew restless.

"It's that miserable book!" she murmured half aloud and with a gust of self-impatience. "I wish I could get the sour taste of it out of my mind."

She fell to brooding sweetly over her own life and contrasting it with that of "Dead Sea Fruit's" heroine. She wished Marcia Kibbe Klaw could know there were husbands like Hugh—husbands who loved their homes, husbands as true as steel to their adored wives, husbands who went out, night after night, to dreary hours of office-work, that their wives might enjoy the luxuries won by extra money.

An odd, willful impulse suddenly seized the woman. She crossed to her little writing desk and sat down. Taking an envelope from a rack, she sprawlingly addressed it:

Mrs. (or Miss) Marcia Kibbe Klaw.

Then she paused uncertainly for an instant, reached for the copy of "Dead Sea Fruit" and, noting the publisher's name, wrote:

Care of Messrs. Schweinhund & Sons,
        New York City.
Personal.
Please forward.

Then, choosing a sheet of letter-paper, she began to scribble—at first haltingly, but soon with a jiggling haste as her feelings bore her along. When she had finished, she read what she had written, correcting or substituting or striking out a phrase here and there. After this she began to read aloud her letter. It ran:

Dear Madam:
I have just finished reading your book "Dead Sea Fruit."
I hate it. I hate it because it isn't true in one single word. Maybe there was once a couple you knew who were like that. But it is wrong to write as if it were so with every couple. And it isn't fair to give the idea that all husbands or even one husband in two thousand is like your Seldon Gwynn.
Because that one man was a beast and wasn't true to his wife, you and your book's heroine try to make out that all husbands are that way. They aren't. And it seems to me a wicked thing to try to make people think so. Nearly every married woman that I know is happy with her husband, and her husband is true to her. I hardly ever knew a woman whose husband wasn't.
So won't you please stop giving young people an untruthful idea of married life? I am writing this to you on the chance you may think you are telling the truth. I want you to know you are mistaken and not write any more such misleading stories.
I have been married for more than six years. In all that time my husband and I have never once been away from each other for an evening or a night—except when he has had to work late at the office or be sent out of the city on business. He loves me just as dearly to-day as he did when we were engaged. He would no more think of being untrue to me than—than I would think of being untrue to him. And

no real man would do such a thing. I know it.

If it is unkind of me to say I hate your book, I am sorry. I don't mean to be unkind. But I couldn't let you go on having such a wrong idea of husbands. Why not make your next book a story of a man and wife who are like real-life people— not like people in a morbid nightmare? Please don't be offended.

LOIS signed the letter, folded it and put it in the addressed envelope. Then, her first crusader-enthusiasm ebbing, she was of two minds whether or not to post it.

And, as usual when in doubt, she telephoned to Hugh. After an interminably long wait, Central droned:

"Broad 09,999 don't answer!"

"Nonsense!" reproved Lois. "It's a big switchboard. All the lines on it can't be busy."

"Not busy—just don't answer," replied Central—and cut short the argument by disconnecting.

Lois hung up the receiver and went back to the living-room, frowning perplexedly. Presently her face cleared. Now she remembered. She remembered she had once before called Hugh up at his office at night, had received no answer and had asked him why. He had explained that the firm's switchboard girl went home daily at six o'clock and that except in emergencies no one was kept at the switch, "after hours."

In her zeal to tell Hugh about her letter, Lois had forgotten this. Of course, Central had gotten no answer to the call. Hugh was in his own office, and there was no one at the switch to connect his wire with the board.

She stamped her letter, dropped it down the mail-chute in the outer hall—and spent several minutes in regretting her action.

She went back to the living-room, worriedly speculating as to whether or not the gifted authorette would bother to answer the letter. (Which, as a matter of record, the gifted authorette never did.)

There was a purr at the door-bell. Lois had let both her maids go out to a dance of the Gentlemen's Sons' Association. So she answered the summons herself, admitting a plump and hatless woman whose chiffon tea-gown would have made a conscientious dry-cleaner's fingers itch.

THE visitor was a Mrs. Winston, who lived across the hall, and who still stuck to the small-town habit of "running in, informally" now and then, on Lois. Lois was not overfond of her next-door neighbor. Yet in her present blue mood she greeted Mrs. Winston with something akin to effusiveness.

"It was good of you to take pity on my loneliness this way," she said as she and her guest went into the living-room.

"I took pity on my own loneliness," disclaimed Mrs. Winston, "not on yours. Harry ran away to his lodge, as usual, and left me stranded."

"Hugh had to go out too," said Lois, "—only, he went to the office instead."

"H'm!" mused Mrs. Winston. "I wonder if Harry's lodge happens to be in Mr. Madden's office, or if Mr. Madden's office chances to be in Harry's lodge."

"Nonsense!" she declared. "Why do you say such things, even in fun?"

"It's fun for them," rejoined Mrs. Winston, "but it's death—or lonesomeness—for *us*. Why, my dear, if all men went to the office or the lodge, after they told their wives they were going there, every window in every skyscraper in New York would be ablaze all night long. And the Masonic Temple would have to be enlarged to cover ten city blocks."

"I wish you wouldn't make that kind of joke," said Lois irritably. "It isn't in good taste. It seems disloyal to your husband to talk so. I feel almost disloyal to Hugh in listening."

Mrs. Winston smiled—as one who hears a far-off melody—or sees two dollars—or recalls a funny story which will not bear telling. It was an annoyingly superior smile. It stung Lois afresh.

"You kindergarten infant!" scoffed the visitor, noting the flush of wholesome temper that jumped through the clear pallor of her hostess' face. "You refreshingly innocent babe in the woods! *Are* you a babe in the woods, or is it just a gallant bluff?"

"I don't understand—"

"Do you actually mean to say you *believe* your husband is at his office? Or that Harry is at the lodge? Call up the office, just for a lark, and ask for Mr. Madden. I'd call up the lodge too, but Harry says lodges have no phones. Call up and—"

"I won't!" flashed Lois. "I wouldn't do such a thing."

"So it *is* a bluff?" chuckled Mrs. Winston in triumph. "And I've called it."

"You haven't! I—"

"Harry told me once that he worshiped me," pursued Mrs. Winston. "He said I'd started something I could never stop! That was when he proposed to me. Well, it wasn't I, but Adam and Eve, who started it. It's been going on ever since. The only difference is that Adam was true to Eve. He was true to her because she was the only woman on earth. Harry used to tell me *I* was the only woman on earth. But since then, he's made the startling discovery that there are a few million others. So has every other husband, including Mr. Madden."

"My husband is splendidly true to me!" asserted Lois with vehemence. "I *know* it. And most other women's husbands are true too. Hugh is never away from me for one single evening or night, except—"

"Except when he is not with you," supplemented Mrs. Winston, "and during the entire day. The days are long, you know. Sometime perhaps you'll wake up to the fact that your husband's business absences may be another woman's business."

"I—that is a horrid, a perfectly horrid, thing to say!" cried Lois, on the verge of tears. "If I thought you really meant one word of it—"

"There is nothing to get excited over," Mrs. Winston assured her, a note of hardness underlying her raillery. "We women must be philosophers—unless we

want to go mad. If only one man on earth had to die, that man would be frantic
with terror. But as all men have to die, all men bear the idea philosophically. If only
one husband were untrue, his wife might be excused for breaking her heart over it.
But since all husbands—"

"They're not!" Lois defied her. "They're *not!*"

"Pretend they're not, then," mildly suggested Mrs. Winston. "You'll be happier
that way. All women are happier that way. That's why most of us dodge the issue
and refuse to prove what we know. We'd rather go on giving our husbands the
benefit of the doubt—even when we know there isn't any doubt. It's easier and
pleasanter all around."

WHEN at last the caller had gone, Lois bravely resolved never to let her own
thoughts stray back to the wretched theme. But it is one thing to slap away a hornet
that has stung you, and quite another thing to forget the sting's hurt.

Lois Madden was profoundly and increasingly unhappy. In vain she scolded
herself for the impression Mrs. Winston and the Klaw woman's book had made
upon her. She could not forget. She was bitterly ashamed of herself for pondering
Mrs. Winston's "The days are long" and "your husband's business absences may be
another woman's business."

She hated herself for the secret disloyalty to Hugh that let such hideous thoughts
live in her mind. She told herself she was not worthy of so glorious a husband—she
who now began to feel a gripping ache at her heartstrings every time he was not at
the office when she called up.

At last it all grew unbearable, and it goaded her into the stark need for action—for
any kind of action at all. Once and forever the cloud must be lifted, if it were not
to blacken all her sweet future. She remembered what *Zira*, in "Dead Sea Fruit" had
done in like case. And she followed the heroine's doubtful example.

The enterprising head of the Skalds Private Detective Agency one morning
received a visit from a young and unusually pretty woman, a woman whose soft
lips were now set in a white line and whose softer eyes were glinted and hard with
pain. The caller wasted no time in coming to the point. Repeating stiltedly an
oft-rehearsed speech, she said:

"Mr. Skalds, my husband is leaving home to-morrow on a three-day trip. He says
he is going to Pittsburgh on business for his firm. He expects to come home again
on Friday night. I want him—followed"—the dry voice breaking ashamedly at the
ugly word—"by the best detective you have, by two of them, if it is necessary. I
want them to keep close track of everything he does and everywhere he goes. Then
I want a full report written out and mailed to me. How much will it cost?" she
ended, her gloved fingers fumbling shakily with her net purse.

"If you care to make a deposit," suggested Skalds, "I will give you a receipt for
it. In fact, it is customary. But I can't tell you how much my bill will be. My charges
are eight dollars a day and expenses for each man I send out on a case. Often the

expenses are larger than the daily eight dollars. Then there is the cost of sending you telegrams, from time to time, reporting progress. And—"

"I don't want telegrams!" she declared. "I don't want to be kept in suspense, half-knowing and half-ignorant. I want you to do this just as I have told you. Have a typed report made out, a *full* report, as soon as my husband gets home, and mail it to me so I can get it the next day—a report that will tell me everything. If the three-day trip is taken up with business,—legitimate business,—tell me all about it your men can learn. If the three days and nights—or any part of them—are spent in any other way, report it in full. Here is seventy dollars. It is all the money I have in my purse. Send me your bill for the rest, and I will mail you a check for it the same day. Understand, please, I want this report to be so accurate and so complete that I can never have any further room for doubt, either way. Here is my card. Here is Mr. Madden's business address, and here is a photograph of him. Thank you. Good morning."

LOIS Madden walked out into the pitiless yellow sunlight of lower Broadway, dazed and nauseated.

"I suppose I've taken the very lowest and most abominable step any woman can take," she heard herself saying aloud in a queer, lifeless voice. "And I'll have to tell Hugh all about it afterward, even if I'm wrong. I can't let him go on without knowing what I've done. Oh, it's so horrible to be alive!"

When Hugh, next morning, kissed his wife good-by, Lois clung to him, weeping helplessly. She felt as if she were taking a last farewell of all that made the world worth while.

"Oh, darling," she sobbed, "darling, *don't* go! For my sake—*Hugh!* Don't go! Give it up!"

"Why, little sweetheart," cried the man, dumfounded, "what's the matter? Are you ill? Has anything happened? I never saw you like this before. Aren't you well?"

"I—I'm all right!" she said, choking back the tumult of sobs. "I'm sorry I was so babyish. Yes, you must go. The sooner you go, the sooner it will be over. It's more merciful that way. Run along. But kiss me again, before you start. Good-by!"

The three-day hell of suspense set in. And the crux of that hell, for Lois, was her sense of unfaith and disloyalty to Hugh. Her only consolation was the thought that, even were he innocent, she would tell him what she had done and would bear, as punishment, his grieved dismay. It would hurt him cruelly, she knew. And she must pay for that hurt—yes, and for her own rash decision to prove or disprove her happiness. Life could never again be quite the same for them. But for that matter, life had never been the same for her since Mrs. Klaw and her book had wrecked the peace of her faith in Hugh. It could never be the same, in any event, until Hugh should be shown guilty or innocent.

So, no doubt, did Pandora reason. So too did *Bluebeard's* wife. So have millions of later women.

When Hugh came back, on the evening of the third day, he was startled at the pallor and the new lines of suffering in Lois' face. She calmed his worries with the world-ancient feminine excuse of a sick headache. On the same excuse she went early to bed.

Next day she arranged to receive the first morning mail in person from the hall-boy, at the apartment door. Among the few letters and circulars was a long bluish envelope, plump and heavy, one corner emblazoned with the imprint of the Skalds Private Detective Agency.

This envelope Lois hid until after Hugh's departure for the office. Then, going to her own room, she shut both doors, sat down in front of the grate-fire and drew forth the long envelope from its hiding-place. Her hands were very cold and wet. Her mouth was very dry and hot.

SHE turned the envelope over and read again the prim advertisement of the Skalds Agency in its top corner. Here between her moist palms lay fate—future triumph, despair, heartbreak, happiness. The tearing of the envelope-end, the withdrawing of the sheaf of typed sheets, a minute's scanning of the report—and she would know everything, whether for good or for ill. She would know whether her life were black and blasted or whether it held a new lease of the perfect happiness which for six years had been hers. In her hands she held her destiny—the secret of existence.

It was characteristic of Lois that she hesitated before she ripped open the envelope and learned the worst—or the best. Now that her weeks of wretched waiting were ended, now that sixty seconds would give her a lifetime of perdition or of bliss, she hesitated. And analyzing her soul, she knew why.

Slowly she forced herself to put into mental words the emotions that swept stiflingly through her. If this report should tell her that Hugh was innocent, that he was the loyal, clean husband of her six-year dream, she must hate herself forever for doubting him without cause. The specter of unfaith must always stand, shadowy and sinister, between her and the man she loved.

If the report should prove Hugh was not worthy of her, then what else in life was left? Self-respect would not let her go on living with a man who had broken his altar-pledge to her. Jealousy would ride her heart to death. With her own hands she would have smashed her idol—smashed all she wanted to live for.

Lois recalled what the serpent in Eden had said to Eve in luring Adam and herself to eat of the Tree of Knowledge: "You shall be as gods, knowing good and evil." They had yielded to the lure, and henceforth their lives had been thick with anguish.

Here in this long envelope lay the secret of good or of evil for her and for Hugh. Who was she, to wrest forth that secret?

If Hugh were guilty—well, she knew that at heart he loved her and loved her devotedly—no matter how far afield his less worthy instincts might have led him. Was her knowledge of his guilt worth the pain and loneliness and disillusion it must entail? She must then leave him—be as a man who has lost his God. There would be no more divinely silly sprees and outings, no more precious home evenings, no one whose daily return from work she looked forward to.

On the other hand, were he innocent—

The sheaf of typed pages, under her trembling fingers, slithered halfway out of the envelope.

Shuddering as in mortal torment, Lois crumpled the sheets and the envelope into

one tight-squeezed lump and threw them into the bed of sputtering coals. Thrusting them down, far out of sight, with convulsive jabs of the poker, she gasped aloud:

"I don't want to know! Oh, I don't! I *don't!*"

"WHAT don't you want to know?" asked Hugh, opening the door from the hall and coming into the room.

She jumped to her feet and stared agape at him.

"I forgot my desk-keys," he explained. "Remembered 'em at the subway and—What's wrong?" he broke off to say, shocked by the stark anguish in her big eyes. "What is it, dear? Another headache? You ought to see Dr. Colfax."

"It isn't a headache," she denied, finding her voice as a rush of fierce resolve swept her. "It's this: are husbands beasts? Tell me! Do they all break faith with their wives? Is it true?"

"What crazy rot are you talking?" he asked, astonished.

"Is the Klaw woman right?" she demanded. "Is Mrs. Winston right? Do all husbands deceive their wives?"

"What an idiotic thing to ask!" he protested, laughing. "Of course not. You know better than that! But what—"

"If I should ask *you*—face to face, eye to eye—if you are true to me, Hugh," she persisted, "could you tell me honestly that you are? Tell me!"

Before he could answer, a swift revulsion of dread seized her.

"No, no!" she wailed, "you mustn't tell me! I don't want you to. I won't listen! I love you so! And I'm not going to have my faith in you shaken. Even if—even if—oh, I *do* trust you, darling. I *do!*"

"Why in blazes shouldn't you?" retorted Hugh. "If I'm not true to you, then no man ever lived who was true to his wife. Of course I am. And you know it. I—"

"Yes," she sighed in utter relief, nestling close to the shelter of his big arms, "of course I know it. I always knew it. I'd know it even if it wasn't so. Because—oh, because it would *have* to be so. I couldn't live if it wasn't!"

you off. What number was you talking to? —Schuyler 4789 is still busy. —It's just twelve-forty-two, by the c'rect time. —Number, please."

Up and down the double rank marched a horribly efficient woman who discouraged repartee and inter-desk conversation. The long room buzzed with the rhythmic droning of fifty voices and with the purring of countless plugs clicked into innumerable sockets.

To end, once and for all, the killing suspense, the room wherein Daisy Reynolds toiled for the first three years of her business career was a telephone-exchange.

And at the three years' end, she was assigned to the job of day-operator at the Clavichord Arms.

THE pay at the hotel was no larger than at the exchange; but there was always the possibility of tips, and the certainty of Christmas-money. Besides, there were chances to rest or to read between calls. On the whole, Daisy rejoiced at the change—as might a private who is made corporal.

The Clavichord Arms is a glorious monument to New York's efforts at boosting the high cost of living. The building occupies nearly a third of a city block, in length and depth, and it towers to the height of nine stories. Its facade and main entrance and cathedral-like lobby are rare samples of an architecture whose sacred motto is, "Put all your goods in the show-window."

When the high cost of living first menaced our suffering land, scores of such apartment-houses sprang into life, in order that New Yorkers might do their bit toward the upkeep of high prices. Here, at a rental ranging from fifteen hundred to five thousand dollars a year, one may live in quarters almost as commodious as those for which a suburbanite or smaller city's dweller pays fifty dollars a month.

And nobly did New York rally to the aid of the men who sought thus to get its coin. So quickly did the new apartments fill with tenants that more and yet more and more such buildings were run up.

Men who grumbled right piteously at the advance of bread from five to six cents a loaf eagerly paid three thousand dollars a year for the privilege of living in the garish-fronted abodes, and they sneered at humbler friends who, for the same sum, rented thirty-room mansions in the suburbs.

And this, by prosy degrees, brings us back to Daisy Reynolds.

THE CLAVICHORD ARMS' interior decorator had used up all his ingenuity and his appropriation before he came to the cubby-hole behind the gilded elevators— the cubby-hole that served as the telephone-operator's quarters. The cubby-hole was airless, windowless, low and sloped of ceiling, calcimined of wall, and equipped with no furniture at all except the switch-board-desk, a single kitchen chair, one eight-candle-power electric light and an iron clothes-hook.

Here, for eight hours a day, sat Daisy Reynolds. Here, with stolid conscientiousness, she manipulated the plugs, that the building's seventy tenants might waste their own and their friends' time in endless phone-chats.

It was dull and uninspiring and lonely in the dark cubby-hole, after the lights and the constant work and companionship of the Exchange. There was much more leisure, too, than at the Exchange.

Daisy at first tried to enliven this leisure by reading. She loved to read; book or magazine—it was all the same to Daisy, so long as the hero and heroine at last outwitted the villain and came together at the altar.

But there are drawbacks to reading all day—even to reading union-made love stories, by eight-candle-power light and with everlasting interruption from the switchboard. So Daisy, by way of amusement, began to "listen in."

"Listening in" is a plug-shifting process whereby the telephone-operator may hear any conversation over the wire. In some States, I understand, it is a misdemeanor. But perhaps there is no living operator who has not done it. In some private exchanges it is so common a custom that the cry of "Fish!" warns every other operator in the room that a particularly listenable talk is going on. This same cry of "Fish" is an invitation for all present to listen in.

(Yes, your telephonic love-talk, your fierce love-spats and your sacredest love-secrets have been avidly heard—and possibly repeated—again and again, by Central. Remember that, next time. When you hear a faint click on the wire during your conversation,—and some-times when you don't,—an operator is pretty certain to be listening in.)

At first Daisy was amused by what she heard. The parsimonious butcher-order of the house's richest woman, the hiccoughed excuses of a husband whom business detained downtown, the vapid chatter of lad and lass, the scolding of slow dressmakers, the spicy anecdotes told by half-hour phone-gabblers—all these were a pleasant variation on the day's routine. But at last, they began to pall. And just as they waxed tiresome—romance began.

THE voice in Apartment 60—a clear voice, girlish and vibrant—called up 9999-Z Worth. And Worth 9999-Z replied in a tone that fairly throbbed with eager longing. That was the beginning. Shamelessly—soon rapturously—Daisy Reynolds listened in.

The voice in Apartment 60 belonged to a girl named Madeline. And Worth 9999-Z (whose first name, by the way, was Karl) spoke that foreign-sounding name *Madeline* as though it were a phrase of hauntingly sweet church-music. He and Madeline had known each other, it appeared, for some months; but only recently had they made the divine discovery of their mutual love. It was then that the phone-talks had begun—the talks that varied in number from three to seven a day, and in length from three to thirty minutes.

Always, now, promptly at nine o'clock in the morning, Karl called up his sweetheart. And always, an hour or so later, she called him up for a return-dialogue. Their talk was not mushy; it was beautiful. It thrilled with a love as deathless as the stars, a love through whose longing ran a current of unhappiness that Daisy could not understand.

Daisy grew to live for those talks. They became part of her very life—the loveliest part. She was curt, almost snappish, when other calls interfered with the bliss of listening-in. More than once she shamelessly broke off the connection when Madeline chanced to be talking to some old bore at a time when Karl sought to speak to her.

Karl, it seemed, was a downtown business man. As scientists reconstruct an entire fossil animal from a single bone of its left hind leg, so Daisy Reynolds built up a vision of Karl from his deep and powerful voice. He was tall, slender, graceful, yet broad of shoulder and deep of chest. Brown curls crisped above his white Greek forehead. His eyes were somber yet glowing. His age was from twenty-eight to thirty. He dressed like a collar advertisement.

Madeline was still easier to reconstruct, from her voice. She too was tall. She was willowy and infinitely graceful—gold-brown of hair, dark blue of eye, with soft-molded little features and long jetty lashes. With such a voice, she could not have been otherwise.

Daisy gathered from their earlier talks that Madeline's family disapproved the match. She even learned, from something Karl said, that there was another suitor—one Phil—on whom the family smiled and whom Madeline cordially detested. Once or twice, too, Phil called up Apartment 60. He had a husky voice and spoke brief commonplaces. Madeline answered him listlessly and still more briefly. But he seldom phoned to her. And she never, by any chance, phoned to him.

SO the ardent, tenderly melancholy love-story wore on. The lovers would make appointments for clandestine meetings—would speak in joyous retrospect of luncheons or motor-drives of the preceding day. Evidently, Madeline's cruel family kept stern watch upon her movements. Daisy used to smile in joyous approval at the girl's dainty cleverness in outmaneuvering them and meeting her sweetheart.

Ever through the glory of their love ran that black thread of melancholy. Apparently all the glad secret meetings and the adoring phone-talks could not make up to them for the family's opposition. Daisy had to bite her lips, sometimes, to keep from breaking in on the conversation and demanding:

"Why don't you two run off and get married? They'd have to come around, then. And if they didn't, why should you care?"

To a girl cooped up alone all day in a stuffy cubby-hole, imagination is ten times stronger than to the girl whose thoughts can be distracted by outside things. To Daisy, immured in her dim-lighted cupboard behind the elevators, this romance of Karl and Madeline was fast becoming the very biggest thing in her drab life.

These two lovers were as romantic, as poetical, as yearningly adoring as *Romeo* and *Juliet*. Karl was as desperately jealous as *Othello* or as the hero of one of Laura Jean Libbey's greatest books. Madeline was *the Captive Maid* come to life again. Oh, it was all very, very wonderful!

Then came the day of jarring disillusionment, a day which Daisy followed by sobbing until midnight on her none-too-soft boarding-house bed, three blocks to westward.

PROMPTLY at nine that morning, as usual, Karl called up Apartment 60.

"Sweetheart," he joyfully hailed Madeline, "I've just bought the new car. It's a beauty. And you're going to be the very first person to ride in it—to consecrate it."

"That's darling of you!" replied Madeline in evident delight. "I'd rather ride in a wheelbarrow with you than in a Rolls-Royce with—with—"

"With Phil?" asked Karl almost savagely.

"With anybody," she evaded. "Tell me more about the car. Is it—"

"I'm not going to tell you," he refused. "I'm going to show it to you instead. Here's my idea: I'll knock off work at noon and bring the car uptown. I'll meet you at the subway kiosk at half-after twelve; we can run up to the Arrowhead to lunch, and then on up to the Tumble Inn for—"

"But I can't, dear—I *can't!*" expostulated Madeline. "Don't you remember? I told you I have to lunch with Phil and those people from Buffalo, at the Knickerbocker, at one o'clock. Oh, dear! I wish I didn't have to. But I—"

"Phone him you're sick," urged Karl. "I've set my heart on christening the new car this way."

"I could get away to-morrow—" she began.

"But *I* can't," he said. "I've a directors' meeting at three. Oh, come along to-day, Beautiful! Tell Phil you're sick and—"

"And have him come rushing up here, in a fidget, for fear I'm going to die?" she suggested. "That is just what Phil would do. No, dear, I—"

"Then tell him you don't *want* to lunch with him," urged Karl, losing patience as a man will when some babyishly cherished woman-plan of his is upset. "Tell him you have to go to your sister's or—"

"I can't, Karl!" she declared; and she added, beseechingly: "Don't be unreasonable, dear boy. Please don't. And don't be cross; it makes me so unhappy when you are. You know how hard I try to do everything you want me to—and how glad I am to. But I *can't* get out of this luncheon. Phil especially wants me to be there. These Buffalo people are old friends of his."

"Why should you have to go there, just because he wants you to?" demanded Karl, far more crankily than ever Daisy had heard him speak. "Why do you? You aren't his slave."

"No," returned Madeline, her own temper beginning to fray, "but I am his *wife*. You seem to forget that."

"I don't forget it half as often as *you* do!" flashed Karl.

At which brutally truthful reply, the receiver of Apartment 60's wire clanked down upon its hook. Nor could all of Karl's repeated efforts bring Madeline back to the telephone.

DAISY REYNOLDS slumped forward upon the switchboard desk, her face in her hands, her slim body ashake. She felt as though her every nerve had been wrenched. She was sick all over. This, then, was the wondrous romance in which she had reveled. This was the melancholy, beauteous love-story which had become part of her own colorless life! A vulgar intrigue between a married woman (not a wife, but a married woman—Daisy now realized the difference between the two) and a man not her husband!

The iridescent bubbles of romance burst into thinnest air. Daisy was numb with the horror and disgust of it all. Even of old she had fastidiously refused to listen in when another girl's merry cry of "Fish!" had told that some such illicit dialogue was on the wire. And now, for weeks, she had been raptly listening to just such talks.

She loathed herself for the silly bubbles she had blown. Their lovely sheen was miasmic slime. They were filled with foul gases. A great shame possessed Daisy Reynolds.

Next morning Daisy came to work swollen-eyed from futile crying over the death of her dreams, and dull-headed from too little sleep. Half an hour later, promptly at nine, Karl called up Apartment 60.

Daisy's hand trembled as she made the connection. She hated herself for listening in. Yet from morbid fascination she did it.

"Darling!" was Karl's remorsefully passionate greeting as Madeline answered the phone-bell's summons. "I'm so sorry! So horribly sorry! I spoke rottenly to you yesterday. Won't you forgive me? *Please* do!"

"Please don't let us speak about it," began Madeline stiffly.

Then her shell of offendedness collapsed, and she went on with a break in her sweet voice.

"Oh, I'm so glad you called up! I was so afraid you wouldn't. And I was going to try so hard not to phone to you. But I knew I'd do it—I *knew* I would—if you didn't call me first. I've been terribly unhappy, dear."

"You've had nothing on me, in that," he made answer. "I haven't slept all night, thinking how I spoke to you. It was our first quarrel. And it was all my fault."

"It wasn't," she contradicted chokily. "It was all mine. I shouldn't have been hurt by what you said about my forgetting so often that—"

"Don't, dear," he begged. "Don't! It was a rotten thing for me to say."

"It was—it was true," she replied, her voice quavering as she fought back the tears. "But you told me yourself that you don't blame me. You know what my life with him has been, from the very beginning. And till I met you I used to wish I were dead. Oh, you *can't* blame me for forgetting him, for—for *you!*"

"You're an angel!" he declared. "I'm not fit to touch your hand. But my love for you is the only thing there is in my life. And it's brought me the only happiness I ever knew. I used to think I'd like to kill myself if it weren't for my mother. And now you've given me something—everything—to live for. I love you so, Madeline! Are you sure you've forgiven me?"

"*Forgiven* you?" she echoed. "Why, Karl, I *love* you."

Yes, the reply was banal enough. But the tone was not, nor was the wordless exclamation of worship with which Karl received it. And to her own self-disgust Daisy felt a stir of answering emotion in her own breast.

Just then she was required to connect Apartment 42 with the market, and at once afterward to put through a long-distance call for the building's superintendent. And when next she sought to listen in, Karl and Madeline were finishing their talk. All Daisy could catch was Madeline's childish query:

"Can't we please try out the new car to-morrow, if the directors' meeting is going to keep you this afternoon?"

And he answered gayly:

"To blue blazes with the directors! We're going to Tumble Inn to-day, you and I, sweetheart—even if New York doesn't get a stroke of business done south of Canal Street all afternoon. Good-by. You'll be sure to call me up later, won't you?"

DAISY sat back in her wabbly chair to take mental account of stock. She was amazed at herself—amazed, and a bit displeased, though not as much so as she could have wished. All her ideas and ideals seemed to be as wabbly as the kitchen chair she sat in. Woman-like, she straightway began to justify herself. True, an hour earlier, she had been filled with contempt for these two. Equally true, she was now irresistibly drawn to them again—which most certainly called for a reason; so she supplied the reason:

Madeline had been forced into a marriage, in mere childhood, with a man she did not love. And had she not said, "You know what my life with him has been, from the very beginning?" That alone told the story—the heartbreaking story of neglected wifehood, of ill-treatment, of a starved soul.

Who was Daisy to blame this pathetic young wife if she had at last let love into her heart after years of bondage to a brute? Daisy recalled Phil's husky voice. From it she built up a physique that was a blend of *Simon Legree's* and *Falstaff's,* with a tinge of *Bill Sikes.* And, her moral sense deserting her, she realized that right or wrong she was steadfastly on the side of the lovers.

During the days that followed, she listened in again, with all her old-time hero-and-heroine-worship. Now she understood the strain of melancholy in these two people's love. It was the hopelessness of that love which made them so sad, in the midst of their stolen happiness.

Once, in a free moment, Daisy slipped from her cubby-hole and into the superintendent's office, to ask for a stronger light-bulb. There on the wall hung a typed list of the house's tenants. Stealing a glance at it while the superintendent's back was turned, Daisy ran her eye down the list until she came to the number she wanted:

Apartment 60—Mr. and Mrs. Philip Caleb Vanbrugh.

Caleb! Yes, that was the sort of middle name her ugly-tempered clod of a husband would have been likely to own. The names *Madeline* and *Caleb* could no more blend than could violets and prunes. Doubly, now, Daisy's heart was with the lovers.

One qualm, only, marred her sympathy. From the fact that Karl always spoke of Vanbrugh by his first name, the men apparently were friends. And to woo one's friend's wife is black vileness. Even Daisy knew that. So she readjusted matters in her elastic mind, and decided the men were merely close business acquaintances, and that friendship did not enter into their relations. Daisy felt better about it, after that—much better.

ONE morning when Daisy connected the wire for the lovers and prepared for her daily feast of listening in, a sharp whir from another apartment in the house drew her back to earth. In her nervous haste to make the new connection and get back to her listening, she awkwardly knocked out a plug or two. Absentmindedly she readjusted them, trying meantime to catch what the second caller was trying to say to her.

This caller was a fussy woman in Apartment 12, who first wanted to know the correct time and then asked for a wire to Philadelphia. A full minute elapsed before Daisy could get back to the lovers. And as she turned again to their talk, she realized with a guilty start that in the mix-up of the various plugs she had left the switch open.

Have you ever called up a telephone-number and been let in on a conversation already going on between the person you called up and somebody else? It gives one an absurdly guilty feeling. And it means the switch has carelessly been left open, so that anybody calling up can tap the wire. That is the condition in which Daisy had chanced to leave the switch to Apartment 60. Eagerly she stretched forth her hand to repair the error. As she did so, three sentences struck her ear. They were spoken in quick succession by three people—as follows:

"Good-by, darling," said Karl. "I'll be there at one."

"Good-by, boy dear," answered Madeline. "I'll call you up again before then."

"Who in hell are *you?*" bellowed a third and huskier voice. "And what do you mean by calling my wife darling?"

Click! All three wires were shut off by one lightning swirl of Daisy's fingers.

SHE sat aghast. The third voice had most assuredly been Phil's—Philip Caleb Vanbrugh's. What had she done? What *hadn't* she done? Then she became aware of a buzzing call.

"Clavichord Arms," she said primly in reply as she sought to rally her shaky nerves.

"That the house operator?" harshly demanded the husky voice. "I called up my apartment—Apartment 60—a minute ago, and my wife was talking over the phone. What number was she talking to?"

"What apartment did you say?" asked Daisy.

"Sixty!"

"Apartment 60 hasn't had a call this morning," solemnly answered Daisy, her throat tightening under the grip of outraged conscience. "Nor it hasn't sent in one, either."

"I'd swear that was my wife's voice," growled the man. "I couldn't place the man's. But it was my wife's, all right. And—"

"It may 'a' been Sarah Bernhardt's voice, for all I know," snapped Daisy. "But it didn't come from Apartment 60. Not any calls have been turned in from there since I came on."

"You're sure?" he asked in sour doubt.

"You can look at my slip here on the desk," pertly retorted Daisy. "All the calls are marked on that."

"No," said the man slowly, "I won't do that—because, if you've lied, you wouldn't be past altering the slip. What I'm going to do is to ask the building's superintendent for an itemized list of all the calls from my apartment for the past month or two. He's obliged to furnish it on demand. That ought to tell me something."

HE hung up. Daisy sat gasping. Before her mental gaze ranged the memory of forty-odd calls a month to Worth 9999-Z. Then she came to a decision. Out into the marble-lined hallway she went. There she corralled the second elevator-boy and bribed him with twenty-five cents to take charge of the switchboard for a few minutes. A moment or so later, a colored maid was ushering her into Apartment 60.

In the middle of a garish living-room stood Daisy, trying desperately to think straight. The curtains parted, and a woman came into the room. Daisy blinked at her in bewilderment—then said:

"I should like to speak to Mrs. Vanbrugh, please. It's very important."

"I'm Mrs. Vanbrugh," answered the woman, eying the girl with curiosity.

"I—I mean Mrs. Madeline Vanbrugh," faltered the girl.

"I am Mrs. Madeline Vanbrugh," was the answer, and now Daisy recognized the voice, "—Mrs. Philip C. Vanbrugh. What can I do for you?"

Daisy could not answer at once. Around her dumfounded head the bubbles were bursting like a myriad Roman-candle balls.

This woman framed in the doorway was Madeline—*her* Madeline? This woman whose dumpy figure was swathed in a bedraggled negligee that had once been clean! This woman whose scalp was haloed by a crescent of kid-curlers that held in hard lumps her brass-hued front hair! This woman with the hard, light eyes and sagging mouth-lines and beaklike nose—this woman whose face was sallow and coarse, because it had not yet received its daily dress of make-up! This—*this* was Madeline!

"What can I do for you?" the woman was saying for the second time, her early air of curiosity merging into one of dawning hostility.

"I am the switchboard operator downstairs," said Daisy faintly.

A LOOK of terror that had all along lurked in the hard eyes now sprang to new light.

"What do you want of me?"

"I want to tell you your husband heard the last part of your phone-talk just now," returned Daisy conscientiously, though her heart was no longer in her mission of rescue. "He called me up about it. I—"

"You told him?" blithered the woman in panic.

"I told him your apartment hadn't had a call all morning."

"You *did?*" cried the woman, her sweet voice sharpening to a peacock-screech of relief. "Good for you! Good for *you!* And you were perfectly right to come directly up here for your pay. What do you think would be fair reward? Don't be afraid to say. You've done me a great service, and—"

"I don't understand you," stammered Daisy. "I don't understand you at all. If you think I did this for money—"

"My dear," laughed the woman nervously, "we do everything for money. So you needn't be ashamed. We don't always *say* it's for money. But it is. That's why I got into this scrape. My husband is the stingiest man in New York. He pretends his business is on such a ragged edge that he can't give me any extra cash. But I know better. That's why I let myself get interested in Mr. Schreiner. He is a widower, and he has more money than he can—"

"Oh!" cried Daisy in sick horror.

"So he'll make it good to you for all that you've done for us," prattled on the woman, without noticing. "He'll—"

"That isn't why I came up here!" broke in Daisy angrily. "And I don't want your filthy money, either. I won't touch it. I came up here to warn you that your husband is going to—"

THE buzz of the flat's front-door bell interrupted her. The woman, too, turned nervously to look. They heard the maid fumble with the knob. Then some one brushed past the servant and into the living-room.

The intruder was a chunky and yellowish man, of late middle years—incredibly bald of head and suspiciously black of eyebrows. He caught sight of Mrs. Vanbrugh, who chanced to be standing between him and Daisy. And he exclaimed:

"I jumped into a taxi and hustled here, as soon as I left the phone. I didn't dare call up again. Do you suppose he recognized me?"

Yes, the voice was indubitably the voice of Karl. But the fat and elderly swain was in anything but a loverly mood. He was a-quake with terror. Beads of sweat trickled down on his brows and mustache. His yellowish complexion was blotchy from fear. He was not a pretty sight.

Daisy by this time should have been past surprise. Yet her preconceived vision of Karl—of young, athletic, hero-featured Karl—died hard and in much and sudden pain. Poor Daisy! Until he spoke, she had mistaken him for the husband.

"If he knew my voice," babbled the man, "we're up against it. I'd better get out of town for a while, I suppose. Maybe he—"

"Don't worry!" interposed Madeline acidly. "You won't have to run away from town and leave me to face it all. This girl has gotten us out of it. She is the operator downstairs. Phil called up and asked her all sorts of questions. And she told him the apartment hadn't had a call all morning. Isn't she a brick?"

A sound like the exhaust of an empty soda-siphon broke from between Karl's puffy lips—a sound of pure if porcine reaction from dread.

"Good girl!" he croaked, still hoarse with recent fright. *"Dandy* girl!"

He sought to pat Daisy approvingly on the shoulder with one pudgy hand. She recoiled.

"How much?" he asked jovially, not observing the stark repulsion in her face and gesture as she shrank away. "How much, little girl? You've done a mighty big stroke of business this day. What do you say I owe you? Or will you leave it to me to do the right thing by you?"

He juggled a bloated wad of bills from his trousers pocket as he spoke. And at his motion something in Daisy's taut brain seemed to snap.

THE girl did not "see red." She saw only two fat and greasy creatures who thought she was as vile as they—who took it for granted that she had done this thing to extort a rich tip from them, for covering up their sin. And wrath gave her back her momentarily lost power of speech.

"Oh!" she cried in utter loathing, "you'd dare *pay* me for trying to help you? If I'd known what you both are, all the money in New York wouldn't have gotten me to lift a finger for you. You horrible—"

"There, there, my dear!" oilily soothed Karl. "You're a little bit excited. Calm down and tell us how much—"

"If you don't want pay," shrilled Madeline, "what did you come here for?"

"What did I come here for?" echoed Daisy, white with rage. "To make a fool of myself, of course. To warn you that your husband is going to get the call-lists for the past month from the super, and find out from them what numbers you've been calling up. That's—"

"Good Lord!" gabbled the woman in crass horror.

Karl's fat jaw dropped upon his fatter throat. He tried to speak. He could only gargle.

"That's why I came here!" finished Daisy, striding past them toward the door. "To warn you. And now I've done it. Your husband's liable to be streaking back home any minute now. And I'm going. And if either of you says any more about money, I'll—"

She was making for the outer door. But for all her start, Karl reached it three lengths ahead of her. He banged it shut after him as he darted out. Through the panel Daisy could hear him ringing frantically for the elevator.

Daisy was following, when a choking sound made her turn back. The woman still stood in the middle of the living-room. Her hard, light eyes were dark and dilated. Her sallow face was haggard and ghastly. Yet her features were unmoved. There was about her bearing and expression a certain hopeless courage that lent dignity to the squat figure.

DAISY hesitated—then turned back into the room. The woman stared dully past her toward the doorway through which Karl had vanished. She acknowledged the girl's presence by muttering, in a curiously dead voice, more to herself than to Daisy:

"Men are queer animals, aren't they? He has sworn to me, time and again, that he'd stand by me to the end."

"Yes," assented Daisy in perfect simplicity, "I've heard him say it to you myself—twice."

"He's gone," went on the woman in that same dead voice so unlike her own. "He's gone. And I'm left to hold the bag. I—I think I'm cured. There are worse things than a husband who loves you—even if he can't give you all the money you want to spend. Phil would never have run away like that, from *anything*—not that the lesson is likely to do me any good, now."

"Here!" exclaimed the girl, shaking the dazed Madeline roughly by the shoulder. "I'm going to get you out of this. I don't know why, but I am. Maybe I've a bill of my own to pay, as well as you have. We've all done some learning to-day, I guess. And learning isn't on the free-list."

"But—"

"Go to the phone right away," commanded Daisy, "and call up the super. Tell him you've got to see him, up here, in a hurry. Act scared. Tell him it can't wait a single minute. Get him up here. That's the main thing. Then—then tell him you want new faucets in the bathroom. Or tell him anything at all. Do as I say. Jump! There isn't much time to waste. Hubby's sure to be hotfooting it home. And when hubby comes, deny everything. *Deny!* And keep on denying. He won't have any proof, remember that. *He'll have no proof.* Pay for the lie by being a whole lot decenter to him, forever-after-amen."

MOVING away from the dumfounded woman, Daisy bolted out of the flat and was lucky enough to catch a down-going elevator. She reached the ground floor just as the building's perplexed superintendent came to the shaft on his way to answer Madeline's urgent summons.

Into the superintendent's deserted office sped Daisy. Going directly to his unlocked desk, she rummaged feverishly amid its drawers until she found what she wanted.

Crumpling and pocketing the telephone-sheets for the past two months, she crossed to the file cabinet, hunted through a stack of dusty papers and drew forth the sheaf of penciled telephone-slips for the preceding year.

Selecting from these the slips for the two corresponding months, she put back the rest of the sheaf. Then, changing with eraser and pencil the date of the year on the two slips she had abstracted from the cabinet, she put them in the drawer. After which, feeling oddly weak about the knees, she started out of the office.

At the door she almost collided with the returning superintendent. Vexed at having been called upstairs in such haste on an utterly trivial errand, he very naturally wreaked his ill-temper on the first subordinate he chanced to meet—which was Daisy.

"What are you doing away from your switchboard?" he snarled. "I won't stand for any loafing. Get that into your mind, once and for all. What did you want in here, anyhow?"

"I came in to see you, sir," was the girl's demure reply.

"What do you want of me?" he rasped.

"I wanted to tell you I'm leaving here to-morrow," said Daisy. "I'm going back to work at the Exchange. I'm lonesome on this job. There aren't enough things happening at the Clavichord Arms. It's too slow—not enough excitement for a live wire like me. That's all, sir."

Don Quixote McGraw

ONE of his ancestors had been a crusader. One had been a civic-reform leader. One had been the original man-who-shared-his-last-crust-with-a-friend. One had been Sir Galahad. One had been Chevalier Bayard. And at least ten of them had been Don Quixote.

This family-tree of Con McGraw's is drawn wholly from deduction. But it is as undoubtedly accurate as is the skilled botanist's deductions as to a flower's ancestry, or as is the scientist's throw-back of the modern horse to the Eohippus of prehistoric days.

Con's family-tree could have been traced back, without any trouble at all, to every one of the illustrious personages I have named—except for one trifling obstacle: his father, Patrick Sarsfield McGraw, began life in a Dublin foundling asylum and with no idea at all who his own parents had been.

Hence the need of deduction, rather than positive proof, in sketching Con's family-tree. But no one who knew Con McGraw could doubt for a moment that all these mighty forbears had gone to make up the sum of his character—especially Don Quixote. Con was ninety per cent Don Quixote.

Con's emigrant father had gone to work, at the age of ten, as tally-boy in the yards of the Daniel T. Greene Smelting Company. At fifty he was superintendent of the works—a self-made man who reverently glorified his maker.

Con himself had been sent to high school and then to business college, and had not entered the Daniel T. Greene works until he was eighteen. Then, he was sent in "to learn the business from the bottom up."

Daniel T. Greene, the big boss and the employer of three thousand men, was Coketown's foremost citizen. A discharged bookkeeper had once spoken of "Dan'l"—thus he wrote his first name—as "a granite shaft topped by a steel trap," which of course was a cruel thing to say, and did not at all do justice to that great and good man. But it came closer to describing him than can any words of mine. So, for lack of a better one, we will let the description go as it stands.

GREENE had but two real weaknesses in his granite make-up: One was the great smelting company he had created out of nothing. The other was his only son, Rolf. There had been a third and supreme weakness—a blue-eyed, sunny-haired Weakness, too soft and fragile for a rough world like Daniel's. She had died in bringing Rolf into life. And, with her—so far as women were concerned—Greene's heart had also died.

Rolf was brought up as a rich man's son, his father pathetically trying to give the boy all the luxuries and good times he himself had had to go without in his own bleak boyhood. As a result the lad was abominably spoiled. And he came home to Coketown, somewhat suddenly, in the middle of his sophomore year at Yale, accompanied by an urgent written request from the dean that he honor the university no longer with his presence.

The disgrace of Rolf's expulsion from Yale smote Dan'l squarely between the gimlet-eyes. He had so counted on his son's acquiring a college education. He had so blatantly bragged to his friends about Rolf's future! And now—

A tempest of unchecked fury swept the Greene home that day, blanching the disgraced boy's face by its blast and well-nigh throwing Dan'l himself into apoplexy. The upshot of it was that Greene refused to send the boy to another college, and curtly drove him into the smelting-works, where—like Con McGraw—he was bidden to "learn the business from the bottom up."

Daniel T. Greene had a profound respect for his superintendent, Patrick Sarsfield McGraw. He admired the style in which the self-made foundling had hammered and wriggled his way upward to the superintendency. He valued the man's services; he even made more or less an intimate of him.

DANIEL liked young Con. There was an honesty, an aggressive Irish pluck, an unselfishness, a snap-and-go to the lad that pleased Greene. He also liked the way Con took hold of his new job.

Over a pipe in the sacred inner office, Daniel prophesied a big future for the boy— to the outward indifference and secret rapture of the old superintendent to whom he made the prophecy. He frankly bemoaned his own son's seeming worthlessness and made a loud moan that he and old McGraw could not swap sons.

"I'd give you half my bank-roll to boot," declared Daniel. "And I'd still be the winner, at that."

"You're a bit tough on young Mr. Rolf, sir," protested the superintendent. "There's no harm to him, beyond a kick of his father's own spirit. You've took yours out in work. He's took his out in mischief. That's the only difference. He's a colt, yet. But he's got the punch. Mark my words, he'll do well, and he'll make you proud of him yet. He's buckling down grand to his work—so his foreman tells me. Don't you be disheartened about him, Mr. Greene. He's all right."

Thereby, with not too great a massacre of truth, did Patrick Sarsfield McGraw seek to repay the compliments his demigod had just been showering on his adored Con.

The two young fellows had gone to grammar school together as children. There they had formed a warm friendship which the separation of twelve years had broken off. Now, meeting again every day in the shops, the old-time friendship was renewed.

Rolf, from the first, liked the ardent, unselfish visionary young Irishman. And Con gradually lifted Rolf to the highest pedestal of worship in his soul. In work and in play, the two workmen became inseparable. Dan'l smiled approvingly on the odd comradeship. As a rule, he disliked Rolf's intimates. But he hoped much from Con's example and influence on the wayward lad. As for old McGraw, he rejoiced as exultantly in the youths' friendship as though his boy had been chosen as a comrade-at-arms by Robert Emmet.

When eighty dollars' worth of half-tempered metal was spoiled through Rolf's carelessness and Con took the blame, old Patrick Sarsfield jubilantly patted his son on the back and vowed to get him a raise of pay. When Rolf, learning of the sacrifice, went straight to his father with the truth, Greene chuckled raspily—and then promoted both friends into a higher shop.

AND so it went on—for a matter of five years. At the end of that time, Rolf was sent out for his initial trip on the road. And Con was assigned to a desk in the sacred inner office. It was the chums' first parting since their entrance into the shops. Up to this point, they had traveled upward, side by side.

Both felt keenly the separation. But Rolf was to spend only six months on road-work; and then Con was to go out on the same traveling job for another six, while Rolf took his friend's vacated desk. After which, the two were to work in the same office until such time as Rolf should go into the firm. So they had a reunion to look forward to.

Rolf did more than fairly well on the road. And Daniel used to listen with an approving grin to old McGraw's praise of the heir's knack at securing orders.

Then came the smash.

One morning, Con was bent busily over his desk. The elder McGraw stood beside him, waiting for Greene to finish reading his mail, before making a report on some new-bought machinery. Daniel himself was glancing over a pile of personal letters with the speed and thoroughness of a conjurer manipulating a card-deck.

His steel-trap face softened as he came upon an envelope in Rolf's loose handwriting. Daniel slackened speed, tore open the envelope and proceeded to grant himself five minutes of leisure wherein to master his beloved son's epistle.

But in much less than five minutes the pleased grin was wiped by magic from his face. His thin lips flew apart in a snarl so ferocious as to bring both the McGraws to his side at a bound.

"What's hit you, boss?" demanded the superintendent in great concern.

Con said nothing. He recognized Rolf's handwriting on the sheet of paper his employer was gripping so fiercely in one big fist. And his own face whitened a bit under its florid color. For a moment Daniel did not answer, but sat glaring in baleful horror at the clenched letter in his hand. Then the flood-gates of speech were flung open.

"THE whelp!" he bellowed. "The thankless, worthless, contemptible swine! The—"

"Hold on there, Mr. Greene!" begged Con as the superintendent still blinked in perplexity at his employer's outburst. "It's your own son you're talking about. And he doesn't deserve a single one of those rotten names. He—"

"Shut up, you!" roared Daniel, purple and writhing. "What do *you* know about it? He's—"

"He's my friend!" retorted Con. "And I won't stand—"

"Shut up, Con!" exhorted the superintendent, shocked at such defiance to the big boss. "Shut up. Don't you hear Mr. Greene telling you to? Be still! What's wrong, Mr. Greene?" he went on, respectfully turning to the sputtering Daniel. "Or maybe is it none of our business?"

"It's anybody's business!" raved Greene. "It's everybody's business. It'll be in all the papers, I suppose. The cur! He's dragged my name in the mud again. The—"

"He—he hasn't got himself locked up, has he, sir?" quavered old McGraw, with all an Irishman's inborn dread of jail.

"He's got himself locked up—for life!" cried Daniel. "That's just what he's done. During this last trip to New York—he's writing from there, now, when he ought to have been on his way to Pittsburgh—during this New York trip, he—he has been married!"

He glared from one of his two hearers to the other, to note their wild distress at the tidings. But as both of them looked merely interested, he remembered he had not told them the crux of the catastrophe.

"He's married an *actress!*" went on the raging Daniel. "An *actress,* d'you hear? A kind of woman who dances in tights, I suppose, and sells herself to—"

"He has not!" flashed Con.

"YOU fool!" snarled Daniel. "Here's his own letter that says so. Not that I blame you for not being able to believe—"

"He *has* not!" declared Con hotly. "Married, he may be. And it's no disgrace to be married. It's nothing worse than a misfortune, at most. And he may be married to an actress too. I'm told there's scores of them that are as clean and as straight as a man's own mother. And I'll stake ten years' pay she's one of those. Rolf's never married the kind of woman you say. His wife's as good a woman as any—"

"Either shut up or else get out of here!" ordered Daniel. "It's black disgrace enough for me to have such a son, without you taking his part. Here I've toiled and sweated and schemed all my life to build up this business, so I could leave a great enterprise for my only boy to carry on, along with my name. And what has he done? He's smashed every plan and every hope and every dream I had. By marrying a dirty—"

"Steady, there!" cut in Con, white-mad.

Daniel glowered on the younger man as if he would have sprung at his throat. But, at the glow in Con's eyes and the hard set of his mouth, Greene swallowed hard and then slightly shifted his own invective's course.

"He's married an actress," he went on, "—a woman I can't receive as a daughter-in-law—a woman I can't ask his dead mother's friends to welcome—a woman who'll teach him that a man's main object in life is to give her all the money she can squander. She'd wring the company's treasury dry and empty his private bank-account, too, if he had any left. And when he had no more money to give him, she'd flit off to some one who had."

"Mr. Greene! I—"

"BUT she won't get the chance!" Daniel shouted, thundering on his desk-lid with his fist and flying into a new paroxysm of blind rage. "She won't get the chance! Oh, I know her sort! And I know her game. They read the papers—her kind of woman. And they study Bradstreet's too. She knows to a dollar what I'm worth. And she knows Rolf is the only child I've got. She thinks she's lighted on her feet in a United States mint. Well, she hasn't. She's overplayed her hand. That's what she's done. She's—"

"There, there, now, Mr. Greene!" soothed the superintendent. "You'll be falling sick if you let yourself get so het up. At your age too, it's dangerous, sir. It's—"

"You'll let my age alone!" fiercely ordered Daniel. "I'm not too old to teach that cub and his chorus-girl wife that it's safer to fool with a rattlesnake than with Dan'l T. Greene. The noon mail to-day is going to take a letter from me to my loving son. He begs me, here, to write to him, at once. Well, I'm going to. I'm going to tell him I can't annul his marriage, because he's of age and has a legal right to commit career-suicide. But I'm going to tell him I'm done with him. I'm going to—"

"Mr. Greene! Boss!" gasped the superintendent. "You'd never do such a heartless thing! Your only—"

"Did he stop to remember I was his father and that he was wrecking my life as well as his own?" growlingly demanded Daniel. "Did he? No! Well, turn about is fair play. He's married. Let him support his wife. And if she kicks him out when she finds I won't surrender, so much the better for him! In either case, I'm done with him for good and all. Not one dollar more of my money shall he ever see. Not one bite of my food shall he eat, if he's dying of starvation. My house is as tight closed to him as it would be to any other tramp. Let him and his—"

"Mr. Greene," interposed Con very quietly, while his father stood aghast at the melodramatic outburst, "Mr. Greene, for your own sake, quit talking like an idiot."

"WHAT'S that?" snapped Daniel, not believing his own large and faithful ears.

"I say, stop it, for your own sake," replied Con. "Angry words are easy enough to spit out. But they're bitter hard to swallow again. And the less you speak along the line you've just been speaking, the less you'll have to swallow, when you come back to your senses. I'm advising it, because I owe you a lot; and because, next to my father, you're the finest man I know, and because I've no right to let you go ahead like that, unwarned, to say nothing of my being Rolf's friend, too."

"Con!" reproved his father, again all but tongue-tied at his offspring's boss-blasphemy. "Mr. Greene, don't you mind what he says. He's young, yet, and he has a queer pig-headed strain to him that's forever making him get into trouble for the under-dog. Overlook it, won't you, sir? He'll be sorry. He means no harm. You heard him say, himself, how he looks up to you."

The father paused in his plea. His quick Irish eyes, studying Greene's wrathful face, told him Daniel was not wholly displeased by Con's impertinence. There was a fighting spirit in Daniel that ever doffed its hat in respect to a fellow-fighter. He knew Con had spoken with the realization that he might be discharged for what he was saying. Yet, fearlessly, the boy had defied the boss who held life-and-death control of his financial destiny.

"Con," said Daniel presently, after swallowing hard once or twice, "if I've said it a single time, I've said it fifty times: I'd give half my pile if you'd been my son, instead of Rolf."

"Then you'd be half a fortune out of pocket!" declared Con.

"I've said it less, of late years," went on Daniel, unheeding, "because I've been donkey enough to think Rolf was beginning to amount to something. But now I've washed my hands of him."

"MR. GREENE, now!" clucked the superintendent, trying to look pained and succeeding very badly. "Mr. Greene, you can't really mean—"

"I mean just what I've said," insisted Daniel. "And I'll prove it. On Rolf's birthday next month, I was going to bring him into the firm, on a one-third partnership basis, and with the job of secretary. I didn't tell him so, because, like the wall-eyed galoot I was, I wanted to surprise him. Well, it's *he* that's done the surprising. But in spite of that, the arrangements for the partnership are all made. And I'm going to replace a worthless son with a worth-while one. Con, I'm going to fill in your name, instead of Rolf's, to the partnership papers."

"Glory be!"

"You *are* not!"

Father and son spoke in one breath.

"You *are* not!" repeated Con, in no wise impressed by the offer or by his father's tearful bliss threat. "You're going to do nothing of the sort."

Daniel grunted, as though some one had butted him in the stomach. Patrick Sarsfield McGraw moaned aloud, in grief at his son's insanity.

"Mr. Greene," resumed Con, "you very well know you'd never think of giving me a third interest in your business, on my own merits. I'm a good man in my place. And I hope, in time, to be a better man in a better place. But on a business basis, you'd never in a thousand years make me a partner in your firm. And you know you wouldn't. And you're not the breed of man to do it out of personal fondness for me, either. If you were as soft as all that, you'd never be where you are to-day."

"Con!" bleated the superintendent, in great misery. *"Con,* lad!"

"You're using me as a club to beat Rolf to a pulp," went on Con. "You want to be able to say to him: 'Not only you're no son of mine, but I've put another son in your place. I've given your heritage to an outsider, to punish you for going against my wishes.' That's what you want to say to Rolf, Mr. Greene. And that's why you're making me this crazy offer. Which same offer, I beg leave to decline without thanks. Rolf's my best friend. I'm not going to let myself be used as a torture-instrument for him. That's final."

DANIEL GREENE'S face went purpler than ever. His mouth opened to let out a torrent of vituperation upon the ingrate. Then all at once he choked back the unsaid words, and his teeth closed with a click.

"I wish, all the more, you were my boy, Con," he said almost gently. "You're a good deal of a man—if something more of a fool. I'm going home now. I'm going to treat myself to a holiday. If I don't feel more like work, to-morrow, I may run out to the lake for a few days' fishing. Good-by."

He stamped out, his hat over his eyes, leaving the McGraws staring after him in amaze. In the memory of neither of them had Daniel T. Greene ever absented himself from work, except on short, specific yearly vacations.

To the elder McGraw came a second shock before he could collect his scattered faculties to the point of speech.

"Having just turned down a chance to make a rich man of myself," airily observed Con, rising and stretching, "I think I'll celebrate by treating myself to a holiday, too. Good-by, Dad."

"By all the saints in glory!" sputtered Patrick Sarsfield McGraw.

But Con was gone. And the office-door shut noisily behind him. In his pocket was the letter from Rolf, which Daniel had flung to the floor during his tirade.

NOW Con McGraw had not worked in the employ of Daniel T. Greene without gaining a fairly accurate knowledge of that sweet-souled magnate's nature. Even as a boxer has a tolerable idea of the next move that will be made by the man who has for years been his sparring-partner, so in this crisis, Con was able to guess at Daniel's most likely course.

The guess was confirmed soon after he had packed a bag and reached the

Coketown railroad station. From behind the waiting-room's grimy window, Con beheld Daniel emerge from a taxi-cab, suit-case in hand, and buy a ticket.

When the noon train pulled out for New York, Daniel occupied a Pullman seat in it, while Con, unseen by his employer, boarded the smoker, far in front.

At four o'clock that afternoon Daniel emerged from the Pennsylvania Station and made his way toward the taxicabs. Con, having studied the uptown address on Rolf's letter, decided he could get to his destination more quickly by the subway—which, perhaps, he might have done, but for a twenty-minute "block" in that temperamental artery of traffic.

Fuming at the costly delay, Con came to the surface of the earth forty-five minutes later on far northern Broadway. He ran, rather than walked, the block and a half that separated him from the address he sought.

He was in a sweat of worry. Daniel had had time enough to burst in upon the two luckless honeymooners and to say and do things that neither of them could ever forget or forgive.

It was to stand between the newlyweds and this assault that Con had risked his own job and his future by running away from work in the busiest season of the whole year. And his sacrifice had gone for nothing.

He had acted on his usual Don Quixote impulse in coming to New York. He had not been clear in his own mind as to what his presence could do in straightening out the snarl. But he was Rolf's friend. Rolf was in dire trouble. And if ever the disgraced youth needed a friend at his side, this was the time.

Therefore, Con had hurried, head-on, to his chum. His only definite plan had been to get to Rolf's flat soon enough to act as a buffer against the old man's first attack. Beyond that, he had trusted to circumstance to show him a way to help.

And now, Daniel must have had a full fifteen-minute start on him. It would probably be too late to undo the harm the father had done. Nevertheless, Con hurried on, all the faster.

THE flat-building he came to presently, and whose number he verified, was the five-story, forty- to sixty-dollar-per-month type that boasts no elevator and whose tenants' names are posted on cards at the top of the double line of mail-boxes in the vestibule.

Con scanned the ten name-slips and found the name he wanted. Not being at all familiar with the push-button etiquette of flat-houses,—which are still a rarity in Coketown,—he looked around for the front doorbell. Failing to find it at once, he gave a tentative turn at the door-handle. The last entrant had left the door on the latch. It opened under Con's pressure. He entered and started upstairs, stopping to read each door-card on the way. Presently he found what he sought.

Pinned to the right-hand fourth-floor portal was a woman's card. On it was engraved: *"Miss Gloria Wesson."* The engraved name had been crossed out, with a pencil, and beneath it had been scribbled: *"Mr. and Mrs. Rolf Venable Greene."*

Con's romantic Irish imagination conjured up the glee of bride and groom as they had thus proclaimed to all possible callers the fact that Gloria was no longer Miss Wesson, and that she and her new-wed husband now occupied her former bachelor-girl flat.

And his fists clenched at thought of Daniel's happiness-smashing intrusion on their bower. He strained his ears for sounds of strife from within. But the unaccustomed noise of the city had dulled his hearing.

Con rang the bell. A woman opened the door.

She was small—almost like a child in her dainty littleness of body. Her black hair fluffed all over her head. Her face was very tiny, and her eyes were very big—very big and very dark.

At one keen look into their childlike depths, Con knew he had been right in giving Daniel the lie when the raging father had sought to rip Gloria's character to shreds.

A glance at the firmly square little jaw, which contrasted so sharply with the softness of her flower face, told him she would not cower meekly under the blast of Daniel's wrath. It was the jaw of a fighter. And Con, being a fighter, recognized it as such, and did homage to it.

He felt much relieved thereat. He had feared to witness the crushing of a butterfly. But here was no butterfly. Rather, a honeybee—sweet, pretty, useful, friendly and harmless when not attacked, yet equipped with a very serviceable sting.

CON breathed easier. From the wholly unruffled aspect of the girl, he saw that no battle had been raging. And he asked, in wonder:

"Hasn't he got here yet?"

They were his first words to his chum's bride. He blurted them as might an excited schoolboy. Gloria's white brow puckered in surprise at the greeting. Before she could speak, he added:

"Mr. Greene, I'm talking about. He hasn't come here yet? I thought sure he must—"

"No," answered Gloria, in a voice with unwontedly sweet and well-trained modulations, "Mr. Greene has not come home yet. He did not expect to get back from business until—"

"Oh, it isn't Rolf I'm asking about," interrupted Con. "It's his father, Daniel T. Greene. He was on his way here—at least, I take it he was on his way here—the same time I started. And I got detained a thundering long time by a wagon or something falling apart on the track, in your underground road. I was sure he'd beaten me here."

"Mr. Daniel T. Greene?" repeated the girl, smiling expectantly, "Oh, you mean my husband's father? He is coming to see us? I'm so glad."

"The pleasure is all yours," muttered poor Con. "Don't count too much on it. And do you mind if I make free to introduce myself? My name is Cornelius McGraw. I'm a friend—"

"You're Con McGraw?" cried Gloria, the smile this time illuminating her whole little face, as she impulsively thrust forward both hands in greeting. "Oh, come in, please! It's so good to see you! Rolf says you're his very dearest friend. He's told me ever so much about you. Come in."

As she talked, she led the way into the flat and on into its pretty living-room.

"Rolf ought to be back in half an hour or so," she said, as Con awkwardly followed her into the room. "It will be splendid for him to find you here. And you say his father is coming too? What a wonderful reunion! We'll all celebrate by going somewhere to dinner. I'm afraid to risk my own poor cooking for such an event."

Con felt a lump in his heart. The girl was unfeignedly delighted at the prospect of entertaining her bridegroom's chum and her bridegroom's father. Her face was flushed and her eyes were shining with the pleasure of the anticipation.

AND Daniel was due to arrive at any moment! Daniel, who had come all the way to New York to cast off his son and to insult his son's wife, in person—because he could do it so much more effectively and satisfactorily that way than by letter.

Con drew a long, long breath and braced himself to the task of preparing this happy bride for the cruel shock in store for her.

"Has—has Rolf told you much about his father?" he began timidly.

"Only that he owns some sort of a factory in Pennsylvania," replied Gloria, as if surprised at the queer question. "You know Dan is here on business for the factory now. That's why he had to be downtown so long to-day."

"At the New York branch-office," said Con. "I know. And he's told you nothing more about the boss—about Mr. Greene?"

"No," she said, after a moment's consideration, "nothing in particular. You see, we haven't known each other so very long, Rolf and I—not much more than two months in all. I met him, through the Bemises, on his first business trip here. And we have had so many things to say to each other that we haven't talked much about our families. But," she added with a return of that same glad smile, "he's talked to me, no end, about *you.*"

"You were married last week, weren't you?" asked Con.

"Four days ago. Yes," she said, "Rolf wanted to wait till he went home, before he told his father about it. He wanted to take me along, as a surprise. But yesterday I persuaded him to write to Mr. Greene. Rolf's father couldn't have gotten the letter until this morning. Isn't it dear of such a busy man to come on here, so soon, to welcome me into the family?"

Con groaned. Gloria, in surprise at the sound and at the visitor's look of utter despondence, jumped to her feet.

"WHY, what is the matter?" she asked.

"Everything's the matter, Mrs. Greene," he made answer, in a spurt of desperate courage. "I'd like to break it to you by degrees. But I haven't time. He's li'ble to be here any minute now. I take it he went straight to the branch-office, to lay out Rolf, before doing the same for you. That must be why I'm here first. Listen to me, please."

"What is it?" she demanded, puzzled and distressed by his manner. "Are you trying to break the news to me that something has happened to Rolf?"

"Something is due to," he responded gloomily. "Here's the idea: Mr. Daniel T. Greene is one of the Lord's own fine men—in his own way. But he's got a will of his own—a will that'd make a pile-driver look like a toothpick. And Rolf's crossed that pile-driver will of his by marrying you. The boss isn't coming here for a love-feast. He's coming to make war-medicine."

"I don't understand. Why should—"

"No," said Con. "And Rolf didn't tell you. I suppose he thought no one could see you without being tickled to death to have you for a daughter-in-law. And no one could, except Daniel T. Greene. Rolf saw how lovely you are. And it made him forget how—how funny his father is, about things—some things. Otherwise, he'd never have written the way he did."

"Will you please try to make it clearer?" asked Gloria, her soft eyes hardening a bit and her jaw taking on a squarer look. "Do you mean Mr. Greene is angry because Rolf has married me?"

"I mean just that," answered Con. "I'm sorry, but—"

"But why should he be?" she inquired in genuine bewilderment. "Rolf is making a living—a good living. He can support a wife. And even if his father's factory should fail and put him out of work for a time, I can always tide him along by going back to the stage until he gets on his feet again. I am not a fortune-maker as an actress. But I've had steady work ever since I left the convent school. And almost any manager on Broadway will pay me seventy dollars a week for ingènue rôles— sometimes a good deal more. So we won't starve. I—"

"It isn't that," expostulated Con, twisting in his chair. "It's hard to explain. You see, he—"

THE pur of the buzzer broke in on his floundering speech. "Ten to nothing that's the boss now!" he said miserably, as Gloria went to answer the summons.

"Miss Gloria Wesson?" boomed a rough voice at the threshold—a voice with a note in it like an angry bull's.

"Mrs. Greene," corrected Gloria. "Are you Mr.—"

Daniel pushed past her into the flat, before the question was finished.

"I've come here to take up ten minutes of your time," he growled. "You'd better spare me that much of it. For it's the last claim I'll make on your time—or on Rolf's, either. I went to the office to see him. But he was out somewhere. So I came here. Is he—"

"Rolf will be back in a little while, Mr. Greene," returned Gloria. And Con could tell she was making a mighty effort not to resent Daniel's bullying tone. "He—"

"Then I'll wait for him," grunted Daniel. "And, meantime, I've something to say to you, too, madam—whether you want to hear it or not. I— Where the devil did you come from?" he broke off, with a bellow, entering the living-room and seeing Con.

"From Coketown, sir," said Con quietly, "on the noon train—same as yourself. I—"

"Get out of here!" commanded the irate Daniel. "I want to talk privately to this woman. We can settle about your deserting the office later. Get out!"

"I *will* not," stolidly replied Con.

"Perhaps it would be better, Mr. McGraw," suggested Gloria, "if only for my sake, it—"

"It's for your sake I'm staying," Con retorted, "—till Rolf gets here, anyhow. If I have to go earlier, it'll be with Mr. Daniel T. Greene on my back. No offense to either of you, but here I'll stay."

DANIEL snorted loudly, glared at the imperturbable Con, then decided to ignore his presence and save all his own wrath for its legitimate object—for this actress-woman his son had married.

"I can say what I've got to say to you in few words," Daniel started in, turning on Gloria. "And what I say is final. You can save your acting for those it will impress. Don't waste any tragedy or pathos on me. It won't serve. I'm a rich man. You know that. That's why you married my son. I'm here to tell you you can keep him, for all of me. I'm through with him. But not one more cent of my money shall he touch, now or hereafter. And, to-morrow his name goes off the company's pay-roll at the same time it goes out of my will. Understand that? It's an ultimatum. And now that I've said it, you can repeat it to Rolf. On second thought, there's no use in my waiting to see him. I've no further interest in him. And I want to go back home. Good day."

He turned, doorward.

"Is that your last word, Mr. Greene?" asked Con, unobtrusively stepping between Daniel and the door. "Because, if it is, it seems to me I'll be doing this lady and my chum a fine big service by dropping you out of the window. You'll drift to the sidewalk in no condition at all to change your will, or to fire Rolf from off the pay-roll, either. Yes," he continued reflectively, "there are worse plans than that."

With no emotion at all, he strode meditatively up to Daniel. Had he sprung at his employer or shown a sign of anger, Daniel's fighting spirit would have flared up at such a challenge.

But at the businesslike voice, the calm face, the unhurried approach, Daniel felt a queer tingling along his spine and his hair-roots. In his own haze of anger, it seemed to him quite possible that the quixotic Irishman would actually carry out his crazy purpose to save his friend's future.

The belligerent old magnate recoiled a step—even before Gloria flung herself between the two men.

"Mr. McGraw!" gasped the girl in horror. *"Mr. McGraw!"*

"Then I'll give him one chance," carelessly agreed Con. "Mr. Greene, you'll not start for that door—not unless you want to go out by the window, instead. You'll sit down and talk with this young lady. And you'll talk with her, as easy and civil as the Lord will give you grace to. If you forget she's a lady and your son's wife, why, the window's still there. Now, miss, just forget to be scared about me. Sit down and talk with him, like I wasn't here at all. Forget I'm anything but a safety-clutch. And keep on remembering that this is your one big chance with him. Talk up now, both of you."

HE strolled to the hallway door and became absorbed in the contemplation of a picture hanging there. Daniel glared from Con's back to Gloria's flushed face. He sat down glumly.

"I've nothing more to say to you," he told her in sulky ill temper. "But if I'm to sit here till Rolf comes back, I have no great objection. Don't let me keep you here if you are busy."

Gloria hesitated; then she sat down opposite him.

"If you don't care to talk to me," she said very coolly, "perhaps you will listen while I speak to you. You need not be afraid of my 'acting.' I am not given to do that except for a living. And even if I were, I see no reason why I should waste my talents on a man who has just insulted me in my own home, and from whom I have nothing to gain or lose."

"Nothing to gain or lose?" echoed Daniel, crankily forgetting his resolve of silence.

"What have I to gain or lose from any man, except my husband?" she asked, still politely, yet with her jaw ever squarer and squarer. "What good or harm can you or anyone else do me? I am sorry you don't like me, of course, but only because it will make Rolf sorry. For I suppose he is fond of you, though I confess I can't see why, if this is the way you always behave. He will be sorry to lose your good will. He may even be sorry to lose his position—though a man of his cleverness can always get another. And I can keep the home going till he does. So what do we lose that is worth 'acting' about? Why should I be silly enough to try to wheedle you into liking me or forgiving Rolf? I don't care whether you like me or not. And if you are casting Rolf off, for no worse sin than for marrying a girl he loves, your forgiveness is not worth having."

Her tone was quiet, even pleasant. She showed no excitement. Yet her every word was incisive. Daniel stared. His armor of aloofness began to crack.

"WHAT have you to gain or lose, eh?" he blustered, stung at her indifference. "You have the fortune and the business of Daniel T. Greene to lose, young woman. Doesn't that seem anything? Doesn't—"

"I don't know whether it's anything or not," she answered simply. "All I know about you is that you run a factory out in Coketown. I don't know whether Coketown is a village or a metropolis. I don't know whether your factory is worth ten dollars a week to you or ten millions. And I don't care. Whatever it is worth, it is not worth our cringing for. Nothing is."

"I fancy you know pretty near to the dollar what my works are worth," said Daniel craftily. "I guess you took a glance through Bradstreet's before—"

A hunching motion of Con's wide shoulders checked him. Gloria replied: "Bradstreet's is a mercantile agency, isn't it? I've heard about it. But as for looking you up in it, Mr. Greene, why, if you'll pardon me for saying so, you are talking nonsense. You may or may not be prominent in Coketown. But, in New York, not one person in a thousand has ever heard of Coketown—to say nothing of hearing of *you*. If I had been angling for a rich man's son, I should not have bothered to look so far afield. There are plenty of them in Manhattan. And if I had married Rolf because his father was rich, I should not now ask Mr. McGraw—as I do—to move aside and let my husband's rich father walk unmolested out of my flat, with no request that he trouble himself to walk into it again. That is all, Mr. Greene."

She rose and, with a curt little nod of dismissal, signified the talk was ended. Daniel rose too. But he did not move to go. Nor was it Con McGraw's presence that held him there blinking dazedly at the tiny woman who was ordering him out of her home.

In all his sixty years Daniel T. Greene had never before been spoken to as his son's wife had just spoken. Others—a very few others, Con among them—had defied him. But they had done it with full knowledge of his power to blast them.

Whereas, this slip of a girl was so wholly unimpressed by his power that she did not even take it into consideration. She simply ignored it. His greatness and the town he had made great—these evidently meant less than nothing to her. She had treated him—him, the all-powerful Daniel T. Greene—as she might have treated any boorishly domineering stranger who had invaded her flat. Any courtesy she had shown him had plainly been due to the fact that he happened to be her husband's father—not because he was Daniel T. Greene.

"WHEN I first told her you were coming," volunteered Con, moving inside his post at the doorway, "she was as pleased as a kid with a Christmas tree. She was prepared to like you fine, boss. Take my word for that. What's come to you, you've brought on yourself. You've thrown away one corking nice daughter-in-law. She don't care now whether you forgive Rolf or not. And if I know Rolf, he won't care either—not after he hears how you've acted to his wife. The doorway's clear, sir, whenever you want to take her tip and go."

Daniel T. Greene did not answer. He stood, frowning heavily—at nothing. All his life his force and his money had smoothed the way for him. Yet here in this one tiny room were two people who cared for neither of those magic talismans.

This square-jawed, big-eyed girl regarded him as an ill-bred brute, and as nothing more. His son—the son he had ruled with iron hand—would think as she thought. Con McGraw too, who had revered the big boss as a superman—even Con was blind to wealth and ambition when right interposed.

With all his money, all his strength, all his industrial mastery, Daniel T. Greene could not sway these two very ordinary people. He all at once felt weak and old and lonely.

Wealth's only use is over people who want it. Power's one use is over people who fear it. These people whom he had tried to hammer into a shape of his own choosing had not only resisted him, but they had overcome him.

UNWONTED tears—not all of them springing from self-pity—welled up in Daniel's gimlet-eyes. Gloria saw them. She took a quick step toward him, her face suddenly growing wondrous sweet and tender. Not since Rolf's gentle young mother died had a woman troubled to look at Daniel T. Greene like that. It went through his lonely soul like the breath of God.

"I'm sorry!" he babbled, ridiculously like a whipped and penitent child, and speaking through no conscious volition of his own. "I'm sorry! I'm *sorry!*"

Then—also like a scared penitent—he caught hold of Gloria's two out-stretched hands.

A latchkey had turned in the flat's door. Rolf Greene came in.

"Dad!" cried Rolf in astonishment.

Daniel T. Greene wheeled about on his son with a ferocious glare that deceived no one.

"I've come here to lug you two worthless, lazy boys back to work!" he shouted. "We start back to-night—the three of us."

"The four of us," meekly amended Con, with a nod toward Gloria.

"The four of us!" Daniel hastily corrected himself. "I *said* 'the four of us.' Anyhow, I *meant* it."

"Con!" exclaimed Rolf, catching sight of his chum for the first time. "What good-better-best wind blew *you* here?"

"Me?" artlessly replied Don Quixote McGraw. "Oh, I just trailed along, to cajole the boss into staying here till you got back from the office and to be the first to tell you he's giving you a partnership as a wedding present. He's a fine man, your father, Rolf—and fonder of you than you know. Why, when he found you weren't here, I had all I could do to keep him from starting right out to hunt for you—by way of the window."

"Con!" rasped Daniel T. Greene. "I'd like nothing better in life than to allow myself the luxury of firing *you*. But"—with a sigh—"I've lived too long without luxuries to begin indulging in them now. So, come on home with—with my family and me."

The Wallflower

A DOZEN of Fairfield's conservatories had been gutted to decorate the country club's rooms for the fourth of the season's Red Cross dances. As it was the fourth of the dances, instead of the first, there was almost no aroma of camphor balls in the men's dressing room.

Outside, from the drive to the veranda, a fluted red-and-white awning sheltered the arriving revelers from the baneful effects of an absolutely cloudless night.

Arrup's Orchestra, at $19.50 an hour, was ensconced in the palm-hidden nook which served by day as an umbrella and raincoat corral. The orchestra was dissecting and vivisecting and clinically macerating the Muse of Melody on the noise-reared altar of the great god Jazz.

Nearly two hundred people were saint-vitusing industriously to the barbaric strains. Two people were not.

Of the two one was a girl with a tip-tilted nose, a fair allowance of freckles and a quantity of indeterminate-colored hair. She was not pretty, and she was not at all homely. A fellow woman, yearning to insult her, might readily have said she had a "good" face.

The other perpetual nondancer was a man in the early thirties. He needs no description, because he looked just like any other man. That was one of his life handicaps.

His name was John Harding. The girl's was Mary Gray. They were not dancing because no one cared to dance with either of them and because they did not care to dance with each other. They were not even sitting out together.

Mary was ensconced in a corner camp chair between two mounds of poinsettia. Harding stood propped against the wall six feet away. He was looking at the dancers with drearily hypnotized boredom. The girl was looking at him in a scaredly speculative fashion.

Presently she scaled her voice to one point above the distant jazzing and called Harding to her. He obeyed the call, foreseeing a plea for ice water or for the opening or closing of a window.

He was not even concerned enough to note that she was visibly bolstering her fright with an effort at bravado.

"Why aren't you dancing?" demanded Mary in the tone of serious accusation.

Harding was mildly surprised at the query. But he braced himself and answered dutifully if awkwardly: "Why, certainly! I'd be glad to if you'd like."

"You wouldn't be glad to," she contradicted in calm positiveness. "And that's why I wouldn't like. I'm not sure I'd like if you were glad to. That's the trouble."

The man stared doubtfully, prepared to grin if the speech should turn out to be a joke.

"I don't understand," he said. "I —"

"That's because you haven't had a month to think it out," she explained. "But I've had longer than that. So I've been doing ever so much thinking. And it dawned on me at the last of these awful dances that you could help me find the answer—if there is an answer."

John Harding's standard-pattern face was blank. The girl, gripping her resolve very tightly indeed, hurried on:

"You see," she said, "it's like this: Suppose you had some mysterious illness? Suppose there weren't any doctor to be found? Suppose you knew that some acquaintance of yours had the same kind of illness? Suppose you wanted to find out all you could about that illness in the hope that you could cure yourself of it? What would you do?"

"Why," pondered Harding, giving up hope of guessing the trend of her queer volley of questions, "I—I guess I'd hunt up the other chap who had it—and—and sort of compare symptoms with him—wouldn't I? And maybe he and I might pool our knowledge of the thing and our ideas for curing it; or—or— Is that the right answer? I suppose not. It generally isn't. It's a new wheeze of some kind, isn't it?"

"No," she replied, taking his queries in reverse order. "It isn't a joke. And it's the right answer. That's why I'm trying to consult with you. You're the only other victim of my malady that I know well enough to—to pool symptoms and cures with. Not that I know you so very well either," she added, fear once more wriggling almost out of the shaky grasp of resolve.

But though he still stared foolishly she clasped her resolution afresh and drove on to the point, her fight with bashfulness making her words more baldly brutal than in their oft-spoken rehearsals.

"My disease," she said, speaking fast, "dates back to Bible days. Leah had it, in the book of Genesis. It is wallfloweritis."

"Huh?" broke in Harding, dazedly curious.

"Wallfloweritis," she repeated stoutly. "An acute and chronic case of being a perennial wallflower. Oh, please don't be polite and silly and deny it!" she interrupted herself as the man's mouth flew ajar. "It's true, and you know it is. So does everybody who takes the trouble to notice. Only you probably notice it more than anyone else because you're in the same boat. I'm being hideously rude, I know; and I'm sorry. No, I'm not sorry, either; because perhaps we can be of some use to each other."

She made her forcedly valiant eyes meet his in something like apology, and she noted that his face was waxing as beet-red as she knew her own must be. Yet she plunged on, speaking more and more rapidly:

"Will you pool symptoms and cures with me? Or would you rather we didn't? Please stop looking at me as if I were saying horrible things! I'm not. I'm just trying to see if there isn't any way to keep us from being the two invisibles at every party we go to. Even if there isn't any cure it can't do much harm to compare notes. Shan't we?"

The crass oddity of the proposal pierced through Harding's swelling sense of self-conscious discomfort and stirred something far beneath it—something in the seldom-dusted recesses at the bottom of his nature. It might have been inquisitiveness; it might have been adventure; it might have been an unconfessed and lonely longing for sympathy. At all events he found himself nodding glum assent, and then wondering why he had done it.

Mary Gray looked relieved. She continued with a closer semblance to ease:

"Good! Shall I begin? Or will you? Suppose I do? Because I'm more interested in my own symptoms than in yours. So I'll begin."

"Begin what?" he babbled stupidly.

She frowned a little at his denseness; then explained:

"I thought we had settled that we are two victims of wallfloweritis who are to compare symptoms, and all that. Well, I'm going to begin with mine. You see, I'm not even asking you never to tell my confession to anyone. I don't know whether it's because I trust you or whether it's because you're a man or because you'd be too shy to tell such a long story. So here goes."

Yet for the instant she did not seem to find the going easy, for she hesitated. And Harding, staring mutely, did not help her.

Then, impatient at herself or at him or at both, she drew a hysterical breath and said: "I wonder if it was my name that started it. If I had been 'Edith Gray' or 'Mary Delorme' the name would have been pretty. And it would have meant something. But 'Mary Gray' has no color in it at all. It's as simple as water and as wholesome as bread. And it is about as inspiring as a mixture of the two. I doubt if Lola Montez and Ninon de Lenclos would ever have been superwomen if they had been named 'Hannah Moore' and 'Susan Jones.' But all that doesn't get me much forwarder in my symptoms, does it?"

"I—I don't know but perhaps it does," argued the man, vastly amazed at his own brilliant powers of analogy. "You see, I've got that same bother too; though I never happened to think of it before. 'John Harding' is kind of in the same class with 'Mary Gray,' in a sense. It's a fine name for the—the—"

"The honest young mechanic or the friend of the family," chimed in Mary. "But not for either of the two men who struggle on the cliff. See?" she added in triumph. "We have one symptom in common already. Only you may think I've an advantage over you because I can change my name by marrying. Well, I can't. I shall be twenty-four next April. And nobody ever asked me to marry. That means nobody ever is going to. So let's pass on to the next symptom. I'd better tell you a little about myself and how it all started, if you don't mind. That will make it simpler."

Without waiting for needless consent she continued:

"It began when I went to dancing school. At least I noticed it first then. I was seven. The day my mother told me she was going to take me round to dancing school I was so happy I almost fainted. I could just see myself all grown up and dressed in pale-pink satin with Killarney roses and with diamond knots on my slippers, and with fifty men clamoring to dance with me. I knew dancing school was the preface to all that. And I could frame a picture of Jimmy Thompson and Tom Hyde and Phil Powers and all that exalted set of youngsters clamoring to waltz with me at parties, just as they did with Annie Stockton and the other baby belles of my youth.

"Well, I don't think any girl ever worked harder at dancing school than I did. You see, I wanted to dance better than the rest, so that the boys would have still more reason for choosing me for partner. That's all the good it did me. Except when Professor Reilly actually ordered some luckless youth to dance with me at the school receptions I had to dance with other girls or else sit by mother. I couldn't understand it at all. It used to make me miserable. But it made me madder. It still does. There's no reason for it. At least, none that I can see. I dance better than a lot of girls. And I'm no homelier than some of them. Yet I honestly don't remember that any man or boy, of his own accord, ever asked me to dance or to go in to supper or called on me.

"There's something I lack. I don't know what it is. Perhaps it's lure or magnetism or charm or—or I don't know what. But it's been this way always. Once in a blue moon I see some other girl who is a chronic wallflower. And I try to figure out why. Because she is another girl I never dare ask her. And nearly always I find she isn't a bit like me. Either she dances like a cattle stampede or like a set of fire irons; or else she is stupid or ugly or sharp-tongued or something like that. I keep on going to places because I'm asked to them and because I won't surrender. But oh, I'd give six years of my life to go to them the way other girls do! That's a silly way to talk, of course. You needn't tell me that... I couldn't confess any of this to a person who wasn't as badly off as I am; and not even then if I wasn't desperate about it."

She caught herself up, tried to laugh, then demanded: "Now, how about you?"

She relaxed her tense muscles, still avoiding Harding's eye. He was silent for a moment. But he was not mustering his forces to hammer aside his lifetime barrier of reserve. Instead he was wondering at his new impulse to speak. Not knowing enough of psychology to realize the infectiousness of confidences he could not understand why he should be willing to open the rusted floodgates.

Yet before he was well aware of it he was talking, talking in a sheepishly disjointed way which gradually merged into naturalness as he forgot himself in his grievances.

"I've asked myself a lot of times why I come to these dances and other places where I'm invited," he said gruffly. "I hate 'em. There's nothing in 'em for me. I don't get scared to death, the way I used to when I was a kid, of course; nor feel sick inside from the minute an invitation comes till the party's over. That's the way I always did when I was little. For years the sound of waltz music used to give me a wrench in the stomach because it reminded me of dancing school. And dancing school was worse torture to me than—"

"I see," she interrupted. "You were just shy. That was it. You had a logical reason for being a wallflower. Now with me it was different. I never was shy. I—"

But the man was too strongly under way to be shaken out of his stride.

"The other fellows used to guy me about it in those days," he said. "They used to steer me up against girls who were shy too. And then they'd laugh their fool heads off at the miserable pair of us... I saw a play once with a shy man for the hero. And all the girls went wild over him. If I could have got hold of the paretic who wrote that play he' d have been shy too. He'd have been shy a nose and half an ear before I was done with him. A girl has about as much use for a tongue-tied shy man as she has for a secondhand typhoid germ or a last year's fashion plate. Especially if he's cursed with too many hands and feet—the way I always am when I get into a crowd like this. I get on all right with other men. But girls!

"I wasn't ten years old when it came to me that no girl would ever want me round.

And I've never changed my mind. I tried to get over it, when I grew up, by dragging myself to call on one or two of 'em. But I didn't have to torment the same girl twice. She always saw to that. I come to dances and things because it'd look queer not to, here in Fairfield, where everyone knows everyone. And it might get me talked about and guyed. I'd rather be kicked than come to these places. But I'd rather be shot than know folks were guying me. That's about all, I guess," he finished, his voice muffled with a sudden return of his bashfulness.

Mary Gray was studying him with a pucker between her brows.

"It's funny!" she commented presently. "You say you're shy. But you didn't talk as if you were, just now. If you talked as eagerly as that when you called on those girls—"

"I didn't," he said sulkily. "I couldn't."

"Then how could you talk that way to me?" she asked.

"Oh," he answered, off guard, "for the same reason you talked as you did to me, I guess. You're as badly off, in your own way, as I am. It's—it's more like talking into the looking-glass, I suppose. I don't know why else. But it's been kind of good to get it off my chest. I never put it in words before. I don't know what got into me to do it this time except—except—"

"Except that I don't count," she supplemented, wholly without offense. "I see. Don't spoil it by apologizing. Well, we have compared symptoms, certainly. It sums up that you are too shy; and that I'm too—too— We didn't decide what was the matter with me, did we? Only that I am a wallflower because I am a wallflower. And that you're one because you're shy. That doesn't seem to bring us much nearer a cure. Thus far our pool doesn't promise many dividends. We—"

"I—I read some advice once, in a newspaper column," he interposed. It was called 'Advice to the Shy.' It said a shy person must forget all about himself and be 'gay and bold and talkative and aggressive, particularly with those of the opposite sex.' Fine and easy, eh? As sensible as to advise a cripple to get well by beating the hundred-yard track record! If a shy chap could forget all about himself he wouldn't be shy. He—"

"He isn't," she declared.

"Isn't what?" asked the puzzled Harding.

"Isn't shy," she replied. "He hasn't been for the past ten minutes. He's forgotten all about himself—except his grievances; and he's been 'bold and aggressive,' too, even if he hasn't been hilariously 'gay.' So you see the advice wasn't so foolish after all, was it? But what about me? I'm more interested in that. We've diagnosed your case and we've found the cure, even if you lack the courage to apply it. But we haven't found why I'm a wallflower. Why? I've helped you. Suppose you see if you can't locate my trouble?"

He nodded. In his present unwontedly expansive mood the request of his fellow victim seemed to him the most natural thing in the world. And he bent his mind in all honesty to its granting.

"Well," he ventured after a pause wherein he scowled with the force of his effort to think, "maybe it's this: Do you know anything about the advertising business?"

"No," she said, perplexed. "Not a thing. You do, though, don't you? Aren't you in an advertising concern? I—"

"I *am* an advertising concern," he corrected. "Not very much of one yet; though we're climbing pretty steadily, this past year. It's been a tough tussle. And I've lived so close to it that it's taught me to think of everything in advertising terms. Get the idea? But of course you don't."

"No," she said with no vast interest, "I don't. And I can't see what it has to do with—"

"I'm getting to that," he told her. "Ever hear of Bunson's Lozenges?"

"No. Yes, I did too! The other day dad brought some home for his cough. I think 'Bunson' was the name. He said he'd been reading—"

"He had," averred Harding. "So had lots more people. I'd been writing."

"Writing what?"

"The things that made your father bring home a box of Bunson's. They did his cold good. As much good as any of six other advertised brands of lozenge would have. No more good. No less good. The point is that he bought 'em because he'd read about 'em. Bunson's Lozenges, between you and me, are nothing to call out the guard for. Nobody much had ever heard of them. The concern went under. It was a little, one-man, two-room business. The receiver got permission to take a mild flyer in advertising; to win them more than eighteen cents on the dollar. That was what they stood to pull out of the wreck. He turned the campaign over to me, with a microscopic appropriation. The creditors have not only hauled down a hundred cents on the dollar but the concern is going on for keeps. And the appropriation has taken a big boost too."

"Very interesting!" she commented in a tone of complete boredom. "But if you'll excuse me for reminding you—"

"That reminds me of something else," he cut in, with no trace of acerbity; "I thought of it before, just dimly. But now it's clearer. Don't you think you might make more of a hit with men if you'd make yourself feel a genuine interest in what they're saying about themselves or their work? I just throw that out as a hint, you know. So don't get sore. You see, a man's business is about the biggest thing in his life. And when a girl gets him started on it—why, it's up to her to score a hit by showing interest, or to queer herself forever with him by—by looking and talking as you do when the conversation happens to slide off your own side of the fence. You won't mind my saying so, will you? Remember, we were to pool our—"

"Yes," she agreed a little breathlessly, yet after only an instant's daze. "I see. And—thanks. Won't you please tell me more about that wonderful campaign to sell Bunnion's—"

"Bunson's," he corrected—"Bunson's Lozenges. I will. The appropriation was so small I couldn't smear the lozenges all over the magazines and papers or cut loose on the line of ads that appealed to me. I had to get my effects with a toothpick instead of a crowbar. It wasn't easy. But I got there by and by. I took a line of goods that nobody had heard of or wanted to hear of—a line of goods that wasn't strong enough to travel uphill without boosting. And I got the public asking for it—enough of the public to lift Bunson's Lozenges out of the failure class. The lozenges stopped being the wallflowers of Coughs-and-Colds Society."

He paused as if expecting her to fall asleep. But she was very wide awake. Mary Gray was a quick learner. From her pose and expression of warm interest one might well have thought she was the original Mrs. Bunson—if ever there were such a woman.

Mary had mastered the first lesson, even though its teaching had vexed her and its long exposition had jarred her from her favorite theme—herself.

"That was splendid of you!" she exclaimed eagerly. "Do go on!"

"I don't need to bore you with any more of it," responded Harding. "I told about it only so you could see how advertising will lift an article out of the discard and put it into the live-ones class; or sometimes into the bonanza division—that is, if the article is worth the boosting."

"How wonderful!" she breathed. "It is as romantic as—"

"Say!" he protested in annoyance. "You don't have to practice on me, you know. I'm just a fellow wallflower. And all the advertising campaigns on earth wouldn't push me into the live ones. But maybe there's a chance of advertising you. That's what I was getting at."

The girl half rose to her feet. She was uncertain whether to be angry or to feel a lofty pity for the brainless dolt. John Harding checked her impending departure by hurrying on to say:

"Don't get me wrong, please! I'm not suggesting that we buy up fifty thousand dollars' worth of print space and an acre of billboards to blow your trumpet. That'd be fine business if you had something to tell the world at large, but you haven't. All the people you want to reach are a few dozen Fairfielders. Less than a few dozen, because if one or two of the right kind get hooked onto the ad the rest will break their necks to follow. That makes it simpler. Never try to reach what you can't handle. That's a mighty good advertising rule. So you wouldn't need to scatter your hits. One little concentrated local campaign would do the trick. If only we could hit on the catchword for the local campaign."

Mary was vaguely aware that her interest in his prattle was no longer assumed. Not that she could imagine at what he was driving. But this ordinarily shy man was at home with his theme—spontaneously and even magnetically at home with it. Advertising was his life work. In discussing it he wholly forgot to be shy or self-conscious. He spoke with keen and compelling authority, an authority which impressed his hearer in spite of herself.

"Go on!" she urged as he paused.

And now Harding could not find a trace of polite insincerity in her tone. He resumed: "I'm not suggesting that we hire a troop of sandwich men to parade up and down Maple Street with signs that read: 'Dance with Mary Gray! Call on her! She's a winner!' I'm not hinting that a two-column ad to the same effect in the Republican would do much for you—beyond landing you in the foolish house. But if you like I'll take a fall out of the problem and see if I can think up anything. What we want to do is what I did with Bunson's Lozenges. We want to show people that you're on earth. After we've done that it's up to you. Would you like me to drop round at your house to-morrow evening if I get an idea between now and then?"

"I think," she said slowly—"I think you are hopelessly insane. And I don't at all follow your plan; at least I don't think I do. But you are the very first man who ever asked leave to call on me of his own accord. So please come! Even if you bring a scheme for me to hang a sign outside our veranda advertising my desirability as a dance partner."

"Hold on!" Harding reminded her. "This isn't a philanthropic freak on my part. A good advertising idea is worth its weight in radium. I'm not going to sprain my mind on your account for nothing. You're letting self-centeredness horn in again. Just cast your memory back and you'll recall this was to be a clinic for 'mutual' benefit. If I can unwallflower you, how about my own case? I won't be any better off than I was before. Didn't you say something about a chance of our being helpful to each other? Where do I come in?"

"If you can help me," said Mary after a moment's puzzled reflection, "I pledge myself to help you any way I can. It's only fair to tell you I haven't the remotest idea how it is to be done. But then, I haven't the remotest idea you can help me either. So it's a draw. Oh, was anything ever so utterly idiotic?" she broke off.

Her impatient exclamation was less for the purpose of discouraging her hearer than to drown any illogical optimism of her own, bred of his calmly certain manner.

"It's a deal," he said tersely. "And we'll take your case first. We'll concentrate on that. Later we'll devote ourselves to mine. I'll call if I get any ideas."

To his own bewilderment Harding realized that he was beginning to take a keen professional interest in the knottily absurd case. For the girl herself—as a girl—he felt no enthusiasm at all. But as a prospective "article" she awakened his ever-smoldering advertiser nature.

"There's another thing," he said as they went in to supper. "It's this: I don't believe you're selfish and self-centered by nature; or bored at everything that hasn't a personal bearing on yourself. I believe it's just because you've had to herd alone so long you've never had a chance to be interested in anyone else's interests. You caught on finely just now when I gave you the tip about it. That means you'll catch on in other things too."

For the first time in the memory of man or woman John Harding was taking a girl in to supper at a dance. Not only that but he was talking to her with evident fluency and excitement.

For the first time, too, in mortal memory Mary Gray had a supper escort who had not been cudgeled into service by a kindly hostess. And she was chatting with him with an interest that did all sorts of pretty and becoming things to her wontedly discontented face.

Full fifty fellow guests gazed in covert wonder. And after supper a man gained an introduction to her and asked her to dance. True, he was a stranger in town. But Mary lured him into talking so interestedly about his new concrete process that he asked her for a second of the after-supper dances. He might have asked her for a third if he had not caught her in a furtive yawn in the most dramatic part of his description of the superiority of white sand over brown for concrete foundations. No one can acquire a complete education in the art of being interested in other people's affairs in a single evening—not even a wallflower who is trying to break into the moss-rose garden. And Mary had done very creditably in spite of the uncontrollable yawn.

Two men at that single dance had shown marked attention to her. Which was a record that did not go unobserved among folk to whom Mary was as much a fixture to the wall at parties as were the electric-light brackets.

The stranger's notice carried weight, as do always the attentions of a newcomer. But more was Fairfield stirred by John Harding's sudden emergence from the silences and from isolation, and by his ardor in conversing with her.

Two passers-by the next night saw him mount the steps of the Grays' Maple Street house; and they spread the tidings. The new drawing together of the erstwhile uncourted couple might perhaps have formed theme for mirth. But there was the verdict of the stranger—the concrete-process man who had danced twice with Mary. And strangers see things in people to which the eyes of those people's associates have become dulled. So the local comment was untainted by laughter.

That was because nobody overheard the dialogue between the advertiser and the advertisee. It began with a query from Mary as to Harding's progress with her case. She spoke in elaborate sarcasm, as one who is weary of the persistent harping on one stale joke and who seeks to slay the theme. But Harding took her seriously; or perhaps he read the worried hope behind the scoffing, for he said:

"I've tried it from a dozen angles so far. Maybe I've struck a scheme. Maybe I haven't. At first I thought of the Desperate Desmond line: For you to go whizzing through town every day in your car at a minimum speed of fifty miles an hour; and get pinched twice an hour for speeding; and build up a name for daredevil driving. Then to buy a pet lion cub and—"

"Dad's only car is two years old," she countered dryly, "and it's of a make that has a maximum pace of something like twenty miles an hour. That's the only flaw in the first plan. That and the fact I don't know how to run a car; and dad won't buy me one. As for romping on the lawn with a lion—"

"Yes," he said. "I know. I told you those were just my first ideas. Like the genre sketch they say an artist makes, to get his hand in for the big picture. Then the Grace Darling angle struck me. To have you save me from drowning some day when there's the right kind of crowd at the beach. Or to dash into a burning hut and save a subsidized and rehearsed child from the flames. I—"

"Thanks, so much!" she murmured frostily.

"That was a genre sketch too," he hastened to say. "Both of them were press-agent stunts. Not straight advertising. And there's an ocean of difference between the two professions. For instance, I'm an advertiser, not an inspired press agent. So I tried at last to reduce the problem to terms of my own trade. Then I got the answer. At least I got *an* answer. Are you any good at cooking?"

"Heavens, no!" she replied, her momentary gleam of hope quenched by the question. "Why?"

"Why not?" he shot back.

"For one reason," she returned loftily, "we have a cook. We always have. Even if it's not the same one for very long. Also because I have better things to do than—"

"What better things?" he challenged. "Except by pitching in and helping the country what better things can be done than cooking? If there's any better way to a man's heart it hasn't been charted yet. I don't mean standing all day over a red-hot range and dishing out corned beef and cabbage, but in having a genius for cooking dainty and soul-satisfying and rib-caressing food. It is an art. Women used to practice it, I guess, a lot more than they do now."

"If your grand idea is for me to hire out as a cook," she commented, "I think I prefer the lion cub or the rescue from drowning."

"I told you this was to be straight advertising," he answered; "not press agenting. How does one advertise best? By waking keen public interest in an article. What interests a man most acutely in a woman? The belief that she can make him happy and comfortable. How is a man made happiest and most comfortable? By super-good food. The woman who can play best on that string of his cosmic harp is the woman who can woo him from half the sirens of history. He may not know it. He probably doesn't. But it's true. Let it be known that a girl is an inspired cook— and the same mysterious force that draws a man toward his dinner will instinctively draw him toward her table. And there seems to be mighty little competition along that line nowadays since girls have learned to believe that home is a place to get away from. It—"

"It is an inspired idea," she agreed with elephantine satire. "The living room can be converted into a restaurant without much bother. And I can make flapjacks in the front window under electric light. And—"

"One minute," Harding stopped her. "If you had indigestion and went to a doctor and he asked to look at your tongue would you slam into him with a call-down about its being your digestion and not your tongue that was hurting you? Well, that's just what you're doing to me."

"I'm sorry," she said stiffly. "But just exactly what is it you want me to do? Suppose we get to the point?"

"The point is this," he said: "I want you to go to town to-morrow, to this address

I've written out for you. I want you to go there every day for a lesson, till you've learned to cook as Paderewski can play. This man I'm sending you to would have got a Ph.D. and an LL.D. and a hundred other degrees long ago if he'd been a professor of anything besides perfect cookery. He is a genius. My father knew him well. Some of his graduate pupils are holding down higher-priced jobs to-day than half the salesmen and storekeepers in America, just because perfect cooking is an art that has a market all over the world. He doesn't take many pupils now. But this note from me will fix it for you. He—"

"But—" began Mary.

"The sooner you learn," went on Harding, "the sooner your triumph can begin. I've written out here the sort of things you are to specialize on. When you are perfect you are to inaugurate a series of Sunday evening suppers. Just little informal affairs with one or two men at each. I'll see to getting the first batch of guests here. After that it will be as easy as going broke. Besides, remember that a lot of men live in boarding houses. And a Sunday night boarding-house supper is a thing from which any man will flee—even to the home of a wallflower. Begin to get the idea?"

"I—I think so," she said, contempt merging slowly into unwilling interest. "But—"

"These little Sunday night suppers of yours," expounded Harding, "will be ostensibly the kind of a pick-up chafing-dish meal that people toss together on the cook's night out. That's what they will seem to be, mind you. But inwardly they will be a set of culinary creations—Sally Lunn, waffles and maple sirup, hot biscuit and honey, sublime coffee, Scotch woodcock, creamed sweetbreads, chicken *à la reine*, scallops Newburg, fluffed oysters—all that sort of thing. The hot breads and the desserts will already be made; but the guests must know you made them. The other things must be made in the chafing dish before their eyes.

"The things that can't be chafing-dished are to be made by you in the kitchen. And the guests must troop out there with you to help. That means the kitchen must have a gay and bright and distinctive air, to harmonize with the dainty cook and with the informal jollity of the supper. The sight of good things cooking has a hypnotic effect on men. How do you account otherwise for the hit that was made by the first restaurants that had griddles and grills at work in their front windows? But remember—one spoiled dish will undo everything. That's where your study time must be made to count."

He stopped. For a long minute she sat, eyes half shut, brain busily turned inward. Mary Gray was anything but a fool. And as Harding had already noted she was quick to catch an idea. Presently she opened her eyes; and he saw they were bright with excitement.

"It's—it's worth the trying!" she said. "Only how—"

"It will be easy enough to get such a reputation," he forestalled her, "and to set men to angling for invitations. Some of the guests will be refined panhandlers who are out for a delicious meal. But some of them will be the real thing. They can scarcely eat your food without calling here, for sheer decency's sake, at other times, and without asking you to dance once or twice when they meet you at parties; can they?"

"It's—it's wonderful!" she sighed in complete and happy conversion. "And it's feasible too! I can see that. You are great, Mr. Harding. Great! I'm going to do it!"

"Yes," he agreed. "It will take you out of the wallflower bed in the old-fashioned garden. I'm sure of that. But where it will land you depends on your own self."

"What do you mean?"

"You have lots of originality and lots of initiative and lots of pluck," he explained. "You proved that by the way you tackled me at the club dance last night. Those are dandy qualities. Just as salt and mustard and vinegar and paprika are dandy condiments. But keep on remembering they are condiments and not a meal. No man would eat them with nothing else. And no man enjoys your qualities of pluck and initiative and originality unless they serve as flavoring for something more palatable. If—"

"You mean," she translated, "if I keep on wanting to talk just about myself and yawn when men talk about themselves, and if I try to say clever or cutting things—"

"You get me!" he approved. "In that case your suppers will still lift you a little way out of the wallflower class. But they won't lift you where you'll be wanting to go as soon as men begin to notice you're on earth. It's up to you. There's no professor in that branch of study that I can send you to. All I can do to help is to remind you that men are four times as vain as women; and that they would rather talk about themselves than about any of the world's other heroes. Let them do it. You'll easily get the knack of starting them in on the subject. And always let them be just a little cleverer than you are. If ever you are lured into an argument be wise enough to lose it; and to admire the giant brain of the man who bests you at it."

"I shall," she promised meekly. "Oh, you have such a marvelous mind, Mr. Harding!"

"Bravo!" he applauded. "That's gorgeous as a start. And if you could manage to ask me in a sort of awed tone 'Where did you get your uncanny knowledge of women?' why, I'd be groveling at your feet. I told you all advertising can do is to get the public interested in an article. After that it's up to the article itself. But if you follow up the line I've just been handing out you can't lose. Why you should want to win I don't know. Why any woman should want to make a hit with men in general I don't know. Especially at the sacrifice of her own brains. We men are called the lords of creation. I guess it's because we haven't the sense to handle any of creation's less exalted and more important jobs. You will start in with lessons to-morrow morning?"

"Yes," she promised.

"Good! When you're ready for your first supper let me know. I'll invite myself as the first guest. And I'll bring along Imlach and Stuart. Both of them are champion *gourmets*. And neither of them can eat an unusually good meal without talking about it for a week afterward to anyone who will listen. I'll give them a hint beforehand about the wonderful food you cook. And afterward you can trust them to press-agent the venture. Your next Sunday night bunch of guests will come a-running."

"But," she urged in belated recollection, "how about your part of the bargain? I was to help you, too, you know."

"So you were," he said. "But I'm afraid I'm unhelpable. A chronically shy man is. But if you can think up any cure for me I'll try it gladly. In the meantime I'll get my pay in the fun of putting over a success; and in one or two of your Sunday night suppers if you'll invite me. You see I live in a boarding house. By the way, it's lucky for you that I'm a wallflower. By sticking against the wall at dances a man hears a lot, and he gets to knowing things about human nature that a popular man never has time to learn—that is, if he keeps his ears open, instead of grouching. It all helped me frame up the scheme I've started you on. But it didn't give me any tip for my own cure. I'm going to drop in here every now and then, if you don't mind, while the cooking lessons are going on. I may be of use in getting rid of the unsuccessful creations and in coaching you to talk of other people's interests instead of your own. Good night, Miss Article."

When Stuart and Imlach at the country club a few months later blurbed deliriously of the most delicious Sunday night pick-up supper they ever had eaten they commanded instant and wistful attention. When they went on to tell where they had eaten it an almost audible grunt of disappointment swept the room.

Mary Gray was still the set's official wallflowerette. This in spite of the tale of John Harding's rather frequent calls at her home and his attendance on her at one or two social happenings.

Yet so vigorously did the two guests defend their manner of spending the Sunday evening, and so glowingly did they descant on the glories of the food their genius-hostess herself had cooked that the contempt died a natural if puzzled death.

Two men who were bidden to the next week's feast shamefacedly accepted—with the air of folk who will try anything once. And two more men that same Sunday chanced to call on Mary dangerously near to supper time. They were asked to stay to the pick-up meal.

After that John Harding's forecast was justified. Men wondered bewilderedly why they ever had been led into the theory that Mary Gray was a dead one. Not only could she cook most divinely but she was actually brilliant in conversation. For instance, she let Mark Townsley talk to her for twenty solid minutes about his suit against the trolley line. When he paused for breath she begged for more details. And other men could boast of like experiences.

Even at other people's houses it was a pleasure to talk to so keenly appreciative an audience of one. Besides which, Mary danced uncommonly well, as male Fairfield suddenly discovered. In brief, she had arrived!

In prehistoric days—a quarter century earlier—informal Sunday night suppers had been no novelty. And the girl who could cook—and cook well—had been almost less the exception than the rule. Yet Mary had rediscovered what was—in Fairfield, at least—a lost art. An art that found scores of worshipers.

One or two other girls observing her victory sought to duplicate it. The only result was to make Mary Gray's new-kindled flame shine the brighter. For these damsels lacked the course of grinding study which had given her a culinary perfection and a multiplicity of dishes. After a try or so at stringy Welsh rabbits and scorched lobster Newburg, men fought shy of Mary's imitators and angled brazenly for invitations to supper at the Gray house.

Now the attentions shown her in public and the theater parties and drives to which she was bidden were no longer mere payments for suppers received. They were bids for suppers to come. They were also tributes to a wallflower emeritus who was fast becoming more or less a belle.

All the time from the side lines John Harding was coaching his pupil, who now needed scarcely a word of coaching, yet who still demanded it of her tutor. Perforce he was present at more of her suppers than were most other men. And at these affairs his zealous interest in his article's success made him totally forgetful of himself and of his shyness.

It was the same when other girls, noting his intimacy with the newly popular Mary, sought to sidetrack him by taking note of his existence. They did not interest him. Therefore they no longer frightened him. He did not care now whether they noticed him or not. His mind and his covert attention were wholly on the girl he was so painstakingly steering to success.

All of which gave him an air of civil indifference to outside blandishments—an air which piqued more than one damsel almost to the point of fascination.

"He's not really shy," a maiden sized up the judgment of her Fairfield sisters. "He's only hard to know. He doesn't care. That's what has made him keep to himself so much. He doesn't think we're worth his trouble. It—it would be fun to make him change his mind, wouldn't it?"

Which change of popular sentiment Harding did not observe in the least— because he did not care, and which Mary Gray observed with heightening annoyance, because she was discovering with amazement that she did care.

Wherefore one Sunday evening she maneuvered him into staying after the rest had gone. And as soon as they were alone together she said: "You haven't been here before in three weeks. Why haven't you? You had time to call on Gertrude Hallett. She told me so. She said she asked you to come and see her about the Red Cross dance and—"

"Very bad!" he interrupted sternly; "very, very bad indeed! And just when I hoped you were trained to the minute! How often do I have to tell you never to ask a man why he hasn't been to see you? There are so many hundred better ways of making him think you've missed him, without letting him feel the yank of the dog collar! And it's still worse to complain to him that he has time to see other girls. You couldn't have done worse. It would have scared any regular victim away for a year.

Besides, you don't have to practice on me any longer. I told you that, months ago. I—"

An angry stamp of her little foot acted on his flow of kindly reproof as on a motor brake, bringing the man to a dead halt.

"I wasn't practicing on you!" she flared. "And I have to be human once in a while, don't I? I've taught myself to be really interested in what interests men who meet me. And I don't think about myself once where I used to forty-three times. But it's different when I'm talking to you. And when you stay away I can't remember to be tactful when you come back. Why, you wouldn't have come here even this evening if I hadn't written to ask you."

"Why should I?" he asked drearily. "My work's done. And I'm not throwing roses at either of us when I say it's done to the queen's taste. Why should I stick round when I'm not necessary? You're cured, Mary."

"So are you!" she retorted in a voice of sharp accusal rather than congratulation. "There's always some girl or other nowadays trying to catch your eye. And you've forgotten how to be tongue-tied. Do you want me to tell you what Gertrude Hallett said to me about you—in this very room, not three days ago?"

"No!" he declared in some trepidation. "I don't. Please don't! Whenever I hear things people say about me it sends queer twingles down my spine. It's a left-over from shyness, I suppose. Yes, I knew I was cured; before you told me. It came to me in a flash, once, when that Forbes girl—"

"Well?" she asked in attempted loftiness as he checked himself. "What about the Forbes girl? Not that I'm especially interested," she hurried on to add.

"Neither am I," he dismissed the subject, continuing: "Yes. We're both cured. Shall we call it a day?"

To her own astonishment as much as to Harding's she wavered in an attempted reply, and found herself crying.

As the weeping fit was not premeditated or foreseen Mary cried very unbecomingly indeed. And she knew it. Wherefore in flaming self-contempt she sought blindly to get out of the room.

But at this effort, too, she was a failure, chiefly because someone had moved between her and the door, someone who detained her by force of arms.

"Say!" she heard her detainer mumbling feverishly into the fluff of hair that had buried itself all unconsciously in the recesses of his coat lapel. "Say! Did you really think I was training you just for the benefit of every other man in Fairfield? Or any other man on earth? Did you honestly think so? Did you, sweetheart?"

Twice-

Over

A T San Francisco's ultra-exclusive Cestus Athletic Club, there was only one middleweight, among all the throng of clever and hard-hitting amateurs, who could hold his own against Phil Shirley. This one talented man was Dallas Graeme, a young fellow of much charm of manner and of apparently easy circumstances. Shirley was the stockier and stronger of the two. But Graeme was the quicker and shiftier; and he had, besides, an unexpectedly heavy punch hidden away somewhere in his graceful body.

The news that Graeme and Shirley were "at it again," in the gymnasium, was usually enough to empty the library and even the restaurant of the Cestus Club and to bring a throng of spectators hurrying to the scene of the bout. It was a real joy to watch these two men box. Even as certain dancers perform best together, on account of mutual suitability of their step, so these crack middleweights were wont to put up the fastest and most spectacular bouts ever seen at the Cestus.

More than one ardent sporting member yearned to see them matched in something more conclusive than a mere friendly competition. Huge would have been the purse and huger would have been the bets on such a contest. But there was no hope of seeing the rivals face to face in a real fight. Not only were they warm friends, but neither belonged to the class from which the prize-ring is recruited. Phil Shirley was a rising corporation lawyer, while Graeme dabbled lazily in real estate. Both were college graduates. Shirley had played good football at Stanford. Dallas Graeme had been a crew-man at a freshwater university.

Their common love for boxing first brought the two together, at the Cestus. And their equal prowess at the same art had formed a further bond of intimacy. While they were not inseparable friends, yet they liked each other and were together nearly every day or evening, at the club.

It was at one of the Ladies' Days at the Cestus, that Shirley introduced Graeme to Eve Shannon, to whom Phil had just become engaged. Eve was an intensely pretty and equally unsophisticated girl, with an inheritance which was already an alluring bait to fortune-hunters. Her parents had died several years before, and her affairs were in the hands of Phil Shirley's uncle, Judge Hull.

Phil was doubtful, for an instant, as to his own wisdom in introducing Graeme to Eve. As a matter of fact, he knew little of the fellow, except for their casual club friendship. And many a man shows up well with other men—as Phil belatedly told himself—who cuts a very poor figure indeed with cultured women. Shirley realized this, just as he had beckoned Graeme across to where he and Eve Shannon were standing. It was too late, then, to back out.

YET, when he noted, presently, how thoroughly agreeable to Eve his friend could make himself, his doubts melted. Eve was most gracious to Graeme, not only on his own account but from having heard Phil speak so often of him. The trio were together, off and on, throughout the reception.

Next evening, Dallas Graeme hunted up Phil, as the latter was finishing his after-dinner coffee in the club grill. Speaking with manifest embarrassment, Graeme drove straight to the theme of his thoughts.

"Miss Shannon asked me, yesterday, to call on her, sometime," he began abruptly. "You've told me you are engaged to her. So I have come to ask your leave, before I venture to accept her invitation."

Phil laughed outright, amused and a little pleased at the man's old-fashioned ideas of punctilio.

"Why, go ahead!" he consented. "I'd like mighty well to have you and Eve know each other better. What a funny question to ask me!"

"No," denied Graeme, "it isn't as funny as it seems. You see, you really know nothing about me—except that I make a good sparring partner for you and that I'm a real-estate man. And some men don't care to carry such chance acquaintanceships into their homes or into the homes of girls they are engaged to. That's all."

"Rot!" snorted Phil. "If you were the sort of man who didn't belong among real people, you wouldn't be suggesting precautions to me, like this."

"Thanks," said Graeme briefly. "And I suppose my past will shape up fairly well with the average. I've done a bunch of things I didn't want to. But I don't think I've done many that I'm ashamed of. Except,"—he hesitated, then went on with a half rueful, half amused burst of confidence,—"except that I let this crowd here believe I'm an amateur boxer. Strictly speaking, I'm not an amateur. That's why I always refuse to go into the club tournaments. I wouldn't mention it now, even to you; but if I'm to call on a girl who is to be your wife—well, I don't want you to hear things afterward that may make you wish you hadn't consented to my going to see her. So

I'd better tell you and let you judge for yourself whether you think—"

"Not an amateur?" queried the puzzled Shirley, his boxing instinct catching at the odd admission before his brain grasped the rest of the other's meaning. "I don't get you."

"IT isn't a thing I'm proud of," returned Graeme. "That's why I keep my mouth shut about it. But, on the level, it isn't a thing I'm ashamed of, either. It was that or worse. And I fought clean."

"You don't need to tell me you fought clean," put in Shirley. "I've boxed with you too often to doubt that. And," he added, swallowing back his curiosity, "you don't have to tell me any of the story unless you want to. I'm willing to—"

"It happened about two years after I got out of college," began Graeme, disregarding the loophole. "I'd gone into a mining deal, back in Colorado. It failed. It left me not only dead-broke, but two or three thousand in the hole. The cash was owed to men who had invested in the deal at my advice. I guess you understand I couldn't let such debts slide."

Phil nodded. Dallas Graeme went on:

"There aren't many ways a man out of a job can raise three thousand dollars in a hurry. But I had heard of one such way, the only way I could capitalize my knack at boxing. Do you happen to remember Cap'n Farrell I brought here once to see the tournament?"

"Big yellow-faced man, with marks on his ears where he used to wear earrings?" asked Shirley. "Yes, I remember him. A queer-looking duck. More like a stage pirate, in looks, than the peaceful skipper of a tramp steamer. I didn't meet him, did I? I think you just pointed him out to me, across the gym."

"I had run across him again, that day," said Graeme. "He's daffy on boxing. He had read about the tournament; and he begged me to get him in to see it. I owed him a good turn. So I paid it that way. His steamer touches here about once in two months, for a week or so; and he always looks me up. Well, that's got nothing to do with my yarn."

"Go ahead," adjured Phil.

"I had heard that captains of tramps and of windjammers, in the coastwise trade, sometimes pick up a wad of easy money for themselves by taking along on their trips some good boxer. The boxer passes for a member of the crew. But all the work he has to do, on board, is to train—and to train mighty hard. When the ship makes a port, the captain goes ashore and brags about the wonderful scrapper in his crew. He gives the idea that the man is just a natural rough-and-tumble scrapper, not an expert. Almost always some other ship or some waterside clique has a fighter it thinks can lick all creation. A match is arranged, and a pretty good purse is scraped together. Then it's up to the boxer to come ashore and hammer the local man. Sometimes the job is a cinch. Sometimes it's gruelingly hard. Sometimes it can't be done. But it averages up fairly well. The captain takes sixty per cent of the purse, generally; and the boxer gets the other forty."

"But—"

"A MAN who is a winner can bulldoze the captain into splitting fifty-fifty with him. If he's only average good, he is lucky to net twenty per cent. If he loses four or five fights, one after another, he is apt to be dumped ashore and left to get home any way he can. Those coastwise skippers aren't lambs, you know."

"And you?"

"I had heard of the custom, as lots of other sea-lovers have. I made inquiries, out here, and I got in touch with Cap'n Farrell, of the *Tigercat*. He tried me out, and he said I'd do. So I made six trips with him. Before the last trip was over, I had paid off my debts and had a little stake left over to start me in the real-estate game. It was a nightmare of a life, while it lasted. But I never fought a crooked fight, and I never bet on myself. I earned all I got."

"Good boy!" applauded Phil, impulsively stretching forth his hand in admiration. "Lord, but I envy you some of your experiences! And do you mean to say you thought I'd be fool enough to want you to keep from calling on Eve, just because you were man enough to go out and fight for the money to square yourself with the world? Why—"

"Thanks, old man!" said Graeme, returning the other's strong grip, and looking thoroughly embarrassed by the eager praise. "Thanks. I'm glad you take it that way. It was only fair to tell you, though."

"It was white of you to tell me," corrected Phil. "But it wasn't necessary. I only wonder you gave up such work, for a tame shore-job."

DALLAS GRAEME laughed. "I didn't want to," he confessed. "At least, I didn't want to do it, till I could make a bigger pile. The life was a nightmare, as I told you. But it was a money-making nightmare."

"Then why didn't you stay at it longer?"

"I had been training too hard, I suppose. I was a glutton for training, because my living depended on it. And Farrell was no man to ease me up on work. In my last fight,—it was with a Monterey greaser,— I got some fearful smashes over the heart. I lasted long enough to put my man out. Then, on the way back to the ship, I fainted. They took me to a port doctor. He looked me over, for nearly an hour. Then he said my heart had got strained from overtraining and from the horrible exertion of my fights, and that the greaser's punches had done rotten things to it. I came back here and saw a big specialist. He said any overstrain or sudden shock might kill me. The heart might be good for years for ordinary use, he said. But it was a wreck, just the same. And some day it would get me. So I gave up fighting, of course. I feel like a mucker, to yammer this way about my infirmities. But—"

"And you've kept on boxing, nearly every night, with a bum heart?" cried Phil, aghast.

"Rot!" disclaimed Dallas. "The friendly little goes, here at the club, keep me in condition. And they don't strain me. An easy three-round bout with eight-ounce gloves is a joke, compared with fifteen or twenty murderous rounds with bare knuckles. No, no, Phil. The silly slapping matches at the Cestus wouldn't jar the heart of a baby."

"Just the same," declared Shirley, "I've boxed with you, for the last time. I'd be scared to death, every time I landed a right-hander on your body."

"Nonsense!"

"Maybe so," acceded Shirley. "But it's the truth. If you want to risk your life, you can risk it against some one else. Besides, I wouldn't be able to box with you again, for a while, even if I wanted to. You remember that Coit Merger business I was telling you about? Well, I got word to-day that it's to be shoved through without waiting for Gregg to come back from Italy. That means I'll have to start for New York, to-morrow or next day. And I may not get back for another three months. Tough luck for a just-engaged man, eh?"

"Vile luck!" assented Graeme in quick sympathy. "Can't you get back here at all, while the work is going through?"

"Not a chance, I'm afraid," grumbled Phil. "It means all sort of conferences and consultations, at all sorts of hours. If it wasn't such a big thing for me, I wouldn't go a step. Eve is a brick about my going, though. And that helps. I'm glad you can drop in on her sometimes, while I'm gone. I'm afraid she'll need all the cheering up she can get."

PHIL SHIRLEY'S stay in New York was decidedly worth while, from a financial view. But it was cruelly hard upon his nerves and his capacity for homesickness. Daily, he wrote to Eve Shannon. Daily, he received adorable letters from her.

But he was overwhelmingly in love. And the exchange of letters made him the more bitterly homesick for her. Two or three times, in her epistles, Eve spoke of Dallas Graeme, and always with a cordial friendliness. Apparently she was seeing Graeme quite often. Just as evidently, she regarded him as an entertaining friend, and as nothing more.

Phil had been in New York for more than two months, and the interminable details of the merger had reached a point where they would not much longer need his personal attention. Then, on a day, he received a letter from his uncle, Judge Hull, who was Eve's former guardian and who still handled the affairs of her very considerable fortune.

"Dear Phil," the letter ran, in Hull's ramblingly nonjudicial style. "There's a pack of trouble here. I think you'd better wind things up in the East, as quickly as you can, and come home—even if you have to make some slight sacrifice to do it. It is your place, and not mine, I think, to straighten matters out. They certainly need it.

"Your friend, Mr. Dallas Graeme, has been making himself solid with Eve, in a purely Platonic way, and has impressed her with his wonderful business sense. He got her interested in a land-development scheme of his. He planned, he said, to get control of a huge tract north of Santa Barbara, and to put into practice some ideas which would make him a multimillionaire in less than five years. Never mind the details. They were so gloriously visionary that I don't really wonder they hypnotized poor little Eve.

"He said he was going to name the new city 'Shirley,' in honor of you, and that he was going to arrange for you to handle all its legal details. He said this would make you a rich man. He was playing, you see, on your scruples against marrying a girl so much richer than yourself and showing her how the obstacle could be cleared away by making you rich, too.

"He told her it was all to be a golden surprise to you; and you weren't to know a thing about it till it was all ready to launch. Then he came to the question of financing the deal. By that time he had got her so thrilled over the notion of making your fortune, and so convinced of his scheme's plausibility, that I verily believe she would have put her whole fortune in his hands.

"BUT Graeme was too clever for that. He knew she would have to consult me, first. So he chose the bird in the hand, rather than the whole nestful in the bush. In other words, he induced her to transfer to him about thirty-five thousand dollars in cash and stock—all she could lay hands on, without letting me in on the beautiful secret.

"I found out about the transfer, by the merest chance, and I managed to get details from her. Then, before notifying you,—which she besought me not to,—I set Marshall and his agency to looking up Graeme's record, so that I might have something tangible to go on. The report has just been handed to me. Here's the gist of it:

"Dallas Graeme was kicked out of Denver for a crooked mining deal. He had to go into hiding, till his father could patch things up. So he boarded a coastwise steamer and picked up a hatful of coin in secret prize-fights at various ports—in the upper rooms of sailors' dance-halls and in wharf lofts and such places. He developed a diseased heart at this pursuit, and came to San Francisco. Since then, under the cloak of a reputable real-estate business, he has put across one or two raw deals which almost landed him in jail. But up to now, he has always managed to wriggle clear, by the skin of his teeth.

"Now, however, a couple of his victims are planning to take their grievance to the District Attorney. And from what I gather, Mr. Dallas Graeme stands a fair chance of doing time, for their case has been bolstered by some evidence which they could not get hold of at the time he fleeced them.

"I went to-day to Eve with the main facts of the report. She won't believe me. The fellow is so clever that he can make people believe in his honesty against a mountain of testimony. He did the same thing in the case of his other dupes.

"Now, there is only one man living, to my way of thinking, whom she will believe.

And that one man had better come out here and convince her, before she can dump any more cash into Graeme's pocket; for if she demands the rest of her estate from me, I've no legal power to refuse. And now that Graeme knows I know, he may try to make her do that."

PHIL SHIRLEY caught the next train for the Coast. In his heart was red fury. He knew Judge Hull well enough to realize that the old lawyer would not have made one of the charges in his letter unless he had ample proof. He could reconstruct, too, the methods whereby the magnetic Graeme had coaxed the money from Eve.

Always her greater wealth had been a barrier between herself and Phil. A dozen times he had lamented to her that he must incur the sneer of being a fortune-hunter, by marrying a girl so much richer than himself. And in her stark ignorance of business, Eve had thought she saw a way to enrich him. Hotter and hotter blazed his murderous wrath against Graeme.

Shirley reached San Francisco at seven o'clock, one rainy morning. He was grimy and unshaven. The hour was too early for him to call on Eve, with his warning. He resolved to go to the Cestus Club for a plunge in the swimming pool, a shave and some breakfast before starting for the Shannon house.

He ran up the club steps, past a porter who was swabbing down the vestibule, and entered the foyer. Several early risers were loitering there, waiting for breakfast or glancing over the morning papers. One of these men was strolling toward the outer door as Phil came into the foyer. Shirley almost collided with him, before recognizing the other as Dallas Graeme.

At sight of Phil,—who, he had thought, was safe in New York, for at least another month,—Graeme's face went bone-white, for an instant. A greenish tinge sprang into his cheek and his lips turned blue. In that one glance, any heart specialist would have diagnosed the seriousness of his condition.

But on the moment, Graeme recovered his poise and lost the involuntary glint of terror which had darkened his eyes. With a smile of welcome, he held out his hand to the red-faced and glaring Shirley.

"Why, hello, old chap!" he said easily. "When did you blow into town?"

AT first glimpse of Graeme, a surge of blind rage had swept over Phil, a passion that choked back his speech and that drove his clenched left fist spasmodically outward and upward.

The blow caught Graeme, flush on the point of the jaw. His feet went up and his head went back. And it was his head which first struck the floor.

There Graeme lay, sprawled supine and moveless on the marble of the foyer floor, while Phil Shirley crouched ferociously above him, waiting for the fallen man to get to his feet and fight.

But Dallas Graeme did not get to his feet. Instead, he lay there, limply lifeless. The rest of the foyer's loungers came running up, shouting confused questions and getting in one another's way. Two of them grabbed Shirley by the arms to hold him back from further assault. Others bent to lift the inert body of Graeme.

One of these—a young doctor—fussily ordered the senseless man carried to the nearest couch and set to work on him.

Phil, meantime, with a gruff word, had shaken off the hold of the two men at his sides. His brain was clearing. He cursed his rash temper for the fix it had got him into. He knew what a place for gossip a club can be. He knew Graeme's calls on Eve were probably no secret. And he, her fiance, had just thrashed Graeme in public. That must lead to a lot of ugly gossip among the Cestus men, and the bandying of Eve's name in bar and grill—and wherever else the story of a supposedly jealous lover's revenge might chance to be told.

The jarring realization cleared Phil's mind of the wrath-mists and set it to working with unwonted clearness and speed.

"This will probably mean expulsion from the club, for me," he said aloud, advancing to the group of men clustered about the couch. "So I want to tell you fellows why I did it. Graeme wheedled me into investing a thousand dollars in a mining scheme he knew was worthless. I stopped over at Denver on the way out here, and found the scheme was a swindle. I found, too, that he had framed it so trickily that I had no legal redress. So I swore I'd take it out of his hide, the next time I saw him. That's why I smashed him, just now. And that's why I'm going to smash him again, as soon as he's able to stand on his feet. I'm going to keep on doing it, till he refunds the thousand dollars he stole from me. He—"

"Shut up, man!" broke in the flustered doctor, in a horrified voice, as he arose from beside the couch. "He's—he's *dead!* You killed him!"

THE group had gathered around Phil, as he told of his imaginary grievance against Graeme. Now, at the doctor's babbled announcement, they shrank instinctively back from him. Shirley did not observe the general recoil. Yet his preternaturally sharpened mind had not only grasped the young doctor's statement, but had also told him that his trial for manslaughter must assuredly bring out Eve's connection with the affair.

As matters now stood, Phil was on record for striking Graeme in revenge for a mining-deal swindle. A court trial could readily expose the falsity of the statement, just as the same court trial would bring out the relations between Eve and the victim. There was only one way—for Eve's sake—to avert such a trial and to make his present statement hold water. Phil, on the instant, chose that one way.

Turning on his heel, he walked out of the club. He did not invoke the hue-and-cry by running. But he walked as fast as he dared. And he was down the steps and in a taxicab before any of the dazed witnesses of the deed had the presence of mind to try to check him.

At five o'clock that afternoon Phil had not only made such changes in his appearance as were possible, but he had tracked down and found the man he had wanted most of all in America to meet. This man was Cap'n Farrell of the tramp steamship *Tigercat,* about to sail for the southern California and Mexico ports with a mixed cargo. Phil—roughly dressed and dirty—was ushered into the Captain's presence in the back room of a saloon.

HE wasted no time in preliminaries, but opened at once on the sullen-faced skipper.

"I'm a boxer, out of luck," began Phil. "I hear you take good men along sometimes and pick up matches for them on the voyage. I want to go."

"H'm!" grunted Cap'n Farrell, with no vast enthusiasm. "Lots of tinhorn amachoors want to go on my voyages. They fair pester me to death, to take 'em along. I'm fixed up with as handy a lad, for this next voyage, as I've seen in a year or more. Not a chance for you, sonny. Don't hang 'round no longer on my account."

"If I can lick the man you've picked out to take," persisted Shirley, "do I get the berth?"

Farrell grinned craftily.

"I don't aim to get Jennings all het up, downin' amachoors, before we start out," said he. "We ain't in the fighting game for our health, him and me."

Phil drew five twenty-dollar bills from his pocket and laid them on the table in front of Farrell.

"Bring on Jennings!" he ordered curtly. "If I don't lick him, keep the hundred. If I do, you take me along instead of him. Is that fair enough for you?"

Half an hour later, in the loft of the same building, Phil Shirley stood, stripped to the waist, in an improvised ring, facing a gorilla-like youth with a split nose and a cauliflower ear. Twenty or thirty waterfront cronies of Farrell's sat in mild interest to watch the bout.

Jennings was the typical dockside fighter—a squat and muscle-bound youth, hard as nails and with a genius for bull-rushes and for the taking of punishment. As a mere boxer, he was a farce. As a fighter, he was reasonably formidable.

Phil, a little to his own surprise, had no trouble at all in avoiding his foe's wild rushes and in keeping out of corners. He hit hard. He hit clean. Jennings' guard was useless against him. He sought out, patiently, the weak spot in his opponent's anatomy and found it presently to be the wind.

By the middle of the fourth round, Shirley's body punches began to do queer things to a waterside system nourished on steam beer and alcohol splits. Jennings wavered under one such mighty stomach punch, and swayed on his heels. This was a signal for Phil to step in and land the blow for which he had been storing so much of his strength. Feinting with his left for the wind,—and thereby forcing the stomach-tortured Jennings to "cover up" with both hands,—Phil sent a lightning half-hook with his right to the undefended jaw.

FIVE hours later, when the *Tigercat* wallowed out through the Golden Gate, Phil

Shirley was an honored (and honorary) member of her crew. In honor of his late adversary, he elected to be known as "Bud Jennings." He had given no name at all, on introducing himself to Farrell. And the latter had asked no impertinent questions.

From his own knowledge of human nature, Shirley deduced that the average fugitive from justice would not be likely to ship aboard a coastwise vessel, which traveled only a few hundred miles in all, between its stops at San Francisco; and assuredly that such a fugitive would not court the limelight by posing as a professional fighter. Hence, he felt fairly safe from pursuit.

For himself, he would not have cared how soon he might be captured. Indeed, left to himself, he would have stood his ground, knowing that a brief prison term was the very worst fate he had to fear. It was on Eve Shannon's account alone that he had fled. It was on her account alone that he must keep out of the law's way until Judge Hall and others of his influential friends should have time to smooth matters over.

In the hour before sailing, Phil scribbled a hurried note to the Judge, explaining why he was running away but giving no hint of his destination or whereabouts. Thus Judge Hull could incur no just suspicion of shielding the hiding-place of a criminal. Shirley also wrote a longer letter to Eve.

The next few months amply indorsed Graeme's statement that the life of a ship boxer was a "nightmare." Farrell kept his champion training mercilessly hard. And the various fights called for all Shirley's stamina and skill.

THE climax came on the return trip. The *Tigercat* was laid up for provisions, for two days, at Ovalle, some seventy-five miles north of Valparaiso. Here Cap'n Farrell had pulled off some of his choicest matches. And he looked forward, blissfully, to a rich harvest. Accordingly, he fared forth to his old dock-region haunts in search of his prey.

But he came back to the ship, surly drunk. It seemed, since his last victorious visit to Ovalle, the sporting fraternity of the town had decided his "amachoors" were suspiciously clever fighters—for untrained seamen. Which fact made the Captain's behavior toward his crew as friendly and lovable as a sick wildcat's.

Next day, Farrell's grief was little assuaged by news that a sailing-ship which had that morning anchored off Ovalle boasted an able seaman who was a wonder in the ring and who sought a match. Farrell met the windjammer's captain in a local sporting saloon, and in an hour the match was arranged.

This was no bonanza, of course, since betting must be chiefly confined to the officers and members of the two crews. But it was better than nothing.

The fight was to begin at eight that evening, as the *Tigercat* was to catch the tide at eleven. Farrell always liked to make a brisk get-away, after his triumphs. The bout was to be staged in a smelly dance-hall conveniently near the docks.

WHEN Phil—wrapped to the eyes in his soiled bathrobe—came out of his dressing-room, the low-ceiled hall was jammed to the doors and was thick-fogged with tobacco smoke. One of the tricks Shirley had gleaned from Farrell was to let the other man get into the ring first—to get there and to wait there as long as the patience of the crowd would permit, before coming, himself, out of his dressing-room. Waiting, under the impatient eyes of the throng, plays havoc with a fighter's nerves and temper and goes far toward fraying the self-control so needful to the winning of a bout.

To-night, Shirley waited even longer than usual. As he strolled toward the ring, he saw his adversary had grown too nervous to sit still, and that he was leaning over the ropes to talk with a fellow-member of the windjammer's crew.

Phil climbed into the ring, nodded in response to a scattering ripple of applause and suffered Farrell to unwind from him the folds of the bathrobe. The other man, he noted, was already stripped for action, and the sweat was pouring in streamlets down his bare body. The heat of the room was stifling.

As he heard the ragged applause that greeted Shirley, the windjammer's champion turned to look at his foe. For the first time, thus, Phil had a view of his face.

Shirley had been in the act of settling himself in the backless deal chair in his own corner. But now he stiffened convulsively to his feet, and he came as near to "seeing red" as does any man outside a novel.

His antagonist was Dallas Graeme.

For a mere instant, Shirley felt not the faintest surprise that the man he had killed should be standing face to face with him in the ring. His only emotion was one of stark fury against the blackguard who had swindled Eve. The same overmastering rage which had made him knock Graeme down, in the foyer of the Cestus Club, now swirled through his brain once more. Fiercely, he exulted at the new chance to punish his enemy.

In another moment, his mind began to work more sanely. He recalled the terrified excitement of the inexperienced young doctor at the club. The callow youth, on superficial examination, had pronounced dead a man who, presumably, had been in a mere swoon. How Graeme chanced to be here, in Ovalle, and matched for a fight, did not interest Shirley in the least. It was enough that Phil now had a chance to settle the old score as it ought to be settled.

A SECOND look at Graeme showed that the last few months had been doing strange things to his once-wiry physique. His springiness was gone. So was the color in his cheeks. The sea-trip had not been able to tan away a certain greenish pallor, nor to put light into his newly sunken eyes.

Dallas Graeme had glanced with no special interest at his adversary, and through the smoke haze, he very evidently had not recognized the swarthy young sailor as his former chum. But now the referee called the men into the center of the ring, and Phil saw a glint of incredulous wonder spring into Graeme's lackluster gaze. With a start that seemed to wrench his every nerve, Graeme stared agape at his opponent.

With a jabbering drone, the referee reeled off the rules, as custom required, taking less than ten seconds for the job. Neither fighter heard. Graeme was swaying, slack-jawed, his drawn face growing greener and sicker, his mouth distorted and drooping. Phil was eying him with a cold fury that had something very like murder in its ferocity.

"Shake hands!" droned the referee, stepping back. "Time!"

The gong rang. The crowd drew a long breath of expectation. But the men did not shake hands.

Graeme's arms had fallen limp to his sides. Noting this, Phil checked himself at the outset of a mad rush and withheld the blow he had started. Before he could make a second move, Dallas Graeme's knees suddenly crumpled under him. Very quietly he slumped to the floor.

The crowd bellowed its disgust. The windjammer's captain jumped into the ring and yanked Graeme roughly to his feet. But the man hung like an empty sack in the angry grasp. Perceiving this, the captain let him slide to the resined floor again and bellowed for a doctor.

TEN minutes later, Phil learned,—this time past all cavil,—that Dallas Graeme was dead. The two port doctors had agreed that a grievously diseased heart had all at once stopped beating, "probably from shock."

That same night, Phil Shirley started back to San Francisco, traveling with all the haste he could command.

As soon as he set foot in his native city, he went to Judge Hull's office.

"Where on earth have you been, you young fool?" roared the Judge, at sight of him. "We've been combing the States for you, Eve and I. What did you run away for? Graeme wasn't dead. It was just a turn his heart gave him. The doctors agree it will kill him, some day. But it didn't, that time. By the way, he skipped, not a week after you did. And there are two indictments out against him. He got wind of them and he lit out. The police can't find a trace of him. He—"

"He's dead," interposed Phil. "And I've been through hell. And now I'm going to heaven. That means I'm going up to see Eve. Good-by. I just wanted to report to you. I'm going to see Eve—thank God! I think I've won the right to."

The Actor-Man

*I*T began with the "Refined and Sidesplitting Minstrel Show," given by the local powder-mill employees at the Odd Fellows Hall, in Paignton. The show netted two hundred and nine dollars for the Thrift-stamp Drive.

Naturally, the Junior Auxiliary of Paignton's Red Cross branch had no part in the minstrel affair, for it was gotten up and performed by persons who were as socially impossible as they were earnest in their efforts for the Cause. Yet the tidings that the minstrels had cleaned up so solid a sum, toward the Drive, rankled in the Auxiliary's collective breast. Hitherto, whenever the Paignton proletariat had raised any substantial amount for a war-fund, the Auxiliary patricians had set to work, with quiet superiority, to show how much more money could be raised in a more exclusive way.

The Auxiliary's members—fifteen strong, of both sexes, and ranging in years from nineteen to twenty-two—met on the Mowbray veranda, and resolved themselves at once into a committee on ways and means.

Viva Mowbray was president of the Auxiliary—for the same reason she was president of her class at college!—for when Viva was available, it never occurred to anyone that there could be another candidate for high office.

Leonard Carter held down, in perpetuity, the dual job of secretary and treasurer. Leonard was twenty-two, and in his last year at Cornell. He had been debarred from starting upon a meteoric career toward the rank of major-general because he was nearsighted and had one flat foot. So, by way of doing his bit and, incidentally, of keeping in reverent touch with Viva Mowbray,—he hurled himself heart and soul into Paignton's various war-fund drives.

It was Viva who suggested the open-air performance. The idea was all hers.

"Why not let's give a play—an open-air performance? Our lawn would be a gorgeous site for it. The stage could be in the half-circle of trees."

That was all. And the Great Suggestion had been couched in language as simple as Napoleon's at Wagram! It was adopted by acclamation.

The site being chosen, the Auxiliary next turned its thoughts to the minor matter of the play itself.

"Let's go slow!" urged Con Hegan. "Remember, we're only amateurs. Don't let's bite off more than we can swallow. Best steer clear of any big play that will take too long to learn. Suppose we pick out some easy little snappy one-act comedy— something simple, like 'Box and Cox' or 'Much Ado About Nothing,' or something like that. How about it?"

It was Viva, as usual, who decided.

"I have it!" she declared after an instant of deep self-communion. "I have it! It just came to me. I wonder I didn't think of it right away!"

Instantly fourteen sets of eyes were focused on her in eager expectancy.

"All our class went over to the Stadium to see it!" she continued rapturously. "And it was altogether the most exquisite thing mortal eyes have beheld. And—and I'm perfectly sure we could do it."

"Oh," hazarded Leonard in no vast enthusiasm, "you mean the time you saw Holt Mallowe and Marise Bayne play their condensed version of 'As You Like It' for the Soldiers' Sweater Fund? But—"

"Yes!" Viva breathed dreamily. "That was it. I have had many experiences in my life, of course. But seeing those two geniuses play 'As You Like It' was the very most supreme experience of all, I think. It haunted me for weeks. Holt Mallowe comes nearer being my ideal of a perfect man than anyone else I can ever hope to see. And Marise Bayne's *Rosalind*—well, I'd rather look and act and be like Marise Bayne than like—like Helen of Troy! She—"

"But 'As You Like It' is a terribly *long* play," objected Edith King. "It would take forever to learn. And—"

"Not the Mallowe-Bayne version," explained Viva. "I read in the paper, the next day, that it lasted just forty minutes. And it was all in one scene. It would be ever so easy for us to learn. And the trees, down there, at the end of the lawn, would make a wonderful Forest of Arden. And—and I'll be *Rosalind*, if you like. I read the part, over and over and over, after I saw Marise Bayne in it. Some of the girls at college said I—I looked a little like her, too. And I remember just how she played it. That ought to help."

SO it was settled. Viva was to play *Rosalind*. Leonard, by virtue of a two-year experience in directing class plays at college, was appointed stage-director, with the rôle of *The Duke,* as a sideline. To big Con Hegan was assigned the part of *Orlando*—to Leonard's grief and to the secret disgust of five other aspiring youths.

Leonard had read, somewhere, of the Players Club. Thither he addressed to Holt Mallowe a very businesslike note, to the effect that the Junior Auxiliary of the Paignton Branch of the American Red Cross proposed to give a condensed version of Shakespeare's comedy, "As You Like It." The play, Leonard added, was to be given out of doors, and all the proceeds were to go to the Red Cross—an organization with whose high humanitarian aims he presumed Mr. Mallowe was cognizant. Leonard concluded his note with a courteous request that Mr. Mallowe would lend the Auxiliary a copy of his condensation of the play.

Viva, to whom Leonard showed the note, before mailing it, daringly added the following postscript:

> Please don't think I am being bold and impertinent when I say I think you and Miss Bayne were perfectly magnificent in "As You Like It." I shall never forget it.
> Gratefully yours,
> VIVA MOWBRAY,
> President.

Three days later came a reply—to Viva, not to the Secretary and Treasurer.

Mr. Mallowe thanked the Auxiliary's president for liking his work and Miss Bayne's, and said he was going to take the liberty of showing her postscript to Miss Bayne—who, he was certain, would be as much pleased by her praise as was he. Mallowe went on to say he would feel honored to give the Auxiliary permission to use his condensation of the play, and that he would not only forward a copy, but a full set of "sides," as well.

"Look!" said Viva, pointing to the address at the top of the actor's letter. "'Hideaway Cottage, Oakland, New Jersey.' Why, Oakland is less than seven miles from here. He must have a summer place, there. I wonder if we dare ask him to come over to the performance? Wouldn't it be gorgeous to be able to say I had played *Rosalind* in the presence of Holt Mallowe?"

"If he ever sees you in it," declared Leonard, "he'll see that you make Marise Bayne look like thirty cents! I never saw her, but I'll bet you'll not only put it over her in looks, but outact her too."

"No," denied Viva with the sweetly modest gravity which Leonard so worshiped in her, "I won't be able to act it *better* than she does, I'm afraid. I can hardly hope to do that. If I act the part anywhere near as well, I'll be content. She is wonderful. Of course, she is ever so much older than I am. She must be twenty-four or even twenty-five, I suppose—though her *Red Book* picture, last month, didn't show much age. But what she lacks in youth she makes up in technique."

"Technique!" snorted Leonard from the depths of his experience in no less than two college shows. "That's just a fetish! All you have to remember, in a stage-dialogue, is that both people change places with each other on the stage every time either of them says anything important. That's what is known as 'crossing.' It's marked in the prompt-books by an X. The one on the left side of the stage goes to the right, and the one on the right walks over to the left. Then, of course, the principal character must stand far enough upstage to keep his face to the audience. And the audience must never see the soles of a player's shoes. Get those three points in mind, and all the rest is easy."

WITH such a stage-director, the rehearsals could not but go well. Upon the wide veranda of Viva's home the Auxiliarians toiled every day. Nightly, at home, they conned the typed "sides."

Leonard went to New York and engaged the costumes. They were to be worn only for the dress rehearsal and for the performance—two days in all. So the rental of ten outfits, at three dollars a night, would eat into the gross profits to the extent of a bare sixty dollars.

The date for the performance was set. Flaring posters of announcement were smeared over every atom of available wall and tree space for miles around. The local proletariat was coy in its attitude toward the great event. The villagers had heard of Shakespeare, but showed no keen zest to witness one of his justly popular plays—at one dollar a seat. The ticket-sale lagged. Among the better-class population, too, there was wholly controllable enthusiasm over the intellectual treat. Old Mr. Ryerson seemed to embody the gist of neighborhood feeling when he remarked boorishly:

"I can stand Shakespeare. And I can stand amateurs. But to stand both of them at once is just an inch or two past my feeble endurance."

Nevertheless the Auxiliary went on right gallantly with its plans. And presently all was ready. The date for the performance was only six days off.

THEN, on the way to one of the final week's rehearsals, Con Hegan fell off his motorcycle and broke his left leg in two places. No one else could possibly learn the rôle of *Orlando* in six days. There would be no question of postponing the perfor-mance, for on the day following it, Viva was going to the Adirondacks for a month.

Leonard, fighting with his back to the wall, changed the wall into a battering ram. How the thought came to him he never could thereafter remember, but it came, and with the vividness of summer lightning flare.

"Viva!" he spluttered, almost beyond speech in his moment of inspiration. "*Viva!* I've got it! It's a ten-to-one shot, but the odds against Napoleon at Austerlitz were more. I dare you to drive over to Oakland with me, this afternoon, and see Holt Mallowe! I *dare* you to!"

"See Holt Mallowe!" repeated Viva dazedly. "What for? We—"

"And throw ourselves on his mercy, and beg him to save us by coming over here, next Saturday night, and playing *Orlando* for us!" shouted Leonard. "It's our only hope. He knows the part. He's played it, hundreds of times, with Marise Bayne. He's a generous chap, and he's interested in charity. Otherwise he wouldn't have helped us out as he has. Besides, actors are out of a job in summer. And Dad says they're an improvident lot. He met one, once. It's likely Holt Mallowe will jump at the chance of earning a little easy money on the side. We'll offer him—we'll offer him twenty dollars! It's a lot to pay out. But it's better than losing the whole show. I wouldn't have the nerve to offer less. How about it?"

Viva's wonderful eyes were aglow as they beamed upon the enslaved Leonard. He read their depths of meaning. He knew she was picturing herself, in advance, as playing *Rosalind* to the far-worshiped matinée idol's *Orlando*. And beneath his thrill he was aware of a nasty tug at his heart. Almost he regretted his inspiration, but by a mighty effort he thrust self aside.

At four that afternoon the little Carter runabout chugged to a halt at the gate of a picturesquely tumble-down old house on the outskirts of Oakland. Very pale, very straight-backed, very tight of lip, Viva Mowbray and Leonard Carter descended from the car and stalked heroically up the interminably long front walk.

AS they mounted the veranda steps, a man got up from a hammock in which he had been sprawling and came forward inquiringly to meet them. He was stocky of build, browned of face and unromantically old. Viva, after a look at his grizzling temples and the lines around his tired eyes, decided he must be at least forty. He was clad most untidily in corduroy trousers, ugly boots and a brown flannel shirt. His clothes were not only worn and shabby but showed traces of garden mold. And anyone could see he had not shaved for a day or more.

The ill-dressed man's tired face broke into a smile of welcome at sight of the two gloriously youthful callers. And by his famed and oft-pictured smile Viva knew him.

"Mr. Mallowe!" she babbled, aghast.

All Viva's dearest air-castles were tumbling about her pretty ears. In her imagination had long been enshrined the vision of Holt Mallowe, radiant with eternal youth, gracefully dashing, resplendent with Elizabethan raiment. And here before her stood the real man—incredibly old, dressed like a day-laborer, disgustingly matter-of-fact. By his wondrous smile alone could she have guessed his identity.

Leonard, expecting less than had she, was quicker to recover a remnant of his senses.

"Mr. Mallowe," he said in the terse captain-of-industry voice he had been at such pains to acquire, "Miss Mowbray and I have had some correspondence with you in regard to our open-air performance of your condensed version of 'As You Like It.' As we told you in our letters, we are ever so grateful for all you have done for us."

"Why, not at all!" broke in Mallowe pleasantly, "I was mighty glad to be of any use to you. Come into the shade and sit down, won't you? It's hot, out here on the steps. You're just in time for afternoon tea. —Betty!"

As he talked, he led the way to a bevy of low wicker chairs deep in the veranda. His call of "Betty!" was addressed to some one whose footsteps could be heard crossing the hall inside.

In answer to the summons a woman moved out through the Dutch doorway onto the porch—a comely woman, somewhere in the thirties, freckled and tanned. She wore a shirt-waist and a corduroy skirt, and had apparently just come in from gardening.

"Dear," Mallowe hailed her, "I want you to meet two fellow-actors of mine— Miss Mowbray and Mr. Carter. This is my wife," he added in careless explanation to the visitors. "And I can tell by the expression of her chin that she is about to order tea served out here for us all, and that she is going to give us some of her own immortal fruit cake with it. Sit down, won't you?"

Viva's brain positively refused to work. The shock of finding the sublime Holt Mallowe an ill-dressed and elderly man was superseded by the greater shock of learning he was married, and that his wife a was a very ordinary and common, sensible mortal of middle age. Were there *no* unsmashable illusions, in all this degradingly sordid world?

Mrs. Mallowe greeted the guests in a jolly, almost motherly fashion, and bustled off to order tea. Whereat Leonard made another effort to get to the point of his call.

"You see," he said somewhat breathlessly, "we're in an awful hole. The performance is—was—is to be next Saturday night. The tickets are out. —We were going to send you two. And now our *Orlando* has just broken his leg, and there's no one to take his place. And we're in an awful hole. And—and we're in an *awful* hole!"

At this stage of the harangue his courage treacherously departed, leaving him gaping and purple and speechless. Which, had he known it, was the very best thing that could have happened to him at that particular moment, for the amused light in Mallowe's tired eyes gave place to a sudden warm sympathy for the pitifully floundering youngster.

(Chronic panhandlers in his own profession had learned to rejoice at that look on Mallowe's face, and had striven artfully to evoke it, for it meant largess.)

Viva forced herself back to reality.

"It means so much for the Red Cross," she pleaded, "and it means so much more for—for *us!* And there isn't any time for any other man to learn the part. And oh, Mr. Mallowe, I know what a horribly cheeky thing it is to ask—we both know. But *would* you consent to come over to Paignton that night—it's only seven miles you know—and—and play *Orlando* for us? You see, it's the only way to save the performance. I'm the *Rosalind*. And I've counted so on—on—"

Here, like Leonard, she found herself deprived of speech. And also like Leonard, she started in scarlet-faced misery at the arbiter of their joint destinies.

As she started, Viva all at once forgot her discovery that her stage deity was an old and slovenly mortal. For the smile had come back to Holt Mallowe's sensitive lips, a smile, this time, that did perfectly beautiful things to his whole face.

"Why, you poor little babes in the wood!" cried the actor with a mighty and utterly non-stagy laugh. "Of course I will! I'll do it gladly. I'll be delighted to. I—"

A wordless gurgle of pure rapture, from Viva, broke in on his acceptance, a million times more eloquently than an engrossed address of gratitude.

"You're a brick!" declaimed Leonard, his voice shaky with joyous reaction. "And Mr. Mallowe," he added, wrenching himself back into his best-loved personification of a Napoleon of finance, "much as—as we appreciate your being so—so magnanimous about it, we plan to put this on a business basis, you know. We are prepared to pay you twenty dollars for the service—the *great* service—you are rendering us.

"The money won't make our debt to you any the less, of course, sir. We realize that. But we shall not feel we are putting you out so unwarrantably, you see. I don't quite know what your regular rates are, but—"

"My 'regular rates' vary a good deal," interposed Mallowe with ponderous solemnity. "So it is hard to strike an average. I am afraid twenty dollars is an exorbitant sum for a single evening's work. It might give managers an exaggerated idea of my value. Suppose we compromise, for the good of the Cause? I will donate my services, and you can turn over the twenty dollars to the Red Cross treasury. Here comes the tea."

BEFORE the visitors went away, all arrangements for the performance had been made. Mallowe had even offered to come over to the remaining rehearsals in order to get accustomed to playing with a strange company.

He seemed to recognize, by instinct, Leonard's efficiency as a stage-director, for he did not suggest coaching the amateurs. Indeed, he listened with approving respect to certain details of stage-direction which Leonard kindly expounded to him. And he was to furnish his own costume—sending to his New York apartment for it, and thus saving the treasury six dollars.

The next morning, at eleven, a super-excited Auxiliary was grouped on the Mowbray veranda, feverishly awaiting the arrival of the great man. Leonard was latest of the members to reach the scene of the rehearsal. He had been up since dawn, driving from one end of the township to the other, affixing to every "As You Like It" poster a flaring strip which announced:

MR. HOLT MALLOWE as *Orlando.*

Leonard fancied Mallowe's name might induce a few more people to buy tickets. He had also ordered a new issue of programs headed by the large-type announcement:

Miss Viva Mowbray and Mr. Holt Mallowe,
in
"AS YOU LIKE IT"

"If we were giving this in New York," explained Leonard as he finished telling of his morning's work, "there would be quite a number of people attracted to the show if they heard Mallowe was to be in it. But up here I don't suppose a dozen natives ever heard of him. I had those strips gotten up, mostly, to let everyone know we had found a substitute for Con, and that the show wasn't off."

"I do hope people won't misunderstand him," sighed Viva worriedly, "when they see him coming to and from rehearsals here. He dresses so terribly, and he is so much older than most actors. But he is fine. I know you'll like him, ever so much."

A CAR came up the drive. At the wheel was Holt Mallowe. He looked no younger or more dramatic than on the day before. But Viva was infinitely relieved to note he had been freshly shaved, and that he wore a strikingly well-appointed lounge-suit of stone gray.

Mallowe did not seem at all ill at ease, on meeting so many strangers. And the rehearsal began.

Then, bit by bit, things happened. No one could tell just how or when the change began. Mallowe did not dispute or defy any of Leonard's directions. Yet—always showing entire deference to the director—he fell to suggesting minor alterations in one thing after another. He did it in such a way that Leonard, half the time, wondered whether the suggestions were not perhaps his own, instead of the newcomer's.

Rôle after rôle emerged from chaos into a semblance of logical coherence. The time was woefully short. Holt Mallowe was achieving miracles, which would have called forth the wondering praise of fellow-professionals, but which his present associates regarded as the most natural things in the world.

Oddly enough, it was from his erstwhile acolyte Viva Mowbray that Mallowe met with his only resistance in the task of smoothing a mass of singsong and explosive declamation into tolerable diction. Their first clash came when *Orlando,* having won the wrestling match, turns to *Rosalind* for his meed of praise. Viva, flinging the chain about his neck, flung with it the ringingly scanned assertion:

" 'Sir, you have wrestled well and over-thrown' " (full pause for end of metric line) " 'More than your enemies.' "

"Oh, Viva," cut in Leonard, "Mr. Mallowe thinks—and I think I agree with him—that you ought not to make that speech sound quite so much like 'The Charge of the Six Hundred,' and more colloquial."

"Something like this," supplemented Mallowe timidly.

He repeated the line in a way that sent funny wiggles through the hearts of several listening girls. He somehow raised the vision of an adoring maiden who tries to say the right thing, yet who is frightened lest she overstep shy modesty.

But Viva was unmoved. She had read her part and reread it, in front of her mirror, every night for weeks, and no outsider was going to upset her clearly thought-out concept of it.

"I'm sorry, Mr. Mallowe," she said with perfect breeding, "but I'm afraid I must read the line as my good taste and experience tell me it should be read. I remember how Marise Bayne rendered that same line, when I saw you two in 'As You Like It.' She was charming, of course. And she is a great actress, probably the greatest in America. But I thought, at the time, that—if there *could* be any criticism of her acting—it was that she spoke that line, and a number of others, just as if she were—were *talking*—as if she were a modern girl, here in America, instead of a Shakespearean heroine. You don't mind my saying so, do you? I—"

"Not at all," replied Mallowe. "You're probably right. We're a hidebound lot, we actors."

FOR a moment Viva's soft brows creased in a half-fear that he was guying her. But Mrs. Mallowe, who had come to this rehearsal with her husband, spoke up before the fear could crystallize.

"Of course Miss Mowbray is right," she averred. "Her reading of the line is very original indeed."

Viva had grown to feel a little sorry for the actor-genius who was fettered to such a prosaic little home-body. She had even wondered how he could endure Mrs. Mallowe's stodgy companionship after his constant association with a divinity like Marise Bayne. Now she decided he was not so much to be pitied as she had feared. Elderly Mrs. Mallowe certainly had brains, brains and discernment. Yet Viva would not have Mallowe think himself snubbed. So she went on sweetly:

"I see your side of the question too, Mr. Mallowe, of course. And from the way you just repeated the line, I can see you must have coached Marise Bayne in it. And I don't doubt that when you first learned the line, years ago, that would have been a simply beautiful way to render it, the *only* way, perhaps. But for *now*—don't you see it isn't quite—well, quite up to date? For us, I mean. When you repeat it in that ordinary way, it sounds just like *talking,* not at all like *acting,* as I understand the term. It sound almost—almost *flippant,* doesn't it? And whatever else he is, Shakespeare can hardy be called flippant."

MEANTIME Paignton was waking up. So was "the Valley," to the north. So was the powder-town just to westward. In fact, to Ridgewood and to Paterson and to Montclair itself the news was gushing—the news that the sublime Holt Mallowe was to play the "lead" in an amateur show at Paignton on Saturday night. And—in droves—people began to buy tickets.

On Friday night the dress rehearsal was held. The actors were to appear not only in costume but in make-up. When Holt Mallowe and his wife arrived on the electric-lighted lawn, they were confronted with a cohort of youths and maidens whose faces ranged in hue from prairie fires to lake sunsets, the carmine tints flaring forth from spectral white.

For the first time, Mallowe despaired. While he still blinked, tongue-tied, his wife came to the rescue.

"Splendid!" she exclaimed. "Who taught you clever children how to make up?"

"I told them how to do it," said Leonard with pardonable pride. "And I made up some of them myself. I learned how, at our college shows."

"But," asked Mrs. Mallowe as an afterthought, "weren't those plays given *indoors?*"

"Why, yes," he answered, troubled by her new air of anxiety. "But what difference does that make?"

"All the difference in the world," was her sorrowful reply. "A make-up that is perfect for the theater would look ghastly at an open-air performance."

"That's true!" spoke up Mallowe in great haste. "Perfectly true. The—the outside air seems to have an altogether different color, even by electric light. If you don't mind, Mrs. Mallowe and I can make the few minor changes in your make-up that will tone it to the outside light. Shall we? We've both had a great deal to do with open-air performances, and—"

"Please do," assented Leonard.

The actor and his capable spouse set cheerily to work. After they had deftly undone Leonard's labor, Mallowe vanished into his dressing-room, carrying his shabby suit-case. Thence, in a bewilderingly brief time, emerged a man whom at first glance they scarce recognized.

He was not a mere grease-paint actor. He was *Orlando,* the poet-swain of the Arden woodlands, eternally young, gloriously handsome, lithe, graceful, high-bred, afire with youthful magnetism. In the soft light he showed no trace of his artistically applied make-up. Nor was there the faintest sign of middle age or of the real Mallowe's everyday commonplaceness.

Leonard Carter saw the worship-glow leap into Viva's big eyes, and he thrilled with something akin to nausea. That look seemed to render ridiculous all hopes of the heavenly reply he had taught himself to dream of Viva's giving him, when—the performance over—he should ask her a tremblingly rehearsed question.

"First scene!" he rasped with *Simon Legree* ferocity. "Miss Mowbray, Miss King, Mr. Ryerson, Mr. Blount! Stage, please!"

Between his own double duties as director and as *The Duke,* Leonard spent a deliriously busy forty minutes. Yet he had time to note—and to note with stark misery—a myriad changes in Viva's acting. For one thing, when she flung the chain over Orlando's shoulders, she said now in adorable diffidence:

"'Sir, you have wrestled well!'"

Then she halted, and with a little catching breath of ecstasy blurted out the sweet confession:

"And overthrown *more* than your enemies!"

Mrs. Mallowe, in the wings, sat up and blinked, much as might a bored music-teacher whose dullest pupil suddenly begins playing with the skill of Paderewski. Leonard wished morosely that he had a sore tooth to bite on, or a mortal enemy to thrash.

"You know," he told Viva as he lingered on the Mowbray veranda a moment after the rehearsal was over, "you know, Viva, you never acted, before, as you acted to-night. You were a revelation!"

Thus much his honesty forced him to say. Then human nature took control, and he continued:

"But don't let yourself forget that Mr. Mallowe is old enough to be your father, and that he's married too—married to a nice little woman, as nice as she's dowdy. Mr. Mallowe—"

To his horror, Viva broke into a passion of tears and ran blindly into the house.

THE performance was scheduled for eight-thirty on Saturday night. As the simple stage was already set for its one scene, and as the actors were dressed and made up before seven, the play began a very little after nine o'clock—which was not bad for an amateur performance.

Yet the delay would probably have whitened Leonard's hair had he still been capable of emotion. But he was curiously numb in mind and body. Mechanically he walked through his myriad duties, trying not to remember—trying, especially, to keep away from Viva and from that awful new light in her eyes.

At last the orchestra began to play. This musical aggregation was made up of Auxiliary members,—four in all,—who mistreated the ukulele, the banjo, the mandolin and another ukulele. Its quartet of musicians had had time to learn only four selections that they could play together. When the fourth of these was played, there was a hopeless stillness from the little orchestra-pit, a stillness that did hideous things to the waiting amateurs' nerves. And then, after a century or more of anguished waiting, the curtain went up.

In the condensed version *Rosalind* comes on the stage a minute after the beginning of the action. Viva's entrance was the signal for polite applause from at least twenty-five pairs of hands in the audience.

Almost directly afterward Holt Mallowe came on. And the audience rose at him, with an enthusiasm that halted the play dead short for a full three minutes, completely throwing Viva out of her lines and filling her with a strange tingling pride.

As Viva had the next speech to make, this caused a shuffling silence on the stage until Mrs. Mallowe's kindly voice, from the front row of the orchestra, whispered the lost line to her. And as Viva delivered it she mentally blessed the good-hearted dame who took such a friendly interest in her talented husband's colleagues. Yet she felt a pang of reasonless guilt at accepting such a favor from Mrs. Mallowe.

AT last it was all over, and the audience was standing up and clamoring for another and still another glimpse of Holt Mallowe. Again and again, the actor was forced to take frantically demanded curtain-calls. And not once would he consent to come before the curtain without Viva. Holding her deliriously trembling hand, he drew her forth with him every time—and always bowed low to her after his bow to the audience.

At length some one yelled:

"*Speech!*"

The cry was taken up by a hundred voices. Still holding Viva's hand, Mallowe took a step forward, drawing her along at his side.

"In the name of the company," he said with his ordinary voice, very pleasant and colloquial, "—in the name of the company, Miss Mowbray and I thank you most heartily for liking our work to-night. We thank you, too, for your contribution to the great cause for which our play was given. The Forest of Arden is an informal place. As we are still in that Forest, I am going to ask you to do something informal: Miss Mowbray and Mr. Leonard Carter deserve all praise for the pleasure you have been good enough to derive here, to-night. Will you give them three American cheers?"

As he spoke, Mallowe took a quick step sideward and clutched the wrist of Leonard, who gloomed, soul-sick, behind the shelter of the low proscenium arch. Mallowe pulled the young director out before the footlights, in time to bow miserably in apathy to the tumultuous triple cheer.

Before the trio could bow themselves behind the curtain again, some one in the middle of the audience pointed excitedly at a woman in the front row and yelled:

"Three cheers for Marise Bayne!"

EVERY eye was turned in the direction of the man's pointing finger. A babel of frenzied cheering arose from the whole audience, while hundreds of necks were craned to locate the worshiped actress. Viva, Leonard, the play—all were ignored in the audience's wild eagerness to gaze on its idol.

Light as a boy, Holt Mallowe sprang over the shallow orchestra pit, leaving Viva and Leonard to look after themselves. Viva had not even dreamed Marise Bayne was to be there. She tingled afresh with the thought of having played *Rosalind* in the genius' presence.

Mallowe had caught some woman by the hand and was gallantly helping her up the three steps that ran from the stage's O. P. side to the orchestra.

"Good Lord!" exploded Dicky Romaine from the wings. "The nerve of him! They called for Marise Bayne, and instead, he's lugging along that wife of his. He—"

His mutterings were drowned in a salvo of applause. Mrs. Mallowe, flushed and laughing and very lovely, stood bowing and kissing her hand in response to the ecstatic welcome.

To Viva, the sickening truth came in one pitiless flash. With a groping gesture she sought Leonard's arm and clung shakingly—lovingly—to him.

"Oh, Len!" she wailed with incoherent fervor as he led her protectingly behind the curtain, a glorious new life pulsing in his numb heart. "I'm glad you act so badly. I'm *glad!* Because I just hate actors! I hate them! Oh, I *hate* them!"

THE YALLER DOG

*I*N THE first place, three times out of four, he isn't "yaller." He is apt to be any or all the colors of the canine rainbow.

And he isn't "yaller" of heart or soul or spirit, one time in forty. But he has been branded as "a yaller dog" in good-natured contempt, because he chances to blend the virtues and brains of two or more breeds, instead of restricting himself to one. Especially in brain.

He is a good fellow, this so-called mongrel—a mighty good fellow. And he deserves a thousandfold better deal than he gets.

A year or two ago, when all the world was upside down, a war dog in the Soissons sector appeared from nowhere in particular one night, limping up to the surgeon who headed a squad of stretcher bearers and the like. The party was scouring No Man's Land for men of their own division wounded in a recent attack on the boche trenches.

As the snipers were busy, it was no sinecure to look for these victims. And word had gone forth that only the wounded were to be brought in. The dead were to be left where they lay. It was an hour for mercy, but not for sentiment.

Up to the surgeon limped the dog, his foreleg shattered by a shell, his furry coat a caked mass of dirt and blood. Whimpering with eagerness, he led the party to a shell hole, from over whose ragged brink protruded a pair of human legs.

The bearers lifted to view a man who seemed dead. After a cursory examination the surgeon motioned the bearers to lay the lifeless body back on the ground and move on. The dog at this signal leaped toward the surgeon, tugging at his tunic and whining as he sought to draw the departing medico back to the supposedly dead man.

Then, releasing the tunic, the dog ran to the still body on the ground and frantically licked the face. The surgeon by some rare luck happened to understand dogs. He proceeded to take this dog's judgment ahead of his own.

He ordered the victim lifted onto the stretcher and carried to the trenches. There, after a few hours' work, the "dead" soldier was brought back to life. The dog had known. How he had known is a mystery. But it was a mystery which saved a human life.

The Cleverest War Pupils

At once when word of the occurrence was forwarded to headquarters—the case is on file in the British War Office—the question was asked:

"What breed of dog was it?"

And the surgeon made answer:

"Half a dozen breeds. That's how he had the stamina to go on with his work after he had smashed a leg. And that was why he had the wit to know there was still a spark of life in the man."

The story of the war is starred with similar true anecdotes of the pluck and the strength and the uncanny cleverness of mongrel dogs. These mongrels were much the quickest and cleverest pupils in the various canine training camps which prepared dogs for their glorious life-saving work at the front. Score One for the yaller dog!

By far the best farm collie in all our rather long experience was no collie at all. His sire had been Sunnybank Lad, our pedigreed collie, of lofty lineage. But his dam had been half bull terrier and half fox terrier.

The offspring of this misalliance was much more like a collie in looks than anything else. But three distinct strains of blood coursed in him. And they made him as hard as nails, as fearless and resourceful as any member of his triple ancestry; cleverer than all three combined.

One lesson, thoroughly learned, was all he needed in order to master any particular line of work. Whether in herding or in driving or in guarding, he was peerless. Blizzard or cloudburst or scorching heat—they made no impression on his compact little frame. For farm work and as a pet he was perfect. Not in spite of being a yaller dog, but because of it. He was but one of fifty like instances that have come to my notice.

The mongrel is worth while. You can save money and acquire a treasure by cultivating him. But begin early in his life. Otherwise the fact that everybody has neglected or ill-treated him on account of his mixed blood may have spoiled his natural talents, as it would spoil yours or mine.

The mongrel of any race is prone to be stronger than is either of his parents.

Take the mule for the foremost example of this. If the mule were not better for three-quarters of the many varieties of equine labor than is the horse or the donkey he would have been allowed to die out centuries ago. He can live where his parents would starve. He can perform labor that would kill either of them. He has a brain that is worth three of the horse's, when he cares to exert it. There is nothing a horse or donkey can do that a mule cannot learn to do in half the time and with double efficiency. Why? Because he is a mongrel.

From barnyard fowls up—or down—the same natural law holds good. Is there any reason why it should not in the case of the dog?

When dog journals and daily papers suggest—as they are forever suggesting—that the canine problem be solved by "destroying all mongrel curs, and keeping alive none but established breeds," they are exhibiting the same profound wisdom as if they advocated the killing off of all mules and nonpedigreed cattle and hens. Utility still counts for something, even in this age of specializing and of pedigree craze. For sheer utility, the mongrel dog has all his pure-bred cousins beaten by a mile.

If the yaller dog has not yet come into his own, then the fault is yours and mine. Not his. In the first place, we value a thing chiefly by what we have had to pay for it. If we have paid several hundred dollars for a blue-ribbon dog with a pedigree as long as the city directory we are likely to treasure him as carefully as we would any other investment of equal cash outlay.

But who ever thinks of paying anything for a mongrel?

John Smith's many-breeded bitch has a litter of fluffy and friendly pups by an unknown sire whose breeding is doubtless as mixed as is her own. The Smiths don't want a lot of great hulking dogs, living at their expense. So they are glad to give away any number of the puppies, because those that don't find homes are fated to be drowned.

One is bestowed on a child who wants a pet. Another goes to a neighbor whose own dog has just been run over by a car. And so on, through the litter. The breeder thinks himself lucky to be rid of them. The recipients prize the pups—as most of us prize the things we get for nothing, the things that are given us because they are of no use to anyone else.

What becomes of that litter of mongrels?

The one that was given to the child as a pet probably gets hauled about and otherwise abused in a way that would not be permitted by the grown-ups of the family if the puppy represented any real cash value or sacrifice. Being a mongrel it can be treated as though it were a Teddybear. Remember, please, that the puppy months of any dog's life are the period when its future character and usefulness are built up or absolutely wrecked.

When Rover stops being a playful little fluff ball and develops a leggy awkwardness, his cuteness no longer amuses his young owner. The novelty has worn off. Puppy has come to the age when a little wise care and education could make him worth hundreds of dollars for utility purposes or for a stanch and clever comrade—or for both. What happens?

As he is a yaller dog and as his baby charm has fled, he is allowed to knock round as he chooses, picking up all manner of lawless habits and meannesses, as would your own child under the same treatment, with all his natural talents warped and gone to seed. Either that, or else he is regarded as a nuisance and is actively ill-treated. Or, perhaps, now that he no longer amuses baby, he is given away or drowned or taken miles off and lost.

Once in a while—being merely a brilliant mongrel and not a pure-bred—he is great enough to overcome all this and to develop into a wonder. But can you blame him if environment often proves too strong for his natural instincts?

And so on, with the whole litter. Perhaps one out of eight of the pups receives something approaching the right sort of upbringing. And when he responds to such treatment in a way to make him the envy of the neighborhood, his master's remarks are always apologetic.

"Of course, he's only just a mutt—a yaller dog, as you might say. But he's a cute little cuss, for all that. Knows as much as a person. Understands everything we say. Lots of help to us round the farm too. If he was a pure-bred he'd be a winner."

But that is the exception. The average pup of the litter is likely to be left to shift pretty much for himself—if he gets no worse a lot in life. If his owner's family moves away there's no use in taking the mutt along. It would mean extra time or bother or money. A new dog can be picked up readily enough in the new neighborhood. Towser is mighty sharp. He can shift for himself somehow.

Hysterical Mad-Dog Rumors

And Towser does shift for himself. He does it as would the average human whose home and friends and lifelong means of sustenance are cut away from him and whom nobody will consent to harbor. He becomes a tramp, a vagabond. He lives by his wits. And, being a mongrel, he has plenty of wits to live by.

Then come tidings of rifled henroosts; of sheepfolds invaded; of food snatched from unwatched kitchen tables.

Then also spring to hysterical life a horde of mad-dog rumors. The wretched beast—deserted and left to starve—perhaps has too much honor to turn plunderer. Driven away from garbage cans, unable to find water to drink, chased perhaps by a gang of boys, he falls sick from heartbreak and loneliness and hunger and fright. His eyes glaze and his tongue hangs out and there is froth on his lip. Down the road he trots—scared, ill, desolate. At once arises the mad-dog yell. He is done to death in peculiarly hideous fashion.

Of all the criminally foolish errors in a world of criminally foolish errors that same mad-dog scare is the worst. A dog loses his owner in the street. He takes a wrong turning and doubles back, seeking frantically for his vanished deity. Fear and worry make him run erratically. He begins to pant—a dog's one way of perspiring—from thirst or nervousness.

Some fool notes that the beast is acting queerly and raises the mad-dog shout that is ever lurking at the back of the human throat. Then follows the chase, the stoning or the pistol shot.

A dog is smitten with mortal sickness and he follows the splendid instinct of his kind to get out of human sight into some sheltered spot where he can die alone without harming or annoying those he loves. In search of such a place of refuge he lurches dizzily along, his tongue out, his mouth slavering. And again the senseless mad-dog drama is enacted.

I do not know whether hydrophobia exists or not. Some vets say it does. Some say it doesn't.

Personally, I have been bitten twice by supposedly mad dogs. Both times I washed out the bites in warm water and painted them with iodine—and proceeded to forget all about it. I have not yet gone mad—to any appreciable extent—nor suffered other ill from the mishaps.

But whether hydrophobia exists as a real peril or is a figment of the medical mind, you may take it as a proven fact that not one supposedly mad dog in ten thousand actually has rabies. The worst bite from a dog can usually be healed, I believe, by the simple treatment I have just described. It has been so in my own case and in those of dozens of other dog fanciers whom I know.

The main point is to put the matter out of one's mind and not to brood or worry over it. By worry the simplest accident can be magnified into a calamity. The nerves and the brain intensify the trifling hurt and put one on the lookout for symptoms. And symptoms have a way of materializing when one is on the lookout for them— whether they be symptoms of hay fever or of hydrophobia.

Fear and hysteria do the damage the bite alone could not have wrought.

All of which is a digression, but it is common sense and perhaps may one day save you from needless terror or from needless cruelty to an innocent animal. And so, back to our yaller dog.

The homeless mongrel turns marauder or he falls ill. He robs or he runs amuck. Which is more or less natural.

From the press at large as well as from the dog journals issues one of the periodical anti-mutt denunciations. It is announced that stray mongrel curs are a menace to sheep and fowls and are in peril of going mad; they should be extermi- nated wholesale, before their misdeeds cast any more discredit on pure-bred canines.

You have read that blatant rot a hundred times. Next time you read it, you have my leave to be as indignant as ever you have been at the same kind of reading matter.

But turn your natural indignation in the right direction. Don't waste it on the friendly and lovable and harmless and useful little mongrel, who is what his master has made him. Turn it on the man who moves away and leaves his dog helpless among strangers. Turn it on the man who has harbored such a dog from puppyhood and who has not taken the trouble to train him to decent canine citizenship. It is ridiculously easy to train him, as a pup, into a self-respecting and useful doghood.

Put the blame where it belongs, not on the dog, who is probably behaving quite as well as would your own son under a similar handicap.

It isn't Rover's fault. It is his owner's. It also is the fault of the man who gave him into such shiftless hands, instead of drowning him at birth. It is the fault of the man who allowed him to be born at all, into a world already overpopulated by unwanted mongrels.

Yes, blame any or all these humans, if you like. And your blame won't be wasted. But why blame the luckless dog himself?

Legislatures are forever hearkening to the mad-dog yell—which is idiotic—and to the complaint of damage done by stray dogs to farm stock, which, alas! is often justified. Then goes forth the murder decree against thousands of dogs which could have been made an asset to the community instead of neighborhood pests.

But, thus far, the average lawmaker has merely strewed disinfectant over the surface of the swamp, but has not bothered to drain the swamp itself. As a result the widespread slaughter of the mongrel is only a momentary solution of the problem. In almost no time—for the yaller dog is a hardy and prolific breeder—the same situation has to be faced all over again.

Make the Owner Responsible

Perhaps it has not occurred to legislators for rural districts to limit the number of dogs a man may own and to make him legally responsible for the training and keeping and disposal of such dogs. It seems never to have occurred to them to limit rigidly the number of female mongrel dogs that shall be allowed to live, and to ordain the painless death of all other such females at birth. Yet that and that alone is the solution.

To make every owner give a strict account of his dog, from the time it is acquired by him, and to make him responsible for its welfare and its behavior throughout the period of its possession by him, to make the willful desertion of the dog by him a misdemeanor, to force an accurate account of all pups born and of their disposal and to limit most carefully all chances of birth rate—these things are feasible and are far simpler and cheaper and more humane than are the present slipshod methods of handling the subject.

Thousands of dollars' worth of sheep and of lesser livestock would be saved from death. The asinine mad-dog scare would dwindle almost to nothingness. People would no longer get a dog to satisfy some passing whim, then turn him loose on the county. The bare fact of having to go through so many formalities in order to become and to remain a dog owner would at once enhance the value of the mongrel pet in his master's eyes and would insure a wiser upbringing of the puppy.

Does one man in sixty, at present, treat a mongrel gift pup as he would treat it if it had cost him $100 or as if he might someday sell it for half that sum? I think not.

Yet the same sense of prideful responsibility could be fostered by such restrictions as I have outlined.

The mongrel could then take his rightful place in life as a genuine asset and as a good comrade. But until the dawn of that era of sanity the owner of a yaller dog can show his own intelligence by ceasing to be ashamed of his pet's mixed blood and by developing the really great qualities which are the average mongrel's birthright. The dog will repay wise training almost as well as does a horse, besides having ten-fold the intelligence of the most sagacious horse ever foaled.

Next time an owner of pure-bred stock looks contemptuously at your fine mongrel, just remind him that two or three of the most popular and high-priced breeds of blue-ribbon dogs to-day are nothing more or less than mongrels. That is all they are—standardized mongrels. And in 1919 one such mongrel received the award of Best Dog in the Show at Madison Square Garden—which means that he was declared, in effect, the best dog on earth.

The dog thus exalted was an Airedale. Not many years ago there was no such dog as the Airedale. But there were otter hounds and bull terriers and Yorkshires and certain other recognized breeds. All these breeds were jumbled together in a presumably scientific way. The result was the many-blooded Airedale. He is really the supreme mongrel of dogdom. For in his veins run more kinds of different blood than in almost any so-called mutt that scratches fleas in the front yard of a negro cabin.

Yet to-day the Airedale is for the moment on the top wave of popularity; all this in spite of his mongrel ancestry, his grotesque homeliness and his villainous temper, together with the queer superstition that Airedales and opals bring bad luck to their owners.

The all-popular Boston terrier, too, is a mongrel; a blend and interblend of several breeds. So are half a dozen other standardized strains that lord it at dog shows.

Indeed, the collie is almost the only pure-bred dog who can trace back a flawless and nonmongrelized ancestry for a thousand years or more, probably for many thousand years before that. He is a genuine aristocrat, whose blue blood has never been sullied by cross strains.

The mongrel has another advantage, too, that is a mighty important one and should not be overlooked. It is Nature's fixed rule to get rid of weaker traits and to intensify the stronger ones. Thus, of the various breeds that go to make up your mongrel, there are the salient traits of all those breeds. The weaker and less vital characteristics have been lost, as a rule; only the strongest have survived.

That accounts also for the yaller dog's more powerful stamina. He represents everything most enduring and salient and predominant in his different breeds of ancestry. It is a survival of the fittest, and a sloughing off of the less worthwhile traits. This in brain as well as in body.

If further proof be needed of his superior cleverness and his quickness to learn, you will find it in the next trained-dog act you see. Not once in a hundred times is a pure-bred dog used in such acts. Practically every trick dog is a mongrel.

The mongrel learns with a readiness that puts to shame the best efforts of the pure-bred. Wherefore his almost exclusive use for the vaudeville stage.

Barbarous Training Methods

And this is but one of the yaller dog's countless misfortunes in life. For, next to vivisection, there is no other form of cruelty so barbarous and so inexcusable as is the trained-animal act. Every trick dog you see on the stage represents something like twenty puppies tortured to death in a vain attempt to teach them tricks. It has been computed that every trick cat represents not less than twenty-seven kittens starved to death during the training process. A dog can be tortured into learning stage tricks. A cat can only be starved into learning them. Bear these gruesome truths in mind before encouraging by your applause another such exhibition.

It is the mongrel and the mongrel alone that has the brain to grasp the idea of intricate stage stunts. He pays dearly for his high intelligence.

As to stamina, he can endure hardships and diseases that would kill any dog more finely bred. To illustrate:

Last week I lost the finest collie pup I had ever been able to breed, the supreme result of my years of experimental breeding. He came back from his first dog show with a bunch of blue ribbons and with two silver cups. He also came back with a most virulent case of distemper, despite the fact that I had had him inoculated against this malady months earlier. He fought the grimly relentless sickness with all his pure-bred soul and nerve. But it killed him, as it has killed so many thousand young pure-breds.

A few years ago I had, here at Sunnybank, a many breeded mongrel. He was stricken with distemper—nobody bothers to inoculate a mongrel—and it hit him in its worst form. He crawled away under some outbuilding, and stayed, hidden, for two or three days. Then he reappeared, somewhat wabbly and thin, but with a fast-improving appetite. And in a week or so he was as well as ever.

The poison that had murdered my great young collie, after the Paterson Dog Show, had had no lasting effect at all on the iron constitution of my young mongrel. And innumerable dog owners can tell you the same story.

After some of the mammoth dog shows at Madison Square Garden hundreds of pedigreed dogs die of distemper. And this despite the utmost care and nursing and the highest paid medical skill. Who ever heard of a hundred mongrels or ten mongrels dying from distemper, even though they had no medical skill to work for them and practically no nursing?

They get sick. They get well. They get well because they belong to the fittest. Compared to them the inbred blue-ribbon winner hasn't a ghost of a chance in the health race.

The mastiff for centuries has stood high on the pedestal of pure-bred dogdom.

Yet the mastiff's very name shows his origin, for mastiff, or masty, is the Early

English word for mongrel. It included all dogs that were of no recognized breed, in olden times. Yet so highly did our ancestors esteem the mongrel that his name was applied later to one of the most honored breeds.

Another ugly nickname for the mongrel is cur. That is Old English too.

With Us to Stay

For some reason, I don't know why, dogs whose tails had been cut off were at one time exempt from taxation in England. People who owned mongrels did not want to pay taxes on them, so docked their tails. The canines thus mutilated were called curtailed dogs, which was shortened to cur dogs and then to curs.

For many hundred years breed after breed has waxed and waned. In our own time we have witnessed the dying out of numbers of these; for instance, the Newfoundland, that could not be spared, and the pug, that could be spared with the utmost ease. No matter what befell the pure-bred, the mongrel has kept on through the ages. Fashion's fickle shifts could not abolish him. The too intense inbreeding, which has wiped out other strains, has had no effect on him. He endures. He will endure till the end of the world. He is with mankind to stay.

Future generations may look in vain for the pointer, the setter, the mastiff. But future generations will have the mongrel at their side. And he will retain all the strongest and best qualities of a hundred vanished breeds in his cosmopolitan cosmos. He is a fixture.

Give Him a Chance

He is what you choose to make him in puppyhood. Give him half a chance and he will serve you to the death—whether in guarding your home or herding your livestock or keeping your barns free from vermin or as a loyal chum. Whatever you may care to teach him to do, he will do; he will do it well.

If you bring him up undisciplined or on kicks and beatings, or if you turn him adrift—well, you can't very well expect him to be a credit to you or to the community, any more than would a pure-bred thus treated or a human child.

Give him the same upbringing that you would lavish on a hundred-dollar dog, and you are fairly certain to get much more than a hundred dollars' value out of him, soon or late.

Above all, don't be ashamed of owning a mongrel. Merely be ashamed of yourself, if you have not developed him as he deserves to be developed. Next time you are tempted to apologize to the world at large for owning a yaller dog, resist the impulse. Be proud of him, for he is worth it. Don't say sheepishly:

"Of course, he's only just a mutt!" Be honest with yourself and say:

"He's the healthiest, strongest, cleverest kind of dog on earth. I'd rather have him than his weight in pure-breds!"

Think more of the quality, less of the quantity, of breeds that are included in his make-up.

Sheer **Weight**

THE Big Fellow stood stolidly still for inspection. He tried not to fidget; not to feel so glaringly undressed; not to wiggle under the coldly quizzical gaze of eight sets of expert eyes. His own glance shifted in covert yearning to the spotty bath robe he had just shucked at Con Vedder's command. His expanse of knotted body was not yet used to long periods of nudity; even in the sweat-compelling heat of the gym.

Almost he wished he had stayed where he belonged, and had not suffered himself to be lured from the warmth and smug respectability of jumper and overalls. Then he forced his brain—a brain built, like himself, for endurance, rather than for speed—to focus on his life goal. And, with a shake of his heavy head, he dismissed the qualmy homesickness that had gripped him.

Coming back to his surroundings, he listened glumly to Con Vedder's glowing lecture to such members of the sporting press as the manager's pleading letters had brought to this first inspection of Con's dark-horse heavyweight.

"Uh-huh," Vedder was declaiming to three late comers in the tiny audience of reporters. "That's how it was. You all remember how I found old 'Spike' Sears hustling bales on a dock. I liked how he rassled them weights onto the ship; and I put him on my string. What happened? Three years later, I'd made him light-heavyweight champ'n, hadn't I? And I'd 'a' kep' him there, yet, if he'd 'a' lissened to me and let the hootch stay in the bottle where it couldn't do him no harm. Old Spike can't buy it any more. He's a poor guy that's seen wetter days.

"Ever since Spike fell apart, I been looking out for a s'cessor to him. Looking ev'rywheres. Because I know how to pick 'em. But it was plenty long before I saw him.

"They don't grow on ev'ry prune vine—like they was southpaws or tenors or short-change artists or bank pres'dents. There's only 'bout one to the ten years. And this one is the one. Take my say-so on that, boys. I never yet picked 'em wrong. And this'll be the third I've shoved up to where the belt was waiting."

The Big Fellow's ample feet waxed uncomfortable. One of his bare knees itched. He reminded himself of freaks he had seen in side show—poor monstrosities who had had to stand up, one by one, in all their queerness, while a leather-lunged lecturer told noisy lies about them.

Con Vedder preached on:

"Then, one day, a coupla months back, I just happened to be going past the baggage room, down t' th' Union Deepo. I stopped to watch a bunch of roustabouts juggling trunks. And in a minute I got a glimpse of Greg Brookins, here. He was slinging a swad of Saratogas and Innovations and six-by-four boxes on an express truck he was chauffing.

"Well, boys, it was a reel joy to watch him. He rassled those big weights like they was the fake cannon balls in a strong-man act. He had all the strength there was. And at that, he wa'n't muscle bound. Strongest feller I'd set eyes on in a year. And I watch 'em all, mighty close. But that wa'n't the half of it."

He paused, for oratoric effect; swept the half circle of bored hearers with anticipatory eye; and added:

"While I was watching him a two-hundred-pound box he had just slung onto the pile on his wagon slipped and come a-cascading down on him. He didn't see it in time to sidestep. It caught him on the jaw, with a wallop like—like hell. I waits for him to qualify for th' hosp't'l. Does he do that? No, he don't. It floors him. But he's up in a second, like not a thing has touched him. And he goes on a-h'isting 'em aboard."

The Big Fellow tried not to meet any one's glance, as a perfunctory murmur of approval seeped through the group.

"That told me all I needed!" proclaimed Vedder. "I see he had the strength and the weight and the nerve; and I see he had the jaw of a reel genius. The jaw a champ'n packs into the ring with him. The jaw you can't crumple with a pile driver. And I upped him off, right away. Green as new-laid grass he was, of course, when I signed him up, first. But I've had him up to the farm for eight weeks of heavy work with 'Bud' Kelleher. Bud's the man can learn 'em. And I've brought him down for you boys to see.

"To-morrow, back he goes to the farm for another two months of training and learning. After that, we're going to start him. When we do, just you watch his dust, that's all. Now—whatcha think of my find? Hey? How about it, boys?"

If there is one thing a newspaper reporter learns earlier than the padding of an expense account, it is the art of minimizing the press-agent's song. To him, the blatant bellow of the barker is a keen insult to the intelligence. And, when he can, he rebukes it in his own particular way.

Thus, for a moment or so, after Con Vedder had concluded his triumph chant, the bevy of reporters stared in cold silence at the squirming giant. Then Burns, of the *Planet,* asked politely:

"How much does he weigh—altogether? Including feet, of course? What's the gross tonnage?"

"He's down to two hundred and twenty-seven, just now," snapped the displeased Vedder. "From two hundred and forty-one. And we'll work another few pounds of fat into iron and whalebone, before we fight him. Six foot three, in his socks. Got the wind of a marathoner. Can't hurt him with an ax. Punch in both hands. Not twenty-four years old till next month. Got—"

"Down to two hundred and twenty-seven!" prattled Wendell, the *Chronicle's* fight reporter. *"Down* to it? That's too light."

"Too—too—" quavered Vedder, bristling at scent of a possible slur. "Why, it is—"

"Too light for a Percheron, I mean," civilly explained the *Chronicle* man. "And too heavy for a chopping block. So I don't just see where your find comes in. If—"

"He might fall on them," hazarded Craig, of the *News*. "Or he might win on a foul, by claiming the other chap kept treading on his feet. There wouldn't be much other space, in a twenty-four-foot ring. Or—"

"Go ahead and josh, all you're a mind to!" grunted Vedder. "I been in this game thirty years. And I never picked a dead one yet. This man's due to win by sheer weight, and by—"

"They said that about big Ed Dunkhorst," yawned Burns. "And Bob Fitzsimmons stopped him in the second round, back in 1900. Dunkhorst went into the ring at two hundred and forty. Fitz told me afterward he'd have put Dunk to sleep in the first punch of the first round, only he got to thinking about a funny story he'd heard and forgot to. 'The bigger they are, the harder they—'"

"Get a new wheeze!" fumed Vedder. "I know what I've found. Watch him, that's all! He—"

A roustabout broke in on the subacid conference by shuffling into the gym with word that a long-distance phone call awaited Vedder in the outer office. Reluctantly, the manager hurried away, promising to put the Big Fellow through his paces with bag and with sparring partner on his return.

Greg Brookins had stood stolid and inert, while the frank comments buzzed through his ears. He was not offended at the criticisms. Apparently, they were a part of the game. And they were as cooing blandishments compared to the line of talk which his trainer, Bud Kelleher, was wont to lavish upon the luckless novice.

As Vedder departed, Burns strolled up to the giant. This, apparently, was to be a comic story. And a few words from the victim might be twisted into a useful addition to the comedy.

"Well, Sandow," began the reporter encouragingly. "I suppose it has been your life ambition, from childhood, to become heavyweight champion of the world?"

"Huh?" queried Brookins absently, as he came out of his armor of shyness long enough to blink downward at his small inquisitor.

"I say," answered Burns, "I say, I suppose you want to be champion of the world more than you want anything else? And of course—"

"I do *not!*"

There was nothing dull nor hesitant about the reply. It fairly exploded into the surprised questioner's face. The rest of the group came to life and narrowed in on the speakers. Here, it seemed, was a fighter who had no ready-made speech to make about his championship hopes, and who promised something out of the routine in the way of a pug interview.

"No?" queried Burns, recovering his breath, and speaking with wily solicitude. "Well, if you wouldn't rather have the championship than anything else, what *would* you rather have?"

The Big Fellow drew a deep breath, and broke into rapid-fire staccato speech.

"I'd rather have a truck!" he declared to his amazed listeners. "A two-ton truck. A Featherstrong truck. Painted red. Best light truck on the market. Goes through the traffic like a—like it was a breeze or a eel or something. Pneumatic tires. Fourteen miles to the gallon. Says so in the circular. Take fishing parties and picnic crowds out in it, Sundays. Painted red; so I wouldn't have to pay out cash to dec'rate it for the Sunday trade."

"But"—stammered Craig, dumfounded— "but a fighter—"

"Painted red," reasserted the Big Fellow, the light of a great vision in his honest little eyes. "Painted red. Pneumatic tires. Like I told you. And you can get at the works from the outside, without taking off the seat. Engine is back, too. Not under the seat. So you don't get all het up, setting on it, hot days. I'd keep it at Raddle's Garage, too. That's on top of the Carston Av'noo hill, you know. Or maybe you don't know. On top of a long hill. It'd save gas.

"All I'd have to do would be to start her and then shut off and let her coast all the way to the bottom. And I got promise of plenty of hauling contracts, right off, whenever I c'n buy her. I c'd clean up seventy-five dollars a week, easy, if I had a truck like that.

"That's what I've been saving for three years now. That's why I signed up with Mister Vedder. I'll make me the price of that truck ten times as quick by fighting than ever I'd make it at my old job. For three thousand two hundred and fifty dollars, I c'n get—"

He snapped shut his eagerly babbling lips. The unfeigned interest of his hearers— their avid attention—confused him. He did not understand why he had let himself go. Never having heard of psychology, he could not realize that stark, homesick loneliness and the crass publicity of the moment had wrought on his shy cosmos; and had made him trot out his life dream on much the same principle that a scolding might send a child running to her best-loved doll for comfort.

It was not like him to babble. But—well, hadn't that tow-headed little rat in the gray suit brought the thing on himself by asking coaxily what Brookins would rather have than anything else in the world? Hadn't he? Well, then! And the Big Fellow glowered challengingly about the half circle, for symptoms of guying.

But every face was grave, even tense. Not with any idea of sparing this big boob from embarrassment, but because the brain behind each visage was busy. This was a story. There were chances in it. And already the reporters were casting it.

Burns opened his mouth to glean more information about the crank who was slated by the great Vedder for heavyweight laurels and who yearned only for a two-ton truck painted red. But the manager came bustling in, and, as he advanced, he picked up the broken thread of his harangue.

"Watch him, I say!" he reiterated. "Watch him, that's all. Sheer weight is one of the biggest points in the fight game—if a bird has the punch and the endurance behind it. And I'm the man who can make ev'ry ounce of Greg Brookins' sheer weight earn a thousand bucks.

"If that sounds like a bluff, wait and see it work out. Jeff had sheer weight. And it licked Corbett's science, and Fitz's, too. And it's been so in a million fights. This lad is due to hold the heavyweight belt in less'n a year. He won't rest happy till he wins it. Will you, Greg," he finished, nudging the sulky giant to reply.

At the nudge the Big Fellow came out of the slumping reverie into which he had returned at sight of his manager.

"I—I wonder will the price of gas begin to go down, pretty soon now," he mumbled vaguely.

"That's the right spirit!" applauded Vedder, scowling hideously up at the Big Fellow and hoping the slurred mutter had gone unheard by the reporters. "That's the spirit! He says they can't come too fast or too hard for him! Now, boys, we'll get to the bag punching."

To the horror of Con Vedder and to the bliss of the sporting public, every metropolitan paper, next morning, carried a full story of the giant who would rather have a truck, painted red, than the heavyweight championship of the world, of the aspirant to whom the price of gasoline meant infinitely more than the name of his first ring opponent.

Such minor details of economics as the hilltop location chosen for the truck, and the money to be saved by owning a gay-colored vehicle instead of having to buy Sunday decorations for it—all these were elaborated on. There is no danger of libel, in attributing weird sentiments to pugilists. So the economies were added to, right fantastically, in nearly every story.

Burns' report of the interview was a newspaper classic, and not only earned him a fifteen-dollar bonus, but was picked up all over America. In a day the tale of the cautious spendthrift who yearned for red trucks rather than for immortal fame was public property. Paragraphers reveled in him. Vaudeville gagsters took up the jest. One shrewd truck builder added to the stock advertisement of his machine, the line:

> This is the kind of truck Greg Brookins is looking for! "Goes through traffic like it was a breeze or a eel or something!"

The joke was not inspiring. It was tenuous. Yet, for some reason, it caught the town. While dozens of cleverer themes went unnoted, the yarn of the Big Fellow and his truck-driver yearnings was amplified and harped on for weeks. It is with the public as with a child on Christmas morning. Passing over more valuable gifts, the youngster centers his adoring attention on some cheap toy. Overlooking innumerable topics for laughter, the public revels in such inane phrases as "Who's looney now?" and, "He seen his dooty and he done it," and, "Let George do it!" and the like.

This same capricious public fairly wallowed in the oft-told and oftener exaggerated story of Greg Brookins. It just happened that way.

Presently Con Vedder stopped swearing and began to pur. The veteran manager saw the wondrous advertising possibilities in the town talk about his novice fighter.

The Big Fellow himself knew little of the laughter he was creating. Back on the training farm he was allowed to see nobody but Bud Kelleher and the handlers. True, there were daily and jocose mentions of him in the newspapers. But the Big Fellow had always found trouble in "reading without glasses." And he had never owned glasses. So, except for the pictures, he seldom picked up a paper.

Which brings us by prosy degrees to Homer Malloy—born Rosalsky.

Malloy would have been a genuine ornament to almost any penitentiary on earth. But it was certain he would never make the error of rendering himself liable to such wholesome confinement. Malloy did not make errors. He preferred to live by the errors of others. Crafty, merciless, ineffably cruel, totally without conscience, he had made his thirty years in life very happy and profitable to himself, and the exact opposite for every one unlucky enough to be associated with him.

He had begun life as a middleweight fighter. Cunning, a boxing genius and an india-rubber constitution had carried him to the top of his division. Having wrung dry the chances of this class, he annexed a few pounds of solid weight and, by dint of speed and consummate craft, began to collect heavyweight scalps.

No one knew better than he that he had not the ghost of a chance to win the heavyweight championship. Not once in many times does that honor go to a man weighing under one hundred and sixty-six. Moreover, Malloy, to his own helpless disgust, was never at top form in any contest, after the eleventh or twelfth round. Not for such boxers is the championship.

Nevertheless, there were rich pickings in the heavyweight division, for a man who knew how and where to find them. There was twice as much cash there, as in the middleweight class. And, by birth and by choice, Homer Malloy was, above all else, a money collector.

Avoiding the top men of his profession, he reaped fine harvests among the second-raters. As a murderously inspired fouler and all-round trickster, he had not his match in the ring. Never did he miss a chance to swell his thick bank roll by the right sort of battle.

When he read the tale of Greg Brookins and noted the growing public interest in the Big Fellow, then Malloy knew once more he was on the track of "the right sort of battle." And he laid his lines.

No pugilist is blind or even nearsighted to the siren charm of the gate receipts. A man most in the newspaper eye is a man who best can command those gate receipts. There were many hundred people who would pay a fair sum to see the eccentric newcomer fight—if only for the possible fun in the situation. Vedder knew this. So, while he stirred up further interest by accounts of Brookins' miraculous hitting power, he kept the Big Fellow screened from all visitors, in monastic seclusion at the farm.

Malloy knew as well as Vedder the value of all this free advertising and the way it must boost gate receipts. He knew, too, that Vedder was probably looking about for the right kind of opponent for Brookins' ring debut. And his money-collector nerve throbbed.

Con Vedder was going carefully over the list of heavyweight fourth and fifth raters, in search of a dead one who would not be too dead to draw a crowd and yet who would not have enough life for a chance blow which might cut short Brookins' championship journey at its very outset.

Vedder had all faith in the Big Fellow's potentialities. A year of grueling work, interspersed with three or four fights with increasingly rugged opponents, would transform him from a slow-moving Hercules to a mighty battling machine. At present, his fistic prowess was still in the making. Yet it irked his manager to think of letting all this Heaven-sent publicity slip away, uncashed. Wherefore his wrinkled-brow scanning of the heavyweight roster.

To the worrying manager, in the thick of his meditations, came Homer Malloy, exquisite of raiment, benevolently gentle of manner, laboriously refined of speech. By these attributes do fighters win the longed-for title of "Gentleman So-and-So," an appellation which Malloy desired above all else save money.

He laid before the blinking Vedder an alluring proposition. In brief, he offered to take on Greg Brookins, for a fifteen-round bout before the local club which should make the best cash proposition.

Now, Vedder was under no delusions at all as to Malloy's character and history. Nor was he in any doubt as to the reason for the offer. Yet, for once, he was overjoyed to play Homer's game for him. Not alone had Malloy a big following among such fight fans as thrill at needless cruelty, but Greg Brookins would suffer no disgrace if, as a mere beginner, he should be knocked out by the famous veteran. Later, on arriving at more of his full power, he could fight Malloy again. And the second bout would not only atone for the first, but would be a greater drawing card because of it.

And, back in Vedder's mind lurked strong doubt that Malloy's punches could batter the iron giant to senselessness. No blow of Bud Kelleher's had been able to do that. And Bud packed a fearsome punch. Malloy, too, was at his worst in a long fight. There was an even chance that Brookins might ride out the fifteen rounds. If he should do so, his reputation would be made.

Vedder fenced for a half hour as to the winner's share of the gate receipts and the purse; compromised on an eighty-twenty basis, and sent for the reporters.

Next day the world was informed that the first battle of "Truck Six," as the press had merrily dubbed the Big Fellow, would be with no less renowned a paladin than Homer Malloy. And straightaway the fight clubs yammered shrilly to outbid one another.

Sporting page archives were combed for such reminiscences as Peter Maher's knockout of the loudly hailed Morrissey in the first punch of the loser's only

American fight, and "Kid" Carter's destruction of the vaunted "Unknown" Smith. Guided by memories like these, the odds on Malloy became at once prohibitive. But there was a brisk sale of tickets for the oddly advertised bout. People who, as a rule, were not interested in the prize ring, bought seats to see the antics of the man who would rather be a truck owner than a champion.

When the Big Fellow was notified, in casual fashion, by Bud Kelleher, that he was to fight his maiden battle, on a certain date, at the Cestus Athletic Club, and that his antagonist was to be "Kid" Malloy, he merely looked thoughtful. Presently he asked what the winner's share of the purse was likely to be.

"The *loser's* share is twenty per cent," responded the comforting Bud Kelleher. "That's the only part of the split you need to bother over. At that, your end of it is li'ble to be close to a coupla thousand dollars, counting Vedder's slice in."

"H'm," mused the Big Fellow, while Bud watched him covertly. "H'm! Pretty near half the price of the truck, in one night. More'n I c'd 'a' saved in five years, at my old job. I—I wonder will the price of gas begin to go down pretty soon now?"

Kelleher groaned aloud in utter despair. Then, by way of precaution, he warned hectoringly:

"If you don't scrap for ev'ry ounce of elephant weight that's in you, the boss is due to tie the can to you. Remember that. If he does, back you go to drivin' for the express comp'ny again. And then by-lo to your measly red truck with red paint on it, tinted red. Keep a-thinkin' of that, if you're nursin' an idee that all you gotta do is walk into the ring and lay down. You gotta fight for all you—"

"The winner's end," smiled the Big Fellow fatuously, emerging from deep mental arithmetic. "The winner's end would—why, gee, it'd buy me that truck and a—"

"Go get into your gloves!" yelled Kelleher, his threadbare temper disintegrating. "Go get into 'em, for our afternoon bout! I don't want to tackle you with my bare fists. And that's the thing I'll sure do if you say 'truck' again. Lord! You're no fighter. You're a warnin'! A horr'ble warnin'!"

The Cestus Athletic Club was so well filled for the Malloy-Brookins bout that Malloy all but wept at thought of the higher price which might profitably have been charged for tickets.

The Big Fellow was first to enter the ring. Down the aisle from the dressing room he plodded, massively yet nervously, midway in an imposing little procession made up of Vedder and Kelleher and several handlers. As he heaved his way between the ropes into the ring, he was greeted by tumultuous applause, through which laughter tingled in a way that would have maddened a more thin-skinned warrior.

Wrapping his spotty bath robe the closer about his bare calves, the Big Fellow nodded to right and to left, as he had been taught by Kelleher. Then he clumped to his seat on a corner stool that creaked under his weight. He hated to have so many folks looking at him all at one time. The racket confused him, too.

Amid the looser babel of applause and chuckles he was almost certain he heard yells that sounded like: "Truck Six!" and "Watch him go through the traffic like a eel or something!" and "Painted red!" and "Hitting on all four to-night?" But as these outcries could not possibly have made any sense, he decided he had heard wrongly and that his own dreams had been responsible for the trick played on him by his fanlike ears.

As the noise sagged a second procession emerged from the entrance to the dressing room. Of this, the central figure was a slenderly swarthy man, classic of feature, and with curling black hair brushed and pomaded to a rich enamel finish.

Homer Malloy bowed comprehensively to the crowd that rose to him in genuine ovation. His gleaming teeth showed an instant from between his thinly cruel lips, as he flashed a smile of thanks to his admirers. Then, his dark face set itself once more in grim lines, and he continued his journey. One toe on the platform corner, one hand on a post top, he vaulted gracefully over the ropes and into the ring. There was something tigerlike and gloriously muscular in his off-rehearsed spring. And the crowd rose to it.

"Just the same," whispered the Big Fellow to Kelleher, "they don't seem to be near as glad to see him as they was to see me. They make more noise. But not a one of 'em's laughing. They aren't even grinning like they did when I come in. I guess they like me best."

He spoke more to cover his own emotions than in brag. A moment later he was eying the doughty Malloy with genuine amazement. Vedder had signed the fight articles for him. So this was the Big Fellow's first sight of his foe.

He had visioned a husky giant, modeled on somewhat his own generous lines; a bruiser with hamlike fists and piano-mover shoulders. But this dapper little antagonist of his looked more like a shipping clerk than a fighter. Such a puny stripling could never stand up under a man-size punch.

Glowingly bright, the winner's eighty percent flickered before the Big Fellow's infatuated vision. Yet, withal, he was sorry to have to thump this little guy around the ring. Then and there, he resolved to be as gentle with Malloy as victory would permit. There was no use in half killing him.

These charitable reflections were still trickling in and out of his slow brain when the referee called Malloy and himself to the center, for final instructions. He looked down in friendly reassurance at the hard-faced victim, whose square chin was a full five inches nearer the floor than his own.

Malloy met the kindly pitying gaze. And he replied to it with a smile of loving good-fellowship. Brookins felt he was going to like Malloy. Indeed, he was beginning already to like him. And he hated the idea of having to thrash him. Only by visualizing a dream truck—painted red—could the Big Fellow steel himself for what was before him.

At the clang of the bell Malloy stepped lightly from his corner. Stripped of the shapeless bath robe, he showed up far better than the Big Fellow had imagined. His muscles were not bunchy or impressive. But they were long and elastic like a cat's; and there was deceptive width to the bronzed shoulders. Brookins was glad of this. The knockout could not be very injurious to a man who was in such grand condition. And he began to feel less compunction.

He could see, however, that his little opponent was flustered. For, as their hands met in the preliminary shake, Malloy pulled the Big Fellow toward him and at the same time loosed his own left glove from the courteous clasp and sent it whizzing to Brookins' jaw. This, assuredly, was a mistake. They should not have begun to hit until they had quite finished shaking hands. Even Brookins knew that. Malloy must have been scared foolish or something. Again Brookins smiled at him in reassurance.

But, this time, Malloy did not reciprocate. Instead, with a bewilderingly swift move, he sent his left fist square into the very center of the Big Fellow's friendly smile. The blow hurt. And under its jarring impact Brookins got down to active work.

Ducking a leisurely and exploratory right swing of Malloy's, he stepped in, with a short right-hander for the heart. But the heart—if Homer Malloy, indeed, carried such excess luggage—was not there. Neither was the rest of Malloy. With ridiculous ease he side-stepped the lunging blow, and sent a ferocious left hook to Brookins' jaw.

The blow rocked the Big Fellow as a liner's wake might rock a tug. And, while he was still recovering his balance, Malloy was at him, in one of the famed tiger rushes that had wrought such hideous damage in their day. The smaller man was all over his clumsy foe. He was here, he was there, he was everywhere and he was nowhere.

To wind, to heart, to throat, to kidney and to liver, and twice to the jaw itself, thundered his fusillade of whirlwind smashes. There was a scientifically cruel and cutting quality to his blows which redoubled the damage done by their mere force. Thus, in fifty fights, had Homer Malloy worn down larger and slower men and had ripened them for early slaughter.

Under the fearful punishment the Big Fellow wavered for a moment, then straightened himself, his slow guard impotently active. And, unflinching, he sought to take the aggressive by hurling himself bodily at Malloy. But, once more, Malloy was no longer there. And, as Brookins paused confusedly in search of him, Homer ducked lithely under the huge outflung arms and poured a punching-bag tattoo of short-arm blows upon the Big Fellow's heart and wind.

Brookins drove heavily at his elusive foe, at close quarters. The glancing punch whirled Malloy halfway around, and, though it had merely grazed his forehead, it set up a detestable singing within his wily brain. Malloy wriggled into a clinch sooner than to risk encountering another such sledge-hammer contact until his dizzy head should be clear enough to avert it.

And, on the breakaway, came the bell for the first round's end.

The Big Fellow plodded back to his corner, the white of his huge body blotched purple or red in twenty places, to receive the eager ministrations of Kelleher and the handlers and to listen to a volley of fast, spoken, cheery counsel from Con Vedder.

"You done fine!" the manager declared. "He give you the best he had. He ain't got anything better than what he give you in them two rallies. And you kept a-going. But don't try to box him. Bore in. You'll likely get him before the tenth round if ever you c'n land square. And keep a-looking out for him. He's as tricky as a weasel pup."

The Big Fellow scarce heard. He was thinking. He was revising his early opinion as to Malloy's unfitness as a fighter. The little man could hit. He could hit to hurt like the very devil. And he had a queer gift of being somewhere else whenever Brookins tried to counter or to lead. Decidedly, this battle was not as one-sided as the Big Fellow had foreseen. And the winner's end of the fight shone less dazzlingly close to his blinking eyes.

Meantime, in spite of the flattering plaudits of the crowd at his brilliant work, Homer Malloy was anything but content. He had seen big novices before. He knew how pitiably vulnerable they were wont to be. He remembered how Jim Corbett had knocked out the awkwardly inexperienced Jeffries, time and again, in the days when Jeff was one of Gentleman Jim's sparring partners at Carson City. And Malloy had poked for still easier prey in his contest with this elephantine truckman.

But all his initial confidence was gone. He had a job ahead of him. A nasty job. Unless—

And Malloy's lips crept wide in a slow smile that did not add to the beauty of his face. Yet what he planned seemed the only safe thing to do. He had slammed Brookins' ribs and heart and wind. And he had encountered a wall of muscles as invulnerable as three-inch planking. He had landed on the jaw with full force, more than once. But—thanks to Kelleher's coaching—Brookins carried his jaw well tucked in and with the neck muscles taut. It is hard to knock out a strong man thus protected.

Yes, there was but one thing to do, unless Malloy cared to face a long and heartbreaking battle with an uncertain issue and the off-chance of one of Brookins' mule-kick blows landing right. The ruse would not add to Malloy's popularity with the crowd. But where money was concerned popularity ran a very poor second.

Malloy glanced across into the Big Fellow's corner. He caught Brookins' mildly wandering gaze. And his own eyes were at once raised perplexedly at the bunch of glaring arc lights just above the ring.

Then the bell rang for the second round. And the crowd, with audible sighs of happiness, settled down again to the slaughter spectacle.

No longer was Malloy's face set and mask-like. As he stepped from his corner he beamed companionably on the Big Fellow. Just before they came together he glanced upward again in worried concern toward the lights.

Nor did he tear into Brookins as before. He stood up and boxed—boxed neither with speed nor with inspiration. When Brookins rushed him he retreated barely fast enough to avoid the blundering leads.

The crowd muttered disappointment. Con Vedder's low forehead and thatched eyes puckered in a perplexity that made him look like a wizened monkey, as he crouched just outside the ropes and watched the tame performance.

Again, Brookins' friendly soul was warming toward this cordial little chap who seemed trying to atone for his cruelty in the first round. Still smiling up at his antagonist, Malloy said affectionately:

"You sure can fight. If I'd known how good you were, they'd never have got me in the ring with you."

There was a note of genuineness to the praise. The Big Fellow expanded. He was trying to think of some fittingly polite come-back, when Malloy glanced upward for the third time. A gape of astonishment split Homer's dark face, and he exclaimed as in real terror:

"For the love of Mike, what's happening to those lights?"

The Big Fellow followed the upward direction of Malloy's excited stare. He himself saw nothing wrong with the blindingly bright cluster of lights, as he raised his head to survey them.

Just then two things happened. Con Vedder and Kelleher shrieked aloud in gabbled warning to their careless giant. And Homer Malloy, setting himself and taking deliberate aim, sent his right fist and all his wiry weight behind it to the very point of the Big Fellow's upthrust jaw.

The punch would have dented a sheet of armor plate. No mortal man could have withstood it. Delivered as carefully as if at a punching bag, it carried the force of an ax blow.

Back flew the Big Fellow's head, in much the most rapid motion any part of his bulky anatomy had ever shown. And the rest of his jarred body accompanied it in degrees of varying leisureliness. Thus his head was the first part of him to hit the roughened canvas, and his roomy feet struck ground last of all. There he fell and there he lay.

Con Vedder squalled incoherent blasphemies and shook both impotent fists at the nonchalantly posing Malloy. Kelleher followed his employer's example, though a more limited vocabulary made him repeat himself oftener. Most of the audience howled and stamped and sprang to its feet in blood-loving rapture. A few sportsmen hissed. But nobody heard them.

The referee took his stand above the prostrate man-mountain in mid-ring. With rhythmic beats the shirt-sleeved man began to rise and fall, an even second to each semaphoric swing.

At the count of three, the Big Fellow's shut lids ceased to quiver. At the count of four, he opened his bemused eyes and blinked sleepily about him. At the count of six, his gaze focused upon the smugly happy face of Homer Malloy. And into Brookins' eyes blazed memory—memory and sudden comprehension. He tucked his wide feet under him and heaved with all his might. The maneuver brought him off the ground and, standing upright, at the count of eight.

Malloy was at him like a rabid cat; attacking ferociously at close quarters. Still not wholly himself, the Big Fellow made no effort to block the assault. Instead, he flung his flaillike arms about the smaller man and fell into a clinch. His two-hundred-and-twenty-odd pounds of sheer weight bore down upon the straining shoulders of Malloy, and he hung there, letting his clinging arms slip inch by inch over the sweating biceps and elbows of his opponent.

This clinch was the Big Fellow's first bit of cleverness throughout the fight. It had been taught him with much accuracy by Kelleher, and was one of the few things he had learned with any ease. It was the same exhausting clinch wherewith Jeffries had worn down and confused Bob Fitzsimmons, in their first championship fight—a clinch that any heavyweight may use to fatiguing effect on a lighter and shorter enemy.

Under its dragging weight Malloy's feline muscles were forced to exert themselves to the full, in bearing up the soggy load. It was at least three seconds before the referee could pry the men apart from their unloving embrace. As he did so, Malloy tore in again, white with fury—only to find himself once more smothered in that nightmare clinch.

"Mister referee!" he snarled as the break was made, "caution this Red Truck from hanging on! He keeps lying down on my shoulders and going to sleep there. He—"

Malloy shut his mouth and prepared to side-step a mad rush from his foe. He miscalculated his distance by the fraction of an inch. As a result, he went staggering six feet backward, from a swing whose force he had not altogether avoided. And this time it was he who ran into a clinch to protect himself. To his disgust he ran into precisely the same sort of clinch he had so bitterly protested to the referee. Only, this time, he had no ground for protest, since very patently it was he who sought the contact.

So ended the round.

The Big Fellow went back to his corner with a look on his mild visage no man had ever seen there. He understood. This pleasant-faced, nice-spoken little chap was a cur. He had played a dirty trick. He wasn't to be trusted. He was to be put out of the way as quickly and as mercilessly as possible.

And, with smoldering rage in his soft heart, the Big Fellow started in to play executioner.

For the next half dozen rounds he pursued the flitting Malloy at every stage of the fight. Slowly, ploddingly, relentlessly, he kept after his man; clumsily chasing the elusive foe, seeking ever to come to hammer blows with him at close quarters or to corner him.

A bull might almost as successfully have chased a hornet. Malloy eluded the Big Fellow with lazy ease, dashing in for a fierce rally and out again unhurt, always on the move, always punishing, nearly always escaping reprisals.

It was a pretty sight—for those of the audience who liked such things. Despite the inter-rounds attentions of his handlers, the Big Fellow's face and body were hideous from their mauling.

Yet ever he kept on. He was not tired. Months of shrewd training had welded his mighty body into a miracle of endurance. True, the punishment hurt. It hurt more and more. But, only on the surface. Dull, cold nerves can endure stolidly ten times the pain that would madden or overwhelm a more highly organized system. Brookins had no definite campaign, except to keep after this measly little cuss until at last he should get him, and, meanwhile, to clinch as often and as weightily as he could.

Malloy held his pose of amused grimness. But, inside, he was anything but amused. The few blows he had failed to block or to duck had shaken him to the very spine. The hang-on clinches had become agonizing in their strain on his muscles. He was tiring. He had not trained for a long fight. There had seemed no need. Nor, even at his best, was he good for a battle whose rounds ran into the teens.

His hair-trigger nerves began to jump. There was something uncanny in this snail-like giant whose elephant body was impervious to the most killing punishment, and who continued to come on and on, unwearied. He was wholly outside Homer Malloy's wide experience. There was something wrong, somewhere. And again, in desperation, the snake-cold brain turned to planning.

The fighters came up for the ninth round. The statuelike immobility of Malloy's expression troubled Con Vedder. He had seen this man in twenty fights. And always that poker face meant something—something that spelled unpleasantness for the other man in the ring.

Leisurely ducking under a lunging left lead, Malloy darted in and smote thrice at heart and wind. As he slipped out, Brookins shoved blindly with his right. The shove caught Malloy under the heart. Luckily for him, he and the Big Fellow's glove were both traveling in the same direction, and at not too-differing speeds. Otherwise, a broken rib or two and a temporarily checked heart must have been the toll. As it was, Brookins' fist banged hard and deep and crushingly against the muscles which laced Malloy's lower left ribs.

A wave of torment, and the intense sickness which follows a heart smash, surged through the smaller man. Scarce had he speed left to roll into a clinch. Scarce had he strength left to keep his footing under that clinch's sheer weight. Yet his brain was as clear as ever. And it cried its command to the shudderingly sick muscles.

The referee parted the two. Malloy staggered awkwardly out of the clinch and to one side. His move brought Brookins' expansive form between him and the referee. As usual, Brookins began at once to bore in at his enemy. In the brief instant, before the referee could come into full view, Malloy sprang forward to meet the rush. His left hand was flourished high, as if seeking Brookins' jaw. This much even the half-hidden referee might see.

Into his poised right, as he and Brookins crashed together, Malloy threw his entire remaining power and whiplash science.

Under the Big Fellow's guard whizzed the punch—well, *well* under it—well under any guard known or needed in boxing. It landed thuddingly against the victim's lower groin.

The foul was worked with infinite cleverness. So quickly was it delivered and so close together were hitter and hittee, that not one person in twenty among the spectators was aware of it. The referee himself had missed the sight. Con Vedder had not; and he squawked fiery maledictions on the fouler as he danced crazily up and down on the ring edge.

Brookins had launched a left hook as he brushed aside the upraised left arm of his assailant. But he forgot to look for the result of this smashing blow. His own armor-muscled body had turned all at once into a swirling hell of pain. Every inch of him was alive with swooning torture.

Even as he toppled writhingly forward, helpless and in unbearable agony, he realized what had happened. And, with the half of his brain not occupied in registering anguish, he resolved to tell the referee how vilely he had been fouled. He knew, from Kelleher, that such a foul would mean the forfeiting of the fight to him. And he wanted that fight. He had gone through hell to get it, and he was not going to be cheated out of it by this murderous trickster.

Thus, half of the injured man's brain; while the other half was trying vainly to keep the giant body from plunging to the floor on its face.

Down crashed the Big Fellow, his forward-toppling body colliding with Malloy's and bringing it to the canvas beneath him. And there the two foes lay, Malloy, lazily moveless, while Brookins struggled groaningly to lift his supine head and shoulders from off his antagonist's stomach.

The house went mad. Outwardly the referee was calm. Inwardly, he was all at sea as to the right procedure to follow when both fighters were on the ground at the same time. Yet he did the one thing left to him to do. Standing over the prostrate pair, he began to count off the ten seconds.

Before he had voiced the third count he was interrupted by the Big Fellow, who had raised a contorted white face toward him and was trying to force gasping words from his pain-contracted throat. Unheeding the referee went on with his count.

Failing to make his lost voice carry for the few feet that separated him from the clocklike referee, the Big Fellow summoned all his strength and energy into an effort to crawl closer to him and whisper the protest he had not the breath to speak aloud.

Like a crab he scrambled free of Malloy and tried to stand up. The attempt was a dismal failure. Battling against the pain that was riving and ripping him, the Big Fellow got his feet under his body and his hands and hips off the floor. But that was the best he could do. Crouching, squatting almost double, like a sick baboon, but with only his huge feet touching the canvas, he tried to waddle across to the referee.

He could not take a step. Then it was he heard the count of—

"Ten!"

"Mr. Referee!" he croaked mouthingly, as the shirt-sleeved man strode up to his bent hulk. "He fouled me. He—"

The referee paid no attention to his protest. Instead he caught the Big Fellow by the right arm. Brookins thought he was helping him to rise. But he was mistaken. All the referee did was to lift Brookins' right glove high in air and let it drop.

At this time-honored victory signal the house shook with screaming and thumping applause, and a cloud of handlers swarmed through the ropes toward him.

The Big Fellow was lifted—not to his feet, but high on the shoulders of a dozen bellowing enthusiasts. As he rose in the air he had the merest glimpse of three bored men, dragging Homer Malloy back to his corner, feet foremost. Brookins' random left hook had done its perfect work on the jaw of a man too eager in the achievement of his own fouling to bother about guarding against such a chance.

Half an hour later, in his dressing room, the Big Fellow had so far recovered from the groin blow as to be able to sit up on the edge of the rubbing table and demand to be told in precise dollars and cents the size of his net winnings.

"It'll run a wee peckle over six thousand dollars," returned Con Vedder, with a new and gratifying respect in his tone. "And you've earned it, all right, all right, Greggy, boy. Weight done it. Sheer weight. That and the wrought-iron jaw. At the count of ten you was on your feet and he wasn't. I never picked a lemon yet. You're still green. But you're no lemon. You're a peach! A reg'lar ol' he-peacherino, with fur on it!

"Another six months will put you so close to the champ'nship that folks won't be able to tell the two of you apart. And now Bud'll help you climb into your clothes and take you round to the Turkish bath. I gotta go see that bunch of noospaper fellers that's waiting for a word about you. They was wild to come on in here. But you wasn't in no shape to see 'em. So they're waiting outside till I get time to go and—"

"Bring 'em in!" commanded the Big Fellow, his faculties recovering a bit from the daze produced by Vedder's magic words about six thousand dollars. "Go bring 'em in! The whole lot. I got something to say to 'em. Chase!"

Obediently the manager trotted out into the corridor. And, presently, he came back, ushering into the dressing room a dozen sporting reporters.

"I told these boys," Vedder informed Brookins, with a flourish, "that you'd see 'em, personal. I said most likely you had some message to give 'em, for the 'Merican public, now that you've started so fine on your champ'nship race."

Having thus prompted the hero of the hour, he stood by to do further prompting if need be. But there was no such need.

Painfully the Big Fellow arose from his perch on the table and faced the reporters.

"Is that right?" he asked eagerly. "Will you folks print in the paper anything I say?"

"Sure!" promised Burns, the spokesman. "Go to it!"

"Then," proudly exhorted the Big Fellow, "put in print that I'm a-going to buy that truck to-morrow. And say that I hope ev'rybody'll remember me when they want any light hauling done. They'll find me at Raddle's Garage. Top of Carston Av'noo hill, like I told you. And—and, say," he ended inquiringly, "I wonder will the price of gas begin to go down pretty soon, now?"

Watchful Wasting

*T*HIS story begins in two places at once. On the "lot" of the Preëminent Film Corporation—just off Hollywood Boulevard, in Los Angeles; and in the New York offices of the same corporation, at No. 999 West Forty-second Street. After which, the yarn follows the course of empire—and takes its way westward.

At Hollywood, the Preëminent people were clearing decks for the second of their Roy McNair features; a picture which, like its highly successful predecessor, was to star the modest young middleweight champion of the world, in what was described as "A Fistic Comedy."

Malachi Ruhl, chief director of the Preëminent, was in artistic throes over the new production. Indeed every one in that section of the lot was infected by Ruhl's thrill. Except perhaps Roy McNair himself. After fighting battle after battle in the campaign toward the middleweight championship the emotions do not respond deeply to the prospect of posturing and grimacing and hippodroming in front of a platoon of punchless cameras. Wherefore McNair went about his all-important task calmly, even amusedly. And he had a queer tendency to grin rather than to cower at Ruhl's bursts of divine rage.

At the New York offices of the Preëminent two bulbous-girthed men sat in grim conclave over a set of newly and expensively audited ledgers. The ledgers had not a tithe of Malachi Ruhl's artistic fire. They were bare of fire and of art. In dull figures they told the sordid truth about the cost of each production. While Malachi Ruhl was glowing to the knowledge that such-and-such a picture had been a triumph and had advanced the progress of movie possibilities, these drab ledgers pointed out that the cash receipts for many of the inspired pictures did not come within fifty thousand dollars of justifying the lavish outlay.

Wherefore the sad conference of the Preëminent's president and treasurer in the corporation's supercostly New York offices. Wherefore too, the summoning of a genie to the conference—a genie whose mission in life was the reconciling of Ledgers to Golden Visions. To end at once the cruel suspense, this genie—and genius—was Hilary B. Banks, the famed efficiency expert, the all-potent, consulting specialist for diseased or anaemic businesses.

The president and the treasurer looked up from their sorrowful ledger-burrowing with something of scared hopefulness as the mighty Hilary B. Banks was announced. And the great man's aspect was enough, by itself, to justify almost any hope. If mortal could save a situation—any situation at all, from fire at sea to an office leak—it was Banks. The first glance at him was enough to convince the world of that.

He was tall. He was about one Jim Jeffries in height and three Jim Jeffrieses in girth. He had the figure of a gladiator whose ancestors included *Falstaff*. He was perhaps the one man in the business world who still wore a senatorial frock coat and a white-corded vest in such a way as to make him look not only tremendously imposing but equally up-to-date. His curling hair was Jovelike. So was his relentlessly piercing, dark eye. His mouth might well have been chipped from a statue of Napoleon. So might his manner. For the rest, he exuded power. Hilary B. Banks could have led armies or sold patent soap from a cart tail; and he could have made a mammoth hit at either vocation.

"Good morning!" gushed the president, with an air so humbly effusive that he himself rebelled at it and added more briskly: "You have been over the books, I hope?"

"That is why I am here," returned Banks, in a tone which carried both authority and reproof.

The president and the treasurer looked meekly at each other, and then at the efficiency expert. Banks was seating himself in the biggest of the room's dozen big chairs and was exhuming from his vest a pale little cigar. The president felt the pettiness of his own query about the books; and he was about to rectify it by some sage remark, as soon as he could think of one. But Banks saved him the trouble. Taking in the wide room with an eagle gaze, the expert said:

"In a minor way, waste stoppage could well begin right here. I note there are no less than twelve of these handsomely upholstered chairs in this room. They cost, probably, on an average, one hundred and twenty-five dollars each. Three chairs of this sort would he ample. Then, if necessary, a half dozen five-dollar cane-seat chairs scattered here and there.

"That couch, too! It must have cost fully two hundred dollars. It has no place in a business office. If you are obliged to work late and need to rest for an hour or so, an army cot in an anteroom, would serve the same purpose. Such can be picked up, now, at any of the various army-stores sales for not more than—"

"But—" blithered the president guiltily, "I—we thought—"

"I notice three highly expensive desks, too," went on the relentless Banks. "I gather that one of them is for each of you gentlemen; and the third—judging from the pads and pencils—for a secretary or a stenographer. A nineteen-dollar combination desk-and-typewriter stand would suffice for your stenographer. The same principle applies to many of these hangings and all but one or two of the paintings. I believe in tasteful decorations, as a legitimate aid to enterprise. But not in costly overfurnishing. Not less than four thousand dollars—perhaps as much as four thousand five hundred dollars—could have been saved in the furnishing of this one room. To say nothing of the rest of the suite.

"Also, in the outer office, I counted eleven employees. Two of them were reading newspapers. Two more were talking. About half your force, out there, seems superfluous. An office boy was scrawling pictures of women's heads on a sheet of embossed letter-head paper. High-priced paper, at that. Five electric lights were burning in an unused dark corner. All this, my one cursory glance told me. A more careful look would, of course, have revealed much more. And if I—"

"It—it never occurred to—to—" began the treasurer, wiggling deeper in his chair.

"If your Los Angeles plant is run on similar principles of utter wastage," continued the remorseless Banks, "I can well understand why you have found it necessary to send for me. This apart from any needless expense in the mere taking of the pictures themselves."

He paused and favored his hearers, in turn, with an eagle glare. He was facing two awed and crushed culprits. His experienced eye told him this. And he resumed magisterially:

"I have jotted down a number of notes in connection with what a study of your books told me. For the moment, I shall not refer to them. It is enough to mention one or two lesser items which seem to me to epitomize the rest. In all the course of a somewhat broad business experience, I have never before come upon such a glaring series of futile expenditures. For example: Under the caption of 'Footage,' I find that it is the custom to take no less than four simultaneous views, sometimes more, of certain scenes. And to 'retake' as often as three times, in some instances. That means the needless hire of several very high-priced photographers—"

"Camera men," murmured the president, loath to interrupt so great a personage, but unable to let pass the crude phrasing.

"And the total and unnecessary waste of thousands of feet of costly film. Moreover the—"

The treasurer plucked up heart to stammer an explanation of the necessity of having one set of films intact in case of mishap to another. He even tried to explain the needful "shooting" of the same scene from different angles and distances. But Hilary B. Banks waved aside his paltry objection, with a curt:

"If four, why not forty? Two cameras would suffice; to obviate the chance of one missing. As for the photographing at different angles, I can better decide on the need of that when I go out there to study the situation at firsthand. In the meantime, here is another item, culled from hundreds: one of your stars, Barry Clive, receives three thousand five hundred dollars a week, it seems, while he is 'working.' And, presumably, he is 'working,' as long as the picture is being made. I find a record of his sitting idle in his dressing room for three entire days, during the filming of a recent picture, because his director was busy trying to film another scene that would not be—"

"But we have to pay him, when he's called to the lot," expostulated the president. "He is likely to be needed at any—"

"Then, again," pursued Banks, "I note that an ex-prize fighter, a Roy McNair, is on your pay roll, out there, at two thousand seven hundred dollars a week. Surely, if it is necessary to introduce pugilism in a picture, there are many impecunious prize fighters who would be glad of so easy a job at seventy-five dollars a week, or even less. And—"

"Hold on!" interposed the treasurer, feeling his cold feet were at last on surer ground. "Roy McNair is a money-maker. He's only been in two features, so far. And each of them has cleaned up big. The fans—"

"Even so. He could be engaged for a mere tithe of that salary. Why, it is more, by the year, than any professional fighter ever made in the ring. And—"

"And we are getting bigger returns from him than any fight promoter ever hauled down from a champion," retorted the treasurer, his back to the wall. "Why, just the story of how he happened to get into the game, out there, has brought a million folks to see his pictures. You've most likely read about it. He—"

"I am not interested in press-agent yarns," reproved Banks. "Which reminds me: the salaries paid to the Preëminent's press staff are—"

"You see," said the treasurer, keen to pass along his favorite story, "it was like this. Barry Clive was our biggest money-maker. Mostly on account of his looks. McNair goes out to the Coast to patch up a bum set of lungs. His cousin, a little cuss named 'Cleppy' Worden, gets McNair a job on the lot, under a fake name. Clive gets fond of Worden's sweetheart, and beats Worden up, to make a hit with her. Then McNair sails into Clive, and puts Barry's good looks into the slag heap; and Ruhl is just going to have McNair pinched, when he finds out who he is and signs him up, instead. And ever since then—"

"Yes," yawned Banks, "very likely. But it's beside the point. Here is my conclusion, gentlemen; I believe, in fact, I know I can put your wasteful organization on a much better paying basis. I can guarantee to cut the overhead and the host of needless expenditures, to the bone. But I must have a free hand. That must be assured to me. And I must go out there, to make at least a three-month study of conditions.

"If the idea appeals to you, I am ready to state my terms. If not—well, my time is limited. Take three minutes, if you choose to decide on my proposition. Here is a rough draft of my plan and the fee I shall require. I'll step into the outer office, while you talk it over."

"But—but only three minutes—" quavered the president. "If you could wait until we—"

"The Magna Charta was signed in just three seconds," said Banks sternly. "And the battle of Austerlitz was won through a fifteen-second decision of Bonaparte's. Three minutes, please. Thank you."

Thus it chanced that Efficiency came to the Preëminent lot, at Hollywood. The first reaction to it was not unlike that caused by tossing a ravenous three-pound pickerel into a pool of busily merry goldfish.

The Preëminent had gone along, like most of the large picture concerns, following the line of least resistance when questions of price arose; and doing its humble share to hasten the hour of drastic readjustment which was to burst upon the movie world a few years later.

In this placidly spendthrift organization appeared a huge personage, in senatorial raiment and armed with almost boundless authority from the home office. To a genius for economical efficiency, he added a cloudless ignorance of the motion-picture industry. And, at once, he acquired all the local popularity hitherto divided between the typhoid germ and the man who devised the income tax.

To the Preëminent's Los Angeles officials, Hilary B. Banks resolved himself into a thing of horror. Beginning with the office force, he swung the sickle among happy heads which had grown large under the authority and sinecure of departmental jobs. The force, in one department after another, was cut down with relentless hand.

The surviving chiefs and subchiefs and workers found themselves buried under the victims' duties, in addition to their own. Gone were the pleasantly dreamy times when five hours of moderately steady labor represented a self-respecting day's toil. Gone were afternoons of golf and of motoring and of sea bathing. Gone were the loafingly luxurious daylight sessions in the lobby or grill of the Alexandria. Gone was everything; except grinding labor. And the laments of the fired were mingled with the despairing anathemas of the nonfired.

Through this scene of wholesale carnage Hilary B. Banks strode in majestic unconcern.

When the average small employer discharges an incompetent or unneeded clerk, he must needs fight against a gloomy wonder as to what is to become of the unfortunate's wife and hypothetical twelve children. No such inefficiently useless thoughts ruffled the gigantic serenity of Hilary B. Banks. He was miles above maudlin sentiment. As justly expect the reaper to shed tears over the bearded grain or the poulterer to sigh above the decapitated forms of his market broilers, as to look for silly compunction in Banks.

True, he sought always to retain the men who had wives and many children; and to discharge the unattached. But that was because the much-married employee can be lashed into prodigies of work at which the independent bachelor would balk or kick, a hungry family being a mighty deterrent to false notions of independence. But sentiment, as such, had no place in Banks' demigod cosmos—as hundreds of luckless Preëminent employees learned with absolutely no loss of time.

Having arranged office matters more to his liking, or less to his disliking, the expert turned his attention to deleting the ghastly overhead and leakage in the artistic departments of the business. Here, he felt, lay the true feast. All the rest had been a mere appetizer.

Roy McNair had been away, for two weeks, "on location." Late one night he returned to Los Angeles and tiptoed to his sleeping porch in the little Figueroa Street home of his cousin, Grover Cleveland—otherwise Cleppy—Worden, with whom he lived.

Roy moved with all the catlike silence of the trained athlete, as he groped his way into the bungalow. He did not at all mind waking fat, little Cleppy Worden.

Indeed, if Cleppy alone were to be considered, Roy would have entered the bungalow with a whoop and would have haled his cousin from bed and made him share a midnight lunch and listen to an account of everything that happened during the ten-day location job out in their old stamping ground in the Imperial Valley.

But, six months earlier, Cleppy had been married. He had married Jean Potter, a lovable wisp of a girl, who also worked for the Preëminent. The two had pooled their incomes and had gone to housekeeping in the Figueroa Street bungalow; taking Cleppy's adored cousin, Roy, to board with them.

Jean had kept on with her work at the lot. But, in a month or so, now, she was going to take a half-year vacation. And it was because of all which this coming vacation implied that Roy now came into the house on tiptoe, lest he disturb the sleep of one to whom full nights' rest were a necessity.

It was not until he and Jean and Cleppy were at breakfast next morning that Roy heard of the advent of Hilary B. Banks. When his host and hostess found that he was ignorant of the great news, both of them began to tell him about it at once.

Roy missed the sense of much of this staccato marital duet. But he gathered from it enough to learn that an elephantine efficiency guy had been sent out from New York and that he had made toad pie of the office force and that now he was starting to raise Cain, out on the lot. And wasn't it the horridest thing Roy ever heard of? And just listen to what he did to poor "Hick" Fallon!

Roy listened eagerly and with what intelligence he could muster. This was something new, in McNair's life—this efficiency business. In his fighting days, his manager had handled all financial details. Since then, Roy had done his easy work for the Preëminent and had drawn and banked his weekly salary—a salary whose magnitude even now dumfounded him. Beyond that, he knew nothing of finance—and cared less. Still, he could see the matter was bothering Jean. And, awkwardly, he strove to turn the talk to some less worrisome channel.

"You two are both working, to-day, aren't you?" he asked, after clucking sympathetically with his tongue against the roof of his mouth as the dual complaint reached a momentary halt. "Because, even if you aren't, you both of you ought to come out there. I want you to see *me*. What do you think I'm going to be? I kicked like a steer when Ruhl told me about it, last week; but he's promised the get-up won't make me sissyish.

"He says the audiences will see it's just a joke, the minute they set eyes on me. Come out and see me be *it*. They're going to have my costume ready by ten o'clock. Ruhl's going to shoot the scene, some time before noon. He doesn't want to give me time to get used to wearing the things. Says the awkwarder I am in 'em, the funnier it'll be. But I kind of hate to do it, at that!"

"Do *what?*" demanded the mystified Jean. "Roy McNair, honestly, I think you can say more and tell less, when you want to, than any three men on the lot. What's it all about?"

Pleased that he had roused her interest and that he had switched the theme from something which made her unhappy, Roy deigned to translate.

"Ruhl's worked a new stunt into that 'With Fist and Brain' picture I'm doing. He thinks a lot of the idea. It doesn't make any kind of a hit with me. The s'ciety chap who proves to his girl that he can handle himself in a scrap as well as the rough-necks, and gets into a cham'nship fight—Lord, but the p'fessional bunch will laugh their fool heads off at that pipe dream!—this chap takes a whirl at being a kind of knight errant—whatever that is.

"That's Ruhl's new scheme. The hero's girl gets insultedlike by a tough, on the street, one evening. So, next night, he dresses up like a girl and sa'nters down that street. The tough sees him and thinks it's a girl. Dim light, you know. And the tough sasays up to him, and the hero pretty near rips him into nine pieces. The tough's all stoopefied to find the classy-looking girl punching him on the jaw. And he—"

"Huh!" grunted Cleppy Worden, in nowise impressed. "Female impers'nation stuff, hey? Rotten! All right for a Sadie-chap. But punk, for a two-handed he-guy like you! You're on the screen to make folks set up. Not to make 'em give you the merry ho-ho. If I was you, I'd—"

"That's what I said to Ruhl," McNair defended himself. "But he tells me I'm dead wrong. This won't be a reg'lar female impers'nation. Just a kind of broolesque. There's to be about fifty feet of me climbing into the she-duds, wrong way; and fifty more of me trying to walk natural in 'em, and breathe without smashing the loose corset. And—"

"Corset!" groaned Cleppy, while Jean squealed joyously. *Corset!* Gee!"

"And," Roy continued, trying not to listen, "then there's just a flash of me, close up, as I start out of the taxi toward the dark corner where the tough is standing. Then a flash of him, getting a glimpse of me in the dark and starting toward me. The rest is to be filmed fifty feet away—where he comes alongside and all—up to the place in the fight where my she-clothes have all slipped their moorings and busted out at the seams, in the whaling I give him.

"I'm not saying I like the notion, even yet. But you know how Ruhl is. Once he gets one of his pet plans, a feller feels like a child beater for refusing to do what he wants. Ruhl takes it like it was the roon of all his life. So I ended up by saying I'd stand for it. And, anyhow," he added defiantly, "it's a heap better than to have to make love down some girl's neck, while the camera close-ups the two of us. That's the part of this game I sure hate."

"That's because you've never been in love," Jean assured him. "And, honestly, you make screen love awfully well, Roy—for a middleweight champion. Reine Houston told me you—"

"Rub it in!" grumbled McNair. "Next you'll be saying—"

"No, I won't, either. And I think it's a fine idea—the dressing you up in girl's clothes. I wouldn't miss seeing it filmed, to-day, if I had to walk out to the lot, bare-foot. I'm going to get within six inches of the camera line and—"

"And guy me for weeks afterward," complained Roy. "I was a happy man, till you started in guying me. You don't seem to have any respect at all for a real live star. Never mind, kid!" he broke off, lest she take his plaint seriously. "I'd rather be guyed by you than flattered by most girls. You're all right. Say, by the way, I spoke to Ruhl about your jumping off the ledge in that 'Golden hearts' picture you folks are working in. And he says it'll be all right about having a 'double' do the jump. He sent a memo to Bemis about it. He said the scene wasn't to be rehearsed, till some time to-day. He wanted Bemis to wait till we came back; because Ruhl wants to go over it with him first. So don't bother your head, any more, about having to do the jump."

He spoke fast, avoiding her eye. But the look of grateful relief in Cleppy's face told him that both husband and wife had been worried over the possible need for this mild feat of acrobatics.

"Thank you, ever so much," said Jean simply, and with no embarrassment at all. "I was sure Mr. Ruhl would make it all right, if you spoke to him about it. And—oh, I do hope we won't be working, at the time of your wonderful scene!"

But, a few hours later, Jean and Cleppy had quite forgotten their amused interest in McNair's female impersonation. They had troubles of their own.

Roy, with the help of his dresser and a snickering wardrobe man, got into his feminine togs. Then, blasphemously, he got out of them; and went to Section 7 of the studio; there to make a conscientiously bungling effort to don them under the battery of two cameras. After which, for the further benefit of the camera, and coached by the delighted Malachi Ruhl, he did a succession of shamblingly ill-balanced steps, which were supposed to depict the pseudo girl's efforts to walk in high heels.

Then Ruhl directed him to the outdoor section where the scene was already set and the characters waiting for the street encounter between the distinguished pugilist and the tough.

Spurred on by the precepts and presence of Hilary B. Banks, Ruhl was trying to obviate some of the usual long pauses between bits of camera action. And he was doing it, with monstrous ill will. Banks was a festering sore in Ruhl's soul. As the chief director himself expressed it: "I'm getting to hate relations of his that I never heard of."

Followed by Ruhl and the two camera men, Roy McNair set off across the lot toward the section assigned for his scene. He was beginning to take a morbid amusement in this weird role of his. And the torment of the more or less mercifully adjusted corsets and high-heeled shoes made him doubly grateful that he was a man. He did not realize how plausible was his disguise—thanks to brilliantly artistic draping and make-up and to the slender grace of his athletic body. At a careless glance, under the mask of cream-colored paint he gave the impression of being a strikingly handsome and somewhat Amazonian woman in her late twenties.

A little to the left of his route to the appointed section, a group of men and women were gathered, in evident keen interest, about some pivotal point. And in the group's center a man was talking, loudly. As Roy paused, idly, he heard a woman's voice make reply to the man's oration. And the tone of the voice was one of frightened unhappiness. Moreover, the voice was Jean's. Hoisting his skirts out of the way of his stride, Roy broke into a run.

It had been a field day for Hilary B. Banks. He had been on the lot since eight o'clock. Apart from the joy of catching a number of employees coming to work disgracefully late, he had found no less than seven major items of extravagance to jot down for future reference. And now, as he was about to depart for lunch, he happened upon a set scene, with several people in make-up loitering around it. Pausing in front of Bemis, who was inspecting an artificial five-foot ledge with a painted ridge of rock behind it, Banks inquired sharply:

"What's the meaning of all this delay? Why don't you get these people to work? The light is good."

"We're waiting for Mr. Ruhl, sir," answered the assistant director, as civilly as might be. "He wants to handle this himself. And just now he's in No. 7, working on a scene in the McNair feature. He'll be here, presently."

"And in the meantime, I suppose—"

Banks stopped midway in a sarcastic retort, to stare at two women. One of them was standing beside a fat little man. The other was sitting on a soft mattress at the foot of the ledge. Both wore decidedly bizarre clothes. And both were dressed precisely alike.

"What's the idea?" queried Banks. "Twins?"

"No, sir," replied Bemis, nodding toward the woman who sat on the mattress. "That is a 'double.' She is doubling for Mrs. Worden, yonder—in the jump from that ledge. The action calls for Mrs. Worden to be escaping from bandits. We took that part, last week, out on location. She comes to a ledge and hesitates; then jumps down. Mrs. Worden is to appear at the top of the ledge and crouch for the jump. Then the double is to do the jump itself. And we're to get a close-up of Mrs. Worden lying senseless at the foot of the ledge, afterward—and of the cowboys finding her there. She—"

"What's the use of the double, then?" rasped Banks. "That drop is a good deal less than six feet. And there's a big mattress at the bottom. Why can't she do the whole thing; and save all the expense of hiring another woman and providing a dress for that woman and all? Why not, eh? It's one of the most asinine pieces of expenditure, in a small way, that I've seen since I've been in this spendthrift hole. She looks strong and healthy. Why can't she do her own jumping, instead of—"

Cleppy had left his troubled wife, and came edging timorously up to the great man. Ranging alongside, he lifted his plump little bulk on tiptoe and whispered mumblingly in the unwilling ear of Hilary B. Banks. Bemis swore, venomously, under his breath. And the "double" cast a reassuringly pitying glance at poor Jean.

"Rot!" stormed Banks, scarce waiting to hear the end of Cleppy's faltering confidence. "Utter rot! If she's well enough to be chased by bandits and to lie unconscious at the foot of the cliff, she's well enough to jump off it. And that's what she'll do. Here, you!" to Bemis. "Send that double about her business. And, after this, see that I'm consulted, before you hire a double, for any part at all."

"But you don't understand, sir!" shrilled Cleppy. "I just told you, my wife—"

"I understand!" snapped Banks. "I understand, all right. And there's something I want you and that woman to understand, too. I want you to understand that I'm not interested in your domestic affairs. You people are here to do your work. If any of you aren't able to do that work, you can stop drawing your exorbitant pay. You're not going to put the Preëminent to the needless expense of hiring a high-priced understudy—I mean, double. Get that, all of you. And you, especially!" wheeling on Jean. "You'll make that jump, when the time comes, or you'll turn over your whole job here to some one who can—"

"I'm sorry, sir," said Jean, trembling. "But Mr. Ruhl was kind enough to—"

"I'm running this place," thundered Banks, furious at the wordless murmur of sympathy and indignation from the fast-increasing group. *I'm* running it. Not Mr. Ruhl or any one else. Get that through your head, once and for all."

"Looka here!" flashed Cleppy. "I don't aim to let any man speak that way to my wife. Cut it out, before I—"

"You're fired," ordained Banks, in his best voice. "Go to the cashier and get your time. I'll not stand for any back talk or bluster here. Not from anybody. Get out!"

"If—if my husband is discharged for defending me," spoke up Jean, very gallantly indeed, "then I—"

"Then you'll get out, too?" flared Banks. "You can bet you will. I'll have no malingerers on this lot, or any one talking back to me. Get that, too. *All* of you. I am in charge here; and I—"

Between him and his scowling audience stepped a strikingly handsome woman. Tall she was and broad of shoulder and deep of chest; and of wondrous athletic carriage. In her make-up and picture hat and exquisitely modeled dress she was a sight to make any one pause.

Hilary B. Banks, like George Washington, "ever had an eye for a fine woman." But his eye was nearsighted, in spite of its Napoleonic gleam. And he would not mar the classic strength of his features by wearing glasses. Moreover this woman had come to a halt with her back to the sun. To Banks, she gave the impression of gloriously vital femininity. And there was a light in her made-up eyes which might well have been taken for a glare.

"Stunning!" said Banks, aloud, in patronizing approval. But his kindly praise went unheard.

"You're firing the Wordens?" she demanded. "I warn you, if they go, I go. Contract or no contract. What's the trouble, anyway?"

"He—he ordered Jean to jump down off that ledge," whimpered Cleppy. "After I'd told him—"

"You swine!" blazed the woman, advancing furiously upon Banks.

Her voice, he noted, was mighty deep for a woman's. It might even have been called a baritone. And her insult had been all but spat in his face. He peered intently at the flashy creature who had dared affront him and whose voice was so ill a match for the dainty costume. And, as his eyes focused on the insulter, he saw that this was no woman but a man in woman's apparel. There could be no possible doubt. The square jaw, the sinewy throat, the big and rough hands, the whole insistent aura of masculinity—all proved that this person belonged to the type of so-called artist, known as a "female impersonator."

By repute and by anecdote, Banks knew of such actors. He had read that they are recruited from among the smallest and most fragile men in the profession. His first twinge of amaze merged into righteous indignation. This whippersnapper had insulted him, here in public; in his own monarchy where he held power of financial life and death. In a second, the indignation had turned to boiling rage,

It was not enough to rap out a dictum of discharge and then to turn haughtily away. He had been spoken to as never before in his triumphant life. The stripling had called him a swine. This demanded something more drastic than a mere discharge—if Hilary B. Banks wanted to keep the reverence and fear of the Preëminent throng. In a trice, the Napoleonic, if flaming mind of Hilary B. Banks was made up. Even while Roy McNair stood blocking his way and with lips parted as if to spit some fresh affront at him, Banks attacked.

Shooting forth a mighty right arm, he gripped the unprepared McNair by the neck, yanked him forward and prepared to throw the mincing female impersonator across his knee for a humiliating spank. Such a public degradation would sting the youth far more keenly than would a fist blow.

But, oddly enough, McNair did not reach his punisher's knee. Somewhere during that brief yanking passage through the air, he melted from Banks' Herculean grasp. Scarce had the efficiency expert's fingers closed on his neckband, than Roy had wriggled free, leaving a handful of valuable dress goods in Banks' fist. And, in practically the same motion, he let drive his left for his assailant's jaw.

Had that punch gone home, the efficiency man would have been totally ineffi-cient for some seconds. But a pugilist's blow is not struck by the arm and fist alone. It is delivered by aid of the entire body, from neck to toe. And in this case, the feet played McNair false. Under the wrench of his effort, both high French heels, already over-strained by clumsy walking, turned under. The right slipper twisted completely to one side, all but throwing McNair off his balance. As a result, his left-hander fell short. Instead of connecting hard with the point of Banks' jaw, it plowed grazingly along the side of his throat, bruising the flesh as it passed.

The blow had a dual effect on Banks. It showed him to his own satisfaction that his opponent had not the strength or skill to hit a damaging wallop. And the quick hurt of it snapped his frayed temper. Into the fight he charged, like a mad bull. And, McNair gave ground at his rush.

Hilary B. Banks was built on lines of great strength. And, in younger days, he had prided himself not a little on his boxing prowess. He still took a moderate amount of athletic exercise; and his two hundred and fifty pounds and six feet two inches of husky physique were far less flabby than the normal business man's. He welcomed this chance to prove, with his fists, what already he had proved with his brain—that he was a master of men. That his present antagonist was six inches shorter and ninety pounds lighter than himself, did not detract at all from his own fierce joy in the battle.

As Banks rushed, McNair not only gave ground, but actually turned and fled. To one side he sprang, barely in time to avoid the other's bull rush. Then he took three floundering steps, and came to a standstill. During the fraction of a second, before his bulkier foe could change direction and charge again, Roy utilized the breathing space to kick his tortured feet free of the encumbering shoes that had made him as slow and as awkward as a novice.

The shoes were off, as Banks bore down upon him. There was no space to side-step or even to get set for punch or parry. Instinctively, McNair ducked and wriggled into a clinch. His lovely picture hat was scraped free of his head—and the fluffy wig along with it—as the top of his skull brushed beneath Banks' deadly swing.

Banks sought to hold on with one arm and to punch Roy's upturned face with the other. He might as readily have held a buzzing, black hornet. McNair was free, and dancing out of reach before the constrictor arm could tighten.

His feet untrammeled, the obstructing picture hat gone from in front of his bothered eyes, Roy at last was ready. Banks came for him anew. This time, McNair did not retreat. His teeth were bared, his eyes were a pair of burning pin points under his thatch of brow. His jaw was tucked into his muscular neck. An impatient tug of one hand had ripped the ruffly skirt from hem to belt. His legs, like his liberated feet, had plenty of sea room. Once more, he was a grimly joyous fighting machine—a figure as menacing as it was ludicrous. Torn finery flapping wide, he met his enemy's onset.

The men came together with a clash. Once more McNair ducked the flailing right-hander, but this time he did not seek a clinch. Instead, his left found its way, with a thud, to Banks' ample meridian. And his right banged jarringly over the big man's heart.

Banks clawed futilely at his elusive foe. Roy was in no hurry to leave the close-quarters range into which he had darted. Before clinching, he landed two more short-arm lefts to the wind and another right to the heart. A woeful grunt of pain and amaze from his opponent gave homage to the battering-ram force of Roy's infighting.

As McNair danced away, now, Banks did not rush him. The efficiency expert was a good judge of efficiency in other matters besides business. And he had discovered that this female impersonator knew how to box. Moreover, that he could hit an unbelievably hard blow for a man of his slight build. Apparently, the fight was not to be won in a single devastating punch, and in the soul of Hilary B. Banks anxiety was born.

He knew, of course, that his enemy was no match for him. But the fellow's skill might prolong the bout to an annoying length. And the rapturous and noninterfering crowd might be treated merely to the unpleasant spectacle of a big and powerful man outfighting a small and weakly youngster and not to the lightning-swift, condign punishment Banks had planned. Instead of striking the assembly with awe, he might well arouse in it the contempt that is the meed of the giant who conquers a game pygmy. Wherefore, Banks awaited Roy's next move, relying on the chance advantage of the boxer who lets his adversary take the aggressive.

McNair did not keep him waiting. Like a whirlwind, he returned. He dashed at his gigantic foe, head lowered. Banks planted himself firmly and struck with his left. A charging fighter is often an easy mark for the cool antagonist who stands and watches. But, somehow, this case seemed an exception.

Banks' well-planned blow whizzed murderously past the ear of the man who scarce moved his head to avoid it and who slackened his pace not at all. And Banks' alert right guard was penetrated with equal ease. Then, before he could clinch or so much as push Roy away, McNair was at his wind and heart with a shower of skilled punches that turned Banks deadly ill.

This was not the first nor the tenth time Roy McNair had fought men much taller than himself. And, instinctively, he was following the accepted tactics for a short man against a tall. Namely, to play for the body until the tortured heart and stomach forced the larger fighter to bend over, from sheer pain, and to leave his jaw exposed and within easy reach.

Sick and dizzy as he was, Banks at last managed to stagger away. McNair was after him like a crazy wild cat. Banks smote with all his remaining strength. McNair had grown careless of the other's awkward leads, and now he paid the bill for overconfidence. He shifted his head, to let the big fist go past him. But, carelessness made him move it too short a distance. Banks' hard-driven left fist caught him full on the cheek bone. Under the tremendous impact, Roy's rush was halted with dismaying suddenness. Roy's head snapped back; and his body followed it. His shoulders struck ground, ahead of any of the rest of him.

This sudden victory went to Banks' head. Craving to avenge his parlous hurts and the spectacle he had presented in being battered helplessly about by his smaller foe, he leaped forward, foaming at the mouth. Back went one of his well-shod feet, for a punitive kick in the ribs of his prone adversary.

McNair might well have passed quietly into dreamland, under the force of the blow that had floored him, if that blow had chanced to land three inches lower.

But the cheek bone is not a vital spot. The impact had knocked him down, thanks as much to his own charging momentum as to anything else, and his head sang from the clout he had received.

But such details are as nothing to a well-trained professional. By the time his body hit ground, McNair was gathering his legs under him and bracing himself to spring up. He had half arisen, therefore, by the time Banks' vicious kick reached him. Thus the swinging boot missed his ribs and caught him alongside the one knee which still remained on the ground.

A howl of wrath from the crowd, at sight of the kick, was echoed by a wild Irish yell from Roy himself. His body left ground and went through the air with the speed of a catapult, straight for the man who had kicked him. The filthy, unsportsmanly cowardice of Banks had succeeded in doing what no professional pugilist had ever been able to do. It robbed McNair of all temper control and turned him into a screaming madman. Yet, subconsciously, his fighting faculties remained cool and as scientifically deadly as ever.

Flying at Banks and brushing aside a ponderous lunge, he hurled himself on the big man. His left and his right in lightning succession sank themselves deep into Banks' stomach. Under that frightful concussion, Banks doubled forward, purple, breathless, agape, his eyes bulging. Before he could right himself or lift his futile guard, Roy McNair had "got set," and had launched the blow for which he had been preparing throughout the fight. Driven with all his science and with all his rage—augmented scientific force, Roy's left fist found its mark. A bare inch to the right of the jaw point it landed. His right fist followed it, coming to anchor higher up on the victim's countenance.

Hilary B. Banks shuddered convulsively, from head to heel. His knee joints turned to hot tallow. With a little gurgling sob, he collapsed in a heap and lay there, still shuddering, his eyes opening and shutting with an unseeing regularity.

Roy McNair nodded, good-naturedly, in response to the shrieked plaudits of the crowd. His fury had departed with Banks' consciousness. He turned away, a bit ashamed of himself. And his glance fell on Jean Worden, standing on a chair at the edge of the exultantly clamorous circle. Frowning, he hurried over to her.

"I'm so sorry!" he blurted. "I—I didn't think of you being here. I didn't think of anything except—except what the cur tried to do. I—oh, Lord, but I hope it didn't shock you or hurt you or—"

"I think," said Jean gratefully, as she laid one little hand on his arm, "I think it did me more good than all the doctors on earth. It was—it was *glorious*, Roy!"

"Good!" exclaimed McNair, grinning as expansively as a mischievous collie. "That was all I cared about. The rest of it was a picnic. Or it will be, when I can get rid of these flappy clothes."

He went over to where Malachi Ruhl and a score of others were striving to restore consciousness to the stricken Banks. Tugging at Ruhl's coat, McNair pulled him to one side.

"That female impersonation stuff is off," proclaimed Roy. "I'm going back to shed this trousseau and get into a pair of honest-to-heaven pants. Sorry to dis'point you but—"

"Disappoint me, huh?" snarled the anguished Ruhl. "Look a' what you done! You've likely killed the poor slob. That'll mean—"

"No, it won't, either," McNair reassured him. "I— Hold on, a second. I'll fix it."

Out of the corner of his eye, he saw Hilary B. Banks shiver all over and struggle to a slumped, sitting posture. Beckoning a camera man to follow, Roy went to the disheveled and bleeding efficiency expert, and stood looking quietly down at him. Banks was blinking dazedly about. At sight of Roy, he straightened. Through a hedge of broken teeth he blubbered, pointing a shaky forefinger at McNair:

"I want that man fired! Instantly! And I want—"

"What you want and what you get, in this good old world," philosophized McNair, "are plenty different. You wanted a cinch victory, just now. And what you got—well, you got it, good and plenty and then a few!"

"Who—what—are you?" blithered the efficiency expert, his hazy vision taking in a glimpse of tiger muscle revealed by the burst dress sleeve. "Who—what—"

"I'm Roy McNair," said the pugilist, choosing his words and speaking with impressive slowness. "And I've given you the licking you've been needing ever since you came out here."

"You're discharged!" bellowed the sick Banks. "And I shall sue—"

"No, I'm not. And no you won't," cheerily answered Roy. "Too many things would get into print. And maybe on the screen, too. This camera man, here, looked out for that part of it. He kept grinding, from the time I spoke to you. The pictures will show the Preëminent's efficiency expert trying to pick on a smaller chap who knocks him out. And don't forget you kicked me, while I was on the ground."

"I—"

"That's what the pictures will show, in court or anywhere else. And the papers will tell a pretty yarn, too, about why you tried to fire poor little Jean Worden; and how you fired her husband for trying to take her part. All that yarn will sound grand in New York, won't it? The pictures will go big, there, too. How about it? Am I fired?"

Hilary B. Banks gurgled, made as though to speak, and fell to nursing his damaged face.

"Am I fired?" repeated McNair.

Slowly, gloweringly, Banks shook his head. Dizzy as he was, he could visualize the screened evidence of what had just happened; and he could hear the Homeric laughter of the world—*his* world.

"Is Jean Worden fired?" pursued McNair. "Is her husband fired? Does she have to make that jump?"

Again the impotently wrathful gurgle, followed by the headshake.

"Good!" applauded Roy. "I've got your word. And I've got the pictures. Better go wash up. That left eye of yours is due to look like it was a thunderstorm, in another hour or two."

He moved away. The camera man pattered after him.

"Say, Mr. McNair," babbled the man. "I didn't like to give you away, back there. But I didn't take any of that scrap betwixt you and Banks. I didn't even have the machine pointed at either of you."

"You know that, do you?" asked Roy.

"Sure, I do. I never——"

"And I know it, too," went on McNair gravely. "And that makes two of us that know it. And here's a nice greasy ten-spot for you, to keep anybody else from knowing it. Least of all, that nice, good Mr. Banks. Something tells me he's due to start East to-night. I'd sure hate to have him postpone his trip, just because you forgot to grind your measly picture box."

The Clean-up

Like many another celebrity, Wolfe Calder had begun his climb by pounding pavements in an ill-fitting blue uniform. He had used brain as well as brawn, in his police job, with the result that he had been shifted at twenty-five from patrol duty to the detective squad.

There, he exhibited no Sherlock Holmes genius. But he showed a bull-terrier alertness and a nose for prey, and an iron tenacity in hanging grimly to a trail till he reached its end. Wherefore, he was much in use, at Police Headquarters. And, from his tireless gift for getting what he went after, a newspaper man named him "Clean-up Calder." The name stuck—not like a burr, but like a medal.

Calder had no political pull. He was ridiculously honest. He was a glutton for work; and he did not have the faculty for making capital out of his exploits. Thus, he saw no future for himself in the Police Department, other than a long life of toil and of peril, with a pittance pension at its end. At twenty-seven, he left the force, to take a better-salaried job as house-detective for the huge jewelry establishment of Ziegerich and Company.

Here, he learned the art of dressing so well that nobody gave a second glance to him, of talking in a modulated voice and with something of the diction of better bred men, and of regarding each and every article of jewelry in the place as a fragment of his own reputation, to be guarded as zealously as his soul's welfare.

His three years at Ziegerich's did not contain as many adventures as had an average three mouths in his police days. During the long lulls between activities, his soul would lave taken on flesh and his wiry brain would have clogged itself with sloth, if he had been the normal hard worker in a soft berth. But there was always something to look forward to.

For example, it was Calder who walked lazily up to the pistol-mouth wherewith an escaping swell yeggman was clearing for himself a path from a rifled jewel-case to the establishment's front door. Deftly, and with no emotion at all, Calder disarmed and collared the desperado.

Calder it was who created momentary

panic, one day, by strolling over to an exquisitely dressed woman who was bending above a tray of rings, and by yanking off her hat and veil and hair, in one comprehensive tug, revealed "her" as a super-shoplifter named Mack Began, whom he remembered from the old days.

Then, after the much-advertised Magnessen necklace was spirited from the supposedly impregnable Ziegerich safe, where it had been deposited for storage and for cleaning, during its fair owner's absence from town, Calder had taken an indefinite leave of absence and had returned six days later with the necklace and with the employee who had stolen it.

Such petty breaks as these, in the routine of wandering with seeming aimlessness from one end of the store to the other, had been Calder's sole diversions, for three long years. Hating boredom and indolence, he had put in his spare time in making himself a really creditable expert in jewelry and in the technique of the business. This meritorious task he had lightened, during the final three months of the time, by making shy but ardent love to Lenore Aken, newest of the Ziegerich stenographers.

For a while, his love story remained to him a mystery more unfathomable than any he had tackled in all his professional work. All his powers of deduction could not tell him whether Lenore's pretty smile of morning greeting spelled encouragement or mere civility.

Being "Clean-up Calder," by nature as well as by nickname, he set himself to the labor of solving this puzzle. And into the work he flung more of himself than had gone into all his professional cases put together.

True to his life-training, Calder, in his study of the case, proceeded to weed out the nonessentials—the men from whom, patently, nothing was to be feared. And this process of elimination thinned down the ranks of his rivals to one, whom he felt to be a really dangerous opponent in the love campaign.

This solitary survival was Moreton, chief of the repair-and-resetting department of Ziegerich's; and, incidentally, Lenore's immediate superior—the department head in whose office she worked. Moreton was a tall and stooping man in the late forties. He had a turtle droop of head and neck, and a perpetual little dry cough. Apart from those trifling oddities, he was much like the other well-clad and well-mannered upper employees of the place.

At first, he had seemed to pay scant heed to his lovely stenographer. But presently he had begun to note her existence. Calder, quietly watching, saw the fellow's new interest in her; and he saw it grow, from day to day, until it obsessed its victim.

From his criminal experiences, Calder was able to diagnose the symptoms as those of a man who, falling in love, past the midday of life, is too old for sanity to temper infatuation.

Now, up to thirty, a lover's strongest card is Youth. For the ten years or so, following that milestone, the absence of Youth may be supplied by technique, by magnetism, by such wiles as experience has taught. But, Satan help the Lothario who reaches the late forties or the fifties and who has not money to back his cause!

For money, at those ages, is usually the only remaining card in the mature wooer's wabbly hand.

Now, Moreton had no overplus of wealth—as wealth goes. But he had something almost as good. He had free access to the most soul-wrecking jewels in all the Ziegerich hoard. And, while there was no shadow of doubt as to his honesty, yet, through his position's advantages, he could and did display these jewels, in all their profusion and gorgeousness, to Lenore Aken.

Calder, happening into his office, not once but several times, in dull moments, caught Moreton heaping on a desk a heterogeneous pile of precious stones, for Lenore's benefit.

The girl—her soft eyes aglow, her breath fast, her lips trembling—stared in a sort of hypnotized ecstasy at the treasures. Timidly, at Moreton's permission, she gathered them adoringly in her white little hands, caressing them and letting them seep through her slender fingers.

Now, by a word to old Ziegerich, the detective could, of course, have put an instant and drastic end to these gem-seances. Ziegerich was paying for Moreton's time, and was paying well for it. He was not paying him to philander, nor to let a comparative outsider dally with jewels whose value was infinitely greater than her salary for a lifetime was likely to be.

But, perhaps through innate squareness, perhaps by reason of his long dealings with underworld ethics, Wolfe Calder preferred to settle his own affairs, rather than to squeal. So he kept his thin-lipped mouth shut—until he surprised Moreton, one day, fastening about the dazedly charmed girl's neck the famed Magnessen necklace, which happened to be undergoing one of its periodical sojourns at Ziegerich's.

At sight of Calder, Moreton hurriedly laid down the little mirror he was preparing to lift before Lenore's wide-gazing eyes, and released the clasp from her creamy throat.

"I was just trying the effect of this new combination of the diamond-and-aquamarine group on the pendant," stammered Moreton, forcing his glance to meet Calder's. "I've been experimenting on that grouping, all week. This time I think I've got it. But it's so much easier to get the effect when it's being worn—especially by a girl as pretty as—"

"I see," interrupted Calder gruffly—adding as he turned to the confused Lenore: "How about a walk, uptown? It's a dandy afternoon. And you were due to leave, fifteen minutes ago. Put on your things, won't you, and come along?"

Now, there was nothing in Wolfe Calder's intonation that suggested the "Come along!" mandate he might have delivered to a prisoner. But perhaps, behind his pleasant voice, there was something of the same compelling authority. For, still confused and avoiding the eye of either man, Lenore nodded and made her way toward the corner where hung her hat and coat.

Moreton, his nervous eyebrows working, picked up the glittering necklace and carried it across to the safe. As he went, his emotion showed itself only in several barked renditions of the hacking little cough that was always with him. Calder did not favor him with so much as a look. Nor did the detective speak again until he and Lenore were side by side in the street, and a block or more on their way uptown. Even then, it was the girl who broke the strained silence.

"You're awfully glum today!" she complained nervously. "I'm not enjoying this walk, one bit. I—"

"Just the same," he cut in, "it's good for you—the exercise and this sharp air and all. A sight better for you than going into a trance over the Magnessen necklace."

"I—" she began, stiffly; but he bored on:

"The first thing a man or woman has got to learn, in the jewelry business, is that jewels aren't jewels. They're only counters in the business game we're playing. It's just as it is in a bank. Until a bank-clerk can get it into his head that money isn't money, but just the counters in the game he's paid to play—until he can get that through his head, he's worthless in his job—and dangerous too. Now, that isn't the first time Moreton's let you fool with the Magnessen necklace. And he's let you handle a lot of other big-value stones, too. And you're dippy about them. That's all wrong. From being dippy about a thing, to wishing it belonged to you, is just one step. From wanting it, to grabbing it, is only one step more. Keep on saying that to yourself, every time you see any of those stones. Keep on, till you've taught yourself what I said about their being counters."

"Thank you, so much!" was the icy reply. "It's so nice of you to warn me! Now, next time Mr. Ziegerich sends for you to find missing jewelry, you'll know exactly whom to accuse."

"No," he denied, with stolid calm. "I won't know. Not if you mean I'd suspect *you*. You're too clean and too white and—and too much—too much *you*—to steal. But it won't do you any good, just the same, to let yourself gloat over that stuff, the way you've been doing. Do you know what would have happened to Moreton if it had been Ziegerich or either of his sons, instead of me, who happened into his office, while he was fixing that thing around your throat? Well, he'd have gotten his. Six months ago, he'd have had too much sense to do such a thing."

"If you are going to begin abusing poor Mr. Moreton—" she began, her voice unsteady.

"I'm not," he made answer. "I'm not a knocker. And if I was I wouldn't abuse Moreton. I'm too sorry for him."

"Because his lungs—"

"No. Because he's crazy in love with you, and because he hasn't a Chinaman's chance. If he had, you wouldn't be calling him 'poor' Mr. Moreton. And he hasn't a Chinaman's chance for another reason—because I'm going to marry you, myself. I didn't mean to tell you so, yet awhile. But when I saw that jewel-doped look on your face, back there, today, I knew it was time."

Lenore Aken stopped dead short and stared up at him, agape. He had stated his intent as coolly as if he were citing an instance in natural law.

"Wolfe Calder!" she gasped, doubtful as to whether she were going to laugh hysterically or cry with anger. "Wolfe *Calder!* Are you daft—or only drunk? I—"

"I'm daft over *you,*" he made stolid reply, "just as I've always been—just as you've always known I was. And as soon as you've said 'Yes,' I'm going to hail a taxi, for the rest of the trip home. Because, you see, it'd look funny for me to kiss you, right out here in the street. Taxies are handy things, that way. Don't go turning your face away, like that, girl! It's no disgrace. Look up at me. I said, look up at me!... Hey, there, *taxi!*"

The taxi had traveled the best part of two fare-devouring miles before Calder was his wonted level-brained and iron-nerved self. Then, talking down into a mass of fluffy hair and a badly damaged little hat that nestled deep into his chest, he said:

"I was going to wait awhile, till I had things shipshape, before telling you, Baby. But, today, I saw it had to be done in a rush or maybe it'd be too late. Now that you've got a real live lover to think about, you won't go mooning over dead jewelry any more—not even the Magnessen necklace."

"It's—it's so—so wonderful, Wolfe!" She protested. "Such a beauty!"

"So is the Statue of Liberty," he argued. "But folks don't go foolish over her. They're content to remember how grand she is, and to let it go at that. Still, it's not for me to knock the Magnessen horse-collar. For that's the thing that's due to put me in a position to marry you. I told you about that time it got stolen, when it was at Ziegerich's. Well, my getting it back made a big hit with Judge Magnessen. He has all the money there is, you know. And he got interested in me. I let out that I was saving, to start a little jewelry business of my own—'way up-town, in the new section that such a crowd of real folk are moving into since the spur road opened. And he's promised to back me and to help me get a first-rate start. Ziegerich is going to help me out, too. I'm leaving the store, next month. I was planning to wait till I got the new place running, before I asked you. But, after today—well, it won't do you any hurt to be lifted out of Moreton's office, and to know a sweetheart's better worth dreaming over than a safeful of jewels that aren't yours and that never can be. With men like Magnessen and Ziegerich behind me, and the good money that's pouring into that new section,—and with *you*,—well, watch me!"

THUS it was that "Clean-up Calder" evolved in due time into the proprietor of the more and more popular uptown jewelry establishment of "Wolfe Calder, Inc." The first few months were hard sledding. But Calder had made no mistake as to the possibilities of his location. He knew his business and he knew human nature. The Magnessen backing tided him over the bumpy beginnings. The Ziegerich and the Magnessen influence were further aids.

The line, "formerly with Ziegerich and Company," on his window and on his business cards, served as a talisman. In the fast-enlarging vicinity, Calder became the fashion. The rest was easy.

In his very early thirties, Wolfe Calder was part and parcel of his chosen community, and was a man of substance and repute. Luck was with him. And his level head and squareness and swiftly sure instincts kept luck from departing. Happiness was with him, too, in ample measure. And that was supplied exclusively by his dainty and still-alluring wife.

At once after their marriage—during the days when the business had to be kept alive by artificial respiration—Lenore had suggested that Wolfe save on at least one salary by letting her work in the store. Indeed, she insisted on it. And the two came perilously near to a quarrel, before Calder could convince her that her work must be confined to their tiny home, and that she was to keep away from the shop.

He knew she was not of the breed—few women are—who could look on his dazzling stock in trade as mere "counters in the business game." And he resolved, at the start, to divorce sentiment from livelihood.

So, during her husband's long hours at the store, she had much time to herself, even after she had wrought over her apartment until it shone...

It was one blistering hot Monday, in early July, during the detective's fourth year as "Wolfe Calder, Inc." Lenore had been fagged by a month of ceaseless heat. Wolfe had sent her that morning to the seaside for a week or two, promising to join her there on Saturday afternoon. This was the couple's first separation during their four-year wedded life. And Calder was unaccountably blue over it.

Business was so dull that he was half-minded to leave the store in charge of his assistant and run down to the shore, to his wife, for the rest of the week.

He was in this glum mood, when a portly old man bustled into the store. The visitor was Judge Magnessen. And he was a piteous mental case. In a spluttering handful of words he explained the reason of his call.

Mrs. Magnessen had once more broken the clasp of her necklace. The Judge, himself, had taken it to Ziegerich's to be repaired, and to have the stones overhauled in search for defective settings. This, on Magnessen's last visit to the city, a week earlier. Today, during a three-hour sojourn in town, he had stopped at Ziegerich's for the necklace.

Old Ziegerich himself had gone to the safe in which it had been placed some days earlier, to draw forth the repaired treasure and to return it to its owner.

He had opened the case, to show the necklace to Magnessen, before wrapping it up. The case was empty.

After Ziegerich's establishment had been ransacked in vain, the Judge had bethought himself of the man who, once before, had found the stolen necklace and the thief who had taken it. Therefore he had posted, with all speed, to Wolfe Calder. With a childlike faith in his detective prowess, Magnessen begged him to find the priceless circlet of gems. Calder, once before, had found the stolen necklace, when the police and high-priced agency men had failed. Therefore, to the Judge's way of reasoning, he could find it again, and could do so much more certainly than could anyone else.

As Magnessen entreated, Calder was amazed and annoyed to note the thrill of the man-hunt pounding again in his blood, to discover that a score of atrophied instincts of the chase were struggling to life within him. Already, he found himself stretching out for clues, and chafing to begin the quest. He had thought himself beyond that kind of thing, long ago, he the sedate and flourishing uptown jeweler!

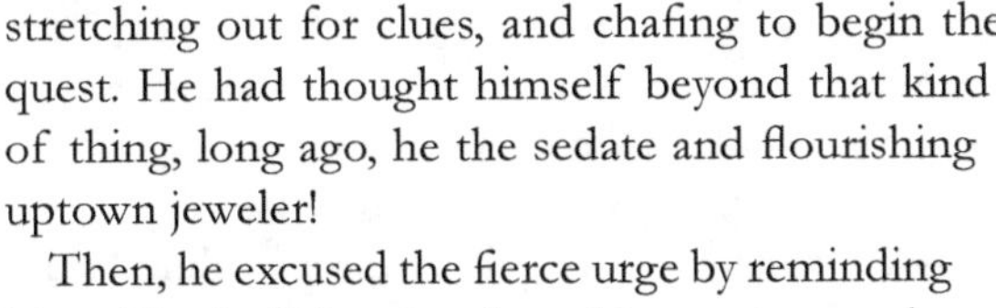

Then, he excused the fierce urge by reminding himself of all he owed to Magnessen; and he decided that the fever of the chase was nothing more than a laudable sense of gratitude to the man who had set him up in business. And, in the end, he awoke the Judge to ecstasies of thanks, by undertaking the job.

A sense of shame prevented him from

sending word to Lenore. He knew she would make all manner of fun of him, for yielding to such a request. And he hated to be laughed at. Time enough,—if he were still on the case then,—to tell her of it when he should run down to the shore on Saturday.

In the meanwhile Mr. Wolfe Calder, jeweler, felt a sense of disreputable pleasure in relapsing for a space into "Clean-up Calder."

His first step, naturally, was to invade the Ziegerich establishment, where old man Ziegerich hailed his advent with heartfelt joy and put at his disposal all the resources of the place. The initial questions and searchings and examinings, at Ziegerich's, threw no light at all on Calder's new-old path.

Not until he voiced the most seemingly banal query of his list, did he strike something resembling a clue.

"Any employees left you, this past week?" he asked at last, adding: "But of course that's the very first thing you'd have told me, if there had."

"Not a soul," replied Ziegerich. "It's even an off-week in the vacation schedule. All here—except, of course," he added as an afterthought, "poor Moreton."

"Moreton?" Calder fairly spat the name at him. "Moreton, hey? Tell me about his going!"

"He left us last Wednesday," said Ziegerich, in very genuine sorrow. "It's a mighty sad case. I wish I could do more for him. Tuesday his landlady telephoned down that he had had another hemorrhage. You know, his lungs have always been affected, more or less. And he took no sort of care of himself. Wednesday morning he came in here, looking more like a corpse than a live man. The doctor had just told him he had a bare six months to live, at best, and that he wouldn't have half that time unless he packed up, that very day, and hurried to Saranac. He came in to say good-by. Poor, faithful old chap! I could see he knew, as well as we did, that he'd never set foot in here again."

"H'm!" commented the detective sympathetically. "Too bad! Got his address, up at Saranac? I'd like to write to him, sometime. It might cheer him up."

FIVE minutes later, Clean-up Calder was hot-footing it to the boarding-house in which for years Moreton had lived. Thence, after a long and authoritative cross-questioning of a landlady (whom he reduced from lofty condescension to tearful spinelessness), he went to an address he had browbeaten her into giving him—and, thence, to three more places, in quick succession. After which, he took a train out of town—but not in the direction of Saranac.

At sunset, the same day, he climbed the steps of a small summer hotel, in a sleepy hill town, and went to the desk. There, he flicked the leaves of the register, for a moment.

He was not looking for a name. He was looking for a specimen of handwriting. A man may choose any of a million names, at will. But he can choose only one chirography. He may—and often does—try to disguise that chirography. But not once in a myriad times can he do so in a way to deceive anyone familiar with it.

Presently Calder left the desk and wandered aimlessly about the stuffy hotel lobby. Twice, he looked at his watch as though expecting some one who was late to an appointment there. Thence, he made his way, unnoted, to the stairs.

As he neared a room at the end of the second-floor corridor, the door of the apartment was opened. A man came out—a stoutish man with a short gray beard, and carrying a black bag.

"Excuse me, Doctor," said Calder timidly, as the man came toward him down the hall. "But how is Mr. Baldwin, this evening? I only just heard he was here. And I'm worried about him. He and I have known each other a good many years. Is he very ill?"

"Yes," returned the doctor, recognizing the half cringing and wholly unhappy manner with which friends of the sick are forever approaching physicians. "He may pull through. Or he may not. He says he has had these hemorrhages before, and has always rallied within a few days. But—"

"How did he happen to send for you?" asked the humble questioner, still more meekly.

"He stopped here, overnight—or for a day or two—on his way to Asheville—down in North Carolina. He fell ill, and the proprietor called me in. The man is not fit for travel. But up to yesterday he kept insisting he must go on. Perhaps you can persuade him to give up the idea for the present."

"Perhaps I can," was the grim response. "Thanks, Doc!"

Brushing past the physician, Calder strode on to the sickroom, entered it, and shut and locked the door behind him.

Then he allowed himself a quick scrutiny of the place.

On the bed, his face green-white except for the cheekbones on which the disease had flung forth its scarlet "No Surrender!" signals, lay Moreton. At the sound of the key in the lock, he turned his languid eyes toward the door. Then, with a gurgle, he sat bolt upright.

"Hello, Moreton!" said Calder pleasantly. "I've dropped in for the Magnessen necklace. You've hid it under your pillow, I suppose? Yes? You would! It's a mistake to get playing with jewelry. It's apt to turn out this way. Jewels are funny things, if once you let them get under your skin."

As he talked, he approached the bed. With one outstretched hand, he prepared to fend off any resistance from the invalid. With the other, he began to grope under the tumbled pillows.

To his bewilderment, Moreton, after that first galvanic start of surprise at sight of him, made no move. But into the cadaverous face crept a grin. It was not a pretty expression. It was not normal. And, watching it spread and ripple athwart the thin lips, Calder was aware of a shivering sense of repulsion.

"Not there!" he muttered, withdrawing his fingers from their futile quest under the pillows, and striving to force back the jarring sensation bred of the other's hideous smile. "Where is it?"

For an instant, there was no reply. Dumbly, Moreton continued to gaze on his captor, his sunken eyes beginning to light up with a strange gleam whose meaning Calder could not fathom—and that dreadful grin of derision spreading and deepening amid the creases of his lower face.

"Come!" demanded Calder, again, half sick with the sight of that cryptic smile and the glint of the pale, deep-set eyes. "Where is it?"

Then, for the first time, the tight-drawn lips parted. The invalid panted, in a cracked and breathless falsetto:

"You're in the wrong pew! You blockhead fool! You can search this place till you're tired. I haven't got it. I had it. But I gave it to—to my—my girl."

He sank back, and fought for breath. Palpably, the man was in agony. Yet never once did that dreadful grin leave his lips, nor the mockingly insane light flicker out of his eyes.

"Ask her for it, you—you cheap bully!" he croaked, between raggedly labored breaths. "You bullied her into marrying you when a better man wanted her. Perhaps you can bully her into giving up the necklace. Even if you couldn't bully her into caring for you or staying true to you. Ask Lenore!"

For a moment the grin gave way to a grimace of rank terror, as Calder towered over him, rocking with blind fury, menacing the helpless figure with upflung hammerlike fists. But at once the look of fear was gone. Moreton saw the raging giant check himself and collapse into a chair by the bed. And he knew the peril of murder was past.

"You lie!" groaned Calder, over and over again, his words a cry of physical pain. "You *lie!*"

How long he sat crouched forward there, head in hands, he never knew. But the twilight had begun to fade when a sound made him lift his tortured face and glance toward the bed.

More than once, before, Calder had heard that same sound. There is no mistaking it; there is no imitating of it. It is the last sound to leave the human throat, driven forth perhaps by the rush of the departing soul.

That Moreton was dead,—that the shock had snuffed out his faint flame of life,—smote Calder with a sense of impotent wrath.

If only the man might have lived! If only he might have gotten well! If only Wolfe might have met him, foot to foot, in fair battle and have torn the lying life out of him with his naked hands! And now—

A tap at the door brought Calder to himself. Mechanically he stumbled across to the threshold and turned the key and the knob. Outside, stood a bellboy.

"Lady to see Mister Baldwin," observed the youth. "Says her name's Mrs. Calder. She—"

"Send her up!" ordered the man, curtly, maneuvering his own body in such fashion as to keep himself between the boy and the dim shape on the bed.

HE stepped back toward the window, and stood there waiting. His mind was still numb. But into it was crawling, like a frozen stream, this confirmation of the dead man's hideous charges. And, out of mind and heart was ebbing the last hope.

The bellboy's clumping feet echoed through the hallway. Between the intermittent thuds sounded the swish of a silken skirt, and a light, elastic tread that Calder knew so well. Followed a knock at the door.

"Come in!" said Calder.

He made no effort to disguise his voice. Yet his own mother would not have recognized it. Even then, he could not concentrate his shattered thoughts.

She had come into the room. The creaking door had swung shut behind her. She was looking around, through the fast fading light. For the first time she seemed to realize that it was a bedroom into which she had been ushered. She took an instinctive step backward.

Then as her gaze roved toward the bed, Wolfe Calder lurched forward. Subconsciously, he was seeking to come between her and what lay sprawled there. So, always, had it been his instinct to stand between her and the harsher sights and facts of life.

The movement drew her eyes to him. A last glimmer of dusk, outside, fell athwart his face as it emerged from the shadows.

Lenore cried aloud. And, even through his dizzy numbness, he was aware of a note of gladness in her cry.

"Oh, Wolfe!" she wailed. "*Wolfe*, darling! I'm so glad you're here! So *glad!* Here! *Take* the horrible thing!"

She thrust into his hand a parcel carelessly tied up in tissue paper.

"Here!" she exclaimed again. "*Take* it! I was in such a hurry I didn't even wait to put it in its box. I hadn't any time. I stuck it in my waist, and borrowed some paper at the station to wrap it in. It's—oh, I forgot, you don't know! It's the Magnessen necklace. Honestly it is! It's been a perfect nightmare to me, all afternoon. I—I never want to see another bit of jewelry as long as I live. Oh, Wolfe, *where* have you been all day? I looked everywhere for you! And how did you ever get here? They said it was Mr. Moreton's room. 'Baldwin,' I mean. That is the name he told me in his letter."

THE incoherent speech was babbled in a vain race to get it delivered in full before the tears should come. Yet something in it swept the numbness from Calder's soul, and brought back consciousness, with a rush that was agonizing. Fighting for self-control, he managed to whisper, brokenly:

"Tell me!"

"It happened, this noon," she said, choking back the sobs of reaction. "I was just going in to lunch. And a messenger boy came. He'd been sent all the way from here. He had a box for me. And a letter. They were from Mr. Moreton. The box had the—the necklace in it. It was a Ziegerich box, too. The letter was ever so much worse than anything I ever imagined. Here,"—fumbling in the waist of her dress and extracting a white oblong. "Read it. And *try* not to be too angry, dear! Oh," she broke off, "I forgot. It's too dark to see. Turn on the light and read it, Wolfe. You *must* read it!"

But he only held her the tighter. And once more he whispered: "Tell me!"

"You can read it later, then," she answered. "Here, take it. It said,—don't be angry, dear,—please, *please* don't!—it wasn't my fault,—it said he had always loved me. Why, he'd only seen me once, since I was married. And that was last week when I went down to Ziegerich's, for you, about the duplicate for the Venetian vase. He stopped me in the aisle and asked me how I was standing the heat; and I told him I was going away and where I was going. That must be how he knew the address."

She paused, as if realizing how incoherent was her talk; then, taking fresh hold on her mentality, she went on:

"He said in the letter he'd always loved me. That he had been planning to join me at the shore today. He said he remembered how mad I was about the Magnessen necklace. (Wolfe, I *loathe* it!) He said he had bought it—he must be richer than we knew—because he had believed my craze for it would make me—make me—well, you'll read it, yourself! Then, he said he was taken terribly ill, here; and that the doctor wasn't sure he'd get well, and he wanted me to have it, anyhow; and to know he—he loved me to—to the death—the beast! And he said he hated you and that he yearned to live long enough to 'make you pay.' I came up to town, right away. You weren't at the store. Todd didn't know where you were or when you'd get back. So—I was all mixed up what to do! I came right here—to throw the miserable necklace in his face and tell him how I despised him. I was so cut up and angry, I

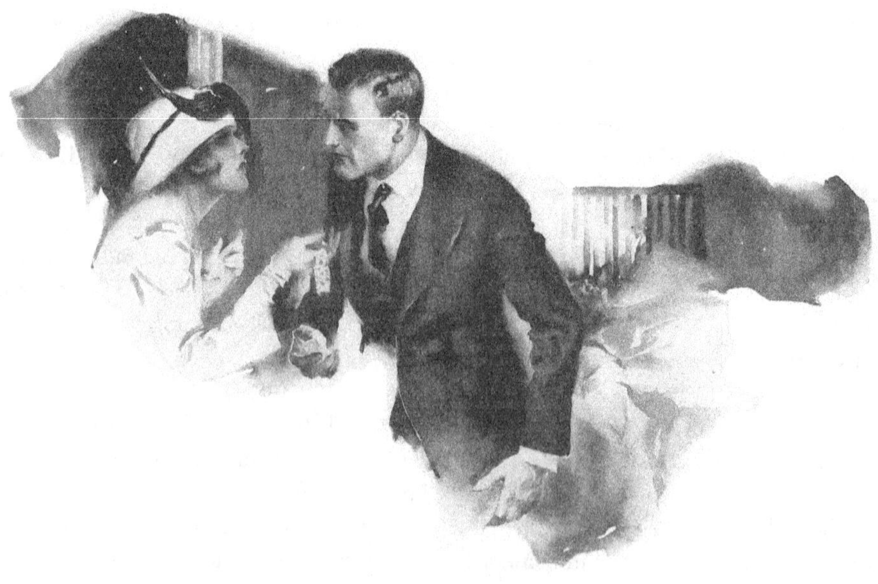

wanted him to know I wouldn't keep the thing he sent me; and I wanted—Wolfe, what's that on the bed over there?" she broke off, nervously straining her eyes through the blackness. "It looks almost like somebody lying there. It—"

"It's nothing," the man assured her, a throb of insane happiness tearing at his heart, as he glanced toward the half invisible bed and realized to the full the venom of the man who had sought to "make him pay," even in the hour of his own death. "It's nothing… Come, darling! We've been in the blackness long enough, you and I. Let's go. Don't look back!"

Appendix

Publication information
for the stories
in this book

The Blizzard Juggler

Argosy, January 1911
No illustrations.
Front text:
How a Big Snow-Storm Was Turned to Account in a Small Town Cut Off from City Connection.
End text: None

The Coney Island Riddle

Top-Notch, September 1911
No illustrations.
Front text:
Age seems unable to wither the charm of the world's greatest seaside playground, or custom stale its infinite variety of wonders. So the author, in choosing Coney Island for the stage of this drama, hit a high place in ever-green popularity. You'll meet bewilderment as you share the adventures of Arthur Dallam—a bewilderment springing not from the whirling, whisking, bumping, thundering, whispering, flaming and darkling "attractions," but from the lost-and-found chase that is the soul of the story.
(A COMPLETE NOVELETTE)
End text: None.
Revision made for this edition:
The following appeared in the original as one paragraph. It was printed in this edition as two:
"Alone?" he asked. "Yes," I said.
Note: Stories in this collection have been presented in chronological order, by publication date—with the exception of the above two.

The Justice of the Sands

The Red Book, July 1914
Illustrations by C. B. Falls
Front text:
Author of "Whose Wife?" etc.
Caption, illustration 1: None

Blurb, 2nd page:

We feel that Albert Payson Terhune is rapidly becoming one of this country's premier short story men. His vividness in writing is in a class by itself. This story takes you into the desert with a Yankee man-hunter, and actually makes you feel the stifling waves of heat of the setting.

Caption, 2-page illustration:

"I take it," he snarled, addressing the Shiek, "that you're the chief of this outfit. Well, sir, let me tell you, I'm Ezra T. Belden,—formerly of Plymouth, N. H., at present attached to the Central Office Detective Bureau in New York. I've got a warrant here for this man's arrest on a charge of embezzling $275,000 from the Aaron Burr Savings Bank of New York City, where he was cashier. And here's his extradition papers, signed at Damascus by your own government. Look 'em over, if you like. I've tracked this crook halfway across the world. And now is the time I take him back with me. So just ask these fellow coons of yours to put down their artillery, will you?"

Caption, illustration 3:

The hot beating of the sun in his face roused Belden. Blinking painfully, he sat up and stared stupidly about him.

End text: None

The Shrimp

The Red Book, September 1914

Illustrations by J. Henry Bracker

Front text:

Author of "Whose Wife?" "The Turnkey," etc.

He was a shrimp physically, but a giant mentally and a demon in love—the man around whom revolves the latest story from this brilliant writer.

Caption, illustration 1:

"You're in love with my wife, aren't you, Allen?"

Caption, illustration 2:

"You'll have to forgive poor frivolous women," she said, "if they are more interested in watching a glorious figure than in watching the workings of f weighty mind such as yours. A Canova gladiator may not be as instructive to gaze on as a twelve-volume encyclopedia, but it is more ornamental—and more thrilling. If Alan had lived in the cave-man days, the roomiest cave and the loveliest cave-girl would have been his."

Caption, illustration 3:

"For God's sake, Doctor!" he croaked. "For God's sake—" "Alan!" broke in Hera, in stark bewilderment. "What on earth!" "He's poisoned me!" bellowed Alan. "I can feel the symptoms. All of them. The dry throat, the chilliness—"

End text:

"Deadlock," by Mr. Terhune, the story of a man and a woman faced with the most difficult decision in life, will be in the October Red Book, on the news-stands September 23rd.

Note: The spelling of "asperin" (used several times) was retained from the original.

Her Faith in Mankind

The Red Book, January 1915

Illustrated by J. Henry

Front text:

The story of the girl who believed what ninety-nine per cent. of the women in the world believe.

Author of "Whose Wife?" etc.

Caption, illustration 2:

She took a furtive step toward the door. But Surles laid a tenderly detaining hand on her wrist. "How would you like—?" he began.

Caption, illustration 3:

"I didn't think *anyone* could be so good!"

"No?" he laughed. "Yet you had no trouble at all in believing that anyone could be so bad."

End text: None

At $32 Per

The Blue Book, February 1915

Illustrator not credited.

Front text:

An exciting battle in a world-old war, that of the sexes. The woman wins and loses—and wins again?

Author of "Marked Cards," "Among the Personals" etc.

End text: None

Note: The following uses the word "women":

If you doubt that, ask yourself if in all the history of law there was ever a women who brought a breach of promise suit, who didn't win her case, no matter how flimsy that case was.

For this book, "women" was changed to "woman."

In His Wife's Name

The Red Book, August 1915

Front text:

Do you tell your wife your business secrets? This is the story of a man who did not. It is the most unusual of the many unusual stories Mr. Terhune has written.

Author of "Dollars and Cents," etc.

Illustrations by Howard Heath
Caption, illustration 1:
He was free; he was rich; he was only a little over fifty-five; and—he was very, very sick.
Caption, illustration 2:
At dawn he awoke and burst into a ribald song.
Caption, illustration 3:
She spent the bulk of her waiting hours sitting just outside the sick-room door.
Caption, illustration 4:
He was a splendid man; so sympathetic and deep-hearted. He even showed her how to write the check.
End text: None

The Other Man

The Red Book, November 1915
Illustrated by Katherine Southwick
Front text:
"How often one hears of the man who has said, "But I love you so much I will teach you to love me." Can it be done? Mr. Terhune here tells, in the letter of a man who has said it, the story of one effort.
Author of "Dollars and Cents," etc.
Caption, illustration 1:
Mildred Kerr, a girl I had loved for years—and who hadn't loved me.
End text: None

The Unbaited Trap

The Red Book, December, 1915
Illustrated by George Baker
Front text:
Author of "The Years of the Locust," etc.
Caption, illustration 1:
Mrs. Dunne herself told Hugh that a man who likes to spend all his evenings at home with his own wife is in danger of becoming a fossil.
Caption, illustration 2:
She had forced back the moss-covered old scruples that threatened to engulf her new ideas of freedom. She had forced them back, after an all-day battle. And now she was here—here in this dim-lit Lovers' Lane of a tea-room, waiting to hear Archer Dunne tell her again that he loved her; that she was the One Woman; that she was a Wonder Girl; that she was his adored Lady of Mystery.

This teaser for the first Lad story appeared at the end of The Unbaited Trap.

Lucrezia Borgia: The Much-Married Siren

Ainslee's, March 1916

No illustrations (other than the elaborate heading).

Front text:

What makes the super-woman? Is it beauty? Cleopatra and Rachel were homely. Is it daintiness? Marguerite de Valois washed her hands but twice a week. Is it wit? Pompadour and Du Barry were avowedly stupid in conversation. Is it youth? Diane de Poictiers and Ninon de 1'Enclos were wildly adored at sixty. Is it the subtle quality of feminism? George Sand, who numbered her admirers by the score—poor Chopin in their foremost rank—was not only ugly, but disgustingly mannish. So was Semiramis. Here are the stories of super-women who conquered at will. Some of them smashed thrones; some were content with wholesale heart-smashing. Wherein lay their secret? Or rather, their secrets? For seldom did any two of them follow the same plan of campaign.

End text:

The March number of AINSLEE'S will contain the next article in Mr. Terhune's Super-Women series: "Rachel: The Woman of Fire."

Note: The end text teaser was mistaken, as this *was* the March issue.

Note: This piece does not appear in the 1916 edition of *Superwomen*.

The Fear of the Job

The Red Book, March, 1916

Illustrated by J. Henry

Front text:

Author of "Whose Wife?" "Dollars and Cents," etc.

Caption, illustration 1:

He didn't tell her she was the first girl he had kissed, because it was not true, and he felt too holy just then to smirch with a lie the mouth she had just kissed.

Caption, illustration 2:

"There, now," he rumbled, slipping an arm around her. "Don't you go getting unhappy. Brace up. It'll be all right."

Caption, illustration 3:

He shrank back from her at almost the same instant, with a dolorous howl of pain and amaze, nursing a pudgy wrist into which a quarter-inch of hatpin had just penetrated. "You she-devil!"

End text: None

The War Bridegroom

The Blue Book, July 1916

Illustrator not credited.

Front text:

"Whose Wife?" "Dollars and Cents" and "A Return to Youth—and Trouble" are some of the stories that have made Mr. Terhune famous. This is one of his best.

End text: None

The Cheat

The Red Book, August, 1916

Illustrated by William Oberhardt

Note: In the original magazine, the first two illustrations were printed in reverse of the order that they are presented in this book.

Front text: None

Caption, illustration 1:

"You've been coming here to see Gracia quite a spell, now, haven't you, Mr. Dorrance?"

Caption, illustration 2:

Mrs. Riker had shared poverty and all sorts of frontier vicissitudes with her husband, and she had thriven on unadulterated luck.

Caption, illustrations 3 & 4:

The stakes are understood, ain't they? If I win, you git out an' you sta out. If you win, you marry Gracia. All ready, dealer."

End text:

There will be another of Mr. Terhune's short stories in an early issue.

Eugénie, Empress Of The French

Ainslee's, September, 1916

No illustrations (other than the elaborate heading).

Front text: Same as for Ainslee's, March 1916.

End text:

The October number of AINSLEE'S will contain the next article in Mr. Terhune's super-women series: "Marie de Brinvilliers, the Woman Without a Soul."

Revisions made for this edition:

William Kirkpatrick was described in the source text as a "Scotch wire merchant." Research showed that this should have read "wine merchant," and that correction has been made for this book.

Note: This piece does not appear in the 1916 edition of *Superwomen*.

The Unknown

The Red Book, February 1917

Illustrated by William Oberhardt

Front text:

The most remarkable short story Mr. Terhune has written.

Caption, illustration 2:

They had their trip for nothing. Professor Van Duyne could give them no tidings whatever of the missing boy and girl.

Caption, illustration 3:

Craig read the confession through a second and a third time.

Caption, illustration 4:

He'd heard the island wasn't inhabited. But on the beach he saw—two natives.

End text: None

When the Devil Was Sick

The Green Book, March 1917

Illustrated by R. F. James

Front text: None

Caption, illustration 2: Dick no longer bothered to resist the impulse to drop in at Mrs. Thorp's for a cup of tea. A kindly solicitous friend, who once met him there, felt it her duty to mention the call to Thetis.

Caption, illustration 3:

"Erdheim has gone," he said brusquely. "He left me to tell you. Said it was no part of his work. Soft-hearted for such a big man! He—" "Tell me!" pleaded Thetis… "My boy," he said kindly, "it's a blow. And you must stand it as God meant brave men to stand such things."

End text: None

Revisions made for this edition:

"with it flood of outsiders" was changed to "with its flood of outsiders"
Erdheim was referred to as "Erdman" in one instance. This was changed to "Erdheim."
The word "dreamly" was changed to "dreamily."

The Girl of the Night-Court

The Blue Book, September 1917
Illustrator not credited.
Front text: None
End text:
ANOTHER STRIKING TERHUNE STORY
"Stretch an invisible cord, knee-high, across the sidewalk at Broadway and Forty-second Street—and in five minutes a hundred prettier girls than Daisy Reynolds will stumble over it." That's the beginning of Albert Payson Terhune's next story, the story of Daisy Reynolds, who was just "The Girl in the Crowd." You who have read "The Girl of the Night-Court" will know that this next story will likewise be refreshingly unusual, true to life and deeply interesting. It will appear in the next—October—issue of THE BLUE BOOK MAGAZINE, on sale September 1st.

Money Thrown Away

The Red Book, September 1917
Illustrations by John Newton Howitt
Front text:
If your husband were untrue, would you want to know it? Or would you prefer happiness at the price of being deceived? A baffling question, presented in a very unusual story of the sort Mr. Terhune writes regularly for The Red Book Magazine.
Caption, illustration 1:
"I've been reading a perfectly horrible book to-day, Hughie," announced Lois, "—a perfectly disgusting book. And not one vile word of it is true. Not one!"
Caption, illustration 2:
Lois clung to him, weeping helplessly. She felt as if she were taking a last farewell of all that made the world worth while. "Oh, darling," she sobbed, darling, *don't* go! For my sake—*Hugh!* Don't go! Give it up!"
Caption, illustration 3:
It was characteristic of Lois that she hesitated before she ripped open the envelope and learned the worst—or the best."
End text: None

The Girl in the Crowd

The Blue Book, October 1917
Illustrator not credited.

Front text: None
End text:
There will be another story by Mr. Terhune in an early issue.

Don Quixote McGraw
The Blue Book, Febraury 1918
Illustrator not credited.
Front text: None
End text:
"Little Mr. Galahad," another of Mr. Terhune's real stories of real people, will be published in out next issue—on sale February 1st.

The Wallflower
Saturday Evening Post, February 1, 1919
Illustrated by LeJaren À Hiller
Note: The two illustrations were presented in the original magazine in the reverse order that they are presented in this edition.
Front text: None
Caption, illustration 1:
"My Disease," She Said, "Dates Back to Bible Days. Leah Had it, in the Book of Genesis. It is Wallfloweritis"
Caption, illustration 2:
How Often Do I Have to Tell You Never to Ask a Man Why He Hasn't Been to See You?
End text: None

Twice-Over
The Blue Book, May 1919
Illustration by Quin Hall (not credited, but signed).
Front text:
The story of two men who were very handy with their fists, and of a strange love-affair, and of a most peculiar fight—an absorbing story, such as only Mr. Terhune can write.
End text:
"The Actor Man," one of the most Albert Payson Terhune of stories, will appear in an early issue of THE BLUE BOOK MAGAZINE.

The Actor-Man
The Blue Book, July 1919
Illustrator not credited.
Front text:

A MOST amusing story of one of mankind's quaintest activities—amateur theatricals. Mr. Terhune well knows how to present the humorous side of life.
End text:
There will be another of Albert Payson Terhune's dramatic stories of real life in an early issue.

The Yaller Dog

Country Gentleman, March 6, 1920
Illustrations by Frank Stick
Front text: None
Caption, illustration 2:
And Towser Can Shift for Himself. And Then Come Tidings of Rifled Henroosts.
Caption, illustration 3:
Give Him Half a Chance and He Will Serve You to the Death
End text: None

Sheer Weight

The Popular Magazine, April 7, 1921
No illustrations.
Front text:
Author of "Najib's 'Yowltide,'" "On Strike," Etc.
Con Vedder sure would have had a ring "champ" in The Big Fellow—if only the latter had not been so keen on auto trucks
End text:
Look for more of Mr. Terhune's work in the future.
Revisions made for this edition:
"In a day the tole of the cautious spendthrift…"
"tole" was changed to "tale."

Watchful Wasting

The Popular Magazine, August 7, 1921
No illustrations
Front text:
Author of "Sheer Weight," "Najib's 'Yowltid,'" Etc.
Hilary B. Banks, efficiency expert, was fine at cutting out. But in the "movie" game he succeeded in cutting out more than he intended
End text: None

The Clean-up

The Red Book, November 1922
Illustrated by Leslie L. Benson
Front text: None

End text: None

Caption, illustration 1:

He Surprised Moreton fastening about the girl's neck the famed Magnessen necklace.

Caption, illustration 2:

"Just as soon as you've said 'Yes,' I'm going to hail a taxi for the trip home… Hey, there, taxi!"

Caption, illustration 3:

Calder was amazed to note the thrill of the man-hunt pounding again in his blood.

Caption, illustration 4:

"Oh, Wolfe!" she wailed. "I'm so glad you're here. So *glad! Take* the horrible thing!"

End text: None

General notes

Most original spellings and punctuations from the source material have been retained for this book, even though they may seem unusual (perhaps even vexing) to the modern reader.

A few exceptions are worth noting.

The word "photo's" was used several times. If this was intended to indicate photos in the plural, that would be JPW (Just Plain Wrong). However, this spelling was retained, as it was quite possibly meant to be a contraction for "photographs." This suspicion is based on the fact that literature of this time commonly used an apostrophe in "'phone" (for "telephone") and "'plane" (for "aeroplane").

The word "won't" in several stories was consistently (and thus, interestingly, deliberately) printed without the apostrophe. I have inserted the apostrophe.

Similarly, the word "aint" was changed to the acceptable and proper English form: "ain't."

Inconsistencies in spelling, hyphenation, and punctuation were found to exist between stories, and efforts were made to bring about consistency, but those efforts were not applied consistently.

The font used for the main text of this book is Garamond 10.5. Table of Contents, story titles (except those taken as graphics from the source publications), and headings for the Appendix are Souvenir.

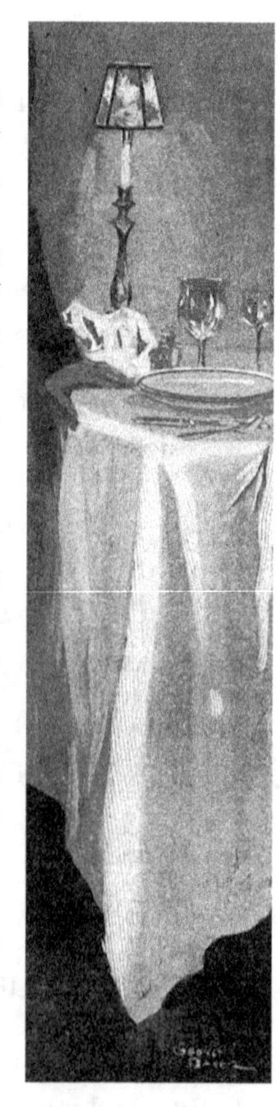